The Play of the Double in Postmodern American Fiction

Gordon E. Slethaug

Southern Illinois University Press
Carbondale and Edwardsville

Copyright © 1993 by the Board of Trustees,
Southern Illinois University
All rights reserved
Printed in the United States of America
Designed by Jason Schellenberg
Production supervised by Natalia Nadraga
96 95 94 93   4 3 2 1

Library of Congress Cataloging-in-Publication Data

Slethaug, Gordon.
    The play of the double in postmodern American fiction /
Gordon E. Slethaug.
        p.   cm.
    Includes bibliographical references and index.
    1. American fiction—20th century—History and criticism.
2. Postmodernism (Literature)—United States. 3. Doubles in
literature. I. Title.
PS374.P64S54   1993
813'.540927—dc20   92-19853
ISBN 0-8093-1841-5   CIP

*For my family—wife, parents,
and sons—who double my pleasure*

Few concepts and dreams have haunted the human imagination as durably as those of the *double*—from primitive man's sense of a duplicated self as immortal soul to the complex mirror games and mental chess of Mann, Nabokov, Borges.

—Albert Guerard, "Concepts of the Double"

There are no "real" doubles in my novels.

—Vladimir Nabokov, *Speak, Memory*

Contents

Acknowledgments

Although a number of students and colleagues assisted me in developing my ideas over the past few years, I would like to acknowledge Stan Fogel and Bill Macnaughton for their comments on an early version of this book and especially to recognize and thank Neil Hultin and Warren Ober, who offered valuable responses at every stage of the manuscript production. Their tireless assistance in reading my analysis and asking helpful questions has improved this book in fundamentally important ways. I owe them a great debt as critics, colleagues, and friends.

*The Play of
the Double
in Postmodern
American
Fiction*

Prescript
Rewriting the Double

During the quarter century since Albert J. Guerard's *Stories of the Double* reminded readers of a rich nineteenth-century literary tradition, stories like Melville's "Bartleby the Scrivener," Stevenson's *Strange Case of Dr. Jekyll and Mr. Hyde*, Dostoevsky's *Double*, and Conrad's "Secret Sharer," with their haunted gothic centers and mysterious, twinned, but mirrored characters, have become fresh once again after having been eclipsed for a time by novels of social realism. Moreover, the idea of the double has seized the imagination of a number of the major modernist and postmodernist writers. Although there are many reasons for the appeal of the double, its continuing importance, Guerard insists, lies primarily in its serious exploration of the psyche: "*Double* literature (if it proceeds from a genuine imaginative act) is rarely trivial, though not infrequently comic. The issues are real and sometimes tragic, the psychomachia definitive or barely survived—whether the experience of seeing one's double lead to a sense of resurrection or to a descent into psychosis, whether to classic split personality or to epileptic episode or to obsessive-compulsive behavior."[1] Elusive as the concept of the double is, a number of modern critics agree that *doppelgängers* are manifestations of psychological phenomena, and Clifford Hallam insists that "the Double (in fiction or otherwise) is directly related to Freud's breakthrough in understanding the human personality."[2] But if Freud made the breakthrough, it was Jung and Rank who gave the most precise analysis of "the mysterious bond between the protagonist and his closest friend, as well as the link between him and his enemy."[3]

1

Recent critics, however, have begun to question the exclusive dependence of the double on some mysterious psychological bond. Tzvetan Todorov, for example, remarks in *The Fantastic* that

> significations can even be opposed to one another, as they are in Hoffmann and Maupassant. The double's appearance is a cause for joy in the works of the former: it is the victory of mind over matter. But in Maupassant, on the contrary, the double incarnates danger: it is the harbinger of threat and terror. Again, there are contrary meanings in *Aurélia* and *The Saragossa Manuscript*. In Nerval, the double's appearance signifies, among other things, a dawning isolation, a break with the world; in Potocki, quite the contrary, the doubling . . . becomes the means of a closer contact with others, of a more complete integration.[4]

Todorov's observations about opposing significations reflect the rich variety of meanings attached to the sign of the double, which has been used to illustrate the desire for unity in the human personality and spirit but now signals double purposes, fragmented understandings, and self-parody in all life and literature. (Robert Rogers calls the self-parodying double a baroque double.)[5]

Traditionally, authors have employed the double to affirm rational humanist views of a unified and stable self and totalized cultures—what Paul de Man calls the self-mystified, transcendent symbol or signified—the coherence of God, self, and the word.[6] We might call this position mimetic, representative, or natural, for as Carl Malmgren points out, the Aristotelian view that art imitates nature usually involves a "higher sense of a unified ethical vision connected in some way with the way we live now."[7] While this view generally informs premodern texts dealing with the double, it is also common to such moderns as Saul Bellow, John Updike, Ursula LeGuin, Toni Morrison, Flannery O'Connor, and John Knowles. Both male and female writers have been attracted to this approach, which strives for pattern and order, values the subject, and emphasizes the synthesis and resolution of differences between dual aspects of the self, men and women, and privileged and repressed. Feminist fiction, especially that of a black writer such as Toni Morrison, is filled with doppelgängers that explore the status of "the other" within a white patriarchal society. Sula and Nel, of Morrison's *Sula*, embody opposite aspects of black women coerced by dominant cultural beliefs and practices into acting against their better instincts. Her *Beloved* presents the emotional and legal difficulties of a black woman who kills her daughter to protect her against her white master, only to discover that she comes back to life to seek the love she was denied. Here the use of the double reveals the complex nature of the sacrifices and love borne by black women.

Recently, however, the double has taken on a new identity: moving away from a consideration of the Cartesian self—an indivisible, unified, continuous, and fixed identity—and universal absolutes, the double in postmodern fiction explores a divided and discontinuous self in a fragmented universe. Its mission is to decenter the concept of the self, to view human reality as a construct, and to explore the inevitable drift of signifiers away from their referents. It assumes that the human being is a locus of contradictions in a reality of conflicting discourses and discursive practices. This formalist, performative position displaces the mimetic stance, values artifice over verisimilitude, substitutes writing for experience, pluralizes narrative points of view, and esteems the autotelic and self-referential in fiction. In recognizing previously marginalized modes of narration and depictions of characters, it confirms the split sign, the split self, and the split text.

It should be made clear at the outset that this study is not an inquiry into postmodernism; it is concerned with how the idea of the double is employed by certain American authors generally considered postmodern. John Barth, Donald Barthelme, Richard Brautigan, Robert Coover, Raymond Federman, Leslie Fiedler, William Gass, John Hawkes, Vladimir Nabokov, Thomas Pynchon, and Kurt Vonnegut, for instance, steer clear of realistic presentation, frustrate the reader's search for coherence, and demystify transcendent symbols of unity. Like the work of other postmoderns, theirs interrogates the present order of things not to present a single, clear-cut new answer but to call into question a rational, consistent order of reality, to transgress social and literary conventions, to debunk a correspondence between the experiential or real world and the text, to raise possibilities of a multiplicity of credible answers, and to use traditional elements of fiction ironically and parodically but without satiric motives. This approach, as Linda Hutcheon suggests, results from the "*postmodern* urge to trouble, to question, to make both problematic and provisional any . . . desire for order or truth through the powers of the human imagination."[8]

For some, like Jean-François Lyotard, Fredric Jameson, and Terry

Eagleton, postmodernism is an art form located within a particular epoch and responsive to historical conditions, though it may choose to ignore the lessons of history. Lyotard thinks that postmodernism is a way of seeing closely linked with existential assumptions and beliefs,[9] but Jameson and Eagleton view it as a product of late capitalism and the postindustrial society in which nothing has value in itself but is nevertheless bought and sold at a frantic pace. History itself has become a commodity; that is, concepts of history are readily incorporated into corporate structures and art and are thus commodified. Although Lyotard makes no objection to postmodernism on these grounds, Jameson and Eagleton do.[10] Because of the blurring of forms, juxtaposing of social periods, and ambiguity and duality of perspective, Jameson finds in postmodern art a depthlessness and commodification, a weakening of historicity, a depleting of contextuality, and a trivializing of culture.[11] Another critic, postcolonialist Helen Tiffin, goes even further in condemning postmodernism, claiming that it is European in origin and "operates as a Euro-American western hegemony," appropriating cultural and historical materials of the marginalized and oppressed everywhere.[12] Linda Hutcheon and Charles Jencks, however, find that its refreshing irreverence for both history and literature implies a recall and reappropriation of the past as well as a reassessment of its relationship to the present. To some extent these two critics exist on the boundary between those who see postmodernism in a political sense and part of the contemporary period and those who regard it as an aesthetic form consisting of various textual strategies and devices. Jencks regards postmodernism as an artistic phenomenon that breaks down traditional codes of art and, when it uses conventions, does so ironically and parodically.[13] It is a peculiar kind of reinvention without a discursive message beyond the confines of art itself.

Although some critics, like Jerome Klinkowitz, assume that structure and theme are likely to be identical in postmodern texts,[14] no such conclusion can generally be drawn: these works are as often as not self-contradictory, self-divided, and fragmented. It is this self-contradiction that Todd Gitlin identifies as characteristic of the movement: "It consistently splices genres, attitudes, styles. It relishes the blurring or juxtaposition of forms (fiction-non-fiction), stances (straight-ironic), moods (violent-comic), cultural levels (high-low). It disdains originality and fancies copies, repetition, the recombination of hand-me-down scraps. It neither embraces nor criticizes, but beholds the world blankly, with a knowingness that dissolves feeling and commitment into irony."[15] Ihab Hassan constructs a similar list, emphasizing pluralism: for example, indeterminacy, decanonization, and carnivalization.[16] These contradictory perceptions of postmodernism bring home fully the issues of plurality, fragmentation, and historical discontinuity that are at the heart of the movement. Although few agree on what postmodernism is or what it accomplishes, I see it as rejecting the existence of consistent personalities and psychological wholeness as well as any stable relationship between signifiers and signifieds. To me, it also emphasizes destabilized and duplicitous meanings, self-reflexivity, discontinuous and polyphonic discourses, arbitrary codes, and inclusion of previously excluded or ignored discourses.

In denying spiritual and psychological completeness or transhistorical, permanent meaning, postmodern authors of the double often make assumptions about culture in general, for personal identity is caught up in the relationship between self and culture, self and history, self and language. Identity, like other linguistic and social codes, is wrapped in the tissue of signification, and it demands de-formation. As John O. Stark suggests, the creation of doubles often "implies that identity is a false category: if two people are alike, or in a simplified double relationship, neither has a unique, well defined identity of his own."[17] Paul Coates similarly finds that the double exists in literature because of our inchoate knowledge that we are incomplete and that we cannot master ourselves.[18] The postmodern double raises questions about fixed categories and constructs, especially about the notion that any human being has a unified identity. As a result, the fiction of the double tends to be antimimetic and anti-epiphanic, undercutting the view that a literary character must of necessity learn something new and grow to maturity and psychological wholeness. It often accomplishes this aim by introducing multiple narrative perspectives or faulty first-person ones, so that the basis of human perception is questioned. For Dick Higgins, postmodernism rejects reality's and fiction's dependence upon stable cognitive underpinnings or goals; this "postcognitive" interrogation of self, as he calls it, is part of a major reassessment of the self within contemporary culture and becomes a metaphor for the interrogation of all formal social structures and discursive practices.[19] For Linda Hutcheon, the metaphor of splitting in Salmon Rushdie's *Midnight's Children* and the doubling effect in

D. M. Thomas's *The White Hotel* help to identify the postmodern emphasis upon multiple subjectivity, cultural diversity, and plural narratives as well as the erosion of "the empirical basis of the humanist and positivist concepts of knowledge."[20]

In exploring these postmodern possibilities for doubles and doubling, my study will deal with representative works of six postmodern American writers: Nabokov, Pynchon, Hawkes, Barth, Brautigan, and Federman. Each in his own way has significantly "de-formed" and "re-formed" the double; each is concerned with the postmodern inquiry into structures and rules of signification in society, fiction, and language; and each is interested in undermining and replenishing them.

Nabokov, Pynchon, Hawkes, and Barth are chosen not only because of their pervasive use of the double but because they are generally considered to be among the most important postmodern American writers; Brautigan and Federman are included because their use of the double is more eccentric, more outrageous, more avant-garde, and less privileged than that of other postmodernists. Other figures, such as Barthelme and Vonnegut, could no doubt be added, but their inclusion would not significantly alter my thesis.

This study will not, and cannot of course, be exhaustive. Neither postmodernism nor the double is a static literary motif, construct, movement, or style. Both contain numerous irreconcilable contradictions, and both will continue to change; readers should rightly challenge some of my implicit assumptions and explicit categories. Still, I have defined postmodernism and looked at the double in ways that I hope will indicate their wide-ranging possibilities and help readers rethink their ways and uses.

The History of the Double
Traditional and Postmodern Versions

1

IN *THE ARCHAEOLOGY OF KNOWLEDGE,* MICHEL FOUCAULT QUERIES the processes that yield historical conclusions. His deep mistrust of series, criteria for periodization, levels of hierarchy, and stratification, as well as associations that lead to causality, prompts him to question how written documentation has been used to create unities and totalities—monuments of history. He even questions the facts upon which assumptions are based because facts cannot, he suggests, be seen as separable from their interpretations. Out of such conviction he argues against closure and teleology, against any certainty in the presentation of the history of ideas, for he finds that history is a reflection of the people who write it and hence invent it rather than a valid, objective interpretation of indisputable facts. He himself prefers the practice of archaeology over history to discover the "silent monuments, inert traces, objects without context, and things left by the past" that can attain meaning and legitimacy only through the reevaluation of historical discourse.[1] In his archaeological method he sifts the "silent" data to present different facts, offer manifold and frequently undecidable interpretations, discover differences, and especially create ruptures and discontinuities—rupture and discontinuity serving as a method of investigation and the product of it. His findings, then, are hesitant, evasive, and inconclusive.

To the extent that my study explores the double, a discourse that is in itself "denaturalized" and consequently one that has been largely ignored, suppressed, and silenced by novelists and critics of realism, it is archaeological. Yet in exploring the history of the double and seeing patterns, my study risks creating origins, installing fixed categories, controlling knowledge, attempting to understand the past through present circumstances and beliefs, and hence defining progress. In that sense, my attempt to locate the double as a subject, clarify contemporary approaches to it, and give unified meaning to them is historical. Such a blending of the evasive and direct, occluding and clarifying, self-differing and analytically categorical, is implicitly self-contradictory, a strategy that is in keeping with the flickering, hologramatic presentation of the double in literature. The double is constituted upon difference, and despite my, or anyone's, attempts to categorize, elucidate, resolve differences, and validate categories through well-poised examples, will always remain duplicitous, dialogic, and relativized.

The sign of the double is an ancient one. It has roots in the earliest Western literature, and it enjoys an astonishing capacity for survival and recombination. Its meaning, like that of any signifier, has not remained constant but has variously emphasized the spiritual, the psychological, and more recently, the process of signifying itself.

The twin, as several critics—Otto Rank, Ralph Tymms, Robert Rogers, Carl Keppler, and Clifford Hallam, for example—have pointed out, is the most ancient and pervasive version of the double, and as John Barth has observed, the twin "signified whatever dualisms a culture entertained."[2] Sir James G. Frazer has recorded stories of twins from almost every culture: North American Indian, European, Semitic, African, and Oriental.[3] Twins are relatively rare, and their existence has traditionally been considered unusual and exotic. Some societies believe that with their own individual talents and gifts, twins bring good luck to the community; other societies banish or kill them as unnatural and intolerable social and spiritual deviants. In certain cases, twins are assumed to possess special spiritual affinities leading to completeness and wholeness uncharacteristic of nontwins; in other instances, twins are viewed as natural antagonists; in still others, the closeness of male and female twins is regarded as incestuous.

Earliest recorded accounts of twins stress their spiritual affinity. Plato, in the *Symposium*, used twinship to explain human origin, deep spiritual divisions, and sexual preference. According to Plato, humans were once whole but of three distinct types: male, female, or hermaphrodite.[4] They possessed double sets of arms, legs, and genitalia, arranged to form a harmonious circle. Punishing them for their overweening pride in their completeness and their effrontery in attempting to mount to the heavens, Zeus split human beings in two. Each individual consequently now longs to be reunited with his or her other half: a male whose original form was male tends towards homosexuality; a female who was joined with a female becomes lesbian; and a male or female whose form was hermaphroditic is heterosexual. This desire for unity is, according to Plato, indicative of human need to move from the world of halves, material forms, and illusions to the realm of wholeness, spirituality, and perfect reality.

Plato finds mankind's deep yearning for an ideal world in still another way.[5] Each human being has a fundamental wish for immortality—whether through offspring, memory of deeds done, or qualities of wisdom or virtue—for thereby a man pursues the good and the beautiful, and his soul is transported from the fleeting material world of the senses to the immutable world of perfect forms. The material world is but a pale shadow, a reflection of an ideal sphere, and man only the remnant of a once perfect whole. Hence, man is torn between the desire for material well-being and that for spiritual beauty and excellence.

The tale of Narcissus has been understood as the epipsychean longing for unification. In the *Metamorphoses*, old Tiresias, always ambiguous, prophesies that the boy Narcissus will enjoy a long life if he does not know himself. But his fascination with his own image in the surface of a pool leads to his early death through self-love. Although Freud has taken Narcissus's mirror image as a projected double that must be acknowledged and understood, the early Neoplatonists saw Narcissus as an individual trapped in human form trying to reach through the mirror surface of physical reality to a primal, eternal form symbolized by the reflection in the pool.[6]

To some extent, the ancient Egyptian belief in the ka also stresses the division between spiritual and material in its assertion that everyone brings into life a double and that every aspect of existence has a shadow double. He who is able to perceive the hidden essence, the double of all life, has magical, prophetic powers. Jewish lore incorporates a similar tradition of the prophetic powers that come to one who encounters his double. Thus, both Platonism and Semitic myth stress the strength that comes with wholeness and unity.

European folklore in general maintains the dualistic view implicit in these myths: the soul is the key to life and consequently the object of demonic attack. It is often identified with the shadow, and many popular accounts narrate the attempts of the trickster-devil to steal it. These *schauerromanen* deal with the horror experienced by a person who casts no shadow, one whose spiritual self has been destroyed. Because the soul is noncorporeal, it is believed to have special powers and while the body is sleeping to be able to roam freely; consequently, the body must remain receptive to the reentry of the soul. As Frazer remarks of tribal beliefs, "The animal inside the animal, the man inside the man is the soul. And as the activity of an animal or man is explained by the presence of the soul, so the repose of sleep or death is explained by its absence. . . . If death be the permanent absence of the soul, the way to guard against it is either to prevent the soul from leaving the body, or, if it does depart, to ensure that it shall return."[7] Perhaps because the soul is said to range outside the body and because it leaves the body at death, human beings who see their doubles, their exact material replications, will according to popular folklore soon die. Among the Scots the fetch or wraith is a ghastly apparition seen just before death.[8] The body and soul together, then, form a perfectible union; deprived of the soul, the body is devoid of meaningful life.

Common to these interpretations is the belief that the spiritual must be privileged over the physical. Even so, spirituality is fully attainable only within the world of pure form. On earth, human beings must be content with an ambiguous relationship between body and soul, material form and spiritual shadow. The separate parts of reality should function cohesively, but division and disunity mar this ideal unity.

Although dating back to Plato at least, this dualism gathered new significance in the eighteenth and nineteenth centuries, involving a doubleness of spirit and matter, of form and content, of reflection and reflected. It included not only oppositions between good and evil, light and dark, creation and destruction, mortality and immortality, spiritual substance and earthly dross, but also such polarities as faith and humanistic rationalism, poetry and science, the individual and society. Where Victorian attitudes were concerned, Masao Miyoshi reminds us, each thing was divided against itself: God utterly opposed Satan; the individual will was unalterably at odds with social responsibility; sensuality was irreconcilable with spirituality; reason and emotion were incompatible.[9] Miyoshi treats all such pairs as legitimate doubles, as does Karl Miller, who considers phantasmagoric doubles, psychic duplication, and division equivalent to philosophical dualism in which "the component parts may complete, resemble or repel one another."[10] Carl Keppler accepts a dualistic basis for doubles but maintains that literary doubles must be personified as first and second selves, as he calls protagonist and antagonist, and divided into the "diabolical and saintly, death-bringing and life-giving, masculine and feminine, hated and beloved."[11] Characters are important both in their own right and as referents and symbols for the underlying ideas.

The German tradition, however, is a notable exception to a belief in a fixed binary opposition. This approach to dualism, greatly influential in nineteenth-century thought, holds that dualistic views, entities, or states of being must be held in continual tension. Friedrich Schlegel and Friedrich Schiller affirm this poetic, paradoxical equipoise and differentiate it from either a fixed dualism in which the elements are irresolvably polarized or a too-easy synthesis in which the separate elements merge, blend, and wholly disappear. For Schlegel, both the Aristotelian mean and the Hegelian synthesis are thoughtless affirmations; for Schiller, "play," one of three basic human drives, maintains an equipoise between the other drives of human abstraction and materiality. Such a paradoxical resolution of dualities is applicable either on the universal or on the personal scale—and applicable either to absolute universal principles or to man himself, whether or not, as Fichte argues, these absolutes are created and sustained only through the human intellect. The universe, governed by both flux and order, is always in a creative state of becoming. The material realm must be balanced with the spiritual world. A human being is also just such a paradox. A physical, moral, and spiritual being, he maintains those properties in a delicately balanced suspension, neither sacrificing one for the other nor conflating them.[12]

According to Schlegel, literature itself is dualistic and depends upon paradox—the delicate balance of the fantastic, the sentimental, and the mimetic, and in a related sense the perfection of classic orderliness coexisting with disruptive, evolving ideas. Schlegel's philosophy, as Hans Eichner observes, emphasizes the integrated doubleness at the heart of literature and reality: "Playfulness and seriousness, intuition and circumspection, the self-intoxication of genius and critical detachment, 'sentimental,' metaphysical content and 'fantastic,' witty form—all these he regarded as different aspects of the same phenomenon, the essential 'duplicity' of art, which reflected the 'duplicity' of man and the duplicity—the infinite plenitude and infinite unity—of the world itself."[13] Doubleness, duplicity, and dualism—these are often interchangeable terms.

Marianne Wain argues that the doubles appearing in Chamisso, Jean-Paul Richter, Hoffmann, and Brentano can be traced back to this "duplicity."[14] Their treatment of the double suggests that a failure to maintain a balanced, united view leads to personal disintegration. Jean Paul's ill-fated doubles, Siebenkas and Leibgeber, encapsulate the principle that the spiritual cannot be separated from the emotional or physical self. In selling his shadow (and hence his soul) for gold and knowledge, Chamisso's Peter Schlemihl loses the spiritual qualities of love and friendship. When Hoffmann's Giglio, in *Prinzessin Brambilla*, allows delusional fantasy about his self-worth to triumph over the realities of his modest rank and income, he comes perilously close to losing the love of the beautiful seamstress Giacinta. These instances of the double function as parables of the need for the paradoxical balance and resolution of opposites on both cosmic and individual levels.

While eighteenth- and early nineteenth-century authors, especially in the German tradition, often deal with the paradoxical resolution of opposites, late nineteenth-century writers rarely do so. They often accept dualistic categories but are able neither to transcend the limitations of dualism nor resolve the discord at the heart of reality. When, in *Ecce Homo*, Friedrich Nietzsche announces that he is a doppelgänger with a second and even third face, he speaks of "dual experiences" and separate worlds that cannot be conjoined.[15] These selves and worlds are equally strong and coexistent, but they are incapable of reconciliation: he is, at the same time, Dionysian and Apollonian, decadent and healthy, German and Polish, but these polarities repel each other. Such unreconciled dualities are also readily apparent in the literature of the period. In Wilde's *The Portrait of Dorian Gray*, the orders of art and morality are judged entirely separate. To forget about their distinctions is to abandon morality and to create bad art. Such is also the case in Melville's "Bartleby the Scrivener," which, although always elusive, can be looked at as a psychodrama,[16] illustrating the irreconcilability of materialism and spirituality, society and the individual, cultural affirmation and personal rebellion. According to Robert Rogers, the story is also about Melville himself and serves a defensive purpose in allowing him to vent his frustration that the reading public will not accept his later literary offerings; it concerns a distinct polarity between author and audience.[17] In these works the desire for paradoxical resolution still exists, though the impossibility of achieving it is clear. The characters, and possibly the authors, remain dualistically split.

Though at only a slight remove from dualism, the psychological conflict between the conscious and the unconscious in Freud and Jung leads to major new developments in the concept of the double. In general, these psychological conceptions concern a normative self and its double or even serial neurotic or psychotic deviations. In "The 'Uncanny,' " "Beyond the Pleasure Principle," and "On Narcissism," Freud argues that one form of neurosis is narcissism, which deviates from the ideal balance between the superego (the reality principle or observance of strictly defined social normatives) and the id (the pleasure principle or erotic, selfish, and anti-social responses). This narcissism results from a child's inability to resolve the conflict between desire for his mother (the familiar) and fear of offending his father (the external, unfamiliar world and alternative sexual drives) and is manifested by the self taking itself as an object of libidinal love.

The ego's desire for a stress-free state results in a narcissism that shuts out the anxiety-generating external world and in extreme cases leads to suicide. Since Freud assumed that an author typically writes of his neuroses, the literary double became in his mind an image of the author's repressed, regressive, autoerotic unconscious. Those who use Freudian premises to explore the double in fiction often write of this view of the unconscious.[18] Such criticism also frequently changes the emphasis from text to author: a literary text can illuminate not only the duality of the world but the duality of the author's self, for as "the playground of the unconscious," the literary text "will reveal unconscious connections, displacements, and condensations of meaning."[19] Rogers has convincingly shown that the motif of homosexuality in *The Picture of Dorian Gray* bears upon Wilde's sexual practices, that the sexuality of the narrator in "The Horla" relates to Maupassant's satyriasis, and that the sexual repression of Spencer Brydon in "The Jolly Corner" serves to illustrate some of James's repressions. Still, as he also indicates, those who employ the double do not only write unwittingly of their own psychological dispositions but consciously or subconsciously perceive deviations in others. Andersen's "The Shadow" and Hawthorne's "Monsieur du Miroir" are probably not about their authors but do demonstrate an understanding of psychological decomposition.[20] Deviations representing the decomposition of the mind are explored through implicit (latent) and explicit (manifest) doubles in which the fragmentation may be both dual and multiple (or composite). In the process of doubling by multiplication, different characters represent the working out of a single ideal, problem, or attitude as opposed to doubling by division in which several characters represent opposing qualities.

Another aspect of Freudian criticism that involves the double is the relationship between thanatos and eros. For Freud, the *process* of doubling, dividing, and interchanging the self is part of his theory of regression. The "compulsion to repeat," to reexperience "something identical," even to play the same game again and again, is a source of pleasure and as much a part of the uncanny as manifest doubles.[21] In "Beyond the Pleasure Principle," Freud defines an instinct as "an urge inherent in organic life to restore an earlier state of things,"[22] to regress to a perfectly protected, tension-free state characteristic of infancy or the inorganic state from which life began. He labels this the "thanatopsis urge," for it is essentially the same as a death wish. Hence, doubling or repeating the stable and familiar may seem to guarantee self-preservation, self-assertion, and mastery, but actually it manifests the will to death.

The thanatos instinct is the double of the eros or life instinct. Erotic dreams include the "doubling or multiplication of a genital symbol which involves a fear of castration or preservation against extinction."[23] Sexual instincts are life instincts and aspects of the will to live. The life instincts and the multiplicity of death instincts are presented in dramatic terms of confrontation in which they take on distinctly human dimensions with independent thoughts and wills. Freud admits that he has posited in this separation of instincts a Schopenhauerian dualistic view of instinctual life: "Death is the 'true result and to that extent the purpose of life,'" while the sexual instinct is the embodiment of the will to live."[24] Doubles functioning in unity and harmony are like superego and id in harmonious balance and present an image of well-being, the so-called immortal self. Antagonistic doubles suggest the opposition between id and superego and imply personal disintegration or decomposition, the so-called second self.[25] In either case, these doubles explore the "sense of the division to which the human mind in conflict with itself is susceptible."[26] In its normal state the self is unified, coherent, and nicely balanced between individual needs and social regulations; in its abnormal state, it is split or decomposed. Psychoanalytic critics argue, then, that the divided self, as a psychological phenomenon, has to be taken seriously.

Several works of American literature with implicit and explicit doubles can be read meaningfully in terms of Freudian psychology. Hemingway's classic *The Sun Also Rises* explores among other things the insurmountable problems caused by narcissistic thanatos instincts. In it the perpetual cycle of unfulfilled desire is never resolved, and Brett's constant attempts to reenact earlier meaningful sexual relationships ironically exemplify the thanatos instinct, for the urge to repeat leads to nothing new and productive in her relationships but only to sterility or death. Although centrally concerned with the important question of race relations in Mississippi, Faulkner's *Go Down, Moses* also presents several characters who function as psychological doubles. The white protagonist, Ike McCaslin, is a rational, reticent, socially privileged, and narcissistic figure, but his foster brother Henry and other blacks in the book reflect a reserve of love and understanding that he lacks. He manifests the qualities of the repressive superego or the conscious, while they represent the requirements of the id or the unconscious. The opposition is complementary in nature and shows what might be possible without primary forms of narcissism.

Bellow's *Mr. Sammler's Planet* concerns the suppression of desire by Sammler, who has seen too much horror and grief to feel or to will anything. His unbroken routine, while seeming to hold chaos at bay, actually numbs him to the vital and spontaneous. He prefers to hear about or voyeuristically witness the affairs of other people. Other males in the book with whom he identifies—the sensual black thief, the pragmatic nephew, the highly intellectual scientist—represent psychological and moral alternatives, ultimately suggesting that a paralyzed id or an overdeveloped superego negates a full life. These are subtly executed works in which the doubles, because they are latent, earn the praise of the psychoanalytic critics who refuse to acknowledge the literary importance of manifest doubles, which they frequently dismiss as meretricious, aesthetically inferior, and too transparent to be taken seriously. As a consequence, they marginalize them in favor of complex forms of literature.[27] This hierarchizing papers over a gap that needs to be exposed by poststructuralist explorations.

Although some would argue that Freud's theory of the id, super-ego, and ego has had a greater impact on interpretations of the double, most would agree that Jung's theory of the shadow has also had significant influence. In his papers "The Ego," "The Shadow," "The Self," "The Syzygy: Anima and Animus," and "The Fight with the Shadow," Jung develops his view that the shadow (or double), the anima, and the animus constitute the unconscious—the unseemly, antisocial, emotional, and spontaneous side of the personality. This part of the personality, Jung argues, has been subjugated by the rationally governed, orderly, and socially acceptable ego. This shadow, sometimes characterized as dark and lurking, at other times is described as light and effervescent, though in both instances perhaps socially unacceptable. The ego governs one's performance in the known and perceptible outer world, whereas the shadow dominates the unknown—or partially known—hidden inner world. When the two are in balance, the self is complete; when they are not synchro-nized—when, for instance, too much emphasis is placed upon reason and order—the necessary tension breaks down, the personality disin-tegrates, and a syzygy or split figure develops. Ironically, at this point the shadow takes over, and socially unacceptable neurotic behavior is the result.

The shadow poses a moral problem in challenging the "ego-personality" since "to become conscious of it involves recognizing the dark aspects of the personality as present and real. This act is the essential condition for any kind of self-knowledge, and it therefore, as a rule, meets with considerable resistance."[28] Resistance originates from both the ego and the shadow. The ego refuses to recognize the reality of the shadow because such an admission would erode its dominion. The shadow in turn resists the moral control of the ego by projecting its characteristics onto another person; hence, the ego can-not recognize and govern this obstinate, manipulative, and ultimately self-destructive force.[29] This tug-of-war between ego and shadow pro-vides the groundwork for Jung's understanding of the double both in the ego's failure to recognize and incorporate it and in the shadow's craving to subvert the power of the ego.

This conception of the shadow has had a powerful influence on recent notions of the double because it seems to square with twentieth-century experience. Jung argues that "the more civilized, the more unconscious and complicated a man is, the less he is able to follow his instincts. His complicated living conditions and the influence of his environment are so strong that they drown the quiet voice of nature. Opinions, beliefs, theories, and collective tendencies appear in its stead and back up all the aberrations of the conscious mind."[30] In an age that still recalls the horrors of two world wars fought by civilized human beings, this description of the shadow has an immediate and powerful appeal.

Another manifestation of the double is, according to Jung, the dream in which all the characters "are personified features of the dreamer's own personality." The dream is "a theater in which the dreamer is himself, the scene, the player, the prompter, the producer, the author, public and the critic."[31] The personae of dreams, fiction about dreams, and perhaps fiction itself are arguably doubles of the dreamer-writer.

Whereas Freud's psychological view of the double is particularly useful in accounting for physical drives and sexual obsessions, Jung's view addresses a broad range of personality situations—disintegration, alienation, insufficient integration, and wholeness itself—of which sexuality is but one aspect. For this reason, literature about the dawning of awareness, whether in children, adolescents, or adults, may helpfully be read in terms of the Jungian interpretation of the double. The relationships between Alice and Cora in Cooper's *The Last of the Mohicans*, Hilda and Miriam in Hawthorne's *The Marble Faun*, Rowena and Ligeia in Poe's "Ligeia," and Huck and Jim in Twain's *The Adventures of Huckleberry Finn* are only a few of the doubles that have been meaningfully analyzed from Jungian perspectives. Other cases in point, which I should like to explore briefly, are Ursula K. LeGuin's *The Wizard of Earthsea*, Joseph Conrad's "The Secret Sharer" and *Under Western Eyes*, and John Knowles's *A Separate Peace*.

In *The Wizard of Earthsea* the shadow may be seen as the hero's dark side, which must be recognized and identified if personal disintegration is to be prevented. LeGuin paraphrases Jung, remarking of her own book "that the first step is to turn around and follow your own shadow . . . on the other side of [y]our psyche, the dark brother of the conscious mind."[32] Furthermore, she argues that "the shadow stands on the threshold between the conscious and unconscious mind, and we meet it in our dreams, as sister, brother, friend, beast, monster, enemy, guide. It is all we don't want to, can't, admit into our conscious self, all the qualities and tendencies within us which have been repressed, denied, or not used." She concludes, "It is inferior, primitive, awkward, animallike, childlike; powerful, vital, spontaneous. It's not weak and decent . . . ; it's dark and hairy and unseemly; but, without it, the person is nothing."[33] Conrad similarly uses the double to describe the need to integrate the conscious and the unconscious, the social instincts and the antisocial instincts. In "The Secret Sharer" this takes the form of an untested captain's vicarious discovery of personal weakness, then strength, through one who is identical to him but has killed to establish order and preserve a ship—Conrad's customary metaphor for society. His *Under Western Eyes*, on the other hand, concerns a man, Razumov, who suffers horribly for failing to recognize and benefit from an alter ego, Haldin. In not responding favorably to Haldin's need for asylum after having killed a corrupt bureaucrat, Razumov pays a terrible personal price for not allowing the unstable, unsafe, and illegal into his life. Psychological disintegration and personal disgrace result from his failure to accommodate and balance differing forces and instincts.

The same is true in Knowles's *A Separate Peace* where the shadow self is actually described in terms of lightness, agility, and beauty, while the rational self is scheming, malevolent, and untrustworthy. A social conformist is unable to accept the Dionysian life and thereby causes unhappiness, destruction, and death. Here the shadow serves as the bringer of light and happiness and the ego as the destroyer of the edenic world. These doubles are sometimes viewed as reflections of one another and at others as realistically drawn separate entities, living records "of imaginative experience, of a relationship given a peculiar electrical excitement by the simultaneous separateness and sameness, attraction and repulsion, of the two beings involved in it."[34]

The conscious and unconscious, or ego and alter ego, lend themselves to allegories of selfhood or universal conflict. Robert Scholes asserts that both Freud and Jung present a new, unseen allegorical world. Notions of universal good and evil and psychological categories may seem far removed from one another, but speculations about the invisible world of human psychology are more philosophical than scientific, and perhaps for this very reason modern people believe in them with the same tenacious faith that past ages gave to Christianity.[35] In that sense, the differences between Freud and Jung are less important than the similarities in their partitioning of the psyche in a way that lends itself to allegorization. Their way of partitioning differs little from the more metaphysically construed dualistic categories. Thus, Otto Rank, in "The Double as Immortal Self," perceives this motif in myth, legend, and fiction as a yearning for wholeness; Carl F. Keppler argues that doubles often suggest "an evil beyond their specific evil: evil on a supra-individual, universal scale"; and Robert Rogers sees specific parallels between Plato's observations and Freud's, remarking that "an almost ineluctable dualism would seem to haunt our categories of the double in literature."[36]

The nature of allegorical doubles has nonetheless undergone a transformation. Reason, seemliness, and conscience in the traditional double were privileged over the irrational, unseemly, and immoral, but the dark side of human beings attains a legitimacy of its own in recent cultural dualism. As a result, affections, strong emotions, sexual inclinations, antisocial desires, and subversive dreams are given prominence. In fact, the soul ceases to be conceived of as a spiritual and rational entity and is associated with deeply felt, irrational, and subversive emotions. Herbert Marcuse has noticed that the signifying power of the term *soul* changed radically during the 1960s with colorations of black "soul" music and irrationality,[37] so that the pure soul, the unconscious self or shadow, and the libido merge to form a new ideal—dark, obsessive, but positive. In general, this new signification has characterized those contemporary French writers who use the double in a psychological sense, including Jacques Lacan and Julia Kristeva, both of whom see the dark and libidinous side as healthy and necessary to counter the overrationality of the ego.

The double has come to stand outside the conventions of the real world in order to assess and counter conventionally accepted psychological reality.[38] To extend Rosemary Jackson's assumptions, the double, like other devices of fantasy, opens a window onto psychological and social disorder and illegality, onto what lies outside the structures of dominant value systems.[39] It is transgressive and exposes an uncontrollable and unpleasurable side of the individual often concealed behind the facade of cohesive selfhood and social and literary convention.

Although Jacques Lacan accepts Freud's basic vocabulary, he too transforms the basic models, arguing that the unconscious is structured like a language in which categories and significations shift and float. Moreover, the modalities and language of the unconscious are so remote and hidden as to be indefinable, and one can never be certain of understanding the true nature of the self. Since the conscious creates the language used to describe the unconscious, any analysis is problematic, and suppositions about dualistic distinctions between the conscious and the unconscious—what Lacan calls the *je* and the *moi*—are untrustworthy. Basing his distinctions on binary patterns with an unusual ability for recombination,[40] Lacan sees the conscious and the unconscious as bound together like the two poles of a metaphor, with transference between them. As with Freud, the id, the *moi*, or the object is identified with the unconscious and the pleasure principle, and the superego, the *je* (the ego ideal), or the subject is identified with the conscious and the reality principle, and although each of these "selves" has a separate language or discourse—the id using the unwritten hieroglyphics of dreams and the superego using the scriptible language of science and rationality (the *cogito*)—their languages and modes are more fluid than fixed, and as a result they influence each other. Lacan further argues that dreams are not necessarily constant, for the language of the unconscious, like that of the conscious, changes diachronically.

What Lacan ultimately seems to find most revolutionary about Freud's view is not only that the unconscious exists separately from the conscious but that their manifestations—in dreams, for example—have neither ascertainable signifier nor signified; they are shifters or floating signifiers. The conscious and the unconscious are less distinct than Freud perceived, and Lacan uses the Möbius strip to illustrate that the conscious contains the unconscious and that their discourses or systems of signification are not discrete but entwined. The subject or "self" is not only opposed to the "other" but is in a subtle way also part of it. Arguing in this Lacanian manner, Paul Coates sees the double as a sign of the ever-alienated and yet aligned unconscious.[41] Lacan's break from both Freud's dualism and his conception of a unified, totalized personality lessens the tendency toward allegorization in its emphasis upon dialectical interaction and transference or paradoxical pluralism.

Of special importance to these new conceptions of the double is Lacan's belief that the unconscious is constituted like a language. For him, the human being can be viewed only through language, so language becomes the basis for all reality. Lacan consequently speaks almost in the same breath of the uneasy relationship of the conscious and the unconscious, of the signifier and the signified. The slipperiness of self and reality is at once the slipperiness and elusiveness of the communication act.

This new Lacanian view of self and language has made untenable traditional ramifications of the psychological double, such as those that concern the way gender roles have been arbitrarily assigned to point to an equation between rationality and maleness or irrationality and femaleness. Joanne Blum thinks that the male-female double discourse in women's fiction reflects an effort to unsettle male-dominated assumptions about gender and to suggest alternative roles.[42] Another assumption undone by Lacanian thinking is that narcissism is necessarily negative. While Freud assumed that homosexuality is one of the primary negative effects of narcissism and a problematic manifestation of the double, current psychological studies of the double often valorize homosexuality. In studying the mother-daughter double in Diderot's *La Religieuse*, for example, Carolyn A. Durham defends the lesbian relationship as unpatriarchal and ideologically liberating.[43]

Lacan's reevaluation of psychological categories and their relationship to the double has even wider ranging effects, for doubts about Freud's psychological categories and the nature of the double fundamentally relate to doubts by poststructuralists about the dualistic premises that have generated such categories. Roland Barthes's comment in *Mythologies* that psychology arbitrarily encodes in language a view of a person that exists apart from the person's real circumstances—that it exemplifies the rich against the poor, the mass against the individual, psychological norms against actual situations—is part of his belief that these dualistic oppositions are built upon a deep-seated, but false, binary principle.[44] He fears that works by Roman Jakobson and Ferdinand de Saussure, which established the foundations of linguistic studies, tend to give binary systematizing a legitimacy it does not deserve and to make it appear natural.[45]

Such reservations appear abundantly in postmodern literature and in poststructural theory. Indeed, it is on the issues of duality, duplicity, and doubleness that literature and theory are most sensitive and intersect strikingly. Although not causally related, postmodernism and poststructuralism both use the arguments and devices of binary systematizing to subvert that logic and influence in modern culture. Both perceive the binary system as the greatest barrier to rethinking ourselves, society, and history. Poststructural critical theory explicitly, and postmodern fiction implicitly, interrogate the duality upon which modernism and premodernism are thought to be centered. They do so not to rehierarchize binary oppositions but to suggest that all systems, hierarchies, and patterns of meaning are human constructs.

Poststructuralist thinkers such as Jacques Derrida and Michel Foucault often argue against a logic based upon binarity in which the first term is hierarchically privileged over the second in such pairings as good-evil, being-nothingness, presence-absence, man-woman, and soul-body; the second term in these instances is regarded as "the negative, corrupt, undesirable version of the first, a fall away from it."[46] Derrida's and Foucault's task is to unsettle the logic that underlies these dichotomies. They are not so sanguine as to believe that we in the Western world can rid ourselves of a concept so deeply engrained in history and culture, one with roots in Plato and Socrates, but their discussions nevertheless cast doubt upon the concept or put it "under erasure." By recognizing and exposing the weaknesses of binarity, by simultaneously using it and refuting it, they assist in its possible demystification.

Derrida regularly uses the term *double* as a means of engaging this theme. His use of the double is best characterized by his tendency to equate it with repetition and the *supplément*. To repeat something adds to the first iteration, but it also changes it in some way, providing a substitution of meaning. This belief leads Derrida to conclude that "pure" repetition or "pure" binary opposition is as impossible as "pure" meaning and further to advocate a new kind of difference, self-difference, or undecidability. "Double, contradictory, [and] undecidable" are thus equivalent terms to describe this process of subverted meaning.[47] In "The Double Session" Derrida speaks of double hymen, double invagination, double vow, double token, and double affirmation to address the issue of repetition, binarity, and undecidability. He playfully repeats himself, doubles the rhetoric, and duplicates the typography, conveying the impression that likenesses and similarities are not necessarily means of producing uniformity nor differences necessarily means of producing opposition. Differences, looked at from a certain perspective, may instead communicate ideas of fragmentation and plurality.[48] His writings are themselves double-voiced: they employ the binary principle in language and thought to undermine it. Derrida's double essay, "Living On: *Border Lines*," can serve to illustrate this process. The format of the essay is double, the top three-quarters of each page given over to one topic ("Living On"), the bottom quarter to another (*"Border Lines"*). The title, the structural format, the content (life and death), all pertain to the double, which is simultaneously divided and joined, used and refuted. Derrida employs the double in this fashion to transgress accepted ways of thinking based upon causality and linearity.

Foucault, in many of his works—among them *The Birth of the Clinic, The History of Sexuality, Raymond Roussel, The Order of Things, Madness and Civilization,* and *Language, Counter-Memory, Practice*—similarly uses the term *double* to imply the numerous possibilities arising out of traditional conceptions of duality and binarity. He frequently compares and contrasts two similar concepts or aspects of a concept, as a structuralist might, but then shows their fissures, ruptures, and inherent gaps, for, he believes, at the heart of sameness, similitude, and analogy is difference. Similarly, at the "center" of a double is a lacuna, so that to double and engage in the play of difference simultaneously means to find less than one and more than two. The term *double* evokes multiplicity, plurality, and absence; it neither refers to a precise parallel between two things nor means "two-of."[49]

To a considerable degree, Foucault's use of the double hinges on his discussion of how human beings are made subjects. One area of his study concerns "dividing practices": "The subject is either divided inside himself or divided from others. This process objectivizes him."[50] While conceptions of insanity, disease, and criminality divide people into groups of sane or insane, healthy or sick, criminal or law-abiding, language itself, Foucault contends, divides the subject, for one's experience is not what can be described in language. The failure of language to express "the thing" or pure experience is further complicated by yet another divider, the fact that language refers to itself. Foucault sees each of us as existing in the "space of self-representation and reduplication" in which alphabetical writing (as opposed to ideographic writing) represents the phonetic signifiers of spoken language and never the signifieds of a thing.[51] Language referring to language is not representational but, like a mirror image or a double, is self-representational and reduplicative and yet distorted or faulty, for writing is not identical with speech. Within this labyrinth or self-enclosed reflection of linguistic repetition and doubled identity exists a gap, illustrating that difference lies at the heart of sameness.

Foucault, in "Man and His Doubles," qualifies this position, calling language one of the real doubles. It binds our notion of reality to experience; it is the linguistic structure that accounts for, even hides, experience itself; and it exists in an infinite order of possibilities of construction, dissemination, and interpretation. Unendingly multiplicitous and duplicitous, language is the medium in which the structure of contraries must be joined and bridged but in which difference must be recognized. The result is a simultaneity of "retreat *and* return, of thought *and* the unthought, of the empirical *and* the transcendental."[52] This view of language seems to stress the paradoxical, but for Foucault the relationship of language to reality is none other than the play of signifier and signified, exemplified by our being born into and produced by language, yet ultimately producing language. In this circular process, we are receivers and producers, subjects and objects. The double movement based upon the redoublings of language inherent in our structuring of internal and external reality heralds the end of "presence" and dualism, and it validates not a unitary or dual self or a transcendent culture but an endless pluralism and duplicity. At the moment of its repetition, it is self-divided; when it appears to expand effortlessly, it is subject to termination and death.

Foucault's warning against either the binarily separated or the paradoxical extends to his discussion of self and other, subject and object, and difference and repetition. One is never altogether separate from the other or object, but neither is one ever united with it. Difference as "a pure event" is impossible, yet difference suppressed or erased to lead to the "generality of the concept" is undesirable. Foucault hopes for "displaced difference," "difference that displaces and repeats itself," and for undoubled doubles and undifferentiated singles.[53] That is, he posits self-conscious repetition that grasps and queries established categories without dismissing the necessity for such categories, and he advocates difference without capsizing into the anarchic.

Finally, according to Foucault, language embodied in writing seems to bear the responsibility of assuring the self of immortality, but he playfully suggests that language is at once life-giving and energizing—like Scheherazade, all tellers of stories hold death at bay—and the bringer of death, for it limits authorial "existence" to the limited values and understandings of readers and their milieus, not the author's self, understanding, and period. Ironically, writing brings about the author's liberation as well as destruction and death.[54]

Derrida's and Foucault's simultaneous evocation and rejection of the traditional significations of the double lead to another permutation of meaning. By problematizing the term within a context of structural doubling, Derrida and Foucault equate the metaphysical and psychological double with the process of doubling. Because "reality" and "identity" are primarily constructs of language, it is a relatively easy step to affirm the linguistic and literary process of doubling instead of treating the double as a separate person or separate aspect of a personality.[55]

This way of thinking about the double returns us to the old story of Narcissus, suggesting that experience or the interpretation of experience mirrors our minds. But this recent notion of the double emphasizes its structurality and process. The double is not a spirit, thing, or person but an ever-elusive, constantly changing mode of conceptualizing through language. This double—Foucault's and Derrida's—is not the double of the past, the *cogito* existing to confirm what we believed.[56] It is no longer predicated upon a belief in balance, order, reason, and wisdom, upon the rationalistic basis of logocentrism. The process now incorporates the elusiveness of thought and communication and introduces a proliferating, multivalent view of life. The *cogito* must now existentially come to terms with the "unthought," the primacy of experience, emotion, amorality, darkness, and the void.[57]

People are themselves, then, not whole beings but "strange empirico-transcendental doublets,"[58] simultaneously experiencing and conceptualizing, living and speaking in no systematic, binary fashion. Captives of conflicting impulses, cultural processes, and discursive practices, they try, without much success, to characterize themselves as "one," though recognizing inherent polarities: heart and soul, good and evil, mind and body. To recognize the self as "two-of" or possibly many more than two-of is to engage in "the world's play at the level of its decentering."[59]

If these new paradoxical doubles and processes of doubling can replace traditional ones—the devil, the conscience, or the id—then so can others, and Barthes, Derrida, and Foucault examine the nature of displacement or supplementarity. By demonstrating that binary opposition is a cultural phenomenon, describing the predominance of dualism in Western thought, and replacing one set of binary oppositions with another, these writers render dualism impotent as a "natural" or necessary metaphysical system and create a new way of thinking about the double. As Derrida notes, when the "structurality of structure" is perceived, the desire for a center is replaced by an infinite number of "sign-substitutions" whereby everything becomes discourse, an infinite "play of the signified" without any transcendental meaning.[60]

This infinite displacement establishes metonymy as one of the keys to the double in postmodernism and poststructuralist theory. Displacement is inherent in Saussure's theory of binary opposition, which suggests that the use of one term implies all the others that might have been used but were not. Behind each term lurks a paradigmatic range of possibilities that could replace it and consequently hover about the one used. In the sense that the term employed (for example, *Ms.*) can be considered only in contradistinction to and differentiation from unused ones (for example, *Miss* or *Mrs.*), the meaning is, in Derrida's sense, deferred. As an instance, Barthes suggests that a reference to a Doric column implies a comparison with the Ionic or Corinthian. In Foucault's usage, the written form of language doubles and provides a parody of the "naive" spoken form, and the written form refers to the spoken forms of the author and to the spoken and written forms of the reader. This process of the double is not static or linear but circular and never at rest. The double, then, has value in exploring the nature of binary opposition itself in comparing one thing or one term and another—or in exploring the serial oppositions between one thing and many others—or in exploring something present and something absent. The double is thus posited on lack or a gap. Consequently, Paul Coates reckons that the double is imagination, cinema, or fiction—whatever is situated upon what is not present or real to the perceiver.[61]

For some postmodern authors, de-forming the double and applying it more broadly to social structures, institutions, and language is a serious matter, useful in decentering cultural patterns and ideological hegemony. This postmodern awareness of ontological instability queries the nature of the world, the human rules in it, and our multiple selves. It also tends to assess cultural matters, increase historical awareness, and address social and political issues despite the postcolonial exclusion of postmodernism and despite neo-Marxist assertions by Frederic Jameson and Terry Eagleton to the contrary.[62] Linda Hutcheon suggests that parody, itself a double, which insists upon linking its self-reflexive discourse to social discourse, is intrinsic to postmodernism. In the postmodern transgression of convention there is a signaling of "ironic difference at the heart of similarity."[63] Her view is grounded in the theory of Mikhail Bakhtin, who argues in *Rabelais and His World* that entertainments in carnivals and fairs of the late medieval and early Renaissance periods incorporated parodies of political issues that could not otherwise have been raised or mocked in public. Performance of this kind, "carnivalization" and masquerade, lends itself to the play of doubleness in postmodern fiction in which parasitic political, social, and literary texts interrupt and transgress their hosts. This doubling of historical periods and texts may comment both on the appropriated period and text or, in self-parodic fashion, the one in which it appears.

Another whom Hutcheon draws upon for this notion is Julia Kristeva, who in *Séméiotikè* refers to intertextuality as the conscious or unconscious inclusion of other artistic documents. For both Bakhtin and Kristeva, then, texts are double, but for Bakhtin this doubling is politically and consciously motivated, whereas for Kristeva it may simply be unconscious or conscious literary play without a political agenda. For Hutcheon, Bakhtin, and Kristeva, this "counterfeiting" helps to create an ironic space between historical fact and interpretation, between authorized interpretation and idiosyncratic or repressed interpretation. Carnivalization, parody, and irony allow writers to recuperate conventional forms of expression and assumptions about culture without valuing them in a conventional way.[64]

Recognizing and refuting the structure of binary oppositions, especially in the metaphorical and metonymical play of language, permits disordering them and dislodges the implicit link between origin and end. Recognition that the binary pattern of language produces dualistic categories and accounts for traditional notions of the double can liberate the double to speak about doubling itself as well as pluralistic possibilities. The designified double becomes a concrete metaphor for metonymical displacement of value amid the desire for unified meaning.[65] By demonstrating that the double is really only a linguistic device, a metaphor, authors can demythologize it and appropriate it for the very process of deconstruction; they can create a metadouble. The double in postmodern fiction can serve to remind the reader that people as social animals are an assemblage of feelings, linguistic habits, and cultural assumptions with no special core identity and that fiction is a linguistic construction.

Poststructuralists and postmodernists do not aim to create a new kind of dialectic that recognizes and resolves contrastive dualities; instead, through an awareness of metonymical displacement, they establish a dialogue of hesitation in which irreconcilable oppositions refer to the very operation of signifying. The lack of thematic unity and order, overall meaning, and total message thus yields to dissemination, the empty locus or decentered center, the "undecidable ambivalence," the "play of the double," and "the process of interminable substitution."[66] Dissemination refuses totalization and recognizes continuing dialogic pressures and stresses. This view of language is typical of the postmodern text, which foregrounds the "ontological *duality* of metaphor, its participation in two frames of reference with different ontological statuses."[67]

The postmodern use and abuse of these challenged concepts typify the carnivalized, ironic discourse of the double and the supplementary inclusion of the process of doubling. History and society are invoked, but they are invoked ironically, to test the assumptions of the past and present. When the fiction is performative, conventions of literature are similarly challenged. This "dual ontology" demonstrates the contradictory nature of self and reality and leads to the use of the double and doubling as primary metaphors of this ontological process.[68] It is a critical rethinking and reworking, not a pure repetition, of established conventions.

Related to the ontology of social and literary codes is the postmodern practice of grammatical ambiguity, syntactical disruption, linguistic indeterminacy, and the assessment of the status of the word. The act of communication, sending a message from the encoder to the decoder, is unstable and double, as instances of double entendre suggest. Each transmission contains not only the opportunity for misunderstandings but the probability that what the speaker-writer has in mind will not be communicated in any pure and essential way. This issue is closely aligned to what David Lodge describes as the primary markers of postmodern fiction: contradiction, discontinuity, randomness, transgression, excess, and short circuit.[69] Douwe Fokkema compiles a similar list of characteristic features—deliberate indiscrimi-

nateness, nonselection or quasi selection, and logical impossibility—
that also call into question the act of communication.[70] Doubleness and
doubling are linguistic and literary devices to break down assumptions
about logical possibility, reason, powers of discrimination, and consistency. Doubleness argues for neither the impossibility of communication nor the assurance of pure "messaging" but for the destabilizing
and ironizing of all discourse.

For many postmodern authors, all splitting or doubling involves
"the play of metaphor and metonomy which would account for the
split of the subject."[71] The play of signification and narration destabilizes traditional hierarchies of expression and action. It frequently
has a serious purpose in undermining "master" cultural narratives,
whether fiction or larger social constructs, but it may also be merely
performative in linguistic and literary features. The double becomes a
linguistic artifact, stripped of psychological or dualistic significance,
used to explore the play of the signifier itself, often through comic or
parodic forms. As John Barth comments, Jorge Luis Borges's stories
of the double "suggest dizzying multiples and remind one of [Sir
Thomas] Browne's remark that 'every man is not only himself . . . men
are lived over again' " through literature and repetitious discursive
practices.[72] In "The Aleph," Borges himself, one of the founding authors of postmodernism, remarks upon the structurality of the psychological structure and so designifies it. His other works trivialize and
render banal the double in order to demystify it. "Borges and I"
concerns the simple and mundane dualistic division between the private self and the public man; "The Other" similarly depicts an encounter between Borges's younger and older selves; and "The Circular
Ruins" tells of one who dreams his double only to find that he himself
is an illusion dreamt by someone else. Such works reject referential
and transparent conventions of traditional literature and advocate self-
referential and autotelic structural systems. The use of minimalist
techniques is an especially effective means of emphasizing self-referentiality in literature.

The deflating of traditional views of the double and the emphasis
upon the play of signifiers is inherent in metafiction, which often
emphasizes textual surface and intertextuality. Some postmodern met-
afictions play with the double as an inherited linguistic and literary
device, both artificial and arbitrary, and useful to counter socially
constructed rules that try to pass as natural. The double becomes a

metaphor used in linguistic-literary play and denies a scheme of meaning beyond or external to language itself. Such fiction calls attention to the structure and perceived meaning of all constructs—literary, psychological, societal, and metaphysical—ultimately announcing to the reader that everything, including the fiction itself, is neither more nor less than the play of language.

For some, the play of language is Plato's "mere play," a fooling with language and other cultural activities without particular rules, structures, or goals. For others, the unclosed and unstructured play of language and texts leads to new structures and goals; in brief, to games instead of play. For still others, the play is not "mere" play at all, but neither is it game. The world-play at its decentering is drawn from theories of play by Friedrich Nietzsche and Martin Heidegger, who conclude that each of us is responsible not only for transgressing and disrupting current cultural attitudes, beliefs, and codes but also for taking the responsibility of setting our own goals and drawing up our individual rules of belief and conduct. This is radical play without fixed direction or ultimacy.

Regardless of the seriousness or playfulness of the works, postmoderns have transformed the double from an alternative self to an ironic literary device that undermines suggestions of universal harmony, essential duality, psychological wholeness, or stable signification. The concept of the double has broken loose from its traditional literary and psychological moorings and now shares common features with poststructuralist criticism—that of Lacan, Barthes, Foucault, and Derrida—that explores, and often rejects, the nature and implications of the binary systematizing of self, social patterns, and language. The literature of the double increasingly speaks of man's employment of, and skepticism about, traditional modes of systematizing, classifying, categorizing, and structuring.

The coincidence of views between postmodern writers and poststructuralist critics relates to a general awareness of the issue of double purposes and functions in literature and language. The desire for central unity, internal coherence, and narrative consistency in literature has by and large been replaced by the awareness that multiple and contradictory ideas, themes, and structures coexist in a text. Recent critical theory and fictional texts disrupt ordinary expectations and frustrate established methods of presentation and reading.[73] One disruption is the blending or crossing over of literary and critical practices. Both Edward Said and Richard Rorty defend the interrogation and dismantling of barriers between criticism and fiction as necessary and healthy.[74] Another disruption that often relates to the double is the blending of forms so that the text is no longer subservient to totalized conceptions of genre. Boundaries disappear between prose and poetry, expository prose and creative writing, and critical theory and fiction. William Gass shapes portions of *Willie Masters' Lonesome Wife* to resemble concrete poetry and splits some of the pages into two or three parallel texts so that no unified vision prevails. Margins cease to be marginalized. This technique, which Brian McHale labels the "schizoid text,"[75] disrupts successive and regular linear prose and introduces simultaneity, blank spaces, discontinuity, pastiche, and collage. In Vladimir Nabokov's *Pale Fire*, footnotes overshadow the text in emphasis and quantity to present parallel but opposing readings. John Barth's *Sabbatical: A Romance* includes unassimilated pieces of journalism from Baltimore newspapers to query claims of journalistic objectivity and fictional subjectivity. By including theory, his *The Tidewater Tales: A Novel* breaks down his readers' preconceptions that fiction does not present critical theory. In *Glas* Derrida presents an essay on Jean Genet and another on Hegel in two columns on each page, simultaneously creating works of literary criticism and philosophical analysis and "putting under erasure" traditional discipline demarcations and textual unity. Especially among university-trained authors, many of whom continue to occupy positions in academe, double purposes regarding critical theory and fiction are important and have become part of the process of doubling.

One way a literary work may stress the play of signifieds is to comment self-consciously on itself as an intertextual variant or double of other literary works. As T. Jefferson Kline observes, Bertolucci's film adaptation of Dostoevsky's *The Double* creates such an intertextual double.[76] This example may seem to stretch the limits of the double, but within the postmodern context such intertextuality or doubling of texts serves much the same purpose as other metafictive doubles. Barthelme's *Snow White*, for instance, simultaneously parodies the original fairy tale and uses it to explore anti-heroism in urban New York. This fiction exemplifies Derrida's ultimate notion of the double: "A double band, a 'double bind,' and a blindly jealous double . . . a 'double blind' ('double blindalley' in 'The Mirror's Secret'). Double proceedings, double *cortège*, double triumph."[77] This postmodern process of doubling and redoubling is a simultaneous construction and deconstruction, a raveling and unraveling.

These postmodern aims, needless to say, are not altogether attainable. Writers who reject Freudian and Jungian psychology, alter human perception, dethrone the *cogito*, deconstruct culture, mock human pretensions, and decenter the dualistic-psychological double can only partly succeed because people are still the double of their culture, created and sustained by it. Despite their struggles to remain objective, they are at best subjective, narcissistic, and solipsistic, spinning the world out of their language and the various social and literary forms that their milieu has to offer. The world is their inseparable double. Consequently, the double is often used to suggest the inherent difficulties and ambiguities of this process. The worlds that humans create are essentially artistic products of their lively imagination and their knowledge of cultural and literary forms, but they are simultaneously their prisons. There are multiple constructs, plural ways of perceiving reality, frames within frames, doubles upon doubles. These have common denominators, deriving from a common context. They depend upon existing forms, but insofar as they come from various individuals, there are quirks, distortions, and aporias in each of them.

Postmodern authors tend to expose the arbitrary nature of human conceptions of self, reality, and language. They undercut conventional fictional epiphanies in which the central figure advances from incompleteness to wholeness, from ignorance to self-discovery and knowledge. They veer away from linear, progressive, and dramatic action and by disrupting those forms, center on their very arbitrariness. They show a human mind that enjoys form and progressive time, even though these ideas are clearly fabrications, however useful and generally accepted. They strip away texture and depth to emphasize insignificant surface detail and designify the signified.

Analogy and the False Double
Nabokov's Despair

2

To SUGGEST THAT MODERN LITERARY BEGINS AT ANY PARTICULAR POINT is hazardous, but Eagleton thinks it may well have begun in 1917 when Viktor Shklovsky published his important essay "Art as Device."[1] Whether or not he is correct, it is certainly true that the designifying process set in motion by Shklovsky's group of Russian formalists and their successors, Roman Jakobson and Ferdinand de Saussure, has continued to alter the nature of critical theory and literary practice in the poststructuralist and postmodern era.

Postmodern American literature, others would argue, may well have begun with Vladimir Nabokov in 1955. Brian McHale considers Nabokov's early works modernist departures from realistic and symbolist writings and his works after 1955 postmodernist in their use of "absolute epistemological uncertainties" and ontological questions.[2] Like the formalists, Nabokov did not accept literature as a means to explore social issues or intimations of divinity through symbols of higher reality. For him, literature revealed no mediate or ultimate truth, no higher form of cognition or " 'theurgy,' capable of bridging the gap between empirical reality and the 'Unknown.' " The poetic word was no "mystical Logos, reverberating with occult meanings," nor was metaphor the " 'parallelism of the phenomenal and the noumenal,' to reveal the latent correspondences between the world of the senses, the 'realia,' and the superior or transcendental reality, the 'realiora.' "[3] Form and content, *signum* and *signatum*, did not form an undivided unity, nor did the sign itself acquire its own symbolical meaning that must be taken into account together with the content.

33

Nabokov affirms instead the value of the word for its own sake, the primacy of form over content, and the principle of self-referentiality. A work of fiction, his novels suggest, is self-contained or at most intertextual. It neither asks nor answers questions concerning the world outside itself; if it does, then it presents the view that without any necessary dependency, fiction is analogous to life. Both are self-referential entities, acknowledging nothing beyond their self-contained, self-perpetuated, autonomous boundaries.

This distinction between referentiality and self-referentiality arises from questions of perception and the function of the literature of the creative imagination. For Nabokov, art dehabituates and defamiliarizes. Not only must it make strange, as Viktor Shklovsky phrases it,[4] but it must also be emancipated from such related disciplines as philosophy, religion, and psychology. Literariness is defined by structural linguistic properties, not thematic unities. By using forms that estrange and by presenting ideas in a critical manner, Nabokov prevents readers from resting secure in their preconceived notions of form and content or the relation of signifier to signified. To underscore the independent significance of writing and to destroy the automatism of perception, Nabokov repudiates artistic economy and coherence, uses "roughened form," and celebrates parody. His entire methodology functions to establish diversity and difference rather than consistency and sameness. In addition, he breaks down a tendency to attribute meaning to circumstantial relationships, connections, and correspondences.

This wish to expose old beliefs, assurances, and structures and to create an existential, fictive world of linguistic play is fundamental to his work. In this regard, he says, "My advice to a budding literary critic would be as follows. Learn to distinguish banality. Remember that mediocrity thrives on 'ideas.' Beware of the modish message. Ask yourself if the symbol you have detected is not your own footprint. Ignore allegories. By all means place the 'how' above the 'what' but do not let it be confused with the 'so what.' Rely on the sudden erection of your small dorsal hairs. Do not drag in Freud at this point."[5] He further characterizes "worthwhile art" as requiring "originality, invention, harmony, conciseness, complexity, and splendid insincerity."[6] By defamiliarizing technique and idea, he teases the reader out of a reliance upon the familiar and leads him to new discoveries within the fiction. By using parody and playing with the reader he avoids heavy-handed moral messages encapsulated in his comment "Satire is a lesson, parody is a game."[7]

The insidious tendency to confuse structure and meaning is the fundamental failure that Nabokov addresses in his fiction about doubles. He strips the double of symbolic significance so that the reader must be simultaneously aware of what the device has stood for in the past and how these uses are now changed and undercut—a pattern, Linda Hutcheon reveals, that is characteristic of postmodern parody.[8] Nabokov uses the double especially to disclose man's need for referentiality and related tendency to see things in terms of meaningful resemblances, correspondences, and homologies.

All of Nabokov's fiction about the double plays with accepted modes of presentation. His psychological and philosophical uses of doubles in *The Life of Sebastian Knight*, *Bend Sinister*, *Laughter in the Dark*, *Lolita*, *The Event*, *Pnin*, *Despair*, and *Pale Fire* have been well documented. Claire Rosenfield uses Otto Rank's theories, Robert Rogers the Freudian and Jungian views of decomposition, and Carol T. Williams the Hegelian dialectic, while Andrew Field, Alfred Appel, Jr., and Charles Nichol, among others, center more on parody—sometimes the idea of psychological identity per se.[9]

Characteristically, Nabokov's use of the double involves a male narrator whose solipsism grows from idealistic-artistic conceptions that are not only untrustworthy but harmful. What begins as a symbolist conception of art as ultimate truth and mystical logos ultimately turns into monomaniacal madness. The narrator imposes his perception and vision upon others, thus undermining or destroying theirs. This imposition is particularly pernicious because it is done in the name of art or philosophical idealism by narrators who fail to distinguish art from life or to call oppression by its real name. Charles Kinbote, of *Pale Fire*, not only urges his own Zemblan cultural background upon the poet Shade but also supposes that he can alter Shade's perception so that his art will conform to Kinbote's vision. Kinbote's published version of Shade's poem does just that—the annotations he adds alter the poem so that it becomes primarily his own. Kinbote's form and content become the shadow or double of Shade's own, footnotes overcoming the text. Albinus, of *Laughter in the Dark*, so fervently wishes art to come off the canvas and "live" that he hires a filmmaker to animate it. Like Pygmalion, he wants images to have a life of their own apart from the constraints of the artist's technique;

he hopes to have the artistic form improved and doubled even as he wants to reanimate and double his life through his tryst with the sixteen-year-old Margot, a hope that is scotched by the cartoonist Axel Rex, who becomes his adversarial double and nemesis.

In *Lolita*, the adolescent Lo is forced to surrender her virginity and freedom to Humbert Humbert's sexual-aesthetic *idée fixe*: nymphets. Although Humbert constitutes Lolita as his double, the embodiment of his fantasy of the nymphet, his other double, Clare Quilty, refuses to be so directed. With no particular motivation and with uncertain movements and goals, Quilty both pursues Humbert and until the end eludes his most ingenious and devious retaliatory schemes. Quilty is Humbert's victimizer, trap, and nemesis, "at once a projection of Humbert's guilt and a parody of the psychological Double."[10] This parody, as Appel argues, assaults "the convention of the good and evil 'dual selves' found in the traditional Double tale," hence the convention of the psychological double. Humbert's and Quilty's wrestling exemplifies the humor of this "fantastic comic cosmos": "I rolled over him. We rolled over me. They rolled over him. We rolled over us."[11] Humbert and Quilty are seen mainly as literary constructs, rhetorical utterances, or verbal products. In a more "writerly" sense, Humbert is the author, trying to impose his will upon a text, whether Lo or Quilty, and having that text resist.

Significant exceptions to this pattern occur in *The Real Life of Sebastian Knight* and *Pnin*, but in both these novels the issue is still the individual's perception as it is affected by others—human beings are presented as the doubles of society. In the first, the narrator, V, is a literary detective or biographical sleuth who tries to determine his half brother's identity from his fiction, the identity of his brother's mistress, and the nature of their relationship. In reading his brother's fiction and meeting his women, the narrator finds his identity coalescing with his brother's, not necessarily a bad thing, Nabokov suggests, for V has learned to question his own world, defamiliarize it, and create new alternatives. In the second of these books, Pnin is caught in a double bind. A decidedly sentimental, nostalgic Russian exile, his artistic sensibility prevents him from conforming to university expectations or adapting to American cultural hegemony. His political exile from Russia and spiritual exile from America are resolved only by another impasse. Pnin is released from his job at Waindell College and given the freedom to roam, or as Ambrose Gordon phrases it, to be "at home in his homelessness."[12] Situations and events are strangely doubled, reversed, and looped. Nabokov's parody of the double's traditional reliance on referentiality, the modernist use of the first-person narrator and the stability of point of view, and his use of puns, word plays, and allusions to other texts paradoxically place his fiction both inside and outside the tradition of the double, finally asserting the triumph of self- and literary referentiality.

Nabokov's statements about the double and his depiction of the double in *Despair* suggest, if anything, an even more formalist stance, one that denies the tendency to turn comparison into ideology. In his interview with Appel, Nabokov asserted that "there are no 'real' doubles in my novels" and, moreover that "Felix in *Despair* is really a *false* double."[13] Although Nabokov emphatically states that he finds the double a "frightful bore," such a disavowal confirms his aversion to the *idea* of the double, with its traditional relationship to psychological "identity" and Platonic dualism. In an interesting use of orthography, Nabokov subjects the word to the indignity of the lowercase, even though Appel's questions are about the "Double," thus diminishing, designifying, and de-idealizing the whole concept.[14] In an off-handed comment seemingly on a different topic, Nabokov hints at his special interest in the formalistic, structural use of the double: "This apartment had been some bachelor's delight but was not meant to accommodate a family of three. Evening guests had to be entertained in the kitchen so as not to interfere with my future translator's sleep. And the bathroom doubled as my study. Here is the *Doppelgänger* theme for you."[15] This comment, exposing the weaknesses of the traditional usage of the double, defamiliarizing it, and reconstituting it as structure, has a particular relevance to *Despair*.

Many critics do see these formalist devices in *Despair*. Robert Rogers remarks on Nabokov's tomfoolery in playing with Freudian analysis and the double but continues to assert that "the psychopathic narrator is a latent homosexual and pathological liar suffering from a castration complex and paranoid delusions of persecution and grandeur."[16] Ann Smock sees the verbal play as central to Nabokov's consideration of the double and writing. She argues that Hermann's killing of Felix explores the nature of crime and retribution in the detective novel (and, one could add, the integral doubling of the detective, criminal, and victim). She discovers a playful correspondence between the form of this detective story and its prototype,

Oedipus, in addition to the characters' quest for identity and their blindness.[17] For Smock, Nabokov's is a metafictive treatment of detective fiction. R. Victoria Arana also argues that the book is about writing, specifically writing that undermines the traditional view of narrative self-objectification in autobiography. She uses Paul de Man's theory of "Autobiography as De-facement" to demonstrate that Hermann fails to achieve objectivity in his views on life and self. According to her, since self-displacement is the subject of Hermann's discourse, the reader is always forced to distinguish between "Hermann-as-agent" and "Hermann-as-reflection," "Hermann as self-characterizer" and "Hermann as self-revealer."[18] Certainly Hermann is parodied as a typical manipulative first-person narrator who reads the evidence in a limited fashion. Dabney Stuart similarly sees Nabokov's repudiation of the realistic double in *Despair* as an aesthetic, epistemological, and moral rejection of the notion of harmony and order.[19]

These assessments are, I think, accurate. While the book may have some bearing on psychological issues, it is about writing and the traditional requirements of harmony and order in story-telling. But I would urge that the book is one of the first, if not the first, to interrogate the conventions of the double within contemporary fiction. Nabokov strips the double of its traditional content and core meanings and in the process criticizes the human tendency to take experience and invest it with unwarranted meaning, to equate experience and art, and to take language and give it mystical signification. Nabokov treats this issue by presenting Hermann Karlovich, his narrator and main character, as one who constantly seeks resemblances, endows them with transcendent meaning, and, acting upon his suppositions, creates what he believes to be a gifted work of art, the murder of his "double" and the writing of his book. Insofar as Hermann feels no sense of wrong about any of the things he has done, he is shown to be as reprehensible as any traditional double—for instance, Dorian Gray. Nabokov both uses and parodies traditional tales by suggesting that such evil does not result from a power outside man, exerting an evil influence on him; rather it is based on destructive idealism that can grow from a faulty view of resemblances and analogues. The book simultaneously exposes a human tendency and a linguistic-literary problem.

Jacques Derrida has recently observed that "analogy is metaphor par excellence" and that "the analogical energy can, itself, give rise only to an analogical concept."[20] He remarks that what begins as a point of comparison becomes a metaphor and is too often transferred into the realm of imagination and ideas. As a result, "analogy, metaphor, the connection of known to unknown, of presence to absence" introduces the danger of "unlimited generality of the principle of analogy."[21]

Metaphor, a purely linguistic and formal equation, ought not be construed as a metaphysic. But insofar as people, Nabokov's Hermann among them, leap from language to "reality" and exhibit a "craving for generality," they become prey to the fallacy at the heart of speculative philosophy and metaphysics.[22] They gather together individual images and experiences according to important or tangential points of resemblance, give them a common attribution and motive, interpret them in a general way, and put them to common use and ideology. If this tendency is viewed playfully as a mere extension of the human need to perceive physical resemblances, little harm can result, but when used to structure all reality, the trope exceeds its limitations. Hermann is strongly given to seeking such resemblances and analogues in every corner of his mind and world, from color to language and finally to what he considers his aesthetically and spiritually based doppelgänger.

In treating his likeness to Felix Wohlfahrt, Hermann equates "resemblance," "mirror," "copy," and "double." He is fascinated by the observation that two things can be alike, and he, like the symbolists, leaps to all-embracing notions of common forms and archetypes to account for these resemblances. Hermann takes some point of resemblance and frivolously uses it as a means of typecasting, implicitly suggesting that people consciously or subconsciously adapt their faces to some preexistent model. Taking a structural similarity and extracting transcendent meaning, he assumes that a brief glance can in fact reveal the underlying archetypal or divine significance.

Nabokov critiques the analogical leap by demonstrating how Hermann piles association upon association to fabricate his ideal. This is done even with a simple detail such as color. Hermann is continually struck with the primacy of color and surrounds himself with fashionable, foppish tones. He drives a blue Icarus at a time when most cars are neutral and somber in color. (The term *Icarus* itself bears deeply mythic and divine connotations, though ironically the automobile is a modern metaphor for the mechanics of form over content.) He wears a dark gray suit with black shoes or mouse gray spats, yellow gloves, and a lilac tie. He sports these colors when he meets Felix, and he dresses Felix in them before killing him. They are also colors which he sees replicated in meaningful ways. The lake near the spot where he kills Felix is blue, the post marking the turnoff is yellow, and the March landscape consists of gray-white patches of melting snow against the black earth; even the "Y-stemmed couple of inseparable birches . . . (or a couple of couples, if you counted their reflections)"[23] are filtered out as gray against the brooding dark pines.

These colors appear in endless variations throughout the text, constantly doubling and multiplying. Hermann's study in mauve (lilac and violet) serves to suggest the particular way he seeks resemblances even on this primary level, confusing nature and human contrivance and allowing life to imitate fiction and advertising. Lilac is a color intimately associated with Hermann's view of his past, his occupation, and his appearance. He remembers his mother as "a languid lady in lilac silks" who "would recline in her rocking chair, fanning herself, munching chocolate, all the blinds down, and the wind from some new-mown field making them billow like purple sails" (p. 14). The fact that he later denies this image of his mother reinforces the impression that it is only a mirror resemblance of his company's chocolate wrapper on which is depicted "a lady in lilac, with a fan" (p. 15). Hermann sports a lilac tie when he first meets Felix, wears a lilac tie flecked with black when they rendezvous in Tarnitz, and places a lilac tie on Felix just before killing him. He also tells a story in which a Mr. X.Y. wears a lilac tie, and by means of a ruse involving Mario, his fisherman double, manages to seduce Mario's fisher girl.

The list of examples goes on and on. Hermann walks through a public garden with "a storm of heaving lilac bushes" (p. 16). Lydia holds a bunch of violets in preparation for Ardalion's departure on the train, and Felix wears violets in his lapel. When Hermann returns to the spot where he has first seen Felix in Prague, he finds there a dead violet, Felix's coiled feces, "a golden cigarette-end," "a scrap of Czech newspaper," and "several emerald flies" (p. 27). This brightly colored and repulsive still life distances the reader from Hermann's perceptions and defamiliarizes the entire scene, so that when Hermann links this scene to the one in which Felix is killed, the reader perceives that the mauve connection—the violets of Felix and the lilac tie of Hermann—may be the only point of resemblance between the two. By depicting Hermann's obsession with color and heightened meaning, Nabokov subverts symbolic attribution and value, and since the colors eventually stand for Hermann, emphasizes metonymical displacement. This displacement suggests the falseness of Hermann's attempts to fix analogical meaning, for that meaning is constantly disseminated.

Even more suggestive of the way Hermann, with a mind that "hankered after reflections, repetitions, masks" (p. 80), tends to confuse the rules of differing modalities and to seek connections and resemblances is his use of language, especially the word *double*, which comes to bear so much significance for him.[24] In the simplest use of the term, *double* refers to two of any given object, and Hermann uses it in that sense when he speaks of that "double, red and blue stripe round the middle" of Lydia's bathing suit (p. 49), when he puts on two layers of clothing in preparation for Felix's murder and calls it his "double cocoon," or again when, feeling light-headed, his "transfigured memory inhaled, as it were, a double dose of oxygen" (p. 212). But signifiers have metataxically shifting meanings, differences at the core of language. So Hermann uses the word in the related but not identical sense of retracing his original steps when, in thinking about the circumstances surrounding the murder, he notes that he "ought to be flustering, scurrying, doubling back" (p. 167). Though tangentially related, this second sense is hardly "two-of." Also related, but still a half turn off, is Hermann's use of the term to mean "bent in half." During a windstorm, he walks in the garden "all doubled up" and also sees the postman "bent double." By describing Hermann's fascination with the word and using it in different contexts with different meanings, Nabokov not only creates enjoyable word play but also demonstrates the extent of Hermann's obsession with the word and the folly of attributing universal meaning to it.

At a further distance from these attributions of *double* are those that are less descriptive and more inherently metaphorical. In one of these, Hermann uses the term to designate an understudy for an actor, a "star ghost." In another, he associates it with betrayal when he berates Felix as a "scoundrel and double-crosser." In yet another instance, he imagines a conversation between Felix and a friend in which he puns on *double* as doppelgänger and the twin images seen by a drunken man:

Later: conversation in a barn on a warm dark night: "Now, as I was saying, that was an odd'un, that bloke I met one day. He made out we were doubles."

A laugh in the darkness: "It was you who saw double, you old sot." (P. 55)

Hermann goes even further than literal and metaphorical meanings when he suggests that he can supernaturally double himself—or rather split himself in two. He conveys the impression that his soul can wander while his body is engaged in intercourse. By parodying the old idea of the soul wandering during sleep, Nabokov simultaneously ridicules Hermann and the symbolist aesthetic. When "dissociation" or the "imp Split" takes over, he claims that he is able from a distance of several meters to watch himself make love to his wife. Supposing that he has accomplished this remarkable feat, Hermann wishes to intensify the mystical sensation: "I longed to contemplate that bedroom scene from some remote upper gallery in a blue mist under the swimming allegories of the starry vault" (p. 38). His wish is never granted, but he *dreams*, "as if seen through a dark glass," that he hangs suspended between a varnished blue-black sky and the ground, watching the road beneath him and his own doubled reflection in a puddle. Hermann has leapt from language and linguistic associations to the magical and mystical. In effect, he becomes an aesthetician who believes that intimations of immortality can be gleaned from nature and that language can communicate these to the reader.

The discrepancy between Hermann and his double, Felix, concretely illustrates the fallacy of such correspondences. The two men clearly come from different social classes. Whereas Hermann (lordman) describes himself as prosperously plump, smooth-shaven, and dapper, a product of the urbane cultures of St. Petersburg, Moscow, and Berlin, he depicts Felix (fruitful or happy) as a lank, bearded, simple countryman from no place in particular. While Hermann deals in chocolates (the delicacies of the rich) and has a house, a wife, and a maid, Felix has no home and nomadically roams from one spot to another with neither family nor steady job to tie him down. Hermann likes rich food and expensive clothing; Felix subsists simply on sausages and apples and dresses in drab, functional clothing lacking buttons, a "gawky disguise for an old-fashioned slumkin-lumpkin fancy dress ball" (p. 19). Hermann is urban; Felix is rural. Physically they bear little resemblance to each other. Although Hermann believes they have the same nose, facial wrinkles, and cheekbones, he has to confess that the rest of the facial resemblance is less exact: "I possess large yellowish teeth; his are whiter and set more closely together, but is that really important? On my forehead a vein stands out like a capital M imperfectly drawn, but when I sleep my brow is as smooth as that of my double. And those ears . . . the convolutions of his are but very slightly altered in comparison with mine: here more compressed, there smoothed out. We have eyes of the same shape, narrowly slit with sparse lashes, but his iris is paler than mine" (p. 27). Since the traditional double that Hermann evokes depends upon an identical relationship between the first self and the second, Nabokov's insistence upon the inexact resemblance between Hermann and Felix undermines the validity of Hermann's conjecture, implying that Hermann's weakness is not just one of distorted sight but a falsification of language.

Not concerned about this discrepancy in background and appearance, Hermann fancies that he and Felix share an affinity more spiritual than physical. He implies this spiritual identity early in his account when he comments disparagingly on twinship, whether contrived by nature or filmmaker: "The likeness between twin brothers is spoiled like an equiradical rhyme by the stamp of kinship, while a film actor in a double part can hardly deceive anyone, for even if he does appear in both impersonations at once, the eye cannot help tracing a line down the middle where the halves of the picture have been joined" (pp. 25–26). This identical twinship, which Otto Rank describes as typical of the double, is too limiting and finite for Hermann, who sees in his resemblance with Felix something archetypal, transcendent, and infinite. He takes the notion of resemblance, passes it through the filter of the photographically identical double, and develops it into a full-blown idealistic, symbolist philosophy and aesthetics with roots in Platonism, Neoplatonism, and German romantic idealism. His craving for generality grows into a philosophical obsession cloaked in the rhetoric of mysticism, ideal forms, and poetic frenzy. From a belief in the validity of one rule, some similarity of appearance, he has posited the existence of a deeply significant metaphysic.

When Hermann first comments on his discovery of Felix asleep on the grass and his dawning perception of him as a double, he does so in terms of philosophical idealism.[25] He loses the rational mode of comprehension and invention, empties himself out in preparation for the divine afflatus, recognizes the immanent divine form or ideal, and acquires the power of poetry to express his new perception: "As for me I was too dazed by the mystery implied. While I looked, everything within me seemed to lose hold and come hurtling down from a height of ten stories. I was gazing at a marvel. Its perfection, its lack of cause and object, filled me with a strange awe" (pp. 17–18). Hermann here does not imply an existential universe without cause or object but something quite different: a universe characterized by a special causality—pandeterminism or pansignification—where, as Tzvetan Todorov explains, everything corresponds to everything, deriving from a great spiritual source: "On the most abstract level, pan-determinism signifies that the limit between the physical and the mental, between matter and spirit, between word and thing, ceases to be impervious."[26] In the language of mystery, marvel, and perfection, Hermann sees himself as a mystical vessel: "I was absolutely empty and thus comparable to some translucid vessel doomed to receive contents as yet unknown" (p. 18). Nabokov's ridicule of form and content as one, as well as the view of inspiration in language, is especially pointed when Hermann emphasizes his oracular insights in "unconsciously tracking" his double and his "frolics of the intuition, artistic vision, [and] inspiration" (p. 18). Todorov explains that this mystical collapse of the boundaries between object and subject, between self and other, is also a characteristic of madness.[27] In a particularly humorous fashion, Nabokov may well be commenting that such symbolist ideals and impressionistic techniques verge on madness, not metaphysical but mundane.

The wonder that Hermann experiences in his fancied resemblance to Felix is so overpowering that for the benefit of his first reader, the émigré Russian novelist, he projects it into a model of universal communism: "In fancy, I visualize a new world, where all men will resemble one another as Hermann and Felix did; a world of Helixes and Fermanns; a world where the worker fallen dead at the feet of his machine will be at once replaced by his perfect double smiling the serene smile of perfect socialism" (p. 169). Hermann projects an entire world of doubles, rank on rank of them, all resembling himself. But to do so, he has to confuse the signifiers. Felix and Hermann must be interchangeable with Helix and Fermann. Instead of being a world of individuals in a pluralistic society with perceivable differences, society becomes the living embodiment of the image and imagination of one man, Hermann, a solipsistic vision based on linguistic and philosophical distortion carried to extremes. Every slight point of resemblance has been magnified and distorted; different signifiers become a single-signified.

Just how destructive this view of life may be is demonstrated by the artistry, inspiration, power, and emotion that Hermann ascribes to his murder of Felix. All the tags of aesthetic and philosophical idealism are used to describe an act of sadistic inhumanity. In regarding himself as an unparalleled artist and Felix as his artistic subject and personal double, Hermann concludes that killing him is the only way to preserve that image before age and decay can alter the likeness. He thinks that if Felix "were to attain old age, . . . his grins and grimaces would end by eroding completely our resemblance which is now so perfect when his face freezes" (p. 85). Forgetting that he too will age and destroy the likeness, Hermann irrationally argues that only through Felix's immediate death will the ideal form and the mirror image merge completely: "At that moment when all the required features were fixed and frozen, our likeness was such that really I could not say who had been killed, I or he. And while I looked, it grew dark in the vibrating wood, and with that face before me slowly dissolving, vibrating fainter and fainter, it seemed as if I were looking at my image in a stagnant pool" (p. 182).

Converting aesthetic idealism to philosophical idealism, Hermann speaks of the details of the murder as flowing and fusing together, taking "inevitable forms" that grow without his assistance. He believes that "the harmony of mathematical symbols, the movements of planets, [and] the hitchless working of natural laws" have a "true bearing upon the subject" (p. 131). He speaks of the accomplishment of murder in the same fashion that Shelley spoke of the creation of a poem as an "image of life expressed in its eternal truth." Indeed, the night before he kills Felix, he accounts to Lydia for this murder and his consequent absence with a false story of his imagined secondary double, his twin brother, a tale that betrays the mystical significance attributed to violent death. Hermann explains that his brother, having lived a horrible, immoral life, wishes to commit an atoning act of suicide: "His soul, which had its mystical side, yearned for some atonement, some sacrifice: merely putting a bullet through his brain seemed to him not sufficient" (pp. 149–50).

This act of suicide in Hermann's version of the words of his imaginary brother Felix amounts to a superb artistic performance: " 'I want to make a gift of my death to somebody,' . . . [the brother Felix] suddenly said and his eyes brimmed with the diamond light of madness. 'Make a gift of my death. We two are still more alike than we were formerly. In our sameness I see a divine intent. To lay one's hands upon a piano does not yet mean the making of music, and what I want is music' " (p. 150). Within Hermann's fabricated tale, this act of suicide fosters spirituality. Twinship, death, and divine purpose are caught together in this statement. When Hermann ruminates on the murder of Felix, he thinks of a creative act arising from divine promptings. The actual killing crystallizes these reflections. He starts at Felix with "operatic force" and imagines that "all was rumble and thunder in the orchestra" between his "vocal outbursts" (p. 173). This "fragment of opera" is part of the greater musical performance in which Hermann is the "virtuoso" responsible for the celestial tones. The death itself Hermann compares to a work of literary artistry, and he looks at Felix, dead on the ground, "like an author reading his work over a thousand times, probing and testing every syllable" (p. 181).

Nabokov's interrogation of the relationship between death and art, a long-standing one in the field of literature, is neatly ironized by changing death to murder. Assumptions that death is poetic and that angst leads to creative insight are shown to be misguided. Brian McHale argues that such an ironizing or parodying of the relationship between death and art is characteristic of postmodern fiction and is often signaled by self-erasure, Chinese box construction, and metalepsis. He maintains that "texts about themselves, self-reflective, self-conscius texts, are also, as if inevitably, about death, precisely because they are about ontological differences and the transgression of ontological boundaries."[28] Hermann's equation of murder and art is especially ironized by his attempt to convince the reader that this murder is superior to other artistic renderings of crimes in fiction by Doyle, Dostoevsky, Leblanc, and Wallace. The difference between Hermann's act and theirs lies in the spirit and execution. Whereas crimes in detective stories have rarely been based on those committed in reality, Hermann brings his crime off the page into the real world and commends himself for it, thinking of it as a sort of unacknowledged tribute to his genius. He considers it a superb avant-garde piece, though of course publicly unrecognized and unacknowledged. Waiting for the moment of artistic recognition, he is proud of his status as a symbolist "maker," a poet in a heightened sense.

In his notion of resemblances, Hermann views himself as more than a maker or shaper, thus deceiving himself even more than he does his readers. He becomes the painter and model, the author and subject, the mover and pawn. He clearly expresses this artistic analogy concerning Felix and himself when he identifies himself as the model and Felix as the mimic or portrait, but he also believes that he can reverse that equation since the two are interchangeable doubles. He attempts just such a reversal when before killing him he dresses Felix in his clothes, making Felix his mimic. He in turn puts on Felix's clothing and passes himself off as Felix. He thus puts his theory into practice by creating a Helix and Fermann. So obsessed is Hermann with this notion of model and mimic that he likes to think of his characters and readers as his mimics, not necessarily a bad trait except as it reinforces his particular tendency to domination: "An author's fondest dream is to turn the reader into a spectator; is this ever attained? The pale organisms of literary heroes feeding under the author's supervision swell gradually with the reader's lifeblood; so that the genius of a writer consists in giving them the faculty to adapt themselves to that— not very appetizing—food and thrive on it, sometimes for centuries" (p. 26). Hermann views himelf as a seer and prophet in whose mind are located the ideal forms that constitute the undergirding structure of ultimate reality. Within this perspective, the mind not only mirrors ideal forms but also becomes an actual part of them.

These idealistic resonances are peculiarly caught in the mirror image itself, which for Hermann reflects divine patterns. He seems to understand that within the double tradition the mirror has often been defined not as an empirically explainable surface reflection of a physical phenomenon but as an intuitively perceived reflection of some underlying significance or divinity, perhaps an active force in itself. The role of the mirror in helping him "split" when making love to Lydia offers a case in point, for the mirror takes over where physical possibility ends. Moreover, when he returns to the room after seeing Felix, he relies upon his hotel mirror to reflect his imagined double: "When at last I got back to my hotel room, I found there, amid mercurial shadows and framed in frizzly bronze, Felix awaiting me. Pale-faced and solemn he drew near. He was now well-shaven; his hair was smoothly brushed back. He wore a dove-grey suit with a lilac tie. I took out my handkerchief; he took out his handkerchief too. A truce, parleying" (p. 24). This image is closely conjoined with his observation that when he offered Felix a hand to rise from the ground, "it provided me with the curious sensation of Narcissus fooling Nemesis by helping his image out of the brook" (p. 23). In all instances, Hermann assures the reader that the mirror can help to capture the essence of a perfect, divinely ordained resemblance, but it fails him. Such is the case when Hermann tries to convince Felix of their doubleness.

What interests Hermann is that the resemblance is "a freak bordering on the miraculous." What interests Felix is Hermann's "wishing to see any resemblance at all" (p. 23). He sees Hermann only as a "doubtful imitator." At Tarnitz too, the mirror refuses to cooperate. After Hermann searches the faces of the waiter and customers at the inn, hoping in vain to detect a hint of surprise at his "doubleness" with Felix, he excoriates the mirror for its failure to embody this resemblance: "Thus we were reflected by the misty and, to all appearances, sick mirror, with a freakish slant, a streak of madness, a mirror that surely would have cracked at once had it chanced to reflect one single genuine human countenance" (p. 99). Nabokov's clever manipulation of Hermann allows the reader an ever-increasing distance from his assumptions and beliefs.

Nabokov ultimately discloses that Hermann's idealism is not grounded on verifiable truths but only upon tropes, for "any poetic invention is, after all, a farrago of words, a delusional system, a form of madness."[29] Nabokov accomplishes this subversion by everywhere including enough contradictory impressions to undermine Hermann's stance. Indeed, Hermann deconstructs his own argument and line of reasoning by suggesting that he really does not believe in the tenets of idealism. By his own denials, he demonstrates the utter falseness of his position and the patent absurdity of creating a mode of idealism from a theory of resemblances: the denials provide a firm basis for Nabokov's parody of idealism.

A seminal problem with Hermann's espousal of idealism is that he does not believe in God as the source of ideal forms. He claims instead that God is simply the best-hidden gamester (or novelist), one that he would like to expose and defeat: "The nonexistence of God is simple to prove. Impossible to concede, for example, that a serious Jah, all wise and almighty, could employ his time in such inane fashion as playing with manikins, and—what is still more incongruous—should restrict his game to the dreadfully trite laws of mechanics, chemistry, mathematics, and never—mind you, never!—show his face" (p. 111). His best thought on the matter is that God has been created "by a scamp who had genius" in formulating views of God and heaven, "that dazzle of argus-eyed angels fanning their wings, or that curved mirror in which a self-complacent professor of physics recedes, getting ever smaller and smaller" (p. 111). Hermann especially objects to this fiction because it is not his; it arises from someone else's mind. Like Ahab in *Moby Dick*, Hermann wants to be the "sultan of . . . [his] own being" (p. 112), creator of his own fiction, and formulator of his own game.

Another problem with Hermann's quest for idealism is his failure to get the facts right. Although he prides himself on the faithfulness of his presentation, his depiction is called into question by his inability to recollect details accurately. Remembering his return from Prague to Berlin, he writes that Lydia was making "goggle-moggle," and he provides an appropriate dialogue concerning this mix as a cure for sore throats. In midstory, however, he announces that she was making coffee, thus casting doubt on his earlier statements. He never resolves this discrepancy, leaving the impression that his memory is not accurate. But these problems bother him little, for he makes a virtue out of lying, at which he claims great skill and for which he has a great "thirst." He even speaks of his lying to Lydia as divinely inspired. Hermann's greatest lie to her is the story of his look-alike brother, which serves to account for the murder of Felix. He will have everyone, including the reader, believe that such lying is merely fiction making, part of his abilities as an artist-actor, a kind of poetic disguise: "Although I have never been an actor in the strict sense of the word, I have nevertheless, in real life, always carried about with me a small folding theatre and have appeared in more than one part, and my acting has always been superfine" (p. 100). Despite such eloquence, Hermann's primary intent is to deceive, and he is indifferent about the distinction between artistically depicting an act of murder and committing one. Such a position demonstrates that he does not really believe morality and truth to have come from a divine source or that they are matters of particular import. It also suggests that for him, experience and language are one. He does not see that all language is metaphor for experience.

Hermann finally has to admit to his failure, though he tries to carry the charade to the very end. Contrary to Hermann's expectation, the death mask of Felix bears little resemblance to Hermann's. The police fail to understand why Hermann has dressed a strange man in his own clothes and can discern no resemblance between the two. Hermann ultimately has to confess after Felix's death that another mirror image, Felix's passport picture, does not resemble his own and that his passport picture, published in the newspaper, does not at all resemble Felix. He finally has to confess that he has failed in his attempt to create the perfect artistic murder. He has been so busy playing the mystic (he even plays on Lydia's misuse of the term) that he misses the stick in the car. His enthusiasm for the idealistic causes him to forget the real.

As a result of his failure to convince the world, Hermann finally decides to eschew the "treacherous world of reflections." He has located what he thought to be a perfect double and killed him; he has invented what he thought was a very clever mystery. But the world refuses to recognize the validity or significance of the doubleness or the construct. As far as the public, both police and readers, is concerned, Hermann is not the idealistic man of genius who has perceived and imitated something in the mind of God but only a madman who has committed a bizarre murder.

What Hermann has done is to use the notion of resemblances as his modus operandi to draw differences together into a false unity. When he applies this method to his ideas about color, the implications are not serious. After all, human beings do tend to group tones into color patterns. But when doubling dominates his imagination as an alleged manifestation of philosophical idealism, he forces the idea of resemblance to irrational—even insane—extremes. When he justifies his murder on the basis of aesthetic idealism, the fundamental dangers of his craving for generality are clear. Hermann has "discovered" a twin, formulated the basis of that double in supernatural, philosophical, idealistic terms, and killed the double as the supreme artistic act of idealistic mimesis. These various activities cannot be vindicated.

That such a faulty, not to say insane, way of thinking can become characteristic of a culture as a whole is one of the terrible inferences to be drawn from the book. When he has Hermann speak of universal communism as the logical extension of his theory of resemblances, Nabokov hints at that conclusion. This conclusion is especially horrifying because the first version of this book was written in Berlin in 1932 when the realization was dawning that the center of civilization could not hold, must fall apart in the face of German nazism and Russian Stalinism. Since Nabokov's other books written in this period address the question of totalitarian repression, it is probable that parody in *Despair*, playful as it is, addresses the frightening thought that a notion of aesthetic and philosophical idealism may share responsibility for the rise of totalitarianism. Nabokov makes this point in his interview with Appel: "I am not particularly fond of Plato, nor would I survive very long under his Germanic regime of militarism and music."[30] Fassbinder's cinematic version of *Despair*, placed in the historical context of Germany in 1929–1930 when "the Weimar Republic was tottering, and the nation was nursing the fertile seeds of National Socialism,"[31] develops the political implications of Nabokov's treatment of idealism. According to Dolores M. Burdick, Hermann is

> a figure of the guilt of the Germany which engaged in genocide while nobody really seemed to see it happen. Felix, in the light of this reading, is the *double* victim of Hermann's madness. First, he is in a sense the German people, who, after all, bought the policy, assented to German expansionism and anti-Semitism, and became accomplices to the war and the holocaust. Second, he is an image of the *victims* of that war and that holocaust. (The perfect crime envisaged by Hermann is one where "the victim is the murderer.") Hermann Hermann in his voracious narcissistic hunger for wholeness, for identity, for escape from exile and guilt, plays out a drama of merger, murder, and madness, which is like the drama of Germany under Nazism.[32]

On a basic level, the book condemns anyone or any system that assents to an idealist-symbolist perspective. A "system," by its very structural inclusiveness, begins to erase individual distinctions, shave the corners from differences, and attribute common causes and motivations to essentially dissimilar terms, experiences, and ideas. The real horror in this story is that Hermann represents the craving for generality that men and nations use to justify the most horrible of crimes against humanity. Nabokov simultaneously employs the double tradition and defamiliarizes it in order to break down any notion of pandeterminism underlying literary texts and traditions. He affirms difference and structural pluralism; he detests sameness and ideological conformity.

Binary Intersubjectivity
Pynchon's Gravity's Rainbow

3

SERVING AS PRECURSORS OF VLADIMIR NABOKOV'S *DESPAIR* ARE AN array of incarnations of the double by Poe, Hawthorne, James, Wilde, Conrad, and others. The protagonist Hermann's obsessive preoccupation with himself, his perceptions of Felix as his double, and his final madness betray similarities to earlier nineteenth- and twentieth-century versions of the double. But there is a difference, and a very important one, between *Despair* and these earlier works. Nabokov's book is not simply another rationalist-humanist iteration of a metaphysical contest between good and evil, of Freudian decomposition, or of Jungian psychological imbalance; it is a duplicitous text, which alludes to, uses, and interrogates previous texts in order to parody them and subvert their desire for truth or transhistorical meaning. It is the carnivalized play of the double, which seeks to tell an entertaining tale while decoding and designifying previous tellings. Such postmodern treatments of the double as those of Vladimir Nabokov and Thomas Pynchon use manifest doubles to play with, subvert, and displace the versions of their predecessors, refusing to allow doppelgängers to serve as the link between analogy, metaphor, philosophical idealism, and transcendental mysticism. This carnivalization embodies a Derridean notion of play. It frees a text from the old rules without necessarily inscribing new ones and decenters old texts without centering new ones. As a sign, the Derridean double of Nabokov and Pynchon is denied presence and subjected to the ever-elusive play of *différence* and *différance* (deferral of meaning).

Nabokov and Pynchon play with texts and decenter them in

part to explore the question of how experience itself differs from perceptions of experience. The perceptions of their central characters illustrate twin approaches to the problem. Nabokov's Hermann prefers to see everything as analogy and similarity; he distorts evidence and warps facts to prove that Felix is his double. Conversely, Pynchon's Slothrop feels himself split in many directions. Lacking a consistent identity and taking refuge in many aliases, he fears that he is wholly controlled by external forces. As a result, he doubts that anything, external or internal, is a unity. Although Hermann believes that he can prove the existence of his double, Slothrop can prove nothing; his search for origins, self-discovery, and causal relationships is painfully (and comically) unproductive. Other characters in Pynchon's fiction may organize experience to find pattern and meaning, but usually they do so in binary oppositions and privileged hierarchies. The double in *Gravity's Rainbow* functions to explore the privileging of white over black, culture over nature, technology over primitivism, male over female, and abstract religion over natural religions. In interrogating binarity, putting it under erasure, and finally affirming binary intersubjectivity, Pynchon alters the function of the double in literature.

For both Nabokov and Pynchon, one of the chief problems in the changing conceptions of reality—and, I might add, the double itself—is the inertia of language, which tends to delimit and focus as it has always done. Nabokov's and Pynchon's perceptions of the ways language interprets, encapsulates, and organizes experience, and therefore creates reality—a double process of experience and articulation and encoding and decoding—are similar. But Pynchon also raises serious questions about the ways cultures, as well as their systems of discourse, are unified and sealed to establish and consolidate power and control over fact and interpretations of fact. He finds that the suppression or conflation of cultural and linguistic differences often restricts and reduces meaning, thereby resulting in oppressive discursive practices at all levels, from the most corporate to the most individual. When differences are observed, Pynchon argues, often the result is to heighten confrontation and ultimately to privilege culturally recognized norms.

Like so many postmodern writers, Pynchon challenges the meaning embodied in and structured by contemporary institutions and explores the infinite dialectic of binary oppositions without either accepting traditional values or establishing new hierarchies, without abandoning familiar language structures or condoning them. He turns from overdetermined cultural normatives and narratives to random and unpatterned experience. Pynchon accomplishes this task by probing and dissecting the assumptions and goals founded on binarity that seem to underlie American society in particular and Western social and political systems in general. His work, like so much of postmodernism, "fundamentally contradictory, resolutely historical, and inescapably political,"[1] succeeds in avoiding capture by any given system. In Marc Redfield's assessment, Pynchon's postmodernism contains "a double gesture of illusion and demystification or, perhaps better, a double affirmation of inevitability: the inevitability of both totalizing pattern and its failure."[2] This double gesture that Redfield discovers in Pynchon's short stories is one of the dominating concerns of *Gravity's Rainbow*, one I should especially like to explore in terms of the slide of signification. This feature of postmodernism facilitates Pynchon's affirmation of pluralism with what Molly Hite calls its "multiple, partial, overlapping, and often conflicting *ideas* of order"[3] (and, I should add, its constant awareness of the reality of disorder).

Postmodern scrutiny, Robert Con Davis argues, overturns Western culture's most deeply held absolutes and "important hierarchies, such as male/female, health/disease, nature/culture, truth/error, philosophy/literature, speech/writing, and seriousness/play." This "intellectual vandalism" wreaks "havoc on traditional economies of understanding and explanation based on these hierarchies"[4] and, ideally, prevents the formation of reverse hierarchies. The "dance of duplicity" and the "erasure of binarity"[5] based upon a dialectic of communication lead to reinscriptions of meaning, a general decentering, and a free play of alternatives. Such reinscriptions are, Foucault asserts, accomplished by disrupting the continuity of discourses and discursive practices and by remaining as much as possible outside them.[6] The very process of definition and displacement of oppositions opens "gaps" and "fissures" in assumptions about concrete meaning and absolute truth, introduces the dimension of undecidability, and grafts new meanings onto the old stocks.[7]

This postmodern way of thinking places particular emphasis on binary intersubjectivity, not merely as it relates to a given discourse but also metastructurally as it relates to all our systems. Language, as the means by which the mind approaches, describes, and creates reality (including human social, political, economic, and religious systems), must yield to scrutiny and partial displacement. Language, as Peter L. Cooper asserts, can lead to new kinds of writing such as Pynchon's counterrealism—writing that helps to reassess the inscribing of reality through language.[8] Abstract systems designed, formulated, and perpetuated by a patriarchal or male-centered society are, as a result, structurally displaced so that the reader can view them differently and question common cultural assumptions. In particular, Pynchon's technique of doubling leads his reader to question the basic structures and implications of received values and systems. The myriad examples of doubles and doubling in *Gravity's Rainbow*—especially the doubling of antisystem and system, culture and nature, and even metaphorically black and white—help to highlight World War II and technology as major twentieth-century problems. Technology is, however, no more the core problem for contemporary society than was Nazi Germany during the 1940s. The fundamental problem is human nature itself and the human compulsion to build systems.

Given the scope and complexity of Pynchon's fiction, his treatment of the double is only one of several important elements in his work, but it is one that especially facilitates his critique of Western structures. Pynchon's continuing preoccupation with dualities dates back to one of his first tales, "Mortality and Mercy in Vienna," in which the protagonist, the American Cleanth Siegel, is invited to a party by a man he perceives to be his doppelgänger, the Romanian David Lupescu. When Lupescu unexpectedly leaves the scene, Siegel is separated from his alter ego and finds himself in the position of host. The offspring of Jewish and Catholic parents, a "house divided against itself," Cleanth feels fundamentally alienated from those at the party, whom he considers spiritually corrupt. As a result, he stages what he considers a purifying massacre. This sense of self-division, alienation, and mistaken dualistic alternatives often characterizes Pynchon's more naive "split" figures.

Pynchon's first novel, *V.*, also depends upon the play of the double, both as alter ego and structure. The character Victoria, for instance, believes in the notion of a wraith or spiritual double. But the book is chiefly concerned with structural doubles. The two principal characters, Benny Profane and Herbert Stencil, are antithetical, Benny living only in the present of 1955–1956 and Herbert exploring the past in an attempt to locate V., a woman who may hold the key to the present. The several incarnations of V. exhibit alternative possibilities of creative and destructive behavior. Stencil's search is mirrored by that of Maijstral, who reflects on the meaning of the intrusion of the past into the present. These are only a few of the doubles, for in *V.*, characters, both female and male, are played off against one another, giving rise to other kinds of dualism that Tony Tanner identifies as "Right/Left; flip/flop; Stencil/Profane."[9] Central to a number of dualities in the book, as Joseph W. Slade remarks, are " 'mirror-worlds,' in which events happen in 'mirror-time.' There are several of these pairs, and each pair asserts the polarity of inanimateness and life, the principal duality of the novel."[10] Also of special importance in this dualistic scheme is the relationship between father and son, especially Stencil and his father. As in the later *Gravity's Rainbow*, the relationship is problematic—it imprisons the son within family structures, social duties, and perceptions but offers him certain open-ended possibilities and opportunities.

As in *V.*, the doubles of *The Crying of Lot 49* tend to be structural. After being appointed the executrix of Pierce Inverarity's estate, Oedipa Maas discovers that just beneath the surface of her normal life is the Tristero, a parallel structure that seems to connect with her own experiences in hidden, possibly sinister ways. Unacknowledged shadow structures and double realities frustrate and confuse her, but they also make her more alert to the various disguises and masks of systems. In becoming aware of herself and her culture, she is forced to look for conspiracies and unacknowledged links as well as a Tristero-like opposition to vested interests. She is caught between an impulse to construct, define, and control reality and a feeling that she is a victim of hidden structures and systems. The "excluded middle"[11] between her freedom and others' control, between order and spontaneity, might have provided a much-needed balance, but Pynchon's works never present perfectly balanced alternatives. They are, in this respect, highly moral, for they require his readers to explore themselves and their assumptions about reality, to be wary of systems and system making, and to subvert those systems that run counter to the public good and humanitarian values, and they never allow his readers to rest complacently in the false assumption that all is well in this best of all possible worlds or that its social constructs and collective actions are easily comprehensible.

Pynchon's *Vineland*, his most recent book after a seventeen-year silence, continues some of the binarity of his earlier fictions, especially in his handling of the antipathy between major characters and social groups. Zoyd Wheeler, an aging hippie, is persecuted by his villainous counterpart, his former wife's current husband, Brock Vond, who represents the suppression of minority opinion by the majority in America. The book explores Californian counterculture in a way that tests familiar assumptions about mainline American society and those about realistic fiction and suggests alternative universes, codes of behavior, and modes of fantastic fiction—in short, new ontological perspectives.

    Gravity's Rainbow is Pynchon's most complex novel—imaginative, well researched, and provocative, presenting various examples of doubles and doublings. Briefly, the book concerns the changing attitudes of Tyrone Slothrop, who discovers that his sexual reflexes may have been conditioned by a multinational corporation and may now be under observation by a behavioral research group. If Slothrop responds sexually to mechanical forces exterior to him, the uniqueness and self-sufficiency of his identity is called into question. This postmodern questioning of the very ontology of the self is, according to John O. Stark, the main function of Pynchon's use of the double.[12] (The importance of these ontological considerations is, according to Brian McHale, that they mark the differences between Pynchon's later fiction and his earlier fiction, which tends to deal with epistemology.)[13] Slothrop's fear that his sexual arousal is linked to the launching of the German rockets sends him from England to the Riviera, then to Switzerland, and finally to the "Zone" of war-torn Germany. In the process he, like Oedipa Maas, discovers hidden conspiratorial networks and so comes to see existence in terms of manipulator and manipulated, oppressor and oppressed. Such polarities, which Douglas Fowler and Thomas H. Schaub believe to be the most important structural links in the book,[14] cause Tyrone to distrust international firms and their representatives. They also serve to induce in him a full-blown paranoia.

    The entire book is founded upon a series of oppositions and what it means to ignore, to synthesize, or to erode them. Numerous critics comment on the dualistic oppositions in the book. Slade sees the important dualities as North and South, "love and death, paranoia and anti-paranoia, sky and underground, the living and the dead, freedom and control, black and white, the Outside and the Inside of the self, gravity and flight, grace and damnation, zero and one, even Rossini and Beethoven."[15] Charles Clerc remarks on the negative and positive poles of some oppositions: "control-freedom, rationality-fantasy, determinism-randomness, mundaneness-magic, supernature-nature, stasis-flux, repression-uninhibitedness, 'modern analysis-savage innocence,' frigid north-tropic climes, fragmentation-connectedness, white-black, Elect-Preterite, They-We."[16] Although Molly Hite does not center her discussion on issues of binarity, she believes that the book pivots on the tension between "fidelity to the secular realm" of largely uncontrolled human actions and "the drive to unify and be as gods" in establishing totalizing patterns and structures, including those of fiction making.[17] Such dualities tend to be clustered around the mirror oppositions that exist between on the one hand nature and natural activities and on the other artifice and unnatural or rational activities. Indeed, man's artifices ("Forces") all but negate and neutralize natural, random, and disorganized processes ("Counterforces"). Although Pynchon uses opposition, he is also highly critical of the binary method, and the book assesses its negative and positive aspects. It is this reappropriation of binarity, its simultaneous evocation and dismissal, that gives *Gravity's Rainbow* its unique postmodern focus.

Pynchon does not see members of binary pairs as perfectly structural, as either opposite or complementary. He refuses to validate Slothrop's ancestor's belief that "everything in the Creation has its equal and opposite counterpart."[18] But, *pace* Slade,[19] Pynchon avoids paradoxical resolution. He is critical of Kurt Mondaugen's creation of a metaphysics of "paired opposites, male and female principles uniting in the mystical egg of the combustion chamber: creation and destruction, fire and water, chemical plus and chemical minus" (p. 403). For Pynchon, life is not so simplistic or resolution so easy; the very notion of the middle as a balance of opposites is called into question.[20] He focuses on the need to escape the traditional privilege given one term or pole and thereby suggests excess and dissemination as desirable means of upsetting the normal balance. Alec McHoul and David Wills refer to this process as Pynchon's postrhetorical method in which dualities are "undercut/rewritten/overruled by another term, which as a result sets up a *second duality* (the words are uttered 'under erasure') between it and the first two terms."[21] The novel's excessive size, its plethora of characters, and its unresolved plots disperse meaning and result if not in entropy at least in a doubled vision. Paranoid and antiparanoid, narrative order and disorder, determinate and indeterminate, pattern and randomness all renew "our awareness of our acts and interpretations as being both conditioned and free, and of ourselves as synthesizing and disintegrating systems."[22] Values of nature and love, which seem in certain respects to be given hierarchical status by Pynchon, are therefore problematic, for they are themselves metaphors for, and doubles and embodiments of, randomness, excess, nonrationality, discontinuity, and indeterminacy. One set of discursive practices slides into another.

Pynchon calls our attention to various sorts of doubles and doubling through a wide-ranging list of the uses of the word *double* and its synonyms, almost all of the examples suggesting that nothing exists by itself with its own pure, self-unified, transcendent meaning. Each "thing" or term is a sign pointing away from itself to some other thing or word. In Gwenhidwy's speaking a "double language" (p. 169), a seemingly innocuous enough usage, the word *double* points to other uses that are not identical. Sammy Hilbert-Spaess's being a "double agent" (p. 217), Roger Mexico's driving his car "double-declutchingly" (p. 626), and Slothrop's being "double-crossed" (p. 598) present a cluster of different attributions relating to the duplicity of language and phenomena. The way one thing signifies and stands in for another is highlighted by the blond doll with lapis lazuli eyes that projects "signs of Katje, and doubles too" (p. 281) and by Max Schlepzig's use of doubles to shoot the bathtub scene from one of his films, *Jugend Herauf!*, although "Greta's double was actually an Italian stunt man named Blazzo in a long blonde wig" (p. 483). (Though the term *Jugend Herauf* does not in itself point up any doubles, it is a corrupted "double" of *Juden, heraus*.) Other uses of the term *double* relating to films and filmmaking reveal a similar slide of meaning. Greta's daughter, Bianca, in certain respects her competitive double, is usually filmed in silver, "warped in and out the violet-bleeding interfaces of Double and Triple Protars" (p. 484). Margherita Erdmann speaks of the moviestudio light that "came from above and below at the same time, so that everyone had two shadows: Cain's and Abel's" (p. 394), creating "Gnostic symbolism" of the "Double Light" (p. 429). As a direct result of the pornographic film *Alpdrücken*, starring Erdmann, men in Germany leave the theater, run home, and ravish their wives, producing "shadow children." Actions pertaining to the military are similarly "doubled" and are equally ambiguous. Chased by Marvy in the tunnel, Tyrone hears the sounds "dopplering" instead of "echoing." Even World War II is, in a bit of doggerel sung by Slothrop, called "Double-u Double-u Two-o-o-o!" (p. 289), and the symbol for the SS is a "double lightning-stroke" or "double integral sign" (p. 300). Scientific uses of the double S have a similar metonymical slide in meaning. The "double integrating circuit" that is part of the guidance system of the A4 rocket and the "double-summing of current densities" that influences the architecture of the underground factory at Nordhausen are compared to the shape of the tunnels in the Mittelwerke, the ancient rune that stands for the yew tree, or death, and the shape of lovers curled asleep, the scientific signified yielding to other signifiers. Loosely drawn together under this double letter, as Cooper has noted, are "fascism, mathematical analysis, death, and love."[23] This flickering "hologram" quality suggests that all—and none—of the versions of the double S are true. Even a trifle such as the drink that Tyrone and Geli Tripping share, the "Schattensaft" (p. 290), is equally problematic in equating the shadow and the double. Such repeated examples of language doubling leave the reader reeling from the contradictions and paradoxes of expression and meaning.

Considering that there are more than four hundred characters in the novel, Pynchon also has ample opportunity to present doubles in characterization that further demonstrate the slide in meaning. The characters, as Stark pertinently remarks, are "often almost indistinguishable one from another, [and] wander around forming unstable bonds with each other and falling victim to stronger forces that mold them at will."[24] That Slothrop himself, among other characters, forms such bonds and falls victim to stronger forces is demonstrated by his various identities within the book: Ian Scuffling, Max Schlepzig, Rocketman, and Pigman. Eventually, he becomes completely fragmented, thus embodying a denial of the idea of a simple and whole identity. His being played off regularly against various other characters implies that differentiation between self and other, subject and object, is artificial and finally false. Slothrop is compared to so many characters that a firm view of him as psychological self or as fictional character does not readily emerge. He is specifically compared to such attractive characters as Roger Mexico and his girlfriend Jessica Swanlake; Geli Tripping, the child witch; Enzian, the Herero black from Southwest Africa; and Tchitcherine, the Russian intelligence officer who wanders the Zone. He is, however, also bracketed with scores of other characters from both the Allied and the Axis camps who are repulsive in their lack of humanity: Edward Pointsman, the behaviorist; Brigadier Ernest Pudding, the English officer; Katje Borgesius, the Dutch girl who is a double agent and uses people narcissistically; the decadent Germans, including the actress Margherita Erdmann, the rocket developer Captain Blicero (Weissmann) with his homosexual lover Gottfried, and the rocket technician Franz Pökler; and numerous lesser characters. These comparisons, however, provide no consistently reliable clues to whether Slothrop is good or evil or whether he is a universal or an idiosyncratic character.

The most significant of these doubles, one that questions the ontological status of the self and demonstrates the nature of the metonymical slide in meaning, is the Russian Tchitcherine. Both he and Slothrop have paranoid suspicions about where they are and why. Slothrop believes himself on a quest for information about Jamf, and Tchitcherine believes his presence in the Zone owes something to his black half brother, Enzian, another double. Both come to have deep paranoiac suspicions about rocket cartels. Playfully, Tchitcherine's horse, Snake, is also doubled, for in the *Weisse Sandwüste von Neumexiko* Margherita rides a horse named Snake, probably acquired by Tchitcherine. Enzian's own double, in addition to Tchitcherine, is Blicero, who now dominates his imagination and consciousness and once dominated him sexually. Each of the doubles has in turn another double: Blicero (or Weissmann as he is also known) is doubled by Gottfried; Gottfried, by Katje; and Katje, by Margherita and Greta. Katje had a brother who so closely resembled her that he was often taken for her twin. Even Lyle Bland has two selves, his physical body and his soul that has the ability to come and go at will.

Events are doubled in the book to problematize ontology by raising questions about the similarity or separateness of phenomena. Jessica and Roger take their niece to see the Christmas pantomime *Hansel and Gretel*, an allusion that is doubled and redoubled in the decaying plaster Hansel and Gretel of Zwölfkinder park and in Blicero's domination of Gottfried and Katje, who are also called Hansel and Gretel. Though with similar linguistic referents, these situations are not at all identical. Something analogous characterizes the several instances of sexual doublings within the novel. Slothrop's first sexual act with Margherita is juxtaposed against and doubled by Pökler's intercourse with Leni, during which Ilse is conceived. Indeed, in Slothrop's mind these sexual encounters certainly double: "Ilse, fathered on Greta Erdmann's silver and passive image, Bianca, conceived during the filming of the very scene that was in his thoughts as Pökler pumped in the fatal charge of sperm—how could they not be the same child?" (pp. 576–77). Also, on one occasion, as Slothrop dreams of Bianca, his sexual partner Solange (an alias of Leni Pökler) dreams of Ilse. But of course each coupling is separate, no matter how much one resembles the other. Here similarity leads to difference, not sameness.

Double events, humans as doubles, and the very word *double* are all used to such excess and mean so many things that meaning is always dissipated. Like all systems in the book, their increasing size and complexity give the illusion of meaning and stability, but at the core, if there is a core, meaning is so dispersed and distorted as to be nonexistent. In this respect, and probably only in this one, there is a correspondence: what is true for the self in the dispersion of meaning is equally true for an organization and society at large. Pynchon's analogies raise serious doubts about the structurality of structures at every level in a way that makes the reader distrust all attempts at projecting and understanding order, and especially at establishing correspondent orders of behavior.

Slothrop as an individual must, then, be contrasted with the secretive, multinational businesses and financial houses that lie behind the war, financing and profiting from it. This motif of person against structure is one of the most important aspects of the structural doublings. Victim and paranoiac, Tyrone Slothrop grows to believe, with good reason, that "They" are out to get him and that he has become the unwitting victim of Jamf's bizarre experiment that links his sexual arousal with the flight and explosion of the German V-series bombs. What he does not know and never finds out is how correct he is in either assumption. He has proof that PISCES (Psychological Intelligence Schemes for Expediting Surrender) wants to control him, and he believes that his father was implicated in a scheme to condition his responses. Even as a student at Harvard, Slothrop felt a sense of a "peculiar *structure* that no one admitted to—that extended far beyond Turl Street, past Cornmarket into covenants, procuring, accounts due" (p. 193). This peculiar structure, with its semantic overtones of America's "peculiar institution," is one that threatens to enslave him, but it is also one whose real masters are hidden. Slothrop's access to information is blocked by the chiefs of the military and the captains of the German and the American General Electric monopoly. In what Foucault would call a system of power relations, all are guilty of complicity, yet none is guilty of individual control. Because Slothrop knows so little and suspects so much, he flees from surveillance and at the same time attempts to determine the origin of his physiological reaction. A contemporary pilgrim, doubled as "seeker and sought" and "baited and bait" (p. 490), he risks being lost in "a great swamp of paranoia" (p. 33) until he himself finally becomes the "genius of meta-solutions—knocking over the chessboard, shooting the referee" (p. 102). He plays someone else's game until he recognizes that he must exercise his responsibility at the level of the world's decentering.

The concept of paranoia itself relates integrally to Pynchon's treatment of binarity, the double, and disseminated meaning, for his paranoiacs believe in double structures. Slothrop's paranoia functions as the psychological fear of persecution when he first considers the possibility that there is a rocket that seeks his death, one "with his name written on it" (p. 25). The group, "They," responsible for this terrible purpose has, he suspects, a wider involvement throughout Europe. When he is given papers that describe his father's connection with IG Farben, he feels as if he has been enslaved by "Them," that he has become "a colonial outpost . . . representing Their white Metropolis far away" (p. 285). This fear that he is the victim of a vast conspiratorial pattern, this "operational paranoia," never disappears, for Slothrop suspects a sinister connection between German rocket launchings and his erections, and he tries to discover the origins of the conspiracy behind it. The book moves, in one sense, backward from the rockets' targets in England to Nordhausen where they were manufactured and fired. But the book also moves forward as Slothrop is gradually initiated into a knowledge of his place in a vast industrial-military complex: "He keeps pushing aside gauze after wavy gauze but there's always still the one, the impenetrable" (p. 359). This forward and backward movement is in itself a kind of structural doubling.

Slothrop finally realizes that it is impossible to discover or reconstruct origins because there may be no conspiracy, because the trail of evidence has been obliterated, or because truth lies in some other realm: "Those like Slothrop, with the greatest interest in discovering the truth, were thrown back on dreams, psychic flashes, omens, cryptographies, drug-epistemologies, all dancing on a ground of terror, contradiction, absurdity" (p. 582).

This operational paranoia is closely related to another kind, the distrust of the visible: the "Puritan reflex of seeking other orders behind the visible" (188). Here nature is perceived as a filter for divine plans and commands. It is, as Ahab said in *Moby Dick*, a pasteboard mask. Taken to an extreme, this particular kind of paranoia assumes double worlds and purposes, an ideal Platonic world, for example, that lies just beyond the real or, again as in *Moby Dick*, the suspicion of an unknown but malevolent force that drives mankind toward some horrible fate. Tyrone Slothrop suspects that circumstances in life are being manipulated and that everything "is really being used for something different. Meaning things to Them it has never meant to us. Never. Two orders of being, looking identical" (p. 202). He reacts similarly when he sees the waves reflecting a light so brilliant that it must be from an "identical-looking Other World." He comes to believe that his memorizing of rocket data is purposeful in the same way that his Puritan ancestors thought their memorizing passages from the Bible enabled them to apprehend an unseen order of reality. He is one of the faithful of rocketry, a pilgrim "along the roads of miracle, every bit and piece a sacred relic, every scrap of manual a verse of Scripture" (p. 391). His is a belief in "the game behind the game" (p. 208), of interconnectedness, simulation, and doubling.[25]

Akin to this "Puritan" paranoia is still another variety, largely of Pynchon's own defining: Western man's ("man's," for this trait *is*, according to Pynchon, particularly masculine) tendency to create networks, patterns, and systems. One typical paranoiac in *Gravity's Rainbow*, for instance, gathers correspondences, shaping them into patterns that can be plotted in parabolic curves. This paranoia is in a sense positive, for it fosters the kind of ordering activity that enables us to go about our daily affairs, to keep us from succumbing to the chaos that always threatens, the kind of rage for order that is equally necessary for the writer and the reader of fiction. This kind of pattern making also permits the creation of new ontological perspectives of the sort that Cooper calls paranoid model building.[26] The negative aspect of this paranoia involves the tendency to believe that each construction or ordering is natural, not fabricated, and the tendency always to build systems and to build them bigger and bigger instead of allowing nature to continue unimpeded or including and recognizing the value of competing systems. This fear of the naturally indeterminate, akin to what Max Horkheimer calls the "paranoia of reason,"[27] leads to a view of reality as a unified totality through control of the production and circulation of knowledge. This control and creation of simulation patterns—or doublings—may well be a response to a fear of the indeterminate or fear of control by others, but it in turn creates situations that others must escape. Thus, control and escape become intertwined and even tautological. There is, then, no neat, linear, binary cause-and-effect relationship, for the effect becomes the cause. (As Leo Bersani points out, this process is true for all tasks, including the reading of Pynchon's novels: "To inspire interest is to be guaranteed a paranoid reading, just as we must inevitably be suspicious of the interpretations we inspire. Paranoia is an inescapable interpretive doubling of presence.")[28] Such "delusional systems" hide the tautology of control and escape.

Human beings can, then, be paranoiac in being system makers; paranoiac in believing that one system reflects another, where *"everything is connected*, everything in the creation" (p. 703), and paranoiac in thinking themselves victims of another system. In each instance, one imagines or creates a system that is one's double. Some of these feelings of paranoia are induced by an already ordered system and some by individuals who attempt to create order and control in their own lives. According to Tyrone Slothrop's fifth proverb, "Paranoids are not paranoids . . . because they're paranoid, but because they keep putting themselves, fucking idiots, deliberately into paranoid situations" (p. 292). As Pynchon presents it, paranoia is an exaggerated form of the Western tendency to see cause and effect, to order reality in a monolithic way according to certain kinds of analytical reasoning. And yet, given Western culture, we cannot escape this condition. Pynchon wants his reader to be aware of the limitations of cause and effect, of grand paranoiac schemes, but the reverse, "antiparanoia, where nothing is connected to anything," is an impossible condition, one "not many of us can bear for long" (p. 434). As Lyotard argues of such paranoiac states, "This realism of systemic self-regulation, and this perfectly sealed circle of facts and interpretations, can be judged paranoid only if one has, or claims to have, at one's disposal a viewpoint that is in principle immune from their allure."[29] One can never completely step outside a system or understand the system from outside, yet it is still possible to imagine other responses and make provisional guesses.

Pynchon uses this concept of paranoia, a belief in double systems, and the opposition to it to rethink customary inferences and conclusions, priorities and exclusions. He suggests new options through his description of paranoid meeting paranoid: "A crossing of solipsisms. Clearly. The two patterns create a third: a moiré, a new world of flowing shadows, interferences" (p. 395). Such interferences prevent people from being able to ascertain whether they are victims. Slothrop himself comes to feel that the Zone contains so many plots and subplots that he (like Pynchon's readers in general, I might add) cannot sort things into neat patterns. No system is stable, no paranoia independent or provable. As a case in point, although Major Marvy has been inadvertently mistaken for Slothrop, arrested, bundled into an ambulance, and surgically castrated, Tchitcherine takes his sudden disappearance personally and assumes it bears a message for him if he can but decipher it. Pynchon's protagonists, therefore, must come to know the existence and complexity of systems, must try to discern whether a given system or network intends them to be victims, must survive by creating countervailing systems of their own, and finally must discover personal responsibility. Part of this responsibility involves the exercise of creative paranoia in forming what Mark Richard Siegel calls "We systems" to counteract "They systems."[30] To achieve whatever limited vision human beings can sustain, Pynchon's characters are forced to recognize, denaturalize, and demystify existing systems, to create alternative systems of their own and to understand that none of the competing systems is necessarily better or more natural than others. All order is humanly created; no given order is transcendent; one order can readily replace another or suffer the metonymical slide of meaning that affects all instances of Pynchon's doubles and doubling.

At the heart of the "They systems" that Pynchon sets out to demystify and even to disprove is the theory of structural opposition derived from I. P. Pavlov, who argued for the presence of these bistable points in the brain. As a child, Tyrone Slothrop was perhaps programmed by the Pavlovian Dr. Laszlo Jamf so that he would experience an erection in response to the sound of a rocket, for "a hardon, that's either there, or it isn't. Binary, elegant" (p. 84). Once programmed, Slothrop's responses can supposedly never again be neutral; he is either programmed for a binary cause-and-effect response or if deprogrammed, will "proceed *beyond* the point of reducing a reflex to zero" (pp. 84–85).

Although Tyrone initially knows nothing of this programming, researchers at "The White Visitation" center discover similarities in the maps detailing Slothrop's sexual conquests and those pinpointing German bomb attacks on London and jump to the conclusion that one is the cause and the other the effect. As a result, researchers for the Allied powers are interested in how they, through experimentation and surveillance, can not only observe this stimulus-response procedure but even subvert Slothrop's ideas of opposites, his ability "to distinguish pleasure from pain, light from dark, dominance from submission" (p. 48). They wish to weaken his notion of opposites, to force him beyond "equivalent" and "paradoxical" states of mind, by starving, traumatizing, and shocking him and thereby push him into the "ultraparadoxical phase." The war itself is to be the laboratory and Slothrop the guinea pig in this "depolarization" or "neurotic confusion." Slothrop is himself to become an ontological problem, a kind of microcosm of postwar Europe, without categories, boundaries, frontiers, subdivisions: "All the fences are down, one road as good as another, the whole space of the Zone cleared, depolarized, and somewhere inside the waste of it a single set of coordinates from which to proceed, without elect, without preterite, without even nationality to fuck it up" (p. 556).

The desire to go beyond opposites is not in itself bad. Certainly, as Barthes and Derrida have pointed out, the bipolar response is inherently limiting in privileging one term of a pair over another: male over female, reason over emotion, white over black, city over country, presence over absence. They assert that such hierarchizing is inferior to pluralistic possibilities and multivalent meanings. Also, according to Barthes and Derrida, the bipolar response leads to a firm belief in cause and effect that precludes other imaginative solutions more random in nature. Rejecting Pavlovian theory, Pynchon's fictional researcher Roger Mexico is one who questions cause and effect, that "damned Calvinist insanity" that construes everything as payment and exchange—one-for-one, retribution springing from sin, effect springing from cause—because he can see other, pararational ways of construing reality, "lunatic" ways such as "survival after death, communication mind-to-mind, prophesying, clairvoyance, teleportation" (p. 58).

Most who wish to strip Slothrop of his ideas of opposition, however, have none of Mexico's consciousness-enlarging, antirationalistic concerns. They do not wish to heighten Slothrop's awareness but to undermine and experiment with it, to manipulate and control his consciousness. To impose their order upon his, they use a certain kind of binary process—cause and effect—to erase difference. They do not understand that as Derrida maintains, without difference there can be no meaning. Without perceiving differences, these pseudoscientists think of analogous patterns as necessarily linked, so that, for example, Leni Pökler's relationship with Peter Sachsa is viewed as identical to Nora's with Sir Stephen Dodson-Truck. Such confusion seems absurd, but equally problematic is the failure to comprehend that certain oppositions share affinities in some nonrational way: "speaker and spoken-of, master and slave, virgin and seducer, each pair most conveniently coupled and inseparable" (p. 88). Researchers at "The White Visitation" do not understand the manifold implications of the binary principle or the limitations of the cause-and-effect process; they are blind to the fact that pure meaning is not possible. Although Pointsman, the Pavlovian, seems to recognize that not everything can be subsumed within the process of cause and effect, he is enamored of "symmetry," of mirror images and "ideas of the opposite" (p. 144). He *wills* to see a relationship between Slothrop's map and the bomb attacks despite Gwenhidwy's equally plausible observation that births during this period also correlate with the bomb attacks and despite Harvey Speed and Floyd Perdoo's discovery that the names on Slothrop's map have no real counterparts. As his name suggests, Pointsman is limited in perceiving reality. He faces in one direction; he has one view of things; he fails to comprehend either the distance or interface between opposing forces, although it is he who establishes directions for others. He understands neither that meaning may be perpetually deferred nor that opposites are of many different sorts and thus cannot easily be lumped together. As a pair, black and white are not the same as dark and light, no matter how similar they may seem. To compare black and white with dark and light or to compare any set of pairs is to use analogy, and analogy always depends upon reducing complex experience to preserve the appearance of harmonious correspondence.

Things, people, and events that are inherently different thus tend by Pointsman's principle of analogy to slide together and resemble one another. This principle of congruity is one use of the double in the book. Because things share certain qualities, people group them together and establish correspondences and units. Such a procedure is not altogether incorrect. To see both difference and pattern is essential for an assessment of life. Slothrop's goal is to discover such differences, especially between the natural and the artificial.

But Slothrop does not identify or discover differences that lead to fulfillment and meaning, for there is no "Real Text" behind the visible orders and serial doubles.[31] Nor can he locate the origins of relationships and systems, because they have no origin. Systems are, as Derrida says, centerless, giving only the illusion of coherence,[32] just as Pynchon's characters are not unitary and self-identical but fragmentary. Not to see links and correspondences, then, is impossible. To become thoughtlessly entrapped in the networks and systems of others is careless, yet to disrupt the apparently seamless systems of logic and order is difficult.

Tyrone Slothrop's great virtue is that he tries to understand the systems of others without becoming trapped by them. The illumination that he seeks, and never fully comprehends, is embodied in the "mirror-metaphysics" or double construction of the book. One side of life consists of those qualities identified in certain ways as natural: nature, sexuality, and religion that takes its spirit from nature, those characteristics identified as "love, dreams, the spirit, the senses" (p. 177). According to Fowler, "One of the most important polarities in *Gravity's Rainbow* is between the tropical and the North, and Pynchon again contrasts this harmonious, organic life of the jungle and savanna, where man still lives in touch with the great Cycle of creation, with the Christian North, 'death's region,' the land of technology, repression, rationalized destruction."[33] While Fowler's distinction is somewhat limiting, it does help the reader to perceive the ways nature is used in Pynchon's novel. Juxtaposed against the natural are replications and simulations of natural processes (especially light), perverted sexuality, abstract religions, and systems that result in military and industrial buildup. These replications or doubles promise "joy and defiance" and appear to move toward a form of the inorganic to avoid being perceived as a "form of death" (p. 579). They constitute a myth of life that seeks self-validation, stability, and immortality, but a myth that is dead.

These correspondences and false resemblances constitute a final aspect of the double and intersubjective binarity. In terms of play and game theory, the urge to codify and systematize arises from the desire to turn the unstructured play of free alternatives (like nature itself) into the structure, systems, and goals of games, which displace and seem to erase freeplay. Pynchon insists that systems bear only the remotest resemblance to nature and that life itself bears only a distant resemblance to an idealized life, that the *wish* and desire for pristine nature, perfect earthiness, and innocent sexuality is itself an illusion. In Lacanian terms, desire is constituted upon an abyss or lack; humans can never realize their fondest dreams; nature itself is never independent of the gaze of the human observers. Differences and doublings are, then, chimerical but must be explored if only to enable us to comprehend our complicity in what Foucault calls relations of power and to explore the nature of our choices.

Given Pynchon's awareness of lack and the problematics of ideas of perfection, unity, and wholeness, his ambivalence toward "nature" is hardly surprising. Constituted upon change and death, nature is not a system and is never as constant and benevolent as humans crave, yet it is accorded a more or less privileged status, not only because it is the original form human beings try to replicate but because its randomness, irregularity, and change contribute to its beauty. Its beauty lies in diversity, not homogeneity. In it, differences are never repressed, and they can never by mastered or controlled. *Différence* is *différance*.

Nature as portrayed by Pynchon is wonderfully abundant, random, disordered, and discontinuous. His most lyrical passages are paeans to it. The seagulls off the Mediterranean are described as "sliding, easy, side to side, wings hung out still, now and then a small shrug, only to gather lift for this weaving, unweaving, white and slow faro shuffle off invisible thumbs" (p. 181). Humankind can only look on in mingled empathy and envy as these birds in their natural habitat rise and sink, float and soar. But soaring is not the sole criterion for acceptance. Birds that cannot fly are equally wonderful. Mauritius and its now-extinct dodoes evoke beautifully sensuous prose: "Ranked in thousands on the shore, with a luminous profile of reef on the water behind them, its roar the only sound on the morning, volcanoes at rest, the wind suspended, an autumn sunrise dispensing light glassy and deep over them all . . . they have come from their nests and rookeries, from beside the streams bursting out the mouths of lava tunnels, from the minor islands awash like debris off the north coast" (pp. 110–11). Such rhapsodic passages often describe remote tropical regions of abundant fertility, although the image of the rainbow suggests that beauty is available everywhere. Every now and again Slothrop is surprised by the beauty of the landscape in northern Europe, especially when it is linked sensuously with the beauty of the women. But those who can truly see the rainbows and thus value a life fully associated with nature are few. Before the advent of whites in Southwest Africa, the Hereros had respect for the land, and their rituals were supposedly designed to invoke and appease the spirits of nature. Theirs was not a religion that divided life into parts and irreconcilable oppositions but sought unity and wholeness: "God is creator and destroyer, sun and darkness, all sets of opposites brought together, including black and white, male and female" (p. 100). Their village, too, was laid out in the pattern of the mandala so that every aspect of life was seen as integrated: "birth, soul, fire, building. Male and female, together" (p. 563). But this is an older, not a modern Africa, and certainly not America or Europe. Pynchon suggests that this ancient mandala has been perverted, first into the cross by the early Christians and, later into the swastika by the Nazis, who used it as a sign of their state and the power of rocketry. "Crosses, swastikas, Zone-mandalas" (p. 625)—all have been altered by the modern orders of civilization. The ancient African life of the Hereros is, then, both attractive and inaccessible. Urban society can never entirely recover its origins in nature, if nature was really ever benevolent and peaceful. Gerhardt von Göll tries in his films to attain this vision of edenic nature—"I can take down your fences and your labyrinth walls, I can lead you back to the Garden you hardly remember" (p. 388)— but it is all smoke and mirrors. Impossible to locate or re-create, the Garden, conceived as an escape from encroaching urbanism and proliferating systems, is only a fantasy; nature as origin and even as process cannot be known.

Europeans, then, are finally denied access to such exotic and ancient natural beauty and natural ways of living, but the wholesome, nurturing side of life is tantalizingly embodied within the Zone by Geli Tripping, the child-witch. Unlike Göll's artificial paradise, hers is presented as apparently real, though unavailable to anyone else and perhaps unavailable to her at any other time or in any other setting, for her situation is the result of having most man-made machinery, constructs, and systems around her destroyed by the war. She lives in the open, seemingly without protection since the roof of her home has been bombed out. Moreover, she opens herself to the elements, embracing the stars, welcoming the owls, making love unpossessively. She is one with the earth and knows the power of natural herbs that made more potent by her incantations can attract the love of the most elusive man. Nature has clearly left its imprint on her: "Nowhere in her eyes is there any sign of corrosion—she might have spent all her War roofed and secure, tranquil, playing with small forest animals in a rear area someplace" (p. 290). She is further described as having winelike "breath, nests of down in the hollows of her arms, thighs with the spring of saplings in wind" (p. 291). What she practices is a religion of the universal Pan, rejected by abstract Western religions. Slothrop's Puritan forbears may have had that power available to them. His ancestor, William, loved taking pigs through the countryside to market, sleeping out under the stars, and becoming acquainted with nature. The great Puritan Thomas Hooker is quoted in *Gravity's Rainbow* as saying, "I know there is wilde love and joy enough in the world . . . as there are wilde Thyme, and other herbes," but he, as a devotee of Christianity, settled for a more arid and, Pynchon suggests, destructive love: "We would have garden love, and garden joy, of Gods owne planting" (p. 22). Historical Christianity imposed abstractions on nature, imposed the Word on the flesh.[34]

This atavistic signification of earthy goodness applies more broadly to the females than the males in the book; they are more open to nonrational possibilities. Although Leni Pökler has been constrained in her life with Franz, upon joining a group of students and finding herself freed from male domination, she feels her sensuality and intellectuality developing together. Freedom to express herself sexually leads to a capacity to free herself from other social and gender constraints and ingrained intellectual ideas. She ridicules her husband's "engineer's devotion to cause-and-effect" and argues for other alternatives: "Parallel, not series. Metaphor. Signs and symptoms. Mapping on to different coordinate systems" (p. 159). In referring to metaphor, signs, and symptoms, she in effect argues for the ever-changing, ever-elusive qualities of language over a more literal and singly focused system. Another such woman, Frau Gnahb, captain of her own vessel, is an unconventional woman who makes her living by disposing of contraband. Daring and uninhibited, she takes risks in undermining systems that no one else would take, and she never sacrifices the helpless to her own purposes. One of the other women in *Gravity's Rainbow*, Jessica Swanlake, seizes an opportunity during the war to free herself from conventional attitudes and restrictions. Once, she casually throws off her blouse while driving down the highway; she leaves her body for the purpose of taking an astral journey; and she always shows regard for the feelings and sensitivities of others. Indifferent to "death-institutions," including psychological conditioning and abstract language, she needs few words to express her feelings. She is also able to turn away from the past without having to project a future. She "was the breaking of the wave. Suddenly there was a beach, the unpredictable . . . new life . . . past all words" (p. 126). Perhaps her flaw is that she is too trusting, so that once the war is over, she automatically assumes that all's right with the world. Her relationship with Roger, invulnerable to falling bombs in wartime, disintegrates in the face of her complacence and acceptance of the seemingly inevitable order of peacetime. Enzian's mother in Africa has also lived according to basic emotions, which in her relationship with Enzian's Russian father were not complicated by sophisticated or analytical language. They were a kind of prelapsarian pair, a nonlinguistic Adam and Eve: "They had learned each other's names and a few words in the respective languages—afraid, happy, sleep, love . . . the beginnings of a new tongue, a pidgin which they were perhaps the only two speakers of in the world" (p. 351). Although *Gravity's Rainbow* is largely dominated by male characters who strive for hegemony in intellectual and social systems, women such as Jessica, Darlene, Mrs. Quoud, and Enzian's mother, who provide pluralism and diversity, are not subordinated to the males' mistaken systems of thought. Yet they are relatively powerless within these systems, so that theirs is an unexplored and unexploited possibility. They are the lesser, the suppressed pole of a binary opposition involving gender and epistemology.

Jessica's boyfriend, Roger Mexico, however, is one male who in wartime acknowledges the value of subjectivity and nonrationality. Sometimes, when his love is predominant, his "heart grows erect, and comes" (p. 120). Once he is described as "off sucking icicles, lying flat and waving his arms to make angels in the snow, larking" (p. 57). Although he curses himself for not working hard enough on fire control or kill rates per ton for the bomber groups, he is intrigued by laws of probabilities (the highly probable arrangement of random distribution) and the "clairvoyants and mad magicians, telekinetics, astral travelers, gatherers of light" (p. 40). He is also the one person who cares enough to follow Slothrop into the Zone to protect him. Too often, however, he denies the nonrational and subjective side of himself. Despite his inclination to play, to acknowledge intuition, and to ignore orderly systems created by rationality, he too is not wholly faithful to those possibilities and takes war, abstract systems, and the logic of causation as his mother. He becomes "the Dour Young Man of 'The White Visitation,' the spider hitching together his web of numbers" (p. 40), a youth of darkness, a "child-surrogate" of the war: "The coincidence of maps, girls, and rocketfalls has entered him silently, silent as ice" (p. 176) and paralyzed his "tropical" "Mexican" nature.

The masculine world that Roger succumbs to consists almost entirely of a hegemony established by abstractions: dreams of cause and effect and visions of purity and consistency. Nature for the males of *Gravity's Rainbow* is not valid in itself; it must be tampered with. Dodoes must be killed; octopuses must be made larger; rats must be used in experiments. Within the male environment, processes of nature are distorted. The beauty of the peacock fanning his tail is replaced by the parabolic arc of the rocket, which "rose off the platform, scarlet, orange, iridescent green" (p. 223). In this unnatural world, love itself is associated with unyielding "masculine" systems: "Love, among these men, once past the simple feel and orgasming of it, had to do with masculine technologies, with contracts, with winning and losing. . . . Beyond simple steel erection, the Rocket was an entire system *won*, away from the feminine darkness, held against the entropies of lovable but scatterbrained Mother Nature" (p. 324). This is a world where plastics have replaced natural substances. In fact, plastic can replicate even the most essential appearance of human desire and fertility: "Imipolex G is the first plastic that is actually *erectile*. Under suitable stimuli, the chains grow cross-links, which stiffen the molecule and increase intermolecular attraction" (p. 699). The three qualities of plastics—*Kraft, Standfestigkeit*, and *Weisse*—are those desired by every Western system. Plastics correspond to man-made systems, which in turn correspond to and distort nature. The nerve center for male-dominated use of medicine, St. Veronica's Hospital, is not a place for curing and healing but for scientific experiments in psychological conditioning. Pointsman's office is a perverted replica of the mystical Delphic oracles: "The tiny office space is the cave of an oracle: steam drifting, sibylline cries arriving out of the darkness . . . Abreactions of the Lord of the Night" (p. 48).

In unmaking and remaking the world, developing concepts and systems, creating lights and agents of death, men, working for the Lord of the Night, believe themselves progressive. Light will scare away the roaches; rockets will make our world safe from the enemy; religion will guarantee eternal life. Pynchon's point is that we deceive ourselves. The enemy is within, part of our way of viewing reality, and what is portrayed as life-enhancing technology is actually destructive of what is really natural in the environment; the inanimate cannot replace the animate.[35] The spirit of Rathenau conjured up at a seance remarks that this view of technological progress and dynamic improvement, which he himself once espoused, is an illusion: "The more dynamic it seems to you, the more deep and dead, in reality, it grows." He adds that such belief in human organization is simply another manifestation of the fallacy of cause and effect: "All talk of cause and effect is secular history, and secular history is a diversionary tactic" (p. 167). Hence, behind military and consumer products, the rocket and the light bulb, lies an ideology, as Foucault would say, hidden and masked. The structure of social power and domination disappears; official sanctions and words mask the horror of the manipulation that lies beneath the surface. Pynchon exposes it. In this book about the Second World War written from an American perspective, the obvious targets, Hitler and Nazi Germany, surprisingly remain relatively unscathed. Pynchon's target is the Western emphasis on reason, progress, and power: "Don't forget the real business of the War is buying and selling" (p. 105). Although one character, Dr. Rozsavolgyi, believes he is assisting in the depolarizing of Slothrop to replace personalities with "abstractions of power" and the intelligent rule of corporations, he does not understand the corporate basis of the war. The orchestrators of the war and postwar society are the American, British, and German scientific and technological industries. Linked together, they have profited from the war, though they manage to keep their association a secret. Instead of centering on Nazi

Germany as the probable cause of the war and the collapse of Western Europe, then, Pynchon blames the entire Western way of thinking. Causes are not so easily identifiable as they seem.

Pynchon decenters our reality by exposing the links between the preferred forms of belief and behavior in Western society. These logocentric beliefs arise from the male consciousness and create systems that are rational, abstract, oriented to words, and suppressive of emotion. Indeed, *logos* is defined as "word, reason, truth," akin to what Lacan calls the Name of the Father, the male way of construing and ordering society. Logocentrism is not the nurturing, earthy power associated with the female; it is the drive to master, control, and exploit on all social levels—ideological, institutional, and informational. Pynchon, passionately editorializing, uses such associations in describing the male perversities of Weissmann and the destruction of the feminine:

> He is the father you will never quite manage to kill. The Oedipal situation in the Zone these days is terrible. There is no dignity. The mothers have been masculinized to old worn moneybags of no sexual interest to anyone, and yet here are their sons, still trapped inside inertias of lust that are 40 years out of date. The fathers have no power today and never did, but because 40 years ago we could not kill them, we are condemned now to the same passivity, the same masochist fantasies *they* cherished in secret, and worse, we are condemned in our weakness to impersonate men of power our own infant children must hate, and wish to usurp the place of, and fail. . . . So generation after generation of men in love with pain and passivity serve out their time in the Zone, silent, redolent of faded sperm, terrified of dying, desperately addicted to the comforts others sell them, however useless, ugly or shallow, willing to have life defined for them by men whose only talent is for death. (P. 747)

The males, "fathers," are identified with the false desire for complete systems. Such systems of oppositions and hierarchical structures are based on the central idea of being as *presence*, "a belief in an ultimate word, . . . essence or reality which will act as foundation for all our thought, language and experience."[36] "Presence" asserts that we have unitary selves, that rationality and rational systems can discover truth, and that our language is capable of defining and communicating precise meanings present in the spoken word. "Presence" also implies that we think in terms of analysis and synthesis; we use our faculty of reason to link disparate systems. In *Gravity's Rainbow*, "presence" means that we of the Western world refuse to recognize intersubjectivity, the slide of signification, and the absence of meaning in our language, circumstance, and life. Although our abstract systems—electricity, whiteness, religion, and the Word—do metonymically disappear into one another, they cannot be treated identically. Their doubling in *Gravity's Rainbow* forces us to comprehend the artificiality of the desire for unity; our perception of their differences forces us to recognize the process by which meaning and signification always shift.

The notion of presence, belief in correspondences and synthesis, which goes back at least as far as Plato, is replicated in many forms in Pynchon's book. Brigadier "Ernest Pudding was," for example, "brought up to believe in a literal Chain of Command, as clergymen of earlier centuries believed in the Chain of Being" (p. 77). The center of "The White Visitation" for psychological testing has a molded plaster ceiling with Methodist versions of Christ's kingdom, synthesizing science and religion. In his hallucination, Pointsman, a researcher at "The White Visitation," believes that he could become the synthesis of the warring elements that he perceives in Roger Mexico: East and West, protagonist and antagonist, Yang and Yin. The integration of technology, the military, and religion is exposed, either implicitly and explicitly, throughout the book because it is generated by the same minds and is part of the same cultural development.

War's true nature as a mask covering integrated systems and beliefs that govern life in Western society becomes explicit when Roger Mexico muses on Christmas Eve about the false unity that the war seems to project. He comes to see that the war actually divides and subdivides lives, "though its propaganda will always stress unity, alliance, pulling together" (p. 130). Furthermore, war is not a *presence*, a truth, but an *absence* that only pretends to be a presence: "Yet who can presume to say *what* the War wants, so vast and aloof is it . . . so *absentee*" (p. 131).

At the heart of system making are the duplicitous false mirrors of nature—the rocket itself and even the more mundane electric light bulb. The rocket is first described as a surrogate sun or new star: "Far to the east, down in the pink sky, something has just sparked, very brightly. A new star, nothing less noticeable. . . . The brilliant point has already become a short vertical white line. It must be somewhere over the North Sea . . . at least that far . . . icefields below and a cold smear of sun" (p. 6). At the conclusion of the book, the ascending rocket launched by Blicero is also described as a point of light (and implicitly the phallus), and so high does it go that the beautiful Gottfried, riding in the rocket's chamber, sees the "first star" hanging between his feet. But the narrator asserts that this rocket "was *not a star*, it was falling, a bright angel of death" (p. 760). The rocket with its power is more than mere weaponry; it is "fantasy, deathwish, rocket-mysticism" (p. 154). Franz Pökler, head rocket engineer, is completely absorbed in his fantasy of rocketry. Devoted only to the rocket, his life is womanless and loveless, and he spends his nights drinking beer, playing card games and chess, and suffering from nightmares. Another involved in the fantasy of rocketry is Katje, who sees rockets as manifestations of "secret lusts that drive the planet and herself, and Those who use her—over its peak and down, plunging, burning, toward a terminal orgasm" (p. 223). For her, it is the manifestation of an infinite order of the erotic. Indeed, many of Pynchon's characters explicitly perceive the rocket as a representation of phallic consciousness, "cruel, hard, thrusting into the virgin-blue robes of the sky" (p. 465). And external to the novel itself but part of its immediate appeal was the timeliness of its appearance in 1973. America's own romance with the rocket had only recently been climaxed by the July 16, 1969, moon shot. What the Germans had begun at Nordhausen was brought to fulfillment at Cape Canaveral.

Because the rocket has such allure and seems to hold the key to such unlimited power and strength, Germany, Russia, the United States, and Great Britain all have coveted access to its inventors and its technicians, not to mention its secret plans. Such is the modern infatuation with technology that the rocket has spawned. But what Slothrop discovers is that the overt competition between nations masks a greater source of power in society—a network of conglomerates such as IG Farben, Siemens, and General Electric, all of whom are involved in rocket research and together began the war, controlled and orchestrated it for their own profit despite the seeming chaos, political anarchy, and random destruction. The links between the Allied and Axis powers belie their supposed binary opposition and form an indictment of the international business community.

The principal genius behind this effort of the cartels to control the affairs of state is Rathenau, who envisions "a Corporate City-state where technology was the source of power" (p. 578), an idea, however, shared by others either consciously or subconsciously. Even Pökler experiences "some nervous drive toward myth he doesn't even know if he believes in—for the white light, ruins of Atlantis, intimations of a truer kingdom" (p. 579). It is this drive for some kind of abstract perfection and ultimate ordering of society, the human race, spiritual life, corporate structure, and systems that drives the Germans to the excesses of fascism and the British, Americans, and Russians to greater industrialization, military fortification, and environmental destruction. Indeed no one in the post-Newtonian age is exempt. But those driven toward the abstractions of this myth do not realize that the drive of the electric companies is toward profit and profit alone; in *Gravity's Rainbow* it is the electric companies rather than the Nazis that are the true Fascists.

Pynchon's description of the sale of electricity makes it clear that he considers electricity the artificial, duplicitous double of natural light, human companionship, and natural systems. The allure of electricity is not just that it represents power through international cartels but that it speaks to a deep-seated yearning to "live forever, in a clean, honest, purified Electronworld" (p. 699), to remake and reform the world in a way that eliminates risk and reduces chaos to order.

Pynchon's allusions to light are frequent, and the power over human life exerted by these cartels is symbolized by the light bulb itself. The "blinding mirror" aboard the Saturnalian cruise ship *Anubis* and Gerhardt von Göll's manipulation of lighting techniques in his sadomasochistic films to produce the "holocaust" of light at the Casino Hermann Goering illustrate the deliberate creation of a desire for artificial light. Slothrop's remark that the word for "electric socket" is the same as that for "mother" in German reveals the complicity of rocket and socket, male and female, mother and father, in this denaturalized profit-making scheme, which blasts the dream of the "cyclical, resonant, eternally-returning" world (p. 412) because it depletes the systems entropically by taking more energy than it returns. The manipulation of the light industry by General Electric is a strong metaphor for the manipulation of human beings by any and all systems.

It is especially the story of Byron the light bulb that illustrates the pernicious nature of electric cartels and other monopolies. "Born" in Berlin in "Bulb Baby Heaven" in a factory owned by Siemens but part of a cartel consisting of International General Electric, Osram, and

Associated Electrical Industries of Britain, which are mainly owned by General Electric of America, Byron is one of twenty million incandescent light bulbs manufactured each year by "Bulb folks [who] are in the business of providing the appearance of power, power against the night, without the reality" (p. 647). The task of Byron (whose name is a visual near-rhyme with Tyrone Slothrop's and who becomes something like a symbol of Slothrop) is to keep the roaches away and thus give the appearance of order and cleanliness. That, metaphorically, is the function of all "illuminating" systems: to present the appearance of order, cleanliness, and harmony—in short, "light"—so that the roaches are not seen. Instead of acquiescing to the purposes of the manufacturers, however, Byron refuses to have his identity defined or his operational life limited to six hundred hours by the corporation: he wants to extend his life indefinitely and even has hopes of organizing all the Bulbs into an Energy Revolution: "Byron has had a vision against the rafters of his ward, of 20 million Bulbs, all over Europe, at a given synchronizing pulse arranged by one of his many agents in the Grid, all these Bulbs beginning to strobe *together*, humans thrashing around the 20 million rooms like fish on the beaches of Perfect Energy" (pp. 648–49). His hopes for revolution are short-lived, but in surpassing his six hundred-hour limit he achieves a glimmering awareness of the possibility of immortality. Because he does not conform, he is put under surveillance by the corporation and targeted for destruction. But he escapes destruction; stolen, traded, transferred from place to place, lost and found again, he becomes a myth with many meanings, a floating signifier whose signification varies from person to person and bulb to bulb. He refuses to remain in place long enough to be given a transcendent meaning. Unlike those who never gain knowledge or understanding, Byron is the Cassandra of the electric cartel, "condemned to go on forever, knowing the truth and powerless to change anything" (p. 655). One light bulb, artificial though it is, can become, so to speak, a tiny sun that highlights and subverts in its humble way the false but seemingly omnipotent systems of illumination.

Whiteness in *Gravity's Rainbow* is closely associated with both the rocket and the light bulb. One might expect whiteness to be equated with the sun itself, but Pynchon uses it to indicate a negation of natural light. As with D. H. Lawrence's white consciousness, Melville's "Whiteness of the Whale," and Conrad's sepulchral whiteness in

"Heart of Darkness," Pynchon's use of white becomes a metaphor for, and takes on meanings of, excessive rationality and intentions to transform and control both the landscape and human behavior. It also brings into perspective the "white" religion of Christianity. Indeed, the quotation attributed to Wernher von Braun that serves as the headnote to the book relates to this view of whiteness—the tendency to view nature as a metaphor for eternity and to attribute to it the power of limitless transformation: "Nature does not know extinction; all it knows is transformation. Everything science has taught me, and continues to teach me, strengthens my belief in the continuity of our spiritual existence after death" (p. 1). This is a view in which all phenomena are unified in one grand design, a view in which the natural is taken not just as a metaphor for the supernatural but as a guarantee of its reality. This attitude allows people to do with nature whatever they choose under the easy assumption that it can be transformed but not destroyed. Pynchon unravels these entwined strands to show that each has its own existence and that it is the desire to erase differences that links them together in the first place.

This vision of infinite transformation underlies what whites have done to blacks in Southwest Africa and on a more personal level what Blicero has done, and Tchitcherine hopes to do, to Enzian. As a white conqueror in Africa, Blicero has forced Enzian to accept the religion of Christ, the language and culture of the West, and the philosophy of the rocket. In addition to being subjected to this domination, Enzian is forced in Africa to service Blicero's sexual desires. Thus, Blicero succeeds in undermining and transforming Enzian's culture and morals. What Tchitcherine wishes to accomplish is comparable; he feels a compulsive "need to annihilate the Schwarzkommando and his mythical half-brother, Enzian" (p. 338). Blicero and Tchitcherine are Enzian's subduing, harmful doubles, forces that seem to be external but are really internal: "Tchitcherine is a complex man. It's almost as if . . . he thinks of Enzian as . . . another *part* of him—a black version of something inside *himself*. A something he needs to . . . liquidate" (p. 499). This is the force of whiteness subduing, and even eliminating, the force of blackness, because black seems different and, to some whites, inferior. Whites also want to subdue or eliminate darkness because it suggests death: "Shit, now, is the color white folks are afraid of. Shit is the presence of death" (p. 688). Conversely, some blacks see the whites as evil: "Manichaeans who see two Rockets, good and evil, who speak together in the sacred idiolalia of the Primal Twins (some say their names are Enzian and Blicero) of a good Rocket to take us to the stars, an evil Rocket for the World's suicide, the two perpetually in struggle" (p. 727). But these people all want to attribute false symbolic meaning to blackness. In reality, Enzian must be seen as a representative of a group of people exploited, repressed, and often annihilated by Colonial systems—a topic, incidentally, that Pynchon covers extensively in his first novel, *V*. Enzian and those Hereros brought with him from Southwest Africa to live in Germany conse- quently have been forced to lead a sterile existence in which the propulsion of the rocket and the suicide of their race are the main goals. But their very existence in the middle of white Germany reminds everyone of blackness. These and associated names—Operation Black Wing, Schwarzgerät, Schwarzkommando, Blackrocket, Black Rocket Troops, Blackdream, Black Apes—affect people with both horror and fascination. Even Slothrop has been called the "Schwarzknabe" and his father the "Schwarzvater," so it is appropriate that the narrator asks of Slothrop: "Is there a single root, deeper than anyone has probed, from which Slothrop's Blackwords only appear to flower separately? Or has he by way of the language caught the German mania for name giving, dividing the Creation finer and finer, analyz- ing, setting namer more hopelessly apart from named" (p. 391). These are part of his "Schwarzphänomen," a force within him that choreo- graphs him. Blackness in Slothrop's unconscious is not something to be repressed and feared; his absurd, illogical dreams and sexual fantasies are more human than the perverted and inhuman hopes of European whites. Certainly, blackness in general is not to be feared. Enzian's half brother, Tchitcherine, has no need to fear him, and Katje has no need to fear the Hereros with their song about paranoia. The blacks do not harm the European whites. The blackness of night is often a time of safety for Slothrop, for then the "Firm" cannot so easily subject him to surveillance. Night is the bewitching time for Geli. Indeed, of the explicitly identifed doubles in the novel—Tchitcherine and Enzian, Blicero and Gottfried, Gottfried and Katje—the black and white combination represents hope and the possibility of harmony. The combination of whites suggests inhumanity and the abuse of nature. Only one example of blackness is to be feared, but this, nuclear blackness, is brought on by the whites; it is blackness that results ironically from too much whiteness.

The description of "The White Visitation" center in London demonstrates the explicitly negative connotations of whiteness: "At 'The White Visitation' the walls read ice. Graffiti of ice the sunless day, glazing the darkening blood brick and terra cotta as if the house is to be preserved weatherless in some skin of clear museum plastic, an architectural document, an old-fashioned apparatus whose use is forgotten. Ice of varying thickness, wavy, blurred, a legend to be deciphered by lords of the winter, Glacists of the region, and argued over in their journals" (pp. 72–73). "The White Visitation" is associated with faulty attempts to condition human beings and with the mistreatment of the dogs and rats used in the experiments—the wish to control both man and nature.

Individuals associated with this whiteness suggest a negation of the finer human instincts, and the sexuality of those associated with the whiteness of "The White Visitation" is perverse. Although Pointsman is delighted to observe and control Slothrop's experiment, he is hesitant to reveal his feelings to women and ends in joyless and loveless masturbation. Brigadier Pudding, his face "whiter than whitewash," is involved in a mutually degrading sadomasochistic sexual relationship with Katje, the Domina Noctura, from which he eventually meets his death. Katje herself, who works for "The White Visitation" and who has previously been forced into sexual relations with Blicero and Gottfried among others, is frequently associated with whiteness, mirrors, mannequins, and narcissistic behavior. She is Blicero's "Golden Bitch" and "leukemia of soul." When she first makes love to Slothrop, the whiteness of her costume sets off her extremely white skin, and the electricity highlights her Dutch blondness: "She wears a white pelisse, with sequins all over, padded shoulders, jagged white ostrich plumes at the neckline and wrists. . . . In the electricity her hair is new snowfall" (p. 194). Having no identity of her own, she is the double of many others and only "plays at playing." She dresses in the uniforms of Gottfried, her "golden games-brother" and "silent doubleganger" (p. 102), watches him masturbating, and is even forced to witness his being seduced by Blicero. Surprisingly, narcissism and voyeurism have little emotional impact on her, and she feels nothing. Her other lovers too seem to mean nothing to her. Captain Prentice, Piet, Wim, the Drummer, the Indian, Osbie Feel, Slothrop, and Pudding—person after person, experience after experience—they are all only games of chance to her.

Her relationship with Gottfried and Blicero, however, has serious implications; it suggests that bondage, sexual inversion, perverse opposition, and doubling are part of the cultural consciousness associated with whiteness. She and Gottfried are a kind of Hansel-and-Gretel pair forced against their will to remain in bondage to the homosexual, cannibalistic, rocket-launching Blicero, who seems finally unable to tell the two apart. He does not know whether "Katje" and "Gottfried" "aren't two names, different names, for the same child" (p. 671): both blond, Katje becomes unnatural in the brutality and force associated with masculinity and Gottfried in the passivity associated with femininity.

Although Katje escapes from Blicero, her conditioning prevents her from transcending those dehumanized responses. And wherever she goes these habits, procedures, and patterns of thought underlie the social patterns, so at "The White Visitation" she must perform even more degrading sexual acts with Brigadier Pudding than those she has submitted to with Blicero. Unnatural systems, attitudes, and modes of thought, then, lead to the specific channeling of energy in unnatural sexual behavior. It is also true that Blicero represents some part of herself, "an old self, a dear albatross" (p. 661), that cannot be blamed on a system. She and Blicero are in some respects the same.

Katje's companion in sexual games, the youthful German soldier Gottfried, is described as an enticing, beautiful victim of Blicero's deviancy, but he is also in his own way poisonous, a physical manifestation of the Western death wish. Pynchon's description of his appearance, at first tantalizing, finally suggests the death at the core of such whiteness: "Fair and slender, the hair on his legs only visible in sunlight and then as a fine, imponderable net of gold, his eyelids already wrinkling in oddly young/old signatures, flourishes, the eyes a seldom-encountered blue that on certain days, in sync with the weather, is too much for these almond fringes and brims over, seeps, bleeds out to illuminate the boy's entire face, virgin-blue, drowned-man blue" (p. 102). This description goes from golden rhetoric to bloodless death. Fittingly, this is imagery of narcissism and of decay, for Gottfried not only shares a homosexual relationship with Blicero but is enamored with rockets, failing to realize that these bear the signature of his death. He is associated with the words "Take me!" and others do take him: the army conscripts him; Blicero seduces him;

Katje uses him; the rocket kills him. Since he is the Object of Desire for others, the reflection they seek, it is not surprising that his face is "reflected in the act of kissing the Captain's boots" (p. 103). Nor is it surprising that he allows himself to be sacrificed in Blicero's firing of the rocket. Like the dogs that Pointsman sacrifices in his Pavlovian experiments, Gottfried—God's peace—must be sacrificed.

"In love with empire, poetry, his own arrogance" (p. 660), Blicero is himself Weissmann, the white one who embodies the greatest degree of unnaturalness and who masterminds such sacrifices. His names—Blicero and Weismann—allude to the town where the rockets were built and to the abstractions of death and whiteness: "The name Bleicheröde [was] close enough to 'Blicker,' the nickname the early Germans gave to Death. They saw him white: bleaching and blankness. The name was later Latinized to 'Dominus Blicero.' Weissmann, enchanted, took it as his SS code name" (p. 322). Self-aggrandizing and bookish, and in love with the words of Rilke, he corrupts Katje, Gottfried, and Enzian. He also furthers the conquest of Southwest Africa and is largely responsible for deploying the A–4 as well as other rockets. The forest witch of folklore, he perceives death as the ultimate erotic experience. As a result, he willingly sends Gottfried aloft in the rocket and identifies himself with the Oven, death. The narrator says of Blicero, "He only wants now to be out of the winter, inside the Oven's warmth, darkness, steel shelter, the door behind him in a narrowing rectangle of kitchen-light gonging shut, forever. The rest is foreplay" (p. 99). The imagery of decay, nature and religion turned rotten, is associated with Blicero. Greta, who replaces Katje in Blicero's final madness, sees him as a werewolf whose humanity has completely abandoned him. That is, even Greta, the habitual murderer of small boys, is struck by Blicero's lack of humanity. Blicero's lack of human decency becomes manifest in the totally white, solipsistic universe of his "Ur-Heimat," which draws everyone to the blankness of death. He sees himself as the embodiment of the "true god [of modern civilization who] must be both organizer and destroyer" (p. 99), a view that is to supplant the primitive African concept of God as creator and destroyer held by Enzian. Blicero destroys Gottfried; he destroys the love of Ilse, Pökler's daughter; he destroys the innocence of the young African boy, Ndjambi Karunga, whom he renames Enzian. He destroys nature and all that is natural in both Europe and Africa. He does so because he sees that he is dying and wants to condemn these beautiful creatures, who might otherwise enjoy a continuing life, to share his annihilation.

The perversions portrayed in the characters of Katje, Gottfried, and Weissmann are not restricted to the war; they are part of a diabolical system of values that undergirds Western society's belief in science, technology, and religion—all require the sacrifice of nature and the natural. This immolation of the self in the system is, Pynchon argues, endemic to Western thought. It pervades, for example, Rilke's Tenth Elegy, in which a young boy is sacrificed to Destiny, and it suffuses the Christian view of the sacrifice of Jesus; it is the systematizing death wish that has replaced the erotic and life-giving instinct.

Ironically, the character who enunciates this Western view best is Enzian, who has adopted the entire system. He thinks of rocketry, sexuality, and religion as strongly intertwined, so that the text of one is the text of the others: "We *are* supposed to be the Kabbalists out here, say that's our real Destiny, to be the scholar-magicians of the Zone, with somewhere in it a Text, to be picked to pieces, annotated, explicated, and masturbated till it's all squeezed limp of its last drop . . . well we assumed—natürlich!—that this holy Text had to be the Rocket" (p. 520). Masturbation, inversion, perversion, and transformation—these are all curiously intertwined. This constellation of images and concepts is presented in a newspaper picture noted by Slothrop which seems explicitly to tie together whiteness, rocketry, phallicism, and Christianity: "a grinning glamour girl riding astraddle the cannon of a tank, steel penis with slotted serpent head, 3rd Armored treads 'n' triangle on a sweater rippling across her tits. The white image has the same coherence, the hey-lookit-me smugness, as the Cross does. It is not only a sudden white genital onset in the sky— it is also, perhaps, a Tree" (p. 694). Maleness, eroticism, rocketry, whiteness, Christianity—they are all packed together in this image. Pynchon specifically equates this religion of the West with masturbatory, narcissistic lives and with death. As Tanner remarks, this equation is prevalent in all Pynchon's fiction. [37]

The Christian way—the male way—emphasizes the primacy of the Word—the divine text—which becomes sacrificial flesh. Christianity begins with a mental abstraction, language imposed upon the material world. This process represents a complete inversion of the witchcraft that Geli practices, which is nature-oriented and therefore mistrusted by Christians. At the center of Christianity, Pynchon suggests, is a celebration of repression, sacrifice, and death, as opposed to life and sensuality. It is informed by the ethic of the ice-saints, "holy beings of ice, ready with a breath, an intention, to ruin the year with frost and cold" (p. 281). Christianity has demanded the surrender of the self and indeed life itself in the hope of greater glory. It has led naturally, Pynchon suggests, to the imperative to sacrifice oneself to history. But because the sacrificial victim was Jesus, who was said to have risen from death, and because it promises resurrection to the faithful, the fact of death is obscured; Christianity is the "Baby Jesus Con Game." This is Christianity's poison; it obliterates the sacrifices from memory: "The true King only dies a mock death. Remember. Any number of young men may be selected to die in his place while the real king, foxy old bastard, goes on. Will he show up under the Star, slyly genuflecting with the other kings as this winter solstice draws on us? Bring to the serai gifts of tungsten, cordite, high-octane?" (p. 131). The real deaths leave behind a wake of emptiness, bridal dresses never worn, hearts never mended, absences never filled. The light promised to the shepherds and the wise men has led only to darkness, to the Lord of the Night and his chaplain, Vicar de la Nuit. For Slothrop, the word *death* and the metaphysical Word are strangely mingled. He seems to intuit the truth of the relationship, though "it's nothing he can see or lay hands on—sudden gases, a violence upon the air and no trace afterward . . . a Word, spoken with no warning into your ear, and then silence forever . . . the Word, the one Word that rips apart the day" (p. 25).

The Word that is God's revelation, the Word that is Christ, the word that science uses, the word that corporations use—all these are the words, the untruths that entangle and bind. The Bible, Pointsman's record of the experiment on Slothrop, company accounts and records, rocket manuals—all these are the books in which the terrible curses are laid upon mankind. They are, Pynchon tells us, records of intolerance, misunderstanding, manipulation, and deceit. They are, he affirms, the words and books that have been generated by a binary system that obscures a necessary opposition by glibly promising the domination of one form by another, promising escape, promising dialectical synthesis.

Why people want to impose a religion of death upon others is not readily apparent; why scientists such as Pointsman want to perform dehumanizing experiments is unclear; but these acts do predicate a certain metaphysical and physiological basis for human behavior. In keeping with that view, Pointsman wants to inscribe his name upon nature, to write his name, his words, upon the tabula rasa of human innocence. It is the thesis of *Gravity's Rainbow* that the processes of scientific experimentation and analysis and the act of writing—Science and the Word—are together used by men to transform and distort nature, to create unity out of diversity, even while conceptualizing that unity into elaborate categories. Rocketry, religion, and language are forms of "name-giving, dividing the Creation finer and finer, analyzing, setting namer more hopelessly apart from named, even to bringing in the mathematics of combination, tacking together established nouns to get new ones, the insanely, endlessly diddling play of a chemist whose molecules are words" (p. 391). But if it is a means of dividing life finer and finer, it is also a means of saying that everything is finally the same, that one thing is just a metaphor or synonym for another. Language itself is a system which pretends to be natural, even as it pretends to be based upon "natural" logic and rational authority. The illogicality of language is demonstrated in Slothrop's discussion with Säure about the terms "assbackwards" and "Shit from Shinola." According to Slothrop, the English language is an "American mystery" that eludes rationalization. But English provides only one of many instances of language's potential for confusion and even evil; after all, it was the Dutch who killed the dodoes because the birds were incapable of speech: "No language meant no chance of co-opting them into . . . Salvation" (p. 110). The whole issue of language in *Gravity's Rainbow* is one of the signifier undermining the signified, for the book is a carefully crafted and highly wrought artifact that does its best to subvert its own medium while testing its readers and trying their patience to the breaking point. The book repudiates at least its own style, challenging the assumption that the massive accumulation of analysis and narrative technique can lead to greater comprehension, understanding, and authority. The medium assaults and undermines itself. It is an attack on the author-authority function, narrative, and language itself. "The poet's responsibility," Charles Russell argues in regard to *Gravity's Rainbow*, "is to reveal the tentative and transitory base of all meaning systems."[38] Tanner substantiates Russell's claim, asserting that "Pynchon's characters move in a world of both too many and too few signs, too much data and too little information, too many texts but no reliable editions, an extreme 'over-abundance of signifier,' to borrow a phrase from Lévi-Strauss."[39] These "aimless signifiers and disconnected signifieds" render the text ultimately unassimilatable.

The Word, in *Gravity's Rainbow*, comes to represent not just the Western believer's abstractions of spirituality and science but the means by which these are conveyed—the abstractions of language itself. Within the context of the book, this mode of communication takes two forms: the creation of maps and books, both of which impose abstract thought and system upon reality, one graphically and the other linguistically. Those who create and use these forms of communication attribute to them something fixed and lasting, something that amounts to truth. As a result, the researchers looking at Slothrop's map of sexual conquests fail to see the playfulness that underlies it. They do not see that he creates the map for no particular reason or that he chooses his colors randomly. The very pointlessness of the map baffles them. Because they believe in intentionality, rational ordering, and fixed meaning, they cannot conceive of a random and uncoded map, so they give it a code and meaning. Language too, while arbitrarily assigned a determination and a fixity, eludes any signification. Much of the zaniness of *Gravity's Rainbow* results from Slothrop's futile attempts to locate meaning within the words of his culture, for as information theory suggests, all communication systems are marred by repetition, ambiguity, irrelevance, and leakage. Nothing can be communicated purely and simply. Between the sender and receiver stands the ever-elusive Word.

Associated with death, the Word is the foundation of the media and hence is closely related to the business activities of the Slothrop family and, by extension, all of America. Toilet paper, banknote stock, and newsprint—"Shit, money, and the Word, the three American truths" (p. 28)—these are intricately linked in Slothrop's ancestral past, and they are at least implicitly present in contemporary American society. As in the bygone relationship between Christianity and the Masonic Order, they are linked secretly and conspiratorially.

In this climate of opinion, words mask reality; authority hides ideology. As Foucault theorizes, "the 'author-function' is tied to the legal and institutional systems that circumscribe, determine, and articulate the realm of discourses."[40] In reading the text of World War II (and there are many allusions to textuality and writing in *Gravity's Rainbow;* John Dugdale, for instance, notes that the allusions create a binary opposition between the art of Modernism and that of the 1940s and 1950s),[41] Pynchon performs a series of "returns" or "*researches*" into the original text in an attempt to discover the author's-authority's mind. He questions the legitimization of views of war that mask the real forms of power, and implicitly shares Foucault's concern with the modes of discourse, their origins, circulation, and control.[42] Pynchon also questions received modes of consciousness and social taboos to unsettle or unground this consciousness. Tyrone Slothrop is not, then, presented as a unified individual living in a unified culture. The Slothropian doubles ultimately lead to the view that he is "plucked, hell—*stripped*. Scattered all over the Zone. It's doubtful if he can ever be 'found' again, in the conventional sense or 'positively identified and detained.' " He has entered and become part of the "Regions of Indeterminacy" (p. 712).

A microcosm of the anarchic Zone and an exemplum of modern man, Slothrop is himself dispersed and centerless, a Humpty-Dumpty of modern society. Not an "integral creature," he cannot be held together by others, and "some believe that fragments of Slothrop have grown into consistent personae of their own. If so, there's no telling which of the Zone's present-day population are offshoots of his original scattering" (p. 742). Not only Slothrop but the various other doubles in the book and indeed the whole system of doubled systems suggest the impossibility either of ascertaining unity or of delimiting reality to sets of oppositions. The binary system in science, business, logic, religion, and language is ultimately shown to be misleading. Doubles within the text consequently point up and develop the theory of opposition, show that each pair should perhaps be kept discreet and demonstrate the inevitability of fragmentation, indeterminacy, randomness, binary intersubjectivity, and metonymical slides in meaning.

Like other postmodern fiction, *Gravity's Rainbow* consists of a series of ruptures. Slothrop's regress is interrupted by interspersed vignettes of sexual liaisons and fragmented episodes in the lives of others. This is an anarchic text that leaves interpretation and pattern making largely to its readers, for in Schaub's words, "The reader is [Maxwell's] Demon inside Pynchon's world, sorting and 'unpacking' the facts."[43] But Squalidozzi's hope that the war in Germany will disrupt the center of civilization and cause it to return to a state of natural anarchy is futile. So enamored of systems and correspondences and so used to thinking, speaking, and writing in certain familiar patterns is Western society that the wish for anarchy and a decentralized openness—for entropy—is mere fantasy. "The Eternal Center can easily be seen as the Final Zero" (p. 319).

The doubles, doubling, and doubleness that provide the basic themes and structural principles of *Gravity's Rainbow* acknowledge differences, but they do not finally restrict reality to binary modes. *Gravity's Rainbow* decenters the privilege that is commonly accorded to the Western phallogocentric principle—to males and all masculine forms of analysis and system that try to stabilize and control reality, whether in peacetime or war—without suggesting that other alternatives are possible or that the female principle is necessarily superior. The diversity and indeterminacy that constitute nature and that typify women as a group receive Pynchon's admiration, but *Gravity's Rainbow* gives no assurance that humanity can really erase the Western cultural legacy of male abstractions and system making.

In the final analysis, *Gravity's Rainbow* is a pessimistic—though never nihilistic—existential manifesto, and as an existential manifesto it denies the authority of Western spiritual and cultural values and systems: abstract religion (especially Christianity), analytic reasoning and science, and unrestrained military-corporate control. It denies the primacy of absolute beliefs, values, and systems—unified and transcendent meaning of any sort—but it affirms humanitarian acts at the most basic, the most personal level. It also suggests that personal engagement, acts of love, acts of resistance, and the luck springing from indeterminate chance can make a significant difference, however small; they provide the only natural light against the tragic darkness. Pynchon argues a moral point: The authors of "the system" want us to stay within certain prescribed boundaries and to follow passively the rules laid down by authority. But inquisitive individuals can and must actively foster diversity of opinion and action, psychic exuberance, and comic resistance. Above all, people must be skeptical of received authority and be willing to recognize their complicity in the relations of power. Only by such means can we save ourselves, however partially, from the cultural and spiritual coercion of tyrannizing ideas, systems, and corporations. To see things as double and to recognize the functions of doubling reveal the possibility that an individual can subvert the tyranny of whatever system holds power. The heroic and human gesture, which still makes the real *différence-*

différance, holds its important place. These means of undermining the system must be fostered and protected in the way that Geli Tripping protects her owl—privately and surreptitiously. Pynchon does not deny meaning itself; he denies the one meaning that systems of authority tend to promote. And he subverts the meaning best through his use of the intersubjective, indeterminate double and its slide of signification.

Eros and Thanatos
Hawkes's Blood Oranges

4

THE STYLE AND CONTENT OF THOMAS PYNCHON DIFFER RADICALLY FROM
those of Vladimir Nabokov, but both authors write in a manner that
defamiliarizes, demystifies, and deconstructs cultural and literary
codes and values. Their use of the double exemplifies this shared
tendency. Through it, Nabokov mocks the human compulsion to seek
unity where none exists, and Pynchon mocks the human compulsion
to group experience into binarily opposed categories, even though
reality is far richer and more complex. Nabokov has nothing to do with
Freud's and Jung's behaviorist theories, which attribute to humans
identifiable qualities, developmental processes, and self-unified personalities. Pynchon too is wary of organizing and labeling human
experience to suggest linear development and causal relationships.
John Hawkes, however, never hesitates to explore human behavior
through the application of psychological theory. But like Nabokov and
Pynchon, he is not content to accept culturally engrained practices
and theories. Instead, he uses the double to deconstruct old categories
of the self and to demystify accepted opinions. He accomplishes this
task particularly through his exploration of the relationship between
the erotic impulse and death.

Indeed, all three authors—Nabokov, Pynchon, and Hawkes—
employ the double in part to explore this fascinating relationship.
In Nabokov's *Despair*, death seems to Hermann his only means of
capturing and preserving his and Felix's affinity. The cold-blooded
murder, which Hermann presents as an act of kindness, love, and
aesthetic integrity, hints at a link between death and repressed sexual-

93

ity. Pynchon is much more explicit about such links. The characters in *Gravity's Rainbow* who take white racial superiority for granted are described by the rhetoric of illuminated whiteness. For them, death and eroticism are explicitly linked. The sadistic Blicero, viewing death as the ultimate erotic experience, sends Gottfried, his favorite companion, double, and lover, off to die in a rocket. Gottfried's death is meant to suggest parallels with the sacrifice of Christ and therefore to define the relationship between Western abstract religion and the eroticized death wish. Eroticism, however, has been turned inward, so that it is masturbatory, solipsistic, and narcissistic—without joy, without love. Europeans' and Americans' infatuation with war and rocketry, their sexual perversions, and their embrace of Christianity are thus seen as inextricably intertwined. If Blicero and Gottfried are doubles, so are religion and war, and so are eroticism and death. Hawkes similarly sees the connection between religion, eroticism, and death. Sketched in the imagery of martyrdom, the suicide Hugh of *The Blood Oranges* bears the burden of self-rejecting Christianity, masturbatory self-love, and death that is borne by Pynchon's characters. Hugh's manifest double, Cyril, despite his emphasis on Mediterranean passion, free love, and fecundity, is likewise caught in the net of death. For Hawkes, this linking of love and death, figured in his depiction of the double, is an integral characteristic of all human beings. These twin drives of love and death are not unique to the West; neither are they as predictable as Freud would have them. Hawkes carefully explores these features in literature, as decentering and demystifying as Nabokov's and Pynchon's.

Although Pynchon and Hawkes both write about love and death, they do so in distinctly different styles. Hawkes eschews Pynchon's grand, sweeping, symphonic deconstructions of cultural and linguistic patterns, preferring, like Nabokov, to present works limited in scope and focus, shorter works that undermine those "enemies" of the novel—plot, character, setting, and theme. However brief, though, Hawkes's deconstructions are subtle and complex. From individual sentence to overall pattern, Hawkes's works are, as Donald Barthelme has remarked, "splendidly not simple."[1] Sometimes hailed as the best American writer,[2] he is justly "grouped with John Barth and Thomas Pynchon as one of the three most important antirealistic novelists in the United States after World War II."[3]

Hawkes is not concerned with verisimilitude and accordingly

sketches in only enough historical background and geographical detail to give the reader necessary bearings. His explorations rarely depend upon fixed time and space or causation but concern themselves with "the things that are most deeply embedded in the human psyche."[4] This position was established with *The Cannibal* (written in Albert Guerard's class at Harvard after the Second World War), which resulted from his experience with and attitude toward the Germany of the Second World War. The book explores the issues of human greed and depravity—of cannibalism—in a way that exceeds the boundaries of war-torn, reconstructionist Germany. Each of Hawkes's novels follows that quintessential pattern of exploring an issue, idea, or moral question without special regard to historical details.

Among those issues that Hawkes judges important are lust for war, nightmarish violence, and human depravity in *The Cannibal*; brutality, ugliness, violence, and decay underlying civilization and especially the American illusion of innocent frontier horizons in *The Beetle Leg*; entrapment, betrayal, sexual fantasies, repressions, and "love breeding terror"[5] in *The Lime Twig*; the relationship between sex and death, beauty and chaos, imagination and perversion in the triad of *The Blood Oranges, Death, Sleep and the Traveller*, and *Travesty*; the contradiction between conscious morality and subconscious desire— man as "cesspool" and "bed of stars"—in *The Passion Artist*;[6] and finally the male, egoistic urge for order versus the female need for love and naturalness in *Virginie: Her Two Lives*. A recurrent theme in the entire canon is the relationship between eroticism and imagination on the one hand and repression and sterility on the other.

Hawkes does not resolve these issues in conventional ways. The good do not defeat the bad, the sunshine does not dissipate the fog, and imagination does not automatically overcome narrow morality and egoism. In *The Cannibal*, the dreams of youth are wholly blighted by the inherited corruptions of the old regimes as a young boy is devoured by an old aristocrat. Similarly, in *The Beetle Leg*, a fetus is cast into a dam reservoir, and the innocent Luke is killed by a motorcycle gang that is never apprehended. In *The Lime Twig* the relatively innocent Michael Banks is pulled into the maelstrom of William Henscher's fantasies and killed, and his wife is beaten and raped, and the villain, Larry, escapes. In these books there is no retributive justice, no common saving morality, no God overlooking the universe, only the sense of universal terror in both the waking moments of consciousness and the dreams of the unconscious. Nor is there a sense of inviolable novelistic traditions. The Western, the detective story, the thriller, and other coded forms of the novel are distorted and upended. Nothing is as the reader expects.

In several of Hawkes's novels, the double plays an integral part in exploring the power of the imagination and central psychological issues. These doubles of person and place are seldom simple mirror reflections or polar oppositions, but they do survey the underside of the human mind. In *Second Skin*, for example, the main character, Skipper, details the history of death in his family and his peculiar innocence by describing twin islands: an imaginary one—warm, fertile, and life-giving—and a real one—cold, sterile, and dead. Here Hawkes himself is quite explicit about the psychic doubling: "I got very much involved in the life-force versus death. The life and death in the novel go on as a kind of equal contest, until the very end, when a new-born baby, perhaps the narrator's, is taken to a cemetery on a tropical island, on an imaginary island. . . . And out of this, I think, does come a sort of continuing life."[7] Hawkes's trilogy—*Blood Oranges; Death, Sleep and the Traveller*; and *Travesty*—also contains a variety of doubles. *The Blood Oranges* presents contrasting males with opposing attitudes toward sex and morality. Hawkes has said that the characters are all "versions of a single figure."[8] *Death, Sleep and the Traveller* presents a dream sequence on a floating ocean liner in which the voyage of Allert, the main character, "takes him nowhere except inside himself, and the reader begins to suspect that all the characters are projections of Allert's psyche. Note the hints of identification: the fish hook that links Ariane and Allert, Ursula and Peter; the similar ages of Allert and Peter; the red rashes of Ursula and Ariane; the fact that both Allert and Olaf are confined to their rooms. As projections within the narrator's night sea journey, the characters act out the dreamer's neurotic wishes."[9] Although we may not want to go so far as to assert that the characters are extensions of Allert, the book is so irreal and the doubling so pervasive as to suggest psychological projection. *Travesty*, the third book of the triad, also deals with such psychological projections. Papa, who drives his car into a wall and commits suicide to prove his theory on the combination of artistic order and chaos, is the sole speaker in the book. The reader only guesses at the existence of other characters, who, like those of Allert, may exist only in the narrator's imagination. Whether in dream or "reality," Papa's wish to possess both his wife and daughter sexually, an act prohibited by the strongest cultural taboos, is fulfilled through the person of the artist Henri, a kind of alter ego to Papa. The two are doubled, in both their sense of artistic design and their wish to possess mother and daughter. *The Passion Artist* uses a barren town as a contrast to a fertile swamp to illustrate the relation of community morality and sensual subconscious, Vost's impotence and the prison women's passion. In *Virginie: Her Two Lives*, a significant doubling occurs since Virginie herself has lived in two separate historical periods. Her encounters with and impressions of men who desire to mold and change women are neatly enhanced by this doubling in time.

Representative in its use of the double, *Blood Oranges* is the richest and most intriguing of Hawkes's works. Critics disagree fundamentally about the meaning of the book and especially about the doubles, Cyril and Hugh. Some suggest that the narrator-protagonist Cyril is trustworthy, writing of his legitimate affection for Fiona (his wife) and Catherine (his friend's wife), both of whom occupy a special place in his tapestry of love. Others, seeing Cyril as an untrustworthy narrator, find more to recommend in the dour Hugh, who is married to Catherine but loves Fiona and who except for his final submission to Fiona refuses to acknowledge the erotic implications of that socially unacceptable love, choosing to remain outside Cyril's vision. While Cyril repeatedly seduces Catherine, Hugh remains aloof and broods upon his wife's breach in morality until his death. Still others, like Patrick O'Donnell, see Cyril as combining sex and death or, as John Kuehl believes, a paradoxical blending of agony and desire, purity and puritanism, love and idealism, and life against death.[10]

Hawkes joins those critics who find Cyril an attractive representative of erotic love.[11] According to him, Cyril is an innocent "natural" man of "sensuous rationality"[12] victimized by Hugh's negative personality, malign mind, and conventional morality. Cyril is honest, true, and even right in asserting "that anything less than sexual multiplicity (body upon body, voice on voice) is näive[.] That our sexual selves are merely idylers in a vast wood" (p. 209). But the opposing group defends Hugh's moral reservations and believes that Cyril, as the first-person subjective narrator, is less innocent. He has, as Hugh puts it in his own vulgar way, "been sucking two eggs at once" (p. 243). Because Hugh dies either from a heart attack or hanging—the cause is not entirely clear—following Cyril's insistently successful attempt to persuade him of his own view of liberated, pluralistic marital love, Cyril may bear some responsibility. Cyril's scorn for Hugh's moral reservations; his obvious dislike of him and his children, especially Meredith, "the sacrificial animal" who knows of his affair; his glorification of marital infidelity; his admission that he is playing games—those traits that lead to Hugh's death cannot be wholly reconciled with Cyril's claim to universal love, nor are the issues of promiscuity versus repression entirely resolved.

Superficially about one man's dream of sexual pleasure and another's resistance to it, *Blood Oranges* is actually about deep psychic disturbance. Hawkes agrees that his writings contain such depths. He says: "I'm not interested in reflection or representation; I'm only interested in creating a fictive world. . . . I want to find all the fluid, germinal, pestilential 'stuff' of life itself as it exists in the unconscious. The writing of each fiction is a taking of a psychic journey."[13] In another interview, he explained this relationship between writer, book, and reader more fully: "I mean that the writer who exploits his own psychic life reveals the inner lives of us all, the inner chaos, the negative aspects of the personality in general. I'm appalled at violence, opposed to pain, terrified of actual destructiveness. . . . It isn't that I'm advocating that we live by acts of violence. . . . It's just that our deepest inner lives are largely organized around such impulses, which need to be exposed and understood and used. Even appreciated."[14]

Blood Oranges, then, is about much more than the conflict between the creative impulse and the puritan ethic. It explores psychological questions first raised by Sigmund Freud in "Beyond the Pleasure Principle" and "The Ego and the Id" and later interrogated by Jacques Lacan in such essays as "Aggressivity in Psychoanalysis" (sometimes called "Narcissism and Aggressivity") and "The Function and Field of Speech and Language in Psychoanalysis." Cyril the sex singer and Hugh the naysayer are manifestations of related dualities—the Freudian eros and thanatos, procreation and death, or the uninhibited sexual and self-preserving ego-instincts. To these we can add the Lacanian dialectic of self and other, subject and object.

Opposite in nature, "the death instincts are," according to Freud, "by their nature mute and . . . the clamour of life proceeds for the most part from Eros."[15] These instincts are inseparable and yet opposing, not unlike Plato's version of the double in the *Symposium*. Also characteristic of Hawkes's *Blood Oranges*, this dynamic opposition depicts a psyche under stress. Lacan also sees the qualities of the double as representing the *"imago of one's own body,"* whether one's individual features, infirmities, or object projections;[16] this psyche under stress is a particular feature of the so-called imaginary stage in which the self tries to control and dominate others and resist acculturation and social morality. For Lacan, a mature human being develops to the symbolic stage, which incorporates social customs and moral imperatives. In viewing Hawkes's characters as opposing projections of the human psyche, readers can see the interplay of such instincts, and the issue of who—Hugh or Cyril—is right becomes less significant, for both act according to their appropriate psychological modes in this complex psychodrama.[17]

Throughout *Blood Oranges*, Cyril, the singer of sex, opposes the force of law, a force Lacan has equated with the death instinct. The instincts of sex and death also resemble Lacan's imaginary and symbolic phases, which are on the whole treated deterministically. Hawkes creates the impression that in Illyria the characters resemble gods and goddesses of a fantastic modern Olympia, reinforcing the deterministic aspects and the mythical overtones of the story. The allusions to art and the timeless quality of the characters and their passions suggest figures from a Grecian urn, as do references to the decaying village as "the smashed shards of the little coastal town" (p. 12). The presence of goats, sheep, rabbits, eagles, a small white donkey, and a young arcadian shepherdess completes this picture.

In this mythical village, Cyril, already "two or three long leaps beyond middle age" (p. 16), nonetheless embodies the spirit of erotic adolescence. Fiona calls him "baby," and Hugh calls him "boy," for he has an air of eternal optimism, spring, and sexuality. Reminiscent of Billy Budd, he is at the same time a kind of aging Pan, for he believes in the "singing phallus" and his "magic" underpants look "like the bulging marble skin of a headless god" (p. 75). Hawkes, in an interview, calls Cyril "a god of love, a kind of eros" who is not reprehensible or manipulative.[18] Preoccupied with sexual conquests, concerned with their harmonious arrangement in his tapestry of love, and characterized by "shaggy shoulders, horns, a lot of experience" (p. 150), he has the air of a satyr. As large as his imagined white bull (another satyr image), he is so massive that Catherine's hands can hardly reach around his back or "preserve their desperate grip" on his "enormous tough rump" (p. 117). A self-confessed devotee of Psyche (he clearly sees himself as her lover, Eros), he is, as his description of the grape arbor implies, also a kind of Dionysus: "The darkness was like a warm liquid poured from the throat of an enormous bird, and above our heads and within easy reach of our mouths vast clusters of stars and tumultuous bunches of black grapes were merging" (p. 99). He adds, "The hard cool globules of the lowest grapes spilled onto the top of my head and brushed my ears. I was relaxed. I was crowned with fruit" (p. 109). Cyril cultivates this godlike image, for he "descends" among the children, "reclines" with them when putting together garlands for his "feast of flowers," and lies "supine" on the ground— images suggesting a godlike presence. He specifically calls himself "the flower god at play" (p. 165) and offers a mental tribute to Iris. He clearly enjoys projecting himself in a godlike capacity and, like the imperial "I," imposes his majesty upon others.

Other characters of this book are also Olympian. Cyril's almost-forty-year-old wife, Fiona, is pixyish and has "the face of a faun, an experienced faun" (p. 11). At one time, she calls herself Circe and asserts that no man can resist her. Large-boned and full-bodied, the forty-three-year-old Catherine is an ample, graying, middle-aged Aphrodite. The mother of three children, she signifies universal sexuality and fecundity. Hugh, also almost forty, is "an indelicate and disheveled god" (p. 65) who has "gigantic deformed shoulders" and a stunted arm, and he carries a camera with a "cyclopian lens." For Cyril, Hugh is a dark god of vengeance or death, a Vulcan or a Mosaic Jehovah in a Greek Arcadia. He attracts and repels, and is the nemesis of the other characters. Like Malvolio of *Twelfth Night* (from which the name of the setting, Illyria, comes), Hugh stands outside the sacred circle of lovers because he is a force not of sexual harmony and integration but of the law that both binds and wreaks chaos, destruction, and death. As Cyril remarks: "Hugh was doomed forever to the extreme left and could never share my privilege of standing, so to speak, between two opposite and yet equally desirable women" (p. 118). The four figures fill the panorama of the stage and are larger than life, for they suggest modes of action and thought that are basic to all forms of life. As Cyril maintains, "We were all four of us imposing in height, in weight, in blood pressure, in chest expansion" (p. 16). He adds, "In our quaternion the vintage sap flowed freely, flowed and bled and boiled as it may never again" (p. 17).

These archetypal figures are not so much driven by their own conscious likes and dislikes as by universal forces that they cannot rationally comprehend but cannot disobey. Cyril speaks deterministically of the "obviously intended symmetry" of the foursome, and in attempting to persuade Catherine to come live with him after Hugh's death, he disavows any personal responsibility in having previously seduced her. Instead he thinks, "Love determined that this woman's shadow was to cross the white path of my capability" (p. 101), and he tells Catherine that "a steady, methodical, undesigning lover like me really has no choice, Catherine. The eyeglasses come off in my hands, the skirts of the dressing gown fall open, I fold the wings of the glasses. No choice. . . . Neither one of us had any choice that first night. It was inevitable" (p. 11). The voluptuousness of his opening comment introduces a vision of love that he tries to sustain throughout his narrative:

> Love weaves its own tapestry, spins its own golden thread, with its own sweet breath breathes into being its mysteries—bucolic, lusty, gentle as the eyes of daisies or thick with pain. And out of its own music creates the flesh of our lives. If the birds sing, the nudes are not far off. Even the dialogue of the frogs is rapturous. (P. 1)

Reminiscent of Count Orsino's opening remarks in *Twelfth Night*, Cyril's defense of himself is phrased to place all responsibility for his actions on the external agency of love. His lack of choice is specifically attributable to sexuality:

> At an early age I came to know that the gods fashion us to spread the legs of woman, or throw us together for no reason except that we complete the picture, so to speak, and join loin to loin often and easily, humbly, deliberately. Throughout my life I have never denied a woman young or old. Throughout my life I have simply appeared at Love's will. See me as small white porcelain bull lost in the lower left-hand corner of that vast tapestry, see me as great white creature horned and mounted on a trim little golden sheep in the very center of Love's most explosive field. See me as bull, or ram, as man, husband, lover, a tall and heavy stranger in white shorts on a violet tennis court. (Pp. 1–2)

He attributes a specific magic to his relationship with Catherine, claiming that "she and I were simply the two halves of the ancient fruit together but unjoined" (p. 126). They fulfill the requirements of the

Platonic notion of male and female conjoined in double symmetry. He is unrealistic about the durability of the sexual drive and opportunities, seeing them as continuing without end: "Ahead of us lay an unlimited supply of dying suns and crescent moons" (p. 45). And he fails to see what Euripides portrayed in *The Bacchae*: joyful sex turning ugly and violent and leading to death. His pagan submission to fate is neither more nor less than sexual instinct, the Freudian biomechanistic revision of Greek cosmological determinism. Both Cyril and Hugh are determined by, and symbolic of, the instinctual behavior.

That these instincts are mutually reinforcing doubles and subject to transference is suggested by various sorts of doubleness in the book and the one primary symbol of the little pink hermaphrodite: the small nude figure of a young girl with a hole drilled into it that accomodates a detachable penis. The "statue's double nature" (p. 171) hints at the doubleness that suffuses the entire book. Such minor instances as Cyril's allusion to the "naked twins" of his and Catherine's "invented constellation" (p. 258), Hugh and Catherine's twin girls, and the double qualities of their other daughter, Meredith—she is both "harmless child" and "spy, who was filled with duplicity and fear of what she took to be my own duplicity" (p. 160)—confirm the presence of doubles and doubling. The landmarks and the landscapes associated with the opposing characters, indeed the very structure of the book present supporting doubles, the most signficant of whom are Cyril and Hugh, Catherine and Fiona, and the couples themselves. Each man is in love with the other's wife, and their "twin villas" are set side by side in Illyria. This opposition has an uncanny way of doubling back on itself, so that opposition becomes likeness. Cyril's sexuality and thrust toward life contrasts with, and yet is part of, Hugh's morality and death wish.

The background and landscape themselves have an important doubleness. The two couples live in crumbling villas that are not only situated side by side but also share the same features. Both are cold, drafty, smoke-blackened single-story buildings with red tile roofs and "fireplaces like abandoned urinals" (p. 2). Cyril's suitcases grow moldy, and his mattress mildews, although he fails to notice these details as long as his dream is intact. Only when the tapestry of desire disintegrates does he see the problems. Dividing the two villas are the trees that Cyril unfailingly calls "the funeral cypresses," a nomenclature reminiscent of death, entombment, and the failure of Cyril's dream.

Doubled too are the landscapes associated with Cyril and Hugh. Cyril's vision is supported by fundamentally pleasing images of nature or culture—pastoral, lyrical, and harmonious. The light upon the azure sea; the lemon, orange, fig, and mariposa trees; a mellow orange sun setting in the evening; the flowers growing in the meadow; the abundant grapes in the arbor of the villa—these are the lambent images of nature associated with Cyril when his dream is intact. When his dream has fallen apart, however, the sea is inhospitable and nature bleak.

Over Cyril's arbor lies the shadow of the Byzantine cross, and across his dream lies Hugh, for "love never had so fierce an antagonist" (p. 240). Accordingly, Hugh is associated in Cyril's mind with negative images drawn from society and occasionally from nature: colorless images of funeral cypresses, dark pines, purplish-black crabgrass, dead pine needles, and black stones strewn on the beach beside the turbulent ocean. Hugh transforms Cyril's "gentle arbor into a cavern of black leaves," changing it from "trysting place" to the "scene of tribunal" (p. 241). He is also equated with false or man-made light rather than the sun or moon. The flashlight he carries into the nearby fortress bears many of the same connotations as Pynchon's light bulb—artifice, control, possessiveness, and manipulation. Above all, Hugh is associated with "the stinking depths of the timeless pestilential" canal filled with excrement where his car first accidentally comes to rest; the dark and decaying building near the canal that he uses for his photographic studio and where he finally dies; the dungeonlike squat church that smells of "wax, dust, flaking wood, rusting iron, all the effluvium of devotion" (p. 20) and that is fitted with windows that give the impression of military security; the cemetery beside the church and the adjacent granite cistern; and the dank, burned-out fortress with its dung-filled pit where he leads his unwilling friends in search of the chastity belt which he places on Catherine.

These are mainly images associated with a decayed, darkly medieval culture, with its negative morality and obsession with death images that (as Fiona remarks of the fortress) are distinctly "masculine" manifestations. Here is Lacan's "name of the Father" at work—the ego with all the accouterments of reason, religion, and culture: "It is in the *name of the father* that we must recognize the support of the symbolic function which, from the dawn of history, has identified his person with the figure of the law."[19] These images are also reflective of Hugh's inner being, for when Cyril sees the fortress, he identifies it with the self-imprisonment, isolation, and "dark caves of the heart" (p. 189) of Hugh's "lean shadow" (p. 191). Cyril says of Hugh: "In all the thoughtlessness of his clearly secret self, perhaps his true interest was simply to bury our love in the bottom of this dismal place and in some cul-de-sac, so to speak, of his own regressive nature" (p. 196). The fortress is Hugh's double, the death or ego instinct, associated masculinity, and regression.

This issue of language is also central to a consideration of the doubles. Cyril speaks English, which he equates with lightness, sensuality, harmony, symmetry, and artistic order. The Illyrians speak a language which Cyril considers dark, dissonant, ugly, and unartistic. These are, in terms of Lacanian methodology, equivalent to the languages of the imaginary and the symbolic, of sexual liberation and cultural necessity. (But Hugh also speaks English yet is equated with death; the opposition is not consistently held.)

The structure of *Blood Oranges* also creates a sense of opposing doubleness. A chapter dealing with Cyril's first encounter with Catherine, for example, is juxtaposed with one dealing with his attempts to revive his liaison with Catherine after Hugh's death and Fiona's departure. The chapters themselves are opposing doubles. The former chapter is characterized by the joy of desire and sexual conquest, the latter by Cyril's "weekly ritual of hope and fidelity" (p. 3). Such alternating chapters move the action back and forth in time as well as mood. Chapters dealing with Cyril's and Fiona's hopes to include Hugh and Catherine in their sexual union are colorful and optimistic. Those treating Cyril after Hugh's death are subdued to the point of moroseness. One is the vision of sexuality, fecundity, and hope; the other, of death, sterility, and failure.

Fiona and Catherine are also doubles of a sort, a contrast to each other and to the men. Fiona is emotional and expressive; she calls everyone "baby" and is forever "kissing flowers, shadows, dead birds, dogs, old ladies, attractive men, as if only by touching the world with her open lips could she make it real and bring herself to life" (p. 20). Sometimes her actions are meaningless and effusive but at other times profoundly significant, "with swift feminine purpose." She is a chatterbox, and it is difficult to assess the person who exists somewhere beneath the banter. Cyril's memory of his wedding night implies that Fiona, a flapper from the 1920s, is more playful than serious. He remembers "the sight of the mid-thigh silver wedding dress, the white stockings, the hot medicinal taste of the brandy I drank rather foolishly perhaps from her silver shoe, the late moment when finally I unzipped the metallic dress and helped her strip off the stockings and then carried her nude to the edge of the warm dark fountain amidst the appreciative sounds of our most loyal friends" (pp. 96–97). At this moment, Fiona asks Cyril not to be a husband, only a "sex-singer," bound not by law but eroticism.

Fiona, large, slender, and childless, usually dresses in lemon yellow, white, pink, or sky blue, Cyril's favorite pastel shades. She seems especially characterized by the color yellow, which at some points in the book signifies innocence and at other times decay. Cyril associates the color with truth, adolescence, and innocence in the mural of the Virgin, but that very mural has decayed. Yellow is also related to the lemon, sweet to smell but bitter to eat. This bitter aspect is suggested by Fiona's "bright severity" and "wildness," and more somberly by her interest in "the cruelest accident, the smallest catastrophe, the gravest incident" (p. 24). Whereas Cyril chooses the brightest, most colorful altar in church to explore, Fiona selects the one of black marble containing the skeleton of a small child. This trait makes her particularly receptive to Hugh's dark personality. She, like Catherine, is caught in the web of men's desire, although Cyril sees her as having more a mind of her own than Catherine.

Large, bulky, amber-eyed, and a mother of three, Catherine stands in opposition to Fiona—quieter, much less sophisticated, and less fashionably dressed, in garments of pea green, gray, or maroon. Although the death of Hugh affects her deeply and causes her to take a vow of silence, before this catastrophe she seemed compliant and complacent, unusually willing to be the passive participant in Cyril's erotic plans. Still, she has courage from the very beginning. It is she who takes off her swimsuit halter, an act that infuriates Hugh and delights Cyril, who assumes that she undid her top especially for him. Her relationship with Cyril is curious; he says that they are interchangeable, "two large white graceful beasts" in an empty field (p. 121). Catherine, like Fiona, is an object to the men; but more than Fiona, she reflects the discourse of others. After Hugh has put the chastity belt on Catherine, Cyril realizes "that never had it occurred to me that Hugh's influence over Catherine might be as strong as mine, and now I could only admit my error since Catherine's tone was suddenly Fiona's tone and Catherine's argument was Hugh's. Apparently all the time I had been grappling with Hugh in the arbor Catherine had been aligning herself with her missing husband in this very room" (p. 254). The men have the will to act, and the women, more passive and receptive, follow their lead. The men, as subjects, view the women as objects.

The most conspicuous opposing doubles are Cyril and Hugh. Driven by sex, Cyril is blond, tall, and heavy. He likes the feel of his body and thinks of himself monumentally: "The knee itself felt like some living prehistoric bone full of solidity, aesthetic richness, latent athleticism" (p. 102). He is gregarious, imaginative, promiscuous, and given to bright colors and trendy clothes. Cyril is the embodiment of the "joy and desire" of the enduring erotic instinct, exotic, exuberant, and colorful. He single-mindedly pursues passion and love, believing that "youth has no monopoly on love. The sap does not flow solely in the young" (p. 16). For him, sex is a game, enjoyable and desirable for its own sake, one that gets the fish "to flow, the birds to fly, the twin heavenly nudes of Love to approach through the night" (p. 257). Touch, the sounds of language and song, and the brilliance of color help to create his aesthetics of sensuality in the "electrified field of Love's art" (p. 15). Such sensuousness is closely bound to an erotic apprehension of nature. Beneath a mimosa tree, Cyril says, "I stopped breathing, I waited, slowly I opened my mouth and arched my tongue, pushed forward my open mouth and rounded expectant tongue until my mouth was filled and against all the most sensitive membranes of tongue and oral cavity I felt the yellow fuzzy pressure of the flowering tree" (p. 54).

Cyril's aesthetic is sexual. His image of "love's pink tapestry" places him firmly in the tradition of Ulysses and Penelope. Known for their bright colors, tapestries (especially the medieval ones Cyril has in mind) are signs of a joyous libido, and he frequently refers to the various animals, large and small, of his "menagerie of desire" that occur in medieval tapestries: doves (Fiona's eyes), small birds (the sparrows Rosella serves him), rabbits (the pets used for Catherine's therapy), fauns (Cyril compares both Fiona and Catherine to them),[20] and goats (one jumps out of Cyril's dream and into the midst of the two families gathered on the beach). Cyril has a lover's firm vision of "love's pink tapestry" and its powers of sexual renewal, and acting as the white bull tupping Catherine, he thinks, "I the white bull finally carried my now clamorous companion into a distant corner of the vast tapestry where only a little silvery spring lay waiting to restore virginity and quench thirst" (p. 117). Cyril too dresses in light exuberant colors that characterize lovers in such brilliant tapestries. In the day he wears white tennis shoes, yellow shirt, white pullover, and beige slacks, or sometimes his white espadrilles, bright green trousers, chocolate-colored corduroys, or magenta swimsuit; at night, he puts on his cerulean pajamas and maroon silk dressing gown. He is attracted to bright colors in any context, and although disliking the squat village church, he has a favorite white marble altar "devoted to gold, to fresh flowers, to the wooden Virgin recently lacquered in bright blue paint" (p. 19). He also likes to see bright colors on others, especially lemon yellow clothes on Fiona.

Even after Hugh's death, Cyril continues to admire and to be affected by bright colors. He loves to describe them:

> The yellow fountain, the orange sand of the courtyard, the white walls and deep-set windows, the tobacco-colored trees with their enormous leaves in the shape of fat supplicating hands, the low balconies, and above everything the pale blue tile roofs that suggest a bright powdery fusion of sky, sea, child's eye, a soft lively blue unlike any other blue I have ever seen. Each week I find all this waiting at the end of the bike ride, and enjoy it, delight in it, my sophistication only enriching if anything the aching candor of the blue tiles.
> (P. 5)

Almost in the same breath, he tells of his attempts to woo Catherine from her self-imposed state of silent withdrawal. He says, "To her, I know, my admonitions were like chocolate stars, chocolate halfmoons, dark balls of honey" (p. 6). After Hugh's death, these images are only the "painted bones of Love" (p. 98), but they suffice for him. As an artist of colorful words, he can take the most negative of experiences, deck it out in gay colors, and transform it to a thing of beauty. A smoker's cough becomes a "thick golden cough"; the "poisonous" smoke becomes "silver cornucopias, silver wreaths, large ghostly horns of invisible rams" (p. 7); his eyeglasses are "golden eyeglasses." Even the decaying wooden arm of the saint in the local church bears "sensual interest" for him.

Cyril is sensual to the point that he does not see dark sides, even his dark side. The problems of the world and the tension of human relationships have little impact on him, and except for one memorable occasion when he lies awake hearing the rust of the bed flaking onto the stone floor, he sleeps soundlessly. He acknowledges that as the "artistic arbiter of all our lives," love does introduce lonely keys, sour notes, and occasional sounds of pain, but no long-lasting sour notes. It is not "true pain" for him, even when his and Fiona's many affairs turn bad. After Hugh's death, Fiona's departure, and Catherine's hospitalization, he confesses that he has never known pain and that his sexuality is still alive and vital, if momentarily dormant: "And dormancy, memory, clairvoyance, what more could I want? My dormancy is my hive, my honeypot, my sleeping castle, the golden stall in which the white bull lies quite alive and dreaming. For me the still air is thicker than leaves, and if memory gives me back the grape-tasting game and bursting sun, clairvoyance returns to me in a different way my wife, my last mistress, the little golden sheep who over her shoulder turns small bulging eyes in my direction" (pp. 35–36). He is, like Hawthorne's Inspector, of "The Custom House," a sensualist who cannot share in the ordinary sorrows of life. He will not have his bright vines stripped, tapestry permanently shredded, or song ended. He will not succumb to sexual possessiveness or aesthetic greed. He remains untouched by jealousy and believes in the "obvious multiplicity of love" (p. 58). His fascination with color, love of naming things, and deep feeling for sensuous, evocative language are fully in keeping with his belief in the sovereign imagination. What he most dislikes is a lack of imagination and impoverished, harsh language.

When Cyril looks at women, he has a way of assessing their physical properties and undressing them in his imagination. Of his wife standing in front of an altar, he remarks, "Her stomach appeared to be unusually small and round above the wide hips and wonderfully frank pelvic area" (p. 22). Of the silent Catherine in the mental institution, he says: "Yet no blanket was thick enough . . . to prevent that large female torso and the arms, legs, hips from taking solid and in a way maximum shape under my first glance" (p. 9). To him, her large, ordinary body and plain face have "classical lines" and the "statuesque design" of some "ancient artist." In all her middle-aged plainness, Catherine becomes a sexual object, and Cyril pursues her with the vigor of Zeus in pursuit of an overblown nymph. It is this sexual vision that turns all of life into erotic fancy for Cyril. Even after he is reduced to celibacy, he can still believe in the possibility of sex. Though he dislikes Rosella, he muses on an "accidental Arcadian embrace," and her eyes momentarily remind him of the "bulging eyes of my long-lost golden-sheep" (p. 48). It takes little provocation, just the simple musky smell of snails or the savor of small sparrows baked with onions and thyme, to conjure up an erotic vision in the pink field of love's tapestry. He passes a "low wall of small black stones that resembled the dark fossilized hearts of long-dead bulls with white hides and golden horns," an image of his own defeat by Hugh's death, and promptly sees the "enormous game birds locked in love. They were a mass of dark blue feathers and silver claws, in the breeze they swayed together like some flying shield worthy of inclusion in the erotic dreams of the most discriminating of all sex-aestheticians" (p. 14). In them he sees a transcendent sexuality of "grace and chaos, control and helplessness, mastery and collapse" (p. 15) where all opposition is paradoxically and magically reconciled in the sexual act—unity and diversity. The link between sex and violence, or as with Fiona between softness and voraciousness, is revealed, but he sees the birds as remaining "true to nature," the same erotic nature that he shares. Cyril looks beyond the barriers imposed by society, beyond experiences and images of death to those of life.

The opposing double and despoiler of Cyril's erotic game, of his tapestry of love, is Hugh, who has his own "game of burial" (p. 214) and moves "to the rhythm of some dark death" (p. 215). Driven by a death wish, Hugh is taller than Cyril but slight, dark, solitary; given to dark, shabby suits; unimaginative and moralistic. Cyril dislikes Hugh's morality and "crippling fantasies" (p. 251), which he equates with his physical deformity, calling the bad arm a stump or flipper and the good arm a claw. Cyril presents him as a kind of Melvillean Ahab, a maimed half man responsible for the demise of his personal Arcadia or a Hawthornian Dimmesdale who feels God's judgment in his chest. Like these literary forebears, Hugh is destined for an early death, and in dying he shreds Cyril's dreams, for he fastens Cyril's "large funnel-shaped white thighs with the fish hooks of their disapproval" (p. 36).

Hugh's very complexion and clothing give a strong impression of his character and death instinct. With black hair, beard, and eyes, he is darkly handsome, and his dark clothes highlight his physiognomy—

black turtleneck, navy slacks, black sailor pants and pea jacket, gray swimsuit, or (reflecting the imagery used to describe the fortress) "penitential denims" (p. 205). His "long thin granite face" (p. 71) with a mouth like an "orifice cut in stone" (p. 252) is "weathered and pebbled, so grained in darkness and cold rain that it resembled stone. Gray stone" (p. 31). His hand of "murderous stone" is described as a "serpent's head." When Cyril secretly observes Hugh on the beach, he refers to him as "a long fish-colored corpse," an allusion reinforced when Hugh chooses that same barren spot for the burial of the dog. His voice is described as a hissing "dark sylvan whisper," and again as a "choking voice" with traces of "black scum." He is restless, and by Cyril's accounts he has "spent all the nights of his life in sleepless writhing" (p. 95).

This description hints at his bleak morality and his death wish: "His long thin legs were the legs of the Christ," and his "spare fishy chest was actually day by day collapsing" (p. 16). He often does collapse, feeling the "hand of death" on his chest. This analogy with an emaciated Christ is supplemented by Cyril's repeated comments associating Hugh with St. Peter. Cyril imagines Hugh's missing arm replaced by that of the wooden St. Peter in the local church, and he sees in Hugh's face the "pointed ears, hard eyes, bitter mouth," "strength and malice" of the stone statue of St. Peter. Indeed, the "thick-lettered unreadable injunctions against frivolity and sex" in the church correspond to Hugh's closely guarded morality.

Despite Cyril's hopes of including Hugh, with his interest in Fiona, in his perfectly symmetrical pattern of sexual extension and domestic multiplicity, Hugh's moral code precludes that possibility. He is the force of repression that prevents the erotic from attaining its goal. Hugh cannot commit himself to an ongoing sexual relationship with anyone but his wife. To do so would be self-betrayal. He enjoys Fiona's company. He can caress her, swim nude with her, but never seduce her, and he objects to her attempts to seduce him, saying to Cyril, "How about a little virtue, boy?" (p. 175), for "manhood rebels at infidelity, it's only natural" (p. 177).

Virtue may be natural (though some argue that all morality is of cultural, not natural, origins),[21] but Hugh's pattern of repetition and personal morality is too deeply ingrained to permit any spontaneous enjoyment of sexuality, not only with Fiona but also with Catherine. Still, such is the death instinct, according to Freud. With Fiona, Hugh always rejects sexuality; with Catherine, he repeats the sexual act, reiterating the same words: "Don't be afraid of Daddy Bear" (p. 153). When Cyril overhears them, he says, "I understood that Catherine was employing a variety of defensive responses, whereas Hugh was saying the same words again and again as if the ease with which he had apparently shifted from Fiona's stimulation to Catherine's struggle justified his use of repetition" (p. 152). Hugh's repeated phrase places this relationship in the realm of the infantile: "this sad and presumptuous appeal from a man who had spent all the nights of his marriage fishing for the love of his wife with the hook of a nursery persona" (p. 153). Cyril's concluding comment here is especially apt in presenting Hugh as the embodiment of the death instinct, which, according to Freud, invariably involves the pattern of repetition. Cyril comments: "Yes, I thought, Hugh had slipped off one schedule but gained another. Their house was in order" (p. 154).

Hugh's rigid morality and loneliness are as violent as the "volcano's chaotic fire" (p. 44). Cyril sees Hugh's actions not solely as an extension of his morality but more importantly as an outgrowth of his torment, tempestuousness, unreasonableness, greed, shame, and jealousy. Since these are manifestations of a death wish, Hugh's actual death finishes the destruction and completely rends Cyril's fabric, destroying all but fragments of the picture, "here the head of a rose, there the amputated hoof of some infant goat" (p. 3). As a result, Cyril loses both Fiona and Catherine, destroying his erotic dreams.

Such an act of retribution against Cyril for disrupting the law of marriage illustrates not only Freud's concept of the death instinct in opposition to eros but also Lacan's notion of the law: "The primordial Law is therefore that which in regulating marriage ties superimposes the kingdom of culture on that of a nature abandoned to the law of mating."[22] This law, identified with language and its governing systems, is also called the "name of the Father" and is manifested in the symbolic stage and the accouterments of culture. According to Lacan, "The neurotic's wished-for Father is clearly the dead Father. But he is also a Father who can perfectly master his desire."[23] In mastering his desire, Hugh has deferred bliss and embraced the reality of decay and death.

Mastery and social constraint also contribute to Hugh's aesthetic, which, unlike the colorfulness of Cyril's, is embodied in black-and-white photography. Like Hugh, the studio is described in terms of darkness, decay, and death. In the plaster are "thick and rusted nails that were more appropriate to beams, coffins, heavy planks" (p. 173). On his shirt are acid stains that reflect his despair and self-created pain. The eye of the camera connotes the cerebral, objective, and analytic (Hugh), not the earthy, subjective, and synthetic (Cyril). The eye consciously records, and "the polished and unmerciful lens" of the camera signifies a failure to discern the hopeful sexual horizons that Cyril sees with his golden eyeglasses. An art form that in this case eschews color, photography depends not upon fanciful imaginative creativity but the mirroring of existing realistic forms. Hugh's photographs of illiterate, virginal peasant nudes (his "unmarried girls of barren countries" [p. 69]) suggest both inherited tradition and social restraint. The "black pebbled carpet" of sheep droppings that Hugh grovels in to get good shots of a nude peasant fully exemplifies for Cyril his debased morality and perverse sexuality, what Cyril would call virginity or pornography.

For Cyril, innocence, purity, and virginity are not cognates. Purity bears the signification of adolescents who are too young to participate in sexual delights; innocence, a guilelessness of attitude, especially in sexual matters; and virginity, the deliberate and willful withholding of love and affection by someone capable of erotic desire and fulfillment. Here, virginity conveys the notion of stunted potential, deformed growth, and "sick innocence" (p. 3). This sick innocence is characteristic of age, absence of desire, and cultural imperatives as opposed to the joyous and unfettered desire of youth. Sick innocence and cultural restrictions are equated with the old man in Hugh and the old woman in even the young Rosella: "It could only be the latent old peasant woman already snoring inside Rosella" (p. 94). Even the skeleton of the dog affixed to a stake in the haystack where Hugh shoots the nude scenes suggests that death is part of this virginal vision of the "old world of sex." In all this, Cyril writes accusingly of Hugh's brutal actions that render a reality that is "aesthetically self-defeating." The self-defeating world of darkness and death is especially embodied in the shepherd and his dog, who resemble Hugh and his dead dog. Cyril speculates that the shepherd has been a familiar partner with death, "that he had slept in dark caves, that he had buried countless dead ewes, that he also knew what it was like to bury children, that only men could work together in the service of death, that death was for men, that now his only interest was in the one-armed man and bare-chested man and the coffin. . . . Only death mattered. He had joined us only because of the coffin" (p. 224).

Although masculinity, the ego, realistic art, and the death instinct are explicitly conjoined, one of Hugh's peasant models, the "little South European maid," continues to embody his moral vision even after his death: "She is a shadow, she is Hugh's last peasant nude" (p. 213). This vision is exemplified not only in her customary dress but in the severity of her moral code. Named Rosella by Cyril, she never smiles; her calves are raw and unshaven; she wears thick gray woolen socks; she wears a black dress. Strong and indifferent, she has a "blunt crippled look in her dark eyes, from wooden pitchforks and the lives of the female saints" (p. 47). She is identified with the grotesqueness of her hunchback companion, who assists in dispelling the magic of Cyril's arcadian dream. She refuses to be touched by Cyril and speaks a language that is to him harsh and uncouth. She also has, in Cyril's opinion, Hugh's "ignorant virginity" of spirit. Rosella and Hugh abort joy and desire, substituting for them emptiness, denial, sterility, and death.

Cyril's vision of sexual liberation seems on the whole preferable to Hugh's and Rosella's mean-spirited and colorless taciturnity. The sexual instinct is preferable to the death instinct. But implicitly if not explicitly this Freudian view is interrogated and problematized not only by Freud's own standards but by Lacanian implications. This is especially true of Cyril since his view of himself is likely to differ considerably from the reader's. It is also true because Cyril's sweeping judgments fail to take into consideration problems or differences.

One of the primary problems is Cyril's eroticism and possible sterility. According to Freud, the erotic instinct exists not primarily for the pleasure of human beings but for reproduction. Cyril tells of his erotic joys, but he and Fiona are childless. Indeed, Fiona snatches Catherine's children after Hugh's death, perhaps to share in motherhood. The childlessness of the couple is not the sole indication of the failure of love and fertility. Hugh's accusation that Fiona has castrated Cyril is another. Fiona defends Cyril's virility against Hugh's attack, publicly when he undoes her halter and later privately. But on the second occasion, their lovemaking takes the form of mutual masturbation, raising further questions about this relationship. Moreover, Fiona's unzipped slacks (themselves a masculine symbol) have "a little blue open mouth" with a "little masculine gold-plated zipper in front" (pp. 74–75). In this context, Cyril speaks of his and Fiona's struggle "to devour each other's mouths, jaws, cheeks" (p. 76). Reinforcing this description is Cyril's comment that Fiona's eyes are "two doves frozen in the hard light of expectation," that her kiss is "cannibalistic," and that his shoulders are soft. This hard-soft, eater-eaten imagery is repeated in several instances and resembles Freud's description of the vaginal dentata of castrating women, suggesting that Cyril is "the headless god," not in the sense of being irrational and driven by love but having narcissistic impulses. Perhaps it is this narcissism that Fiona really refers to when she tells Catherine that Cyril is "different from other men." His wish to live with Catherine in "sexless matrimony" certainly suggests emasculation. These questions undermine Cyril's sexual claims and illustrate Lacan's contention that one caught in the imaginary stage is fundamentally narcissistic and sexually impotent.

Eroticism manifested in symmetrical patterning is also problematic. Cyril wants everyone and everything to fit into his pretty picture of words and deeds. He wants sexual symmetry, and he tries to weave the lives of his associates into the tapestry of his desire. The force of the book strongly links eroticism and imagination, but as Lacan remarks, within an individual's narcissistic structure, the role of spatial symmetry is especially important, the result of a mirror projection onto the field of the other. This tendency results in a narcissistic distortion of the erotic instinct. Reproduction is "psychologically subordinate to the narcissistic fear of damage to one's own body."[24] The desire for sexual extension and artistic symmetry becomes, according to Lacan, equated with fear of death.

Hugh's daughter Meredith presents another interrogative discourse within the text. Disliking Cyril for seducing her mother, she in turn senses Cyril's dislike of her and defends her father: "It's not my father who doesn't want us around. It's you" (p. 156). Like Hugh, Meredith refuses to conform to Cyril's "concepts of playful sport" (p. 162) and his solipsistic ideas about reality. Her reservations are confirmed by Donald Greiner, who finds in the flowers Cyril and the children weave emblems of Cyril's egotism. He chooses all the best flowers with positive emblematic meaning, leaving to Meredith and the twins the poorest flowers with painful connotations of regret, bad luck, abandonment, and death.[25] Cyril even hints at his poor motivation and judgment when he admits to having "erred somewhat in the size of Meredith's little queenly crown so that it sat low on her slender brow and obscured her eyes[.] And . . . the other two were hastily made and were identically composed of nothing more than leftovers" (p. 166). He tries to project an image of selflessness, but he implicitly demonstrates the kind of selfishness that particulary marks Lacan's imaginary stage.

Cyril's sense of self-importance also casts his assertions into doubt. Whenever he describes himself, he does so with a generous amount of self-congratulation. He speaks of his "large and sympathetic lips," "unlimited gentleness," "richness of feeling," patience, tolerance, and "systematic personality"—traits that others do not necessarily find in him. His perceptions frequently differ from those of others, though he always says to them, "Trust me." On many occasions, Cyril takes what is explicitly negative and construes it as positive. In certain respects, this tendency can be considered constructive optimism, but sometimes it shows Cyril as obtuse or wrong. When Catherine looks at Cyril, he cannot tell whether she feels "love or indignation," and when Hugh puts his hand in her halter, Cyril, astonishingly, does not know whether the act springs from "love or viciousness." Cyril's concluding statement in the book is a glittering generalization that he knows from his own experience to be untrue. He says, "In Illyria there are no seasons" (p. 271). At times, the seasons do seem confused in the book: Fiona leaves a bouquet of hyacinths upon the arrival of Hugh and Catherine, and yet the grapes are ripe. This confusion could be a result of faulty memory, momentary confusion, or creative imagination at work, but to say there are no seasons fails to take into account the reality of the decay that surrounds him and the metaphorical winter that blasts his vision of eternal sexual joy. Cyril's statement cannot be reconciled with his earlier account of his spiritually and sexually impoverished life with Rosella and the way chaos and decay overtake him. When he and Rosella look for snails, he comments about the "senseless clumps" of grass that have grown against the walls and into his flower beds, which are "nearly invisible now under thickets of crab grass, dead brambles, translucent yellow weeds that turn to powder at the slightest touch" (p. 45). When Catherine is clearly in pain over Cyril's reference to their affair and Hugh's death, he says, "But when the shades of pain were drifting across Catherine's face, as they were drifting now, there was nothing else to see, to marvel at, to desire. Catherine's pain was her beauty"

(p. 12). To construe pain as beauty suggests insensitivity at best and sadism at worst. In a similar misinterpretation, when in church Fiona says sharply, "Cyril, baby, why don't you put out the cigarette? For God's sake," he softens the force of her comment with "and I smiled to hear Fiona's voice clipped and imploring, harsh and sweet, a mere whisper filled with richest possible sounds of assurance" (p. 18).

These comments suggest the incredible egotism of an infant taken up with self-gratification. Statements that have the ring of falseness relate closely to other questions about Cyril's judgment and motivation: his self-confessed "pompous lyricism"; his "deception, selfishness, showmanship" (p. 158) in making flower crowns; his confident assurance that he knows what Hugh is dreaming when he sees him sleeping and writhing on the beach; and his encouragement of Hugh to go farther into the fortress by saying, "our wives don't want to admit how much they like this little dangerous hunt of yours" (p. 198). Cyril's glasses may have importance in this respect, for of all objects identified with him, they are the most ubiquitous. Yet by his own admission they do not suggest insight. During his first seduction of Catherine, Cyril claims to have clarity but not understanding, but in removing his glasses, he symbolically disregards clarity too.

Another problem is that Cyril seems neither to recognize Hugh's better qualities nor to acknowledge how much he has absorbed the worse ones. As writer of the account, Cyril gives Hugh practically no credit and becomes aggressive toward him when the two talk in the grape arbor. Such aggressiveness is, according to Lacan, a sign of narcissism and deeply rooted paranoia.[26] On occasion Cyril neglects to censure one of Hugh's positive comments or actions. When the small goat comes into the midst of the two families, it is Hugh who romps and frolics with it, causing Fiona to say of Hugh: "Isn't he wonderful? I want him for my own, I really do" (p. 94). Since Cyril does not disparage Fiona and her judgment and since she sees such qualities in Hugh, Cyril's constant denigration of him is suspect.

Immediately after Hugh's death, Cyril assumes many of his qualities. He becomes a creature of ritual and repetition: every day he puts on his shabby black suit, tight-fitting vest, white shirt, and faded tie and rides his "pathetic" rusty bike with rotten wheels to visit Catherine. In the evening he puts on his "nearly ruined black dinner clothes" and eats alone. He gives up traveling, leads a sedentary life, and allows his old cowhide suitcases to become moldy. Surrounded by decay in his villa, he grows noticeably older, giving the impression of having moved rapidly from youthful vitality to decrepit old age. He also speaks of his "moody psychic organization" (p. 167), which refutes the buoyancy he earlier claims. Even when he and Catherine resume their relationship, it survives only on memories. His vaunted tapestry becomes a map, something familiar and charted but at the same time abstract and lacking immediacy. He says of the map, "I know well its contours, its monuments, its abandoned gardens, its narrow streets, and Catherine is beginning to know them too. In an atmosphere of peaceful investigation we are traveling together from sign to sign, from empty stage to empty stage" (pp. 167–68). This is not a clarion call to exploration and desire but wistful recapitulation and memory—important manifestations of Freud's death instinct and Lacan's name of the Father.

Still, the need for pattern and repetition was there even before Hugh's death and Fiona's departure. The first time that Catherine and Hugh fail to come visiting, Cyril records his and Fiona's morning ritual, "how the day had passed, true to form" (p. 180). He then notes that "unspoken traditional decorum was always the handmaiden of unconfessed anticipation" (p. 181). Cyril's life may be one of erotic games and flowing time, but it too has "timeless" patterns of ritual and decorum.

The sort of transference between the erotic and the death instincts and the imaginary and the symbolic stages that Lacan speaks of also characterizes Hugh's and Cyril's need to control. In his attempt to enforce a conventionally moralistic view of marriage, Hugh tries to control Fiona's actions (in addition to his and Catherine's) by changing her "into a lifeless and sainted fixture in his mental museum." He tries to impose his will on Catherine by forcing her to see to a crying twin on one occasion and having her make the children stop playing on the dog's coffin on another. Placing the chastity belt on Catherine is only the most barbaric and extreme example of Hugh's frequent attempt to control others. But Cyril also attempts to control others. He wants Hugh to become involved with Fiona, an act that will justify his affair with Catherine and complete the symmetry and coherence of the four-pointed relationship. When Hugh finally does sleep with Fiona, Cyril ecstatically sees it as the fulfillment of his desires: "He had proven my theories, completed Love's natural structure, justified Catherine's instincts, made Fiona happy when she had given up all her hopes for happiness. What more could I ask?" (p. 260). He similarly tries to exert control over the children, requiring them to make flower crowns in the meadow. But neither man can maintain control. Cyril admits that the violets he tries to arrange perfectly in the vase defy "the aesthetic pattern" he had in mind, and Hugh refuses to continue the *ménage a quatre*. All attempts at control lead to entropy and death. Sexuality and morality, aestheticism and pragmatism, lead to the same end.

This undermining of Cyril's vision raises questions about sexual roles and social attitudes. Cyril embodies the erotic instinct but nonetheless is subject to death and decay. Sexual instinct cannot remain isolated from and unrelated to the death instinct. When Cyril describes the snails in his decaying villa, it is apparent that darkness and decay are part of the life force: "The snails were plentiful and the sticky silver trails crept down dead stems, climbed over exposed roots, disappeared under black chunks of decomposing stone. Everywhere the snails were massing or making their blind osmotic paths about the villa, eating and destroying and unwinding their silver trails. They were the eyes of night, the crawling stones" (p. 47). Death too has an element of eroticism of which Cyril seems largely unaware. One of his final revelations is that Hugh has a special erotic side: "Hugh's despairing use of that iron belt must have occasioned a moment more genuinely erotic than any he had known with Catherine, with his nudes, or in his dreams of Fiona" (p. 257). (Of course, this view is Cyril's, and he tends to see everything as erotic. What it was to Hugh is unknown.) Sex, violence, and death—they are closely related and integrally connected.

Hugh and Cyril, then, share many characteristics. In his compulsion to repeat the sexual act, Cyril shares with Hugh the basic instinct of the ego for repetition and recurrence. Indeed, in view of Hugh's interest in photographing virginal nude peasants and especially his need to clutch one such picture at the time of his death, it is certain that he shares the erotic instinct. When playing the grape-tasting game, he too recognizes the grapes as "nipples" and feels uncomfortable about the implications. Moreover, although Cyril criticizes Hugh for "propelling himself about in crablike motions for the sake of angle, light, depth, expression" (p. 69), he does virtually the same thing in trying to find his place in the tapestry of love and to give his account of that experience in his narration of *Blood Oranges*. Each of the men finally crosses over to participate in the characteristics and behavior of the other. They share the same water and the same earth, like the pear tree and the cistern into which Cyril throws the wooden arm stolen by Fiona and Hugh. This is the phenomenon of intersubjective transference in which two opposites influence each other.

The mixture of life and death, beginnings and endings, pleasure and pain, is exemplified in the launching of a boat that Catherine and Cyril witness. In an ancient ritual, the villagers use coagulated blood to lubricate the launching conveyance, which youths push down the streets into the water, whereupon a disreputable, goat-faced naked old villager gambols about the prow of the boat, making loud, lascivious comments. Sex and death, youth and age, are combined in a ritual that embraces power, fecundity, and death. From participating in such an experience and simply being human, Cyril should have recognized the conjoining of sex and death, the transference between the imaginary and symbolic modes.

The broader context of the imagery of the blood orange further exemplifies this purpose. Rare and highly valued, the blood orange, with its sections clustered around a vaginal center, is a potent sexual symbol, as the illustration of the New Directions edition of the novel makes clear. In Cyril's mind, such an exotic fruit is intricately related to the human faculty of expression. He says that "if orgasm is the pit of the fruit then lyricism is its flesh" (p. 210). Cyril plays upon such a meaning when he and Catherine see the boat launched in the sunset while the water turns red from the coagulated blood. The orange sun blends with the water, creating "a diffusion of thick erotic color" (p. 132), and the life-giving quality of the sun is reflected in the "fleshy waves." On a separate occasion, blood oranges are equated with Fiona's breasts, which hang "unimaginably free" in the setting sun. This scene, however, is fraught with tension, for Hugh is uncomfortable with Fiona's nakedness and immediately accuses her of castrating Cyril. "That enormous smoldering sun" lying "on the horizon like a dissolving orange suffused with blood" (p. 37) also suggests to Cyril a predestined death, so that the vision of joyful sexuality and fecundity is mingled with one of joyless sterility and death. These colors are also picked up in Cyril's description of the burned-out penitential fortress, and he notes the "intestinal pink, lurid orange, great blistering sheets of lifeless purple" (p. 192). The description of the chastity belt found deep inside this fortress similarly involves "the brown and orange color of dried blood and the blue-green color of corrosion" (p. 207). Blood orange, then, embraces life and death, life-giving nature and soul-destroying culture, eroticism and repression, female and male.

Like the eagle soaring above the couples' heads, the characters, places, and image patterns of the novel are "doubly significant" in blending "correct and incorrect," "right and wrong," "the breath of dead kings" and the sunrise (pp. 138–39). Doubles and doubling in Hawkes's work demonstrate not so much unequivocal polarization and opposition, even paradoxical blending, as the intersubjective transference between sex and death instincts and between the imaginary and symbolic modes. Both Cyril's and Hugh's alternatives are to some extent correct, but sex and death cannot easily be separated, for they are integral parts of the human activity. Cyril is wholly attractive in his desire for sensual and sensuous delights, but he errs in assuming that sexuality will triumph in the battle with Hugh's morality, monogamy, and death wish. His mistake lies not in pursuing the erotic but in misunderstanding the nature of the Other. Although Hugh is less attractive than Cyril, he represents the necessary awareness of decay and death in the human condition. In the dialectic of the body, sex tries to ignore death, and the law of the Father tries to preempt the law of desire, but they are inextricably connected. In this book, Hawkes employs and decenters the Freudian model, providing some tentative solutions but leaving numerous questions unanswered. Hawkes may want to assert the triumph of eroticism and imagination over death and conventional morality, but willy-nilly his book implicitly supports the Lacanian view of the double.

"Neither one nor quite two"
Barth's Lost in the Funhouse

5

LIKE MANY OTHER LITERARY FORMS AND DEVICES, THE DOUBLE CAN SERVE serious purposes by means of a comic style. Renowned for his playful, witty prose and his frequent disavowals of serious intent, Nabokov uses the device of the double not only to reflect self-consciously on previous uses of the double in literature but also to critique the metaphysics of analogy, metaphor, and mysticism. He creates a false double in order to stress the necessity for stripping the device of its accumulated cultural baggage: conventional psychological and dualistic interpretations. The double, Nabokov indicates, is no more than a playful metaphor, one that admittedly lends itself to profound views of people and the universe but that does not have to affirm meaning outside the text itself. The text alone is a sufficient game. Still, Nabokov sees in the tendency to attach meaning to literary artifacts evidence of a pervasive weakness in human beings, the inclination to draw logical necessity from mere analogy or meaning from metaphor. Possibly more ludic than Nabokov, Pynchon employs elaborate doubles and doubling to explore ways the individual fell victim to industrial and technological conglomerates and unholy political alliances during and following World War II. But, like any other literary device, the double, Pynchon believes, is never finally able to encompass a totalized structure, meaning, or origin, nor can it embody more than fragmentary knowledge. Darker, more concerned with brutality and decay, and more oblique in his humor, Hawkes plays with the traditional double in a way that sheds light upon the complexity of human psychic imbalances, patterns of social interaction, and aesthetic pleasure. He

121

perceives the gaps between fact and language and fact and "reality," and sees that the self is conditioned by the Other as much as the self affects the Other.

Exhibiting black humor in his early short novels, John Barth reveals a more elaborate, gleeful, and self-conscious sense of play in his later treatments of the double, demonstrating a Nabokovian distrust of metaphysics, a Pynchonesque fear of the manipulation of national values and activities by government and business, and a Hawkesian interrogation of the self. For Barth, especially, culture becomes the double of literature just as literature becomes the double of culture—they echo and reflect each other but are not the same. As a result, when Barth designifies the double in his fiction, when he indicates that it is only a self-referential literary device, he is also designifying society, culture, and history.

While nineteenth- and early twentieth-century American versions of the double were generally portrayed by authors with little if any formal background in higher education, later twentieth-century writers are almost invariably products of the university and in many cases have earned academic appointments. Nabokov taught at Cornell; Hawkes teaches at Brown; and Barth teaches at Johns Hopkins. In many respects, Barth's choices of style and topics reflect his academic interests. His style, characterized less by "naturalness" than "artifice," is in keeping with his background and his interest in the eighteenth-century origins of the novel. But his choice of topics shows an awareness of contemporary language theories, modes of irrealist writing, and political and environmental issues currently of interest in universities. In addressing these issues, Barth indicates a deep distrust of binary systematizing, a suspicion that he shares with Nabokov, Pynchon, and Hawkes. Barth's method of "double postulation" employs the traditional signs of culture and literature to explore their inherent gaps and infinite supplementations.

John Barth's double postulation, the simultaneous use and displacement of signs,[1] is overtly literary and nonbinary, grounded in his concept of orchestration and improvisation.[2] He "arranges" established signs, discourses, and cycles, inscribing upon them his own mark or signature. Barth maintains that his interest in reorchestration, the replaying and doubling of forms, is attributable to his being "an opposite-sex twin" whose "books come in pairs,"[3] a playful comment at once highlighting the homologous structures he sees in music, literature, and his personal life[4] and indicating the way he typically destabilizes those forms through overextended comparison. By playing upon their shared basis in human experience and the importance of artistic technique in each, Barth undermines naive understandings of life and art. Human life and technique, "fire" and "algebra," constitute "passionate virtuosity."[5] Only partially about the human situation, Barth's fiction is by his own admission "always also about itself."[6]

With that awareness, he calls into question the relationship between life and art, his work and tradition, or, in the case of the double, between his literary doubles and traditional psychological and dualistic ones, implying that although signifying systems share structural isomorphs such as regression and return, theme and variation, they cannot be metaphysically linked. By this distinction he makes the reader aware of the discrete boundaries between signifying systems, their arbitrariness, and the gap that exists between them. Of postmodern fiction, his is the most comprehensive and systematic use of the double. It pervades every work and, as with so many other literary devices, changes radically in signification from such earlier modernist treatments as *The End of the Road* to such later postmodernist ones as *The Tidewater Tales*. Although all his works warrant at least brief comment, the latter half of *Lost in the Funhouse* is arguably his most radically innovative work, the one that marks the outset of his postmodern period.

To be aware of communication systems and their gaps is to perceive that language is not only a powerful tool but also incomplete.[7] When authors self-consciously play a semiotic game, as Barth has, the endeavor is not teleological; it has little if anything to do with our notions of completeness, final goals, or happiness.[8] The characteristics, laws, and goals of semiotic play correlate with Barth's views of literature and treatment of the double. As one form of game, literature may mirror other signifying systems, but the nature of its rules must ultimately be appropriate to itself. As early as 1960, Barth argued that a "novel is not essentially a view of this universe (though it may reflect one), but a universe itself; that the novelist is not finally a spectator, an imitator, or a purger of the public psyche, but a maker of universes: a demiurge. At least a semidemiurge."[9] According to Heide Ziegler, this view of author and text is one of the most enduring in Barth,[10] each work telling the story of its own creation and speaking of its own existence.[11]

Barth has not ruled out fiction's dependence on and contamination by other signifying systems—the experiences of the real world or the devices of mimetic and modern fiction. He is of the long-standing opinion that fiction does not have to abandon the realists' use of place, linear narrative, and continuity to maintain a unique form of signification. He is also of the opinion that literature can use modernist conventions. He admits that his own works contain realistic and modernist conventions,[12] though in his most recent ones he challenges them by using the techniques metafictively, employing parody to distance the readers from those conventions and creating games whose stakes are aesthetic success or failure. While he accepts Barthes's comments from *Writing Degree Zero* that "the whole of literature, from Flaubert to the present day, . . . [becomes] the problematics of language," he confesses that like cultural myths, literary conventions are subject to diachronic changes and "are liable to be retired, subverted, transcended, transformed, or even deployed against themselves to generate new and lively work."[13] As a consequence, although his fiction uses realistic and modern conventions, the value he assigns them differs. In that sense, the gap between his signification and the original may seem to create a structure of oppositions.

But he has recently espoused the "synthesis or transcension of these antitheses" for his "ideal postmodernist author neither merely repudiates nor merely imitates either his twentieth-century modernist parents or his nineteenth-century premodernist grandparents."[14] Despite Barth's use of the term *synthesis*, he seems more preoccupied with perceiving the gaps between oppositions and neutralizing them than in constituting a third term and arriving at a solution. This is his way of arriving at undecidable, polysemic meanings and pluralistic interpretations of reality. By means of "a double gesture, a double science, a double writing," he helps to overturn classical oppositions and to produce a general displacement of the system.[15] He helps us to see that balanced equations and binary oppositions are not innately human but only the result of a certain cultural view.

Gaps between formalistic literary themes and devices and their specific uses in one text, between form used straightforwardly and form used in a parodic way, create "double-voiced discourses," the "intersecting of two voices and two accents"—the author's and another. In an unironic "stylization," an author uses another voice for its own projects, while in parody "the second voice, having lodged in the other speech, clashes antagonistically with the original, host voice and forces it to serve directly opposite aims. Speech becomes a battlefield for opposing intentions."[16] Both stylization and parody, especially postmodern parodic intertextuality, mine the vein of literature self-referentially; each in its own way is a tribute to a previous form and adds length to the broad avenue of literature but functions in a different manner. Generally speaking, Barth's earlier works reflect more stylization than parody, but *The Sot-Weed Factor*—substantially a stylization of, and a tribute to, the eighteenth-century novel—has its own twentieth-century voice that parodies aspects of content and form. This use of stylization is also true of later works, including *LETTERS*, in which the epistolary form is palinodically used and displaced, as well as *Sabbatical, The Tidewater Tales,* and *The Last Voyage of Somebody the Sailor* in which voyage literature is invoked, but it is parody which Barth foregrounds in *Chimera* and *Lost in the Funhouse* as a means of highlighting the gaps within the structure. Moreover, Barth's treatment of the double changes considerably in his works, extending from modernist to metafictive uses and ranging from emulation of original significations to a parody of them.

In Barth's first novels, *The Floating Opera* and *End of the Road*, the double is a stylization reminiscent of Victorian mimesis. In *The Floating Opera*, Todd Andrews weighs life and death in the balance in a thirteen-year inquiry into his father's death before attempting suicide. Following this abortive attempt, he views suicide as neither better nor worse than life itself. Todd also convinces one of his doubles, the elderly Mr. Haecker, to commit suicide by playing upon his fear of old age. Todd and Mr. Haecker are more or less traditional contrastive doubles playing upon familiar dualistic categories and binary oppositions—youth and age, death and life, mind and body, rationality and irrationality—which, Charles B. Harris argues, merge, implicitly "suggesting an integrated unity."[17] Something similar can be said of Todd and his friend Harrison Mack, who share not only similar masks or changing views of life but the same woman. Their similarities and even their differences suggest a kind of integrated unity.

In Barth's second novel, *End of the Road*, rational and irrational modes are more central issues. Philosophically a nihilist and morally a relativist, Jake Horner sees little in life that is rationally coherent or fixed; even grammar, of which he is a teacher, cannot be prescribed or systematically described. Like the law that Todd practices, grammar is a product of historical convention and observance. Both are self-contained structural systems and self-referential discourses with their own internal rules, which are fundamentally inexplicable outside themselves. Jake believes language to be so self-referential that it falsifies experience. Opposed to Jake's arguments against reason are those of Joe Morgan, who is convinced that everything can be systematically explained without betraying experience. An embodiment of a Western logocentrism that differs little from Pointsman's in *Gravity's Rainbow*, he tries to exert control over himself and events by exaggerated rationality. Joe and Jake, binary opposites, join battle in the field of rationalism. As in so many other contests, however, it is the unengaged and innocent who fall victim. Joe's wife, Rennie, who believes implicitly in his Godlike rationality and wisdom, is seduced literally and metaphysically by Jake. The constant "whipping" of her head from side to side (reinforced by the metaphorical comparison of her to a horse) graphically illustrates the tug-of-war between two approaches to rationality. Jake and Joe, as the similarity of their names implies, are contrastive allegorical doubles who represent opposing ideologies, and Rennie is the body that suffers from both.

In suggesting that the doubles of this book form a psychodrama of the narrator, Charles Harris is not far from asserting that the characters of *End of the Road* are emanations of the author, who plays out different roles or attitudes that simultaneously exist within him,[18] an opinion suggested by Barth's self-analysis—"I've always been impressed by the multiplicity of people that one has in one . . . I've never been impressed by any unity of identity in myself"—and his essay on authorial selves in fiction.[19] The author of a novel has the opportunity to project and explore his various real or fictive selves and ideologies—his several doubles.

This notion of doubles as playful extensions of the author's imagination (not schizophrenic manifestations or Freudian extensions of the author's biomechanistically determined psyche) accounts for the extraordinary play of the double in *The Sot-Weed Factor*, where Barth drives "a hundred characters through eight times that many pages."[20] A number of these characters are doubles, proliferating at such a rate that the concept of the double entropically loses power and significance. It is what Barth calls "dual *regressus.*"[21] In this book Barth begins to draw a clear line between the traditional double and his parodic imitation to show that "identity is a false category" and to underscore these characters as fictive.[22]

Some critics object to Barth's use of parody—the gaps in the doubles discourse that permit ironic distancing. An early reviewer for the *New Yorker* complains that Barth's stories "are parodies in a quite destructive sense; they are like the doodles and wisecracks a schoolboy scribbles across the pages of his textbooks. Mr. Barth cannot improve on the original works; he merely wants to remind us of his presence."[23] But other critics, such as Earl Rovit, Russell Miller, Gerhard Joseph, and John O. Stark, comment appreciatively on the nature of parody in Barth, though Stark thinks his parody is more "a holding action" against a dying novel than a form of replenishment.[24] It is Robert Alter who best describes Barth's use of parody as renewing and transforming jejune literary forms and Robert Rogers who is especially appreciative of Barth's ability to parody the virginal maiden-temptress duality "out of existence" in *The Sot-Weed Factor*.[25] To recognize or create a gap within the signification system of fiction is paradoxically to change the context and give fiction new life.

The possibility that parody can create a gap between signifying systems or within a signifying system and provide replenishment is nowhere more observable than in *The Sot-Weed Factor*. In this book the most self-evident and traditional use of the double is that of the hero, Ebenezer Cooke, and his sister, Anna. Playing on Burlingame's account of the historical signification of geminology and the folkloristic belief that opposite-sex twins have a morally questionable symbiotic relationship, perhaps even having coupled in the womb, Barth raises the question of the licitness of Eben's love for Anna that remains unresolved at the conclusion, which finds them sharing the ancestral home at Malden. Fittingly, even the silver seal ring (given by their father to their mother, Anne Bowers) that Anna places on Eben's hand brings their names into anagramatic conjunction—"ANNEB" or "EBANN"—when viewed on the circle of the ring. The sign bears the traces of the traditional meaning, but humor threatens that stable relationship.

The destabilizing influence of humor is heightened by another double: Henry Burlingame III, who licitly or illicitly loves Anna and Ebenezer in equal measure. Although the central character is Eben, who in his youth fixes upon an identity of poet and virgin, Henry dominates this romance and specifically alters the signification of the double. Burlingame, whose name combines *burl* (jest) and *game*, is Cooke's opposing double and contrasts with him in almost every way.[26] Without parents and therefore without pedigree, Burlingame has no fixed identity and assumes a succession of masks. Whereas Eben tries desperately to contain reality in a single vision, to hang onto his chosen virginity and compose his romantic vision in end-closed couplets, Burlingame alters, Proteus-like, at every turn, donning the guises of Colonel Peter Sayer, Tim Mitchell, Nicholas Lowe, Lord Baltimore, John Coode, Francis Nicholson, and Monsieur Casteene. For Burlingame, life is a constantly changing drama without closure, and he claims to be the "Embracer of Contradictories," the essence of paradoxical resolution. Although Ebenezer's essentialist absolutism is to Burlingame's mutations as Joe Morgan's firmly held logocentric rationalism is to Jake's rationalistic relativism, Burlingame's role changes exceed Jake's. While Jake's depend on existential ethical relativism, Burlingame's quixotic changes denote the absence of any identity or ideology. Burlingame is the embodiment of the freeplay of "infinite substitutions and permutations" where sign leads to sign and signifier replaces signified. One meaning replaces another in uninterrupted circulation.[27]

This question of semiotic values is made explicit in relation to Henry's name and Eben's reading of the *Secret Historie*. When Eben is captured by the Indian tribe, he inadvertently mentions Henry's name, causing a stir among the Indians, whose chief after John Smith's departure was Burlingame's ancestor. Once Henry discovers that his history is bound to the Indians, he surrenders to it and disappears in it. His original lack of signification is replaced by a fixed one. Burlingame, though unaware of it, has born the "trace" of his ancestry in him. When his "trace" has a fixed point of origin, Burlingame, as a sign, disappears into it, having lost his "absence" by the intrusion of "presence." Burlingame's disappearance reminds us of the danger of believing in fixed, unalterable signification, but it also suggests that literary signification systems (such as the *Secret Historie*) can affect the actions of human beings. One signifying system can exert an influence on another, although the two will never be wholly aligned. The "signs"[28] that Eben discovers in the *Secret Historie* are neither easily interpretable nor consistent.

The double in *Giles Goat-Boy* is more comprehensively structural.

The story concerns a dualistically divided campus, WESCAC (America) and EASCAC (Russia), and dualistic characters that include the bucolic, natural goat boy versus his sophisticated adult self; the lecherous, sexually free, black-skinned Croaker versus the cerebral, voyeuristic, white-skinned Eirkopf; Stacey versus Lacey; the capitalist Ira Hector versus the Communist Classmate X; the rationalist and self-controlled Lucius Rexford and the antirationalist, anarchic, entropic Maurice Stoker; and the false, apparently evil Harold Bray versus the true, apparently salvific George Giles. Naturally, these oppositions raise the age-old duality of country-city, ignorance-knowledge, sexuality-rationality, comedy-tragedy, and good-evil. These oppositional categories, as critics have noted, exist to deny the validity of dualism and support pluralism and paradox. Throughout, Barth refines an effect tried earlier in *The Sot-Weed Factor*—the doubling not only of character and theme but of literary form. A recreation of eighteenth-century style, if not precisely of enlightenment sensibility, *The Sot-Weed Factor* is by and large stylization, a tribute to and reinvigoration of an exhausted form. *Giles Goat-Boy* reflects more forcefully the actual structures of fiction, ranging from the mythic conventions of the wandering hero, Giles, to the application of the ancient and venerable genres, epic and tragedy, to a university setting in the computer age. The epic format of the book, the reinvention of *Oedipus Rex* under the title "Taliped Decanus," and the presence of the framing story all specifically point to form itself, placing more emphasis on the doubling of structure than the doubling of character. The "teller and the extraordinary circumstances of their telling" and "the narrative convention of the framing story"—these generate a metamythical or metaformal text, myth that calls attention to itself as myth and form that calls attention to formalistic qualities.[29] This metastructure creates a gap between the original code and its new application.

This emphasis on the structure of the double brings Barth's work into the postmodern context, what Barth calls "the 'performing' self-consciousness and self-reflexiveness of modernism," "fiction that is more and more about itself and its processes, less and less about objective reality and life in the world." It is important nevertheless to note that as much as Barth enjoys the postmodern technique and temperament—"disjunction, simultaneity, irrationalism, anti-illusionism, self-reflexiveness, medium-as-message, political olympianism, and a moral pluralism approaching moral entropy"—he is quick to add that "these are not the whole story either."[30] In recognizing and opening the gaps in the double discourse, Barth simultaneously uses and displaces significance, abides by and questions the rules of the game of fictional doubles.

This intertextual dependence upon and transposition of previous textual systems is nowhere more evident than in *Lost in the Funhouse, Chimera, LETTERS, Sabbatical, The Tidewater Tales,* and *The Last Voyage of Somebody the Sailor.* Unlike earlier novels, which are relatively continuous narratives with consistent points of view, the later books consist of short stories or epistles connected by similar or identical characters, myths, and techniques. Individual stories are linked not only intertextually to *The Narrative of Arthur Gordon Pym of Nantucket, The Thousand and One Nights, The Odyssey,* and *Huckleberry Finn* but intratextually to Barth's other works. The discourse of the double in one story plays upon the other stories in the same volume and, in the case of *LETTERS,* upon all of Barth's preceding fiction. These books do not reflect the real physical world but reduce the world to the activity of writing: the world as text.[31]

Although *Lost in the Funhouse* remains to be discussed extensively, it is important to note at this point that it is the first book by Barth in which the matter of the gap between sign and referent, signifier and signified, and signifying systems is especially rich and metafictive in its handling, woven throughout every story. Influenced by the fiction of Borges,[32] the work explores the difference between signifier (literary conventions) and attributable signification. Ambrose, of "Ambrose His Mark," regales the reader with the history of his mark or "naming-sign" and observes that "I and my sign are neither one nor quite two." He and the conventional associations of the birthmark or the linguistic mark, "Ambrose," are hardly one.[33] Although the book includes traditional significations of the double, it adds defamiliarizing instances, including double narrators and repetitive vocabulary and structures. Consequently, characters such as Ambrose in "Ambrose His Mark" and Anonymous in the "Anonymiad" are doubles in their authorial capacities; the forms of "Menelaiad" and "Frame-Tale" double in their unfathomable cyclicalness; and in some tales such as "Anonymiad" and "Title" narrators and structures double one another. Such alternatives stress the fictionality and interdependency of the fictions.

Chimera also reveals just such inter- and intratextuality. All the

tales—"Dunyazadiad," "Perseid," and "Bellerophoniad"—reorches-
trate ancient stories and as such confirm the ambiguous cyclical intertextuality of fiction. As the narrator of "Bellerophoniad" muses, "Thus
begins, so help me Muse, the tidewater tale of twin Bellerophon,
mythic hero, cousin to constellated Perseus: how he flew and reflew
Pegasus the winged horse; dealt double death to the three-part freak
Chimera; twice loved, twice lost; twice aspired to, reached, and died to
immortality—in short, how he rode the heroic cycle and was recycled.
Loosed at last from mortal speech, he turned into written words:
Bellerophonic letters afloat between two worlds, forever betraying, in
combinations and recombinations, the man they forever represent."[34]
By rehearsing the production and structure of these myths, Barth
demonstrates that they are as relevant to and dependent on modern
tidewater Maryland as ancient Greece. Myth is as present in the individual as in the texts of society and writing. For Barth, it is a matter
of recognizing that presence and thereby putting a different value on
it. This point is evident in "Dunyazadiad," Barth's evocation and
stylization of *The Thousand and One Nights*, where the question of sign
and signification is similarly addressed, not only by Scheherazade but
by those who learn technique from her—the sister, Dunyazade, and
Barth himself. These narrators are linked not only by the narrative
process (signifier) but also by their difficulty in telling a story (transmission) and ascertaining the meaning of the product (signified). As the
Genie (an avatar of John Barth) tells Scheherazade: "I've lost track of
who I am; my name's just a jumble of letters; so's the whole body of
literature; strings of letters and empty spaces, like a code I've lost the
key to." By admitting to the loss of a code and to the existence of empty
spaces, the fiction opens itself to reversals of traditional meaning. Time
and transmission have altered the context and hence the signification.

The parody of traditional doubling—Scheherazade and Dunyazade as sisters, Shahryar and Shah Zaman as brothers, the two couples
as lovers—raises questions concerning the origin and transmission of
literature. As the one who dreams Scheherazade and Dunyazade into
existence, the narrator considers himself their brother, but as the
reader of *The Thousand and One Nights*, he can tell them the stories,
and thus rescue them from their personal and narrative dilemma. The
question of where the book actually begins, with Barth as reader or
Scheherazade as teller, is irresolvable. The cycles of literature have
neither origin nor telos but exist with endless permutations. In this

way Barth combines "the double, the voyage in time, the contamination of reality by irreality, and the text within the text."[35] This small
unit thus suggests that author and reader or teller and listener are,
regardless of separation in time and space, doubles of each other,
interchanging roles at will. For the story's triple narration, the glue
that binds them all together, the "Magic Key" that unlocks the treasure
chest of narrative, is not the transcendent Word, the Alpha and Omega
that breaches time and space, but simple words. In short, the endlessly
repeatable telling of story suggests that the sign itself is significance
enough. The gap between signifier and signified becomes so great
that it annihilates the signified and makes of every mark only a chain
of differential marks. The binary opposition, or *différence*, is postponed
and deferred.

The annihilation of significance is especially characteristic of doubling in *LETTERS*. Here Barth brings many of his former characters to
life, allowing them to interact in a different context—or perhaps they
allow him to interact with them, for they seem to have as much
independence and authority as the author. "Alive" again are Todd
Andrews, Jake Horner, Joe Morgan, and Ambrose Mensch, along with
the descendents of the Cooks and Burlingames. These characters live
again in fiction just as the author lives again through his fiction. Their
lives are all doubled in time and fiction. Barth's system of echoes and
allusions in *LETTERS* insists "upon its status as a *mise en abyme*, a
Derridean plexus of intertextual traces."[36] By this inter- or intratextuality, Barth patently demonstrates that each work is not self-contained
in form or meaning but can be resurrected and transformed into
another piece of art with different signification. Barth can no more
claim full credit as originating author of these fictions than could
Scheherazade as the inventor of *The Thousand and One Nights*. As Harris
observes in *LETTERS*, Barth denies his works originary authorial status, for

> *The End of the Road*, we learn, was derived from Jake Horner's dis-
> carded manuscript "What to Do Until the Doctor Comes" . . . ; *The
> Floating Opera* sprang from a conversation a young Barth had with
> Todd Andrews at a New Year's Eve party in 1954 . . . ; parts of *Lost
> in the Funhouse* are from Ambrose Mensch's abandoned novel *The Am-
> ateur* . . . ; the plan for "Perseid" came from Ambrose . . . , for "Belle-
> rophoniad" from Bray . . . ; and, according to the disputed claims of

Cook and Bray, *The Sot-Weed Factor* was borrowed from the former, *Giles Goat-Boy* from the latter.[37]

In one specific instance, the character Ambrose writes to the character-author Barth, giving away the plot of *Chimera* together with the rationale for it. (This statement of intention supposedly takes the search for meaning away from the critic since the signification is now transparent, therefore virtually nonexistent.) Since a character of Barth's creation ostensibly gave Barth the idea for the book, the question of authorship is meant to be just as vexing as in "Dunyazadiad." The origin and telos of creativity cannot be charted in linear progression but in a complicated manner is shared by author and character, writer and reader, past and present—all doubles. Significance can never inhere to a work as such but is shared and exchanged in transmission.

Barth's attention to pattern making reinforces this notion. As he notes, the book depends upon the abundance of the number seven: "*Letters* is a seven-letter word. *LETTERS* is my seventh book of fiction. The letters in *LETTERS* are from seven correspondents . . . , and they're dated over the seven months from March through September."[38] Even Ambrose's relationship with Germaine has seven stages. The proliferation of sevens is no different in kind from the proliferation of characters. All are part of structuring or pattern making. All emanate from the author's-culture's-character's collective mind. And none have any "real" signification beyond demonstrating the prevalence of the production of form within fiction. This is the real double of *LETTERS*.

Sabbatical: A Romance is arguably Barth's most successful experiment with the designifying process. Here Barth achieves what he wholeheartedly admires in Marquez's *One Hundred Years of Solitude*: "the synthesis of straightforwardness and artifice, realism and magic and myth, political passion and nonpolitical artistry, characterization and caricature, humor and terror, . . . a masterpiece not only artistically admirable, but humanly wise, lovable, literally marvelous."[39] As in Barth's other aesthetic fantasies, this one makes use of character doubling in several ways. Both Fenn and Susan double as the heroes of the text; they conceive a set of twins that Susan aborts; and both are "same-sex dizygotics." Fenn and his brother, Manfred, who may be a double agent for the CIA and whose likely death is mirrored by that of another CIA agent, fit the classic paradigm of twins as rivals in both their oppositional descriptions and styles of life. But Barth draws the same-sex dizygotics still further: Fenn is not only Susan's husband; because his brother married her mother, he is also her uncle. Count may thus be Susan's stepfather as well as brother-in-law, and Susan's mother becomes Fenn's sister-in-law and mother-in-law. This convoluted, if not incestuous, doubling calls attention to its structure.

The references to the Byronic myth at the back of the book also introduces the use of intertextual doubling, but with distortions. Barth recalls the legend of Byron's Manfred as a means of centering upon the literary quality of the brothers' doubling. In Byron's *Manfred*, there is only one male sibling who loves his sister (Astarte) incestuously. In Barth's version, Fenn and Manfred love Marilyn Marsh. In referring to Homer, Virgil, Cervantes, Melville, Poe, Twain, and Conrad, Barth also comments on the seemingly endless number of travel voyages that form the literary code-context for this work. But he also includes intratextual doubling with self-conscious references to "Night-Sea Journey," of *Lost in the Funhouse*, and allusions to the heroic journeys of *The Sot-Weed Factor*, *Giles Goat-Boy*, and *Chimera*. Even the yacht serves as a vehicle for the plot's action, a device going as far back as *The Floating Opera*. These verbal signifiers draw from the sign-structures within and outside Barth's *oeuvre*.

Barth has, however, another, more abstractly formalistic sign that multiplies the signification infinitely in the text. Embedded within the title page of the hardcover edition of the book is a design or logo resembling three wedges of pie arranged in a circle. Between each of these pieces is a gap leading to a tiny circle in the center, the design forming a Y shape. This logo is not immediately meaningful, nor is it ever wholly determinate within the context of the book, for this is a floating signifier, an appropriate device for a book dealing with a yachting tale.[40] Its design cannot be totally described or its functions defined. This mark literally resembles the helm of the yacht and the map of the route the boat follows up the Chesapeake, and serves metaphorically to describe the multiple narration (first Fenn, then Susan, then both simultaneously), the choices that Fenn and Susan must make ("We're at a fork in our channel," says Fenn),[41] and even the apparent pattern of the galaxy. The logo is consequently a homogram whose various paradigmatic possibilities and significations are simultaneously present; one does not displace the other.

The interrupted circle that contains the Y shape is also important as a signifier, for it contains all choices. As the narrator points out, while "our galaxy looks like the capital letter Y, 'in reality' it is a disc of stars, a flat swirl or Saturn-like ring" (p. 235). In this way the design promotes the view that systematizing is not a closed option. In keeping with this, the route up the Chesapeake follows the binary pattern for only a limited period before Fenn and Susan discover that all choices are multiple, not binary. They can sail left, right, downward, or stay at the center. A triadic or ever-expanding form replaces the binary one, emphasizing the value of pluralistic possibilities and polysemic meanings that go beyond an easy Hegelian synthesis. This seemingly insignificant sign, an integral feature of the title page, consequently functions as the double of meaning, though that meaning is multiple in signification.

The Tidewater Tales: A Novel is an even more complex book on doubles and doubling than *Sabbatical*. These books are indeed twins.[42] Not only are both sailing narratives with recurrent characters, but *The Tidewater Tales* is about the process of conceptualizing and drafting *Sabbatical*. Even though *Sabbatical* was published first, *The Tidewater Tales* claims to predate it because it tells of how Franklin Key Talbott (à la Fenn Turner) developed an interest in writing *Sabbatical*, an interest fostered by Peter Sagamore, the narrator of *The Tidewater Tales*.

These books are not only complementary in the sense of their real and supposed authors but also play with binary oppositions, as the subtitles of the books imply: *Sabbatical: A Romance* and *The Tidewater Tales: A Novel*. Although various definitions of these modes apply, in the romance problems are generally resolved, love requited, and the structure governed by marvelous occurrences and coincidences. The novel usually emphasizes realistic events, deals with the sociopsychological makeup of the main characters, documents the culture of a given period, and depends upon cause and effect. To some exent, these polarities do apply in the two books. *Sabbatical* is about the relationship of Fenn and Susan, their maturing love for each other, and mutual decision to let their lives be extended through fiction rather than offspring. These decisions, as with previous major ones, are marked by the magic of the ever-returning boina, an event supplemented by the even more fantastic sighting of Chessie, the sea monster. *The Tidewater Tales*, conversely, deals with family life, especially the heroine's, the circle of friends that gather to hear the telling of tales as well as the major social and political issues currently affecting the lives of Americans. Obviously fantastic elements such as the sighting of Chessie are omitted, and the boina, which moves from story-teller to story-teller, becomes the badge of narration. The book does, however, indeterminately deviate from the realistic to present the appearance of Peter's double and the figures of Odysseus, Nausicaa, Don Quixote, and Scheherazade.

The narrators of this book are also indeterminate doubles of a sort. Husband and wife, they are equally responsible for furthering the plot and interpreting reality and fiction. Katherine and Peter Sagamore are the parents of fiction, and they will give birth to twins. Barth consequently does more than double his books; he doubles the elements within them to disrupt the binary principle. He does this primarily by suggesting that one thing is not opposed to another but always inside it. The twins are inside Katherine; the books are inside Peter; and *Sabbatical*, the nucleus of a clever and innovative frame tale, is inside *The Tidewater Tales*. To have a single book that is the central frame of a frame tale revealed in the second book demonstrates the inherent limitations of the binary principle while employing it. In using structural doubles, Barth plays with binary opposition, considerably extends the limits of the frame device, and centers both books on the development of the literary imagination.

Barth's most recent book, *The Last Voyage of Somebody the Sailor*, extends the limits of this framing technique even further. It is never quite clear which is the outside or the inside of the frame. "Somebody" (Simon Wheeler Behler) of Maryland is the most contemporary character, and his narration embraces that of Sinbad and Scheherazade. But since he falls into the life and narrative of Sinbad, a character in Scheherazade's story (herself a narrator in someone else's), it may not be fair to say that they are encompassed within Behler's narrative. Nor perhaps is it accurate to say that all of this narrative is Barth's when so much of the language and technique has been garnered from *The Thousand and One Nights*. Author and work, narrator and narrative, text and reader, reality and fiction—all of these are questioned in a way that is amusing and disconcerting. Barth allows no easy resolution of these questions; he never allows a continuing binary opposition, nor does he permit a resolution. This is a dialectic of unending possibilities in which reality and fiction are both inseparable and are richer than might be imagined. *The Last Voyage of Somebody the Sailor* is, then, both a continuation of issues raised in *Sabbatical* and *The Tidewater Tales* and a further freeplay of signfication.

The use of the double to undermine the binary principle is most innovatively explored in *Lost in the Funhouse*, Barth's first explicitly postmodern text. Indeed, Carl Malmgren believes it to be the most "exhaustive compendium of all the metafictional tactics and graphotechnics" that characterize a certain kind of postmodern fiction. These include overdetermination of motifs, interpolation of ironic metalingual statements, parody of narrative conventions, the self-conscious play on letters of the alphabet, and the parody of fictional space.[43] Although almost all the stories, including "Menelaiad" with its cloud Helen and real Helen, deal with doubles, Barth's handling of them is most complex and innovative in "Frame-Tale," "Lost in the Funhouse," "Echo," and "Petition," stories about intertextuality and how the characters reflect literary forms while they interpret and add to or subtract from them—the double postulation. This game of the double is essentially a manipulation of language and literary codes as derealized universals. Barth repeats a sign—a word, a motif, a character, a form, or a structure—with endless parodic variations. Arbitrary and parodic repetition exposes a gap in the signifying process that Barth utilizes metonymically to substitute sign after sign. He plays with and against the rules, abiding by and distorting arbitrary linguistic and literary processes. The double is only one of a host of such arbitrary "poetic" signs that, as Philip Stevick suggests, function around the principles of "formal contrariety" and "formal perversity," but an important one.[44]

Barth begins *Lost in the Funhouse* with a clever, humorous, and writerly use of the double, one that stresses the coercive nature of forms, cultural and literary, and one that is clearly a game of repetition meant to engage and challenge the reader. In interacting with the text, the reader becomes an author (*scripteur* or *écrivain*), seeing the world differently and altering it in some literary way. In this "Frame-Tale," one portion of the page bears the words "ONCE UPON A TIME THERE," which is to be joined by the readers to the reverse side of the page on which appears "WAS A STORY THAT BEGAN" (pp. 1–2) to form a Möbius strip. The page is not, however, a full loop unless the readers follow the rules. By instructing us to cut the page and join the ends to deliver language from immobility, Barth encourages the readers to respond and generate meaning. Consequently, this strip functions as both message and medium. Form, lacking fixed content or signification, doubles and repeats itself ad infinitum if the reader permits; within what appears a self-enclosed tale there is no enclosure, or within an endless tale there is complete enclosure—as the reader chooses. Written by an author, a story can be vitalized only by a reader. Author and reader, their conventional responsibilities and significations eroded, simultaneously generate the work. The lines drawn between author and reader, subject and object, begin to disappear, though a gap necessarily continues to exist. The gap here is explicated by the nature of the Möbius strip itself. If the readers walked this strip, coming back after one revolution to the point where they began, they would be upside down. Form repeats itself, but every revolution incorporates slight distortions or gaps. This is the freeplay of repetition, carrying with it the power to distort and subvert.[45] Barth advocates "iteration-with variation," open-ended spiraling "retracements, recapitulations, rehearsals, and reenactments" that result in the reorientation of the reading process.[46] Barth's repetition denies a given authorial certainty, a determined signified, or a univocal statement.

Barth's use of "Frame-Tale" illustrates precisely Derrida's view that to identify the structurality of structure, whether in myth, literary form, or idea, is thereafter to deny the desire for thematic center or presence.[47] Space encircled by the Möbius strip is a nonlocus, a hole, a loss, the absence of a center or subject, a labyrinth, a universe of discourse where an infinite number of sign substitutions come into play, where nothing contains everything, and where a gap constitutes the subject. The center or subject is consistently fading, so that no unitary meaning is possible. "Is not the center, the absence of play and difference," asks Derrida, "another name for death?" He adds that death "has begun with repetition. Once the center or the origin have begun by repeating themselves, by redoubling themselves, the double did not only add itself to the simple. It divided it and supplemented it."[48] In Barth, "the center is decentered, origins are denied, and destinations are deferred."[49]

"Frame-Tale" and the other stories of the collection consequently deny the transcendental signified of the double. The gap between the *langue* of the genre or idea and the *parole* of Barth's discourse is widened to permit an infinite number of substitutions of signifieds. This discourse of the double depends upon the differences that Barth incorporates into that context, not upon previously existing signification. Accordingly, Barth uses the form of the Möbius strips to introduce the initiation-quest pattern, form doubling form. There is precedent for this. Bruce Morrissette has demonstrated that Möbius strips, like mazes and labyrinths, are an important part of *artifex ludens*[50] and illustrate how reality and fiction are self-enclosed, self-perpetuating games. Such a doubling designifies the traditional signifier-signified relationship. These literary forms, infinitely repeatable, bear out Barth's point that no piece of fiction can strictly speaking be original or used in an originary sense, although the devices of fiction can be put together in new shapes, changed, modified, and distorted. Barth thinks that a human "is primarily a linguistic animal, a creator of systems of signification" and that "playing with words may compromise their very status as linguistic signs, revealing their inadequacy to relay accurately or completely the 'realities' they purport to designate." This is what Barth means when he says that the story, "Once upon a time there was a story that began 'Once upon a time,' " is about "life."[51]

Like bookends, an opening frame tale usually has a companion at the end of the volume, and "The Anonymiad" complements "Frame-Tale" that way. But "The Anonymiad" too has its own internal double, having both a "Headpiece" and "Tailpiece" supposedly written by its author on two halves of goatskin hide. "Anonymiad" doubles the "Frame-Tale" not only by its position but also by its concern for perpetual attempts at communication and in the aporia at the center of all communication. Abandoned on a lonely island, the anonymous minstrel discovers his ability to write and plans perfectly unified pieces that he hopes to send off in his amphorae to readers across the world. But the writing neither happens in the way he wishes nor contains the unified language and ideals. Halfway through his effort he announces, "Part Three, Part Three, my crux, my core, I'm cutting you out; _____; there, at the heart, never to be filled, a mere lacuna" (p. 183). At the heart of the heart of Anonymous's fiction is no center, and the author cannot be certain that anyone will receive his amphorae. He has enciphered a script, but it has no totalized meaning or sure audience. All he has done is to construct "snares, pitfalls, blind mazes" with no clear egress. His namelessness suggests that the entire text is without demonstrated subject or object and focuses our attention upon a secret, a vanishing point, an undiscoverable name.[52] Anonymous himself thinks of his story "as lacking a subject and thus a name" (p. 198). Neither author nor tale has personal or cultural identity, only language.

Barth's stories reveal the inadequacy of attempts to communicate "reality." Although "Night-Sea Journey" follows the pattern of Ulysses's quest for meaning in *The Odyssey*, it distorts that classical presence through the use of a loquacious sperm who on its way up the fallopian tube swims with a host of questing spermatozoa. This feature parodies the quest-wanderer motif in Western literature, focusing attention on the "structurality of the structures" rather than content. Similarly, in the title story, "Lost in the Funhouse," Ambrose's journey through and confusion in the house of mirrors playfully reiterates the journeys of Ulysses, Theseus, Arthur, and Huck Finn and their similar quests and initiations. Even "Autobiography," a metafictive tale commenting on itself, suffers the same fate. These repetitions designify the quest and, as a replacement, elevate the process of doubling. The sperm, Ambrose, and the narrator of the self-reflexive tale are not just doubles of Ulysses but, given the entire context of the doubling and distorting of standard quest features, privilege this particular textual doubling over the psychological or dualistic.[53]

Virtually all of the stories double this quest-initiation pattern,[54] and their characters redouble themselves. Almost every story has a threesome consisting of the archetypal protagonist, antagonist, and personified object of the agon or quest: the sperm, the Maker, and She in "Night-Sea Journey"; Ambrose, Tommy James, and Peggy in "Water-Message"; Ambrose, Peter, and Magda in "Lost in the Funhouse"; Hector, Karl, and Andrea in "Ambrose His Mark"; the narrator, his twin, and Thalia in "Petition"; Narcissus, his reflection, and Echo in "Echo"; Menelaus, Paris, and Helen in "Menelaiad"; Anonymous, Aegisthes, and Merope in "Anonymiad"; the author, his book, and his lover in "Life-Story"; and the author, the reader, and the text in "Frame-Tale." Not only does a pattern repeat itself, but even the prose echoes itself, so that a comment from one of the characters becomes a comment by other characters centuries removed. Of course, the elements of the *pacte de la parole* are altered; the subject, audience, and moment cannot be the same. One story serves as text for another, and it matters little who is considered ultimately to be the author. In "Night-Sea Journey," the Maker produces the sperm, which in turn reflects the Maker's image and creates his immortality. Similarly, in the interaction between the author, his work, and the reader, each is created and sustained by the other. The author writes the book; the book creates the author's fame and ensures his immortality; and the reader necessarily sustains both their immortalities and in turn uses their substance to help create, apprehend, and sustain his own world: "If Sinbad sinks it's Scheherazade who drowns; whose neck one wonders is on her line?" (p. 121).

This hero-quest-initiation pattern, so typical of modernist fiction, becomes a chessboard where narrator, hero, and narratee, or character, author, and reader, play against one another, demonstrating the very nature and enjoyment of a self-consciously played, unending signifying process. In this metaphoric-metonymic interplay, the *pacte de la parole* continually recombines with endless shifting, displacement, and substitutions. *Ménage à trois*, narrators and protagonists as doubles, and repetitions of the quest format can never be structurally dissected and tallied to create a "totalization," for as Derrida maintains, the play of language depends on repetition as well as chance and discontinuity.[55] Barth empties this doubles game of prior significance and forces the reader to see that the value of literature lies in its multitudinous signifying structures. The key to the treasure is the treasure.

In this short-story cycle, Barth demonstrates that all fiction, realistic and unrealistic, consists of supplementarity. Realistic tales and characters are replaced by unrealistic ones that are replaced by formal structures. The *bildungsroman* is the same as the *künstlerroman*. Self-conscious heroics yield easily to authorial self-consciousness.[56] As Barth's tale laments of its author: "I'm . . . [Dad's] bloody mirror!" "Which is to say, upon reflection I reverse and distort him" (p. 37). A form reflects a person; literature reflects history; and history reflects literature. Constant repetition and distortion of analogous situation, character, language, device, and motif raise fundamental questions about the impact and applicability of conventions that once purported to signify reality. Like funhouse mirrors, they reflect and reinforce each other and depend on one another for interpretation, for their part in the common myth, but they should not be accorded unquestioned credibility. Forms coerce only insofar as people grant them authority, and once a work such as *Lost in The Funhouse* shows the nature of the artifice through the process of supplementarity, it loses its authority.

Supplementarity and its entropic effects are central to "Echo," the retelling of the traditional double tale of Narcissus and Echo. Here blind old Tiresias, the seer, projects the future of Narcissus, but he has too many histories and biographies at his disposal to approach that of Narcissus freshly. In addition, his prophecy concerning Narcissus repeats the history of his own impotence. His story and those of Oedipus and other Greeks ultimately displace the particularity of Narcissus, so that Tiresias feels a sense of "saturation: telling the story over as though it were another's until like a much-repeated word it loses sense" (p. 98). With Tiresias at the center of prophecy, all prognostications sound the same, but they become empty of constant meaning, so that those who repeat his words actually change the signification. The problem of Tiresias's self-reflexive visions is similar to that of Narcissus, who looking in the pool can perceive only a reflection. His mistake lies in failing to perceive that he and the re-flected image are not one and that they are not entirely different. Though the likeness must be acknowledged, so must the difference; there is the unbridgeable gap.

The failure to perceive the gap, however, is the fundamental human dilemma, for the viewer cannot see beyond that reflection: "Like the masturbatory adolescent, sooner or later he finds himself. He beholds and salutes his pretty alter ego in the pool; in the pool his ego, altered, prettily salutes" (p. 102). This self-reflexive self-referen-tiality that each person necessarily embraces characterizes most of the protagonists of the book, who lose themselves in their reflections. They may consider themselves objective, but their observations mirror themselves: they are the true subjects of their discourse. Even the sperm of "Night-Sea Journey" announces, "No matter which theory of our journey is correct, it's myself I address" (p. 3). But which self does he address? The very splitting of the subject has become an issue of the double for poststructuralists and postmodernists.[57] When lost in the house of mirrors, Ambrose also finds that he can see only a certain part of the self: "In the funhouse mirror-room you can't see yourself go on forever, because no matter how you stand, your head gets in the way" (p. 85). He adds, "Even if you had a glass periscope, the image of your eye would cover up the thing you really wanted to see" (p. 85).

Willy-nilly, human beings are substantially self-reflexive, and there is no clear-cut distinction between subject and object or within the split subject, but it is important to try to distinguish the gap. Barth illustrates this dilemma in "Petition," the tale of a distraught narrator joined belly to back with his Siamese double. The narrator complains that because he is attached behind his brother, his brother refuses to acknowledge his existence: "My attempt to direct our partnership ended in my brother's denying first my efficacy, then my authority, finally my reality. He pretended to believe, offstage as well as on, that the audience's interest was in him as a solo performer and not in the pair of us as a freak" (pp. 64–65). The narrator's brother deconstructively denies that ideal forms underlie the signification process, refuses to grant authority to the sign-system, and finally claims only self-reflexive vision. The narrator himself is unable to see clearly and accurately. He is always forced to see his brother from the back, never from the front, and he remarks in his petition to "His Most Gracious Majesty Prajadhipok, Descendant of Buddha": "If my situation has any advantage it's only that I can see him without his seeing me; can therefore study and examine our bond, how ever to dissolve it, and take certain surreptitious measures to that end, such as writing this petition" (p. 63). His is quite literally what Jean Rouillon calls the relative voice of the *vision par derrière*, the "view from behind," by a first-person narrator who has limited understanding and historical perspective but nonetheless dominates the action and governs the interlocutory relationships.[58] Whether in fiction or in more realistic circumstances, seeing and telling are finite and superficial, basically restricted to a single plane or surface. The bawdy brother can only look ahead; the narrator can only see the back of that brother. Context restricts content, and signifier ultimately governs signified.

The repetition or doubling in Barth's stories reveals the impossibility of going past that reflection to see meaning and the necessity of having to be content with the signifiers. So long as the maturing characters, like Ambrose of "Water-Message," remain uninitiated, sincerely believing in the value of social forms, they have a measure of blissful ignorance, but once they begin to mature, they cannot readily be carried forward by consistent, unified, and totalizing rites of passage. While in "Lost in the Funhouse" Ambrose remains uninitiated, he accepts the prevailing social premise of a romantically perfect relationship in part based upon traditional dualism and in part upon Freud's. He romantically imagines that Magda loves him instead of his brother Peter and fantasizes about the loving attitude the two will adopt when married. Like any true hero, Ambrose will show himself calm, studied, devoted, protective, and magnanimous. Magda will in turn be caring, slightly submissive, deferential to his authority and wisdom, and devoted to their relationship. His vision of life is primarily a literary one, based upon Arthurian romances. As a sign, Ambrose is marked and supplemented by a literary system. He learns that an awareness of supplementarity is necessary to curb his youthful idealism and turn his new knowledge to advantage. Because he has been supplanted in his love relationship by another, because like the narrator of "Petition," who cannot achieve disjunction, he cannot *do* something, cannot love, Ambrose elects another alternative: "He will construct funhouses for others and be their secret operator—though he would rather be among the lovers for whom funhouses are designed" (p. 97). He will be the one to set in motion the process of supplementarity.

For Ambrose, it is the awareness of the gaps—elements of surplus, ballast, or indeterminacy—prevalent in language, fiction, or life that finally allows him a certain measure of freedom. Despite all the ways he is caught as a pawn in someone else's game—God's, his brother's, his author's—his manipulation of language gives him a measure of distance between himself and conventional cultural significations. His love of such terms as "initiation" and "breaking out in a cold sweat" (p. 52) makes him aware that reality has been rendered literary as much as literature has been rendered real, that words create an artificial construct in which experience may be located but in which, as in a mirror, that experience is distorted. Speaking candidly, Barth agrees with his character on this matter: "It is not speaking mystically to say that our dreams dream us; that our fictions construct us, at least as sub-contractors." We are, like Ambrose, "the man of metaphor," the poet who "plays on the multiplicity of signifieds."[59] As a poet, Ambrose stands aloof, feeling "an odd detachment, as though someone else were Master. Strive as he might to be transported, he heard his mind take notes upon the scene: *This is what they call* passion. *I am experiencing it*" (p. 84). He recognizes that he cannot confront his experiences and feelings directly because his culture (or his master, the author) has inscribed his character with certain linguistic and literary signs. And he becomes aware of the confusing and self-contradictory signification shifts. When as a young child Ambrose tries out the signifier "fact" in "facts of life," he gets a laugh. When he sees it in a magazine called *Facts About Your Diet* and tells his mother, she does not laugh, though he expects her to. Each context shifts, though the signifier itself seems constant. Language is unstable, and as the narrator resignedly notes in "Title," a tale about the process of constructing fiction, the signifiers that we use to convey experiences, feelings, and attitudes are, after all, really rules, forms, grammatical apparatuses: "In this dehuman, exhausted, ultimate adjective hour, . . . every humane value has become untenable, and not only love, decency, and beauty but even compassion and intelligibility are no more than one or two subjective complements to complete the sentence" (p. 107).

The sperm of "Night-Sea Journey" ("*Love* is how we call our ignorance of what whips us" [p. 5]) and Menelaus of the "Menelaiad" find just such difficulty with the problems of signification when they try to apprehend the word *love*. In fact, Menelaus indirectly causes the Trojan wars because he questions too long the signification of Helen's statement that she chooses him for love. He cannot fathom what Helen means by a term that has been rendered virtually meaningless by the successive layers of culture. He goes to the far ends of the earth trying to find the answer to the question, in the process wrestling Proteus to the ground. Says Proteus: "Beg Love's pardon for your want of faith. Helen chose you without reason because she loves you without cause; embrace her without question and watch your weather change" (p. 161). Proteus's answer implies that cultural conventions and history are too deeply embedded in the term *love* for it ever to signify anything distinctly personal. In fact, the layers of history in "The Menelaiad" indicated by the layers of dialogue and italics cannot be rationally fathomed, separated, or understood. They form a centerless maze that Menelaus and the readers never meaningfully negotiate. Finally, Menelaus has little choice but to sit quietly by Helen's side in his dotage, accepting only the signifiers themselves—Helen and *love*—the apparent truth of her dedication and even her excuse that she never eloped with Paris. He must accept her view that she was spirited away to Pharos and that her double, "Cloud-Helen," served to trick Paris. Menelaus finds that language may obscure rather than disclose and that it reflects only his consciousness and knowledge, not any kind of objective reality lying pure and untainted outside himself.

As much as Menelaus and Ambrose try to avoid the shifting "faded distorting mirrors" of sign mirroring sign, they are restricted to this culturally generated condition. As the older, wiser narrator-

Ambrose notes of the youthful initiate-Ambrose: "Stepping from the treacherous passage at last into the mirror-maze, he saw once again, more clearly than ever, how readily he deceived himself into supposing he was a person. . . . It's not believable that so young a boy could articulate that reflection, and in fiction the merely true must always yield to the plausible" (p. 93). The plausible is dependent upon the culture, and mere fact gives way to conventionally attuned utterances and interpretations.

Because the conventionally plausible replaces the "merely true," one recognizes too late the absurd and often capricious relationships and situations that exist outside the self-reflexive frame. To illustrate this point, Barth includes "Two Meditations," double paragraphs on the difficulty of seeing and beyond that the impossibility of acting in a coherent, rational, or "natural" way. The first of these paragraphs is unintelligible babble, pure signifier, but the second perhaps serves as its signification, suggesting that only after a sign has been made, a deed done, a fault created, can signification be attributed: "The wisdom to recognize and halt follows the know-how to pollute past rescue. The treaty's signed, but the cancer ticks in your bones. Until I'd murdered my father and fornicated my mother I wasn't wise enough to see I was Oedipus" (p. 104). Sight, insight, or signification is only *a* perception of culture and language after the catastrophic fact.

Despite the barriers, splits, and gaps that self-reflexiveness creates in self, language, and culture, Ambrose's solution is, after all, the only one: "The only way to get out of a mirror-maze is to close your eyes and hold out your hands. And be carried away by a valiant metaphor, I suppose, like a simile" (p. 111). The linguistic imagination, valiant metaphor and simile, is always at work, operating on experience, collecting, organizing, dissecting, and, most important, spinning new worlds out of old signifiers. With finite insight and knowledge and self-limiting cultural and linguistic rules, we can use the old forms, retrace their perameters, turn them upside down, let them mirror their own reflections. Solipsism and narcissism are identified in current theory and practice with the power of the artistic imagination to generate literary fabrications and constructs. Limited though the artist's sight may be, it can create wonderful pictures and joyful entertainments.[60]

This pursuit of the artistic is most fully illustrated in "Echo," a story that analyzes the limitations and possibilities of art. A character who like Ambrose is refused love, Echo turns life into art: "Afflicted with immortality she turns from life and learns to tell stories with such art that the Olympians implore her to repeat them. Others live for the lie of love; Echo lives for her lovely lies, loves for their livening" (p. 100). As with all members of a culture, the words, the linguistic rules, are not hers alone but come from an anterior source or voice. This source is the voice of the Father, the law, which is the formulated code that the child mimics and distorts.[61] It is the grounding or myth that fiction uses and that the artist Echo "edits, heightens, mutes, [as she] turns others' words to her end" (p. 100), effacing "herself until she becomes no more than her voice" (p. 101). She reflects the signs of her culture, provides a focus for them, and becomes their double, their clouded reflecting pool. Even as she is the shadow of others' voices, so culture is her shadow, for as Roland Barthes maintains, a literary text (and author) bears the cultural double or shadow: "There are those who want a text (an art, a painting) without a shadow, without the 'dominant ideology'; but this is to want a text without fecundity, without productivity, a sterile text (see the myth of the Woman without a Shadow). The text needs its shadow: this shadow is *a bit* of ideology, *a bit* of representation, *a bit* of subject: ghosts, pockets, traces, necessary clouds: subversion must produce its own chiaroscuro."[62] In this respect, it is hard to "tell teller from told. Narcissus would appear to be opposite from Echo: he perishes by denying all except himself; she persists by effacing herself absolutely. Yet they come to the same: it was never himself Narcissus craved, but his reflection, the Echo of his fancy; his death must be partial as his self-knowledge, the voice persists, persists" (pp. 102–3). Echo's voice is not original (no voice of the culture ever is), but it can transform. Shackled by the cultural views and expressions that she tries to expose and escape, she continues the process of narration, giving it an appropriate shape or form, changing the shape of the signifiers, editing out some ideology and distorting the signification:

> I can't go on.
> Go on.
> Is there anyone to hear here?
> Who are you?
> You.
> I?

Aye.
Then let me see me!
See?
A lass! Alas. (P. 101)

The artist distorts and by the doubling of signs (A lass! Alas) alters the original form, plan, paradigm, myth, or game. Repetition, alteration, and distortion create gaps and lead to different angles of vision and successive voices that induce provocative supplementations. The echo's "dual character of repetition and displacement"—their supplementations—reflect the linguistic tendency of signs to stretch "out infinitely and indefinitely, all in the same plane, without any priority being attributed to a particular one." This process, characteristic of aesthetic fiction that participates in myth, exposes it, and escapes it, insists on simultaneous presence and absence of meaning.[63]

Barth's paradigm for artistic supplementarity, the desire for symbolic renewal, and a warning against static signification is effectively handled in "Petition," the most obvious treatment of the doubles in the book, and the most self-reflexive and parodic. As noted above, the cerebral narrator permanently fastened to his satyric brother launches an effete and pedantic petition for medical disjunction. Although he believes that the two could have worked in tandem and harmony like the Carolina woodsmen cutting logs, employing the technique called the "double chop" (p. 60), the narrator's double will have none of that, and their differences become insurmountable:

> We are nothing alike. I am slight, my brother is gross. He's incoherent but vocal; I'm articulate and mute. He's ignorant but full of guile; I . . . [am] reasonably educated. . . . My brother is gregarious: he deals with the public; earns and spends our income; tends (but slovenly) the house and grounds; makes, entertains, and loses friends; indulges in hobbies; pursues ambitions and women. For my part, I am by nature withdrawn, even solitary: an observer of life, a meditator, a taker of notes, a dreamer if you will . . . stoical, detached. (P. 62)

He continues in this vein, personifying himself as a disembodied Apollonian *écrivant* writing his letter to change reality and his brother as a Dionysiacal *parleur* whose language is all vulgar play. They are the narrator and narrated but also to a degree the allegorical embodiment of writing and speech, with writing regarding speech as its inferior shadow and speech maintaining the opposite. But as Derrida affirms, the dichotomy between speech and writing is utterly false, for "oral language already belongs to this writing."[64]

Narrator and brother, writing and speech—their differences must be recognized but their sundering deferred indefinitely. This petition to Prajadhipok should not succeed, for no single justifying significance exists. Corresponding or isomorphic signs and structures cannot be interpreted in identical ways. The metaphor of the double delivers this point forcefully, for its signification has been supplemented throughout the ages, dependent upon the prevailing cultural myth. Where the code of Christianity is operative, the irreconcilable opposites allegorize that old vexing question of dualism, the debate concerning the relative importance of the body and soul in which one cannot be detached from the other but both ought to work in harmony for their mutual welfare. In this case, the narrator wrongly pleads for a radical separation, and his brother wrongly emphasizes the flesh over spirit. Within a Neoplatonic or Manichean context, the narrator's complaints are valid; within such a context it would be appropriate for the king to grant his request for separation. The twin's grossness can only hinder the narrator's spiritual development.

Following the modus operandi of the Freudian discourse, however, neither of the twins has the right to seek a disjuncture or to deny the claims of his double, for the id and superego are both legitimate, natural parts of the personality. One or the other may have to be trimmed or developed further, but they are mutually dependent. Similarly, if the arguments in the letter are to be judged against the standard of the Buddhism of Prajadhipok, the narrator is again guilty of a sort of monomania. Seen from the Buddhist perspective, the problem of the narrator is baseless because all things in life are necessarily one. Taken together, these views imply the floating quality of the signifying process: signified replaces signified just as sign replaces sign. The question of sign is further complicated when the narrator mentions that Thalia, the woman whom both brothers love after their fashion, has a double too, "a Thalia *within* a Thalia, like the dolls-within-dolls" (p. 70). Insofar as Thalia is traditionally the muse of comedy, the doubled Thalia is doubly comic. This parodic double of the male Siamese twins serves as a clever metaphor of our ultimate inability to see, understand, or interpret reality. Everything seems outrageous, bizarre, and fantastic, and no one set of discursive practices or system of signifieds—Christian, Neoplatonist, Freudian, Buddhist—can satisfactorily resolve the dilemma. The petitioner can only be known by his letter, his written sign. He is folded within his own text, the writerly shadow of his brother-master-author. And his relationship to the reader or listener is no more definite.

This subject-object, me-other, body-soul dilemma that the narrator invokes is the dualistic opposition which an assessment of the structurality of structures undoes. Such an assessment allows the reader to reject the complacency of what Jake in *End of the Road* calls "the Janusian ambivalence of the universe, . . . the world's charming equipoise, its ubiquitous polarity."[65] The "external line of cleavage" disappears, collapsing distinctions between signifier and signified, significance and meaninglessness, spiritual and material phenomena, superstructure and infrastructure, culture and nature, meaning and raw material.[66] Barth's fiction is ultimately a poststructuralist allegory asking for a fuller recognition of the basis for and process of the signifying system.

Barth's works abound with structural, autoreferential, and self-reflexive doubles. They present the gaps between fact and language and fact and "reality," demonstrate the diachronic variations in the signification system, and show that literary signs have affected other sign systems. For Barth, culture has become the double of literature just as literature has become the double of culture. They echo and reflect each other but are not the same. As a result, when Barth designifies the double in his fiction, when he indicates that it is only a self-referential literary device, he is also designifying society and history. His "double postulation" employs the traditional signs of culture and literature to explore their inherent gaps and infinite supplementations.

Minimalism, Metadoubles, and Narcissism
Brautigan's Hawkline Monster

6

IN OTHER HANDS THE SIMULTANEOUS USE AND DISPLACEMENT OF SIGNS that is John Barth's embodiment of Derrida's notion of the freeplay of signification could result in the reader's disorientation because of the artist's failure to distinguish between the origin and end of the narrative, teller and tale, writer and reader, text and reality, or myth and mimesis. Such an exploration of the labyrinthine issues involving life and text might easily prove confusing, especially given the typically elaborate structure and daunting length of Barth's works, but happily Barth's deft writing rarely leaves his reader in the lurch. His narrative control, like that of Nabokov, Pynchon, and Hawkes, is unerring, and his amused tolerance of human folly makes his fiction accessible to a surprisingly wide readership. Perhaps because he sees so little distinction between the techniques and themes of modernism and those of postmodernism or for that matter between art and life, his writing has an astonishingly appealing richness of texture.

Richard Brautigan raises similar questions about traditional views of art and the relationship of art to life, but his style, though equally intriguing, is neither rich nor evocative. He destabilizes the reader's conceptions of art by means of irreal journalism. His sentences are short, and his words are those of the morning paper, but the context defamiliarizes the known and accepted. This defamiliarization does not have its roots (unlike Barth's) in the expansive eighteenth-century novel or (unlike Pynchon's) in the nineteenth-century American epic or (unlike Nabokov's and Hawkes's) in the grotesque. It is

151

grounded primarily in modernistic minimalism. Nabokov, Pynchon, Hawkes, and Barth all have at one time or another been called modernists, but not one of them has been affected with the minimalist spirit in quite the same way or to the same degree as Brautigan. His mentor is not James Joyce; his precursor is Gertrude Stein. Like her, he is brief, elliptical, unconventional, and disconcerting. But if Brautigan's technique is that of modernist minimalism, his play of signification is inherited from Friedrich Nietzsche and Martin Heidegger. It is designed to short-circuit a system, to oppose and unsettle, but never to reinstate. Brautigan's doubling cancels the basic rules governing literary games and reduces the play to zero. His is anarchic play, which denies the value of the signified and affirms only the play of the signifier.

Unlike John Barth, Richard Brautigan left no record of his views on poetics or his place within artistic movements, but Marc Chénetier asserts that he is "oddly placed . . . on the margins of 'metafiction' and 'post-modernism' (margins being where Brautigan likes to be)."[1] John Barth also considers the flat, irreal, prosaic quality of Brautigan's fiction, the "radical manipulations of narrative viewpoint, dramatic form, or format," postmodern.[2] Brian McHale views him as typically postmodern in his anti-illustration and parody that "foreground the ontological opposition between the fictional world and the material book."[3] This aspect of postmodernism, evident in all his works, reflects the circulation of signs and the play of signifying references that, "strictly speaking, amounts to destroying the concept of 'sign' and its entire logic."[4] To designify the "concept of sign" is to dismantle traditional patterns and systems of writing, to refuse to set seriousness above frivolity.

Brautigan effectively destroys the concept of sign by playfully distancing the reader from the text and debunking literary and cultural myths, not the least of them the double. The designifying of "historical icons and discursive monuments" is "an assault on all fixed representational forms, from myths and codes to moral messages and ideological assertions."[5] His works provide an especially good illustration of "parody as repetition with critical distance that allows ironic signalling of difference at the very heart of similarity."[6] Rather than enforcing similarity, Brautigan's iconoclastic books play with language and disrupt conventional meaning, value, and significance. They self-consciously acknowledge their parodic nature and do not try to make readers identify with or sympathize with traditional values in literature or life. Previously straightforward values can, with a "double-voiced," parodistic quality,[7] playfully serve new aims, among them the celebration of fiction itself and a new regard for narcissism. Brautigan's works are playful and still intellectually pleasurable, undermining conventional literary, social, political, and religious ideologies. They provide pleasure in pointing out breaks and aporias in life and art and collapsing the boundaries between antipathetic codes.[8] They simultaneously query our perception of the real world and textual activity itself.[9]

Given this ambitious purpose, Brautigan's books have sometimes frustrated critics who object to their "littleness," for these small books appear to trivialize culturally sanctified ideas. The extreme brevity dispenses with social realism, psychological complexity, and dramatic climaxes, instead emphasizing the values of the quixotic and capricious imagination. When *The Hawkline Monster* first appeared, critics, almost to a person, labeled it trivial and cute, a view recently reiterated: "We have learned to expect so much from Brautigan," Edward Halsey Foster says, "that we are not liable to be satisfied with yet another silly innocent, forever tripping over his own shoelaces."[10] While this criticism has some validity, it unduly values the serious over the comic and fails to give sufficient credit to the artistic underpinnings of the work's intellectual foundation and its presentation of narcissism through the device of the double.

Generally underestimated and largely ignored, *The Hawkline Monster* has special value when understood as minimalist and postmodern. Terence Malley, one of the few early critics to discern that Brautigan was not attempting conventional writing, acknowledges that "Brautigan seems fairly close to John Lennon's view that art is all a con-game anyway and that anyone who looks into a song or a poem or a painting is making a fool of himself."[11] Brautigan has indicated that he is not interested in such conventions of realistic fiction as "character delineation,"[12] though he would not dismiss all meaning. To some, minimalist postmodern works are boring or foolishly ahistorical in their rejection of historical meaning, significance, referentiality, and large-scale, symphonic complexity in favor of the microtonal clarity of the self-referentially minimal.[13]

Whatever the artistic medium—the fiction of Robbe-Grillet, films of Jean-Marie Straub, paintings by Frank Stella, the sculpture of Sol

Lewitt, or the music of John Cage—minimalist postmodern works are often characterized as antilinear, uneventful, flat, deliberately trivial. They emphasize direct, unadulterated experience in art minus symbolic meaning.[14] With its origins in fantastic folktales and antimimetic fiction, the device of the double is especially pertinent to this reductiveness. Brautigan's simplicity and diminishment of narrative form and the doubles tradition are in keeping with purposeful minimalist endeavor and achievement, and his related affirmation of narcissism cuts against the grain of acceptable communal values. His self-conscious attention to formalistic elements, especially metaphor, the flattening of character, and the repetition of the double on various levels "are driven by an obsessive interrogation of the fossilization and fixture of language, and by a counter-desire to free it from stultification and paralysis."[15]

This rejection of those literary conventions that provide the basis for realism is part of a broad reassessment of artistic form, ranging from the role of artist to that of the reader and the conception of form itself. Postmodernism deemphasizes the artist's role and stresses the performance itself, the reader or user taking on important new responsibilities as the creator of textual meaning. This technique discourages authorial determination and encourages active reader participation. The reader is asked to enter into the performance and imagine other textual possibilities. Brautigan's opinions on this matter are fairly clear from his fiction. His narrators are gentle, passive, bemused at the absurdities and indeterminacies of the world. His fiction is full of warnings about the danger of too much control and ego involvement in the artistic process. And the flatness of his fiction prompts the reader to flesh it out imaginatively and give it meaning. *In Watermelon Sugar* denounces the sense of will and power that underlies the overdeveloped and misused ego, whether in artistic creation or elsewhere in life.[16] This is certainly the dilemma of the mad scientist in *The Hawkline Monster*, who tries to exercise too much control in creating his own doubles.

The scrupulous avoidance of excessive control is noticeable also in the structuring or "space" of Brautigan's fiction. *Trout Fishing in America* is a particularly good example, for Brautigan fully deconstructs linear movement in it and presents instead a collage of incidents that create a vision or mood of potentiality and disenchantment. The disruption of space is perfectly in keeping with the distortion of the pastoral ideal. Even the flooded landscape at the end of *The Hawkline Monster* rethinks space and light, especially abandoned artificial landscapes.[17] The newly created lake, which has become an art object in its own isolated space, makes the reader aware of the fluidity of all forms.

The rethinking of space in minimalist postmodernism is frequently accompanied by a reconsideration of light and movement. Distorted light in art destroys typical conceptions of linear time and enclosed space, forcing the spectator to "abandon the closed, definitive, static state of older attitudes."[18] Moving water and light, "whatever shifts, sparkles, glows, illuminates and radiates," have a special relationship with the forces of life in Brautigan's fiction and are opposed to the static, immobile, and petrified in culture and writing.[19] The play of the double in *The Hawkline Monster* illustrates this reevaluation of the role of light, for the monster itself is a mischievous pool of light and his double a beneficent shadow. In depicting the monster and his conscience in this way, Brautigan reverses the typical conception of light and darkness as equivalent to good and evil. By inverting the analogy, Brautigan empties it of any inherent value, designifies all such culturally coded relationships, and opens the door for a reconsideration of such cultural taboos as narcissism.

Minimalist postmodern techniques have important implications in deconstructing "bourgeois perceptual ideology" and breaking down "conceptual order into visual chaos";[20] they undermine conventions of artistic perception to underscore the limitations of individual perception and the falsity of an artistic process based upon liberal humanism. Minimalist postmodernism, art that is specifically about art, attacks the foundations of liberal humanism, psychology, and history. As Robbe-Grillet comments, it turns the world around us "back into a smooth surface, without signification, without soul, without values [in which] . . . we find ourselves once again facing *things*."[21] Such postmodern art opposes the traditional "realistic" and dramatic narrative patterns in which "dualism plays a large part: high/low, rise/fall, fast/slow, climax/stasis, important/unimportant, . . . sound/silence, colourful/monochrome."[22] Characterized by "strangeness and mystery and otherness," it levels out traditional emphases so that antithetical modes such as tragic and comic are indistinguishable; this in turn inevitably affects the conclusions of narratives, for no ending is preferable to any other. Brautigan's *A Confederate General from Big Sur* presents five alternative endings but suggests that others can be generated at 186,000 per second. This nonclosure and indeterminacy are inherently related to new kinds of perception. As John Clayton observes of *Trout Fishing in America*, discontinuity, evident in metaphorical transformations and illogical connections, is not only part of the magic of the book but indicates Brautigan's lack of interest in character, psychological insight, interpersonal dynamics, materiality, time, and causality.[23]

Pleasurable mockery is especially typical of *The Hawkline Monster*'s playful deconstruction of fiction and "reality." Brautigan compares the exploded Hawkline house and ice caves and subsequently formed lake with a scene from a surrealist painting by Hieronymous Bosch. This reference, coupled with similar disjunctive, surrealist images such as Miss Hawkline's standing in front of the formal Victorian house in frontier Oregon with her coat flowing like a waterfall and her patent leather shoes sparkling like the adjacent coal pile, stamps this work's comic affinity with a demythologized view of reality. Brautigan uses these metaphors to call attention to their fabricated nature. His "rupture of narrative itself with a display of self-conscious metaphors . . . sunder[s] the elements of story in favor of virtuosity on the page"[24] and establishes the view that metaphors are not "natural" highly suggestive, idealized relationships but products of a writer's fancy that grow out of cultural semantics. Strange juxtapositions and metaphorical comparisons raise questions about the perception of what is normal and real, an appropriate response for fiction about the double, but traditional perceptions of the double are also raised by Brautigan.

At issue in the transvaluation of perception is not only the leveling out of modes and values but also "the inversion of the personal and the public. What was once private (nudity, sex) is now public, and what was once the public face of art at least (emotions, opinions, intentions) is now private."[25] Thought by some to be sexually offensive, *The Hawkline Monster* is neither especially erotic nor pornographic; sex is treated as a routine part of the characters' lives, and the decorous eastern-educated Victorian ladies are certainly as libidinous as the men. Sex is a comic ritual, part of everyday life, but Brautigan's use of it helps to overturn conventional perceptions of sexuality in fiction.

Minimalist postmodernism also insists that narcissism, usually portrayed negatively, can be positive, especially given the fact that humans perceive themselves only within the prison of language. In his essay "Serial Art, Systems, Solipsism," Mel Bochner forges this link between perception and solipsism. For him minimalist art exists because "viewed within the boundaries of thought, the random dimensions of reality lose their qualities of extension. They become flat and static. Serial art in its highly abstract and ordered manipulation of thought is likewise self-contained and nonreferential."[26] This emphasis on perception and solipsism is by all odds the most important element in any approach to Brautigan, for central to his minimalist text is his emphasis on narcissism.

In *The Hawkline Monster*, the double becomes a metadouble, one that self-reflexively uses the conventions of the double to parody dualistic assumptions and pose new views. Brautigan's metadouble calls attention to its literariness and disputes the negativism implicit in the Freudian link between narcissism and the double. This book has so many pairs of doubles that they multiply in every direction, doubling for the sake of doubling, calling attention mainly to themselves rather than to any exterior frame of reference. The book has two towns, Brooks and Billy, the respective locations of twin groups, the sheepmen and the cattlemen. The man hanging from the bridge is probably the twin of a man with whom Cameron got drunk. The giant living butler is magically transformed into a dead dwarf. The professor for most of the story exists only as an elephant-foot umbrella stand, though we come to know about his other doubles, his scientific experiments. The twin cowboys, Cameron and Greer, are the heroes of the book. The two indistinguishable Hawkline sisters, Susan and Jane, have another double, Magic Child. The hard-hearted monster of light has a good-hearted shadow of darkness. Finally, the monster and shadow are transformed into a handful of diamonds and their shadows. Brautigan provides an endless procession of characters doubling and redoubling; he even provides a series of romance subgenres (the gothic, the Western, science fiction, fantasy) that transform rapidly from one to another and in the end lapse into realism—a doubling of forms of fiction. Even the title of the book, *The Hawkline Monster: A Gothic Western*, points the readers in a double direction—to the monster itself and to a self-divided narrative structure.[27] This proliferation effectively reduces the significance of the double to zero, a decidedly entropic state.

This process of doubling leads to a destabilized philosophical view of literature or life. It is in short a parody of previous doubles without any conventionally reforming purpose in mind, "the grotesque without the vision of a perfection of form, irrationality without the possibility of reason, bad taste without the possibility of good taste."[28] The transformations entertain without acquiring socially acceptable value. Miss Hawkline is not more psychologically whole after her double, Magic Child, fading out and "dying," allows the "real" person to emerge. The heroes and heroines are not better for destroying the luminous monster. The book is not more interesting or fruitful for the metonymical displacement of genres. Nor does the return from the fantastic ice caves to the "real" world signal normalization for the characters; if anything, the real world is more deadly than that of the Hawkline monster. As the author piles double on double, the reader's pleasure increases with an awareness of the self-conscious process of doubling, the clever uses of language, and a recognition of the intertextual references to such gothic texts as "William Wilson," *Dr. Jekyll and Mr. Hyde*, and *Frankenstein*, and the undermining of normatives.

Enjoyable in themselves, the minimalist doubles also comment on a traditional signification—narcissism—but as in Barth, with a twist or distortion. In fact, narcissism in this text has a double signification, partly negative but mainly positive. The most obvious, prevalent, and traditionally negative use of the doubles with relation to narcissism in *The Hawkline Monster* concerns the way the monster tries to twist all reality to conform to its pleasure, and the positive aspect relates to the self-centered nature of human perception and the self-referentiality of the artistic process.

The Hawkline monster, deliciously malevolent, is unconcerned about general social good and is intent upon altering the world to conform to its own ideas. Capable of extraordinary mental and physical feats, it can suspend a piece of pie in the air, cover the furniture with green feathers, metamorphose the professor into an elephant-foot umbrella stand, transform the giant butler into a dead dwarf, and change one of the Hawkline sisters into an Indian maiden, a truly malicious act in a turn-of-the century white Western society. It also bends the minds of the heroines, so that they are unable to think properly or come to terms with their monster-guest. The monster's ultimate objective is to transform the Hawkline sisters and the gunmen heroes into auxiliary shadows of libidinous, unrepressed, antisocial behavior. Here, paradoxically, is a narcissistic monster of light whose main quality is bound-less energy and power of transformation, with no social or moral con-science and no hesitation about altering, maiming, or killing. Its activity, however, seems harmlessly buffoonish in view of all the killing that goes on in "real" life. Its "motion, magic, life" is opposed to "whatever does not move any longer—whatever is consumed, past, over, set for all time . . . the monumental and the eternally fixed."[29] Its anarchism and constant energy are a source of delight.

In effect, the presentation of this monster parodies the monstrous protagonists of Poe's "William Wilson" and Wilde's *The Picture of Dorian Gray*, who are so bent and warped that an identical counterpart emerges to serve as foil, conscience, and avenger. This monster of "dark invention"[30] is plagued with a "shadow companion," a con-science whose aims are dedicated to moral absolutes and the reestab-lishment of the past: "The shadow was a buffoon mutation totally subservient to the light and quite unhappy in its role and often liked to remember back to the days when harmony reigned in The Chemi-cals and Professor Hawkline was there, singing popular songs of the day" (p. 129). This shadow, functioning as a superego, bitterly resents having to serve as an accomplice in the monster's missions of terror. But follow along it must. When the monster lights on a spoon, the shadow must light on the gravy; when the monster lights on the flame of the fire, the shadow rests on the log. What the light does, the shadow must reflect.

Still, as the gothic genre traditionally dictates, the shadow is not a mere reflection, for it has unique feelings and a moral code, a code that when increasingly violated finally thwarts the monster's worst intentions. Sentimental and wracked with nostalgia, the shadow at-tempts to put a stop to the light's energy. From the playful monster's point of view, this shadow is an annoying, retrogressive nuisance. From the moral shadow's point of view, the monster is an evil that must be deflected. In fact, it would like to kill the evil monster and function independently for social good, not realizing initially that to destroy its host is surely to destroy itself.

That the shadow is governed by affection for the Hawkline sisters is also part of the gothic discourse. It loves to twine itself around their necks and move through their hair, and it is surprisingly protective of them. In this way it bears intertextual "traces" of nineteenth-century gothic fiction. Some doubles, for example, Hans Christian Andersen's

"The Shadow," plot to steal the affections of women, deviously plan character assassinations, and finally manage real assassinations. In those instances the shadows become pursuers, overreachers, and usurpers; in Brautigan the shadow simply loves the sisters and nostalgically wills to return life to its predictable, stable—and dull—routine. When Cameron and Greer, the hired monster killers, are about to do battle with the monster, the shadow reverses its normal position, stepping into the path and blocking the monster's vision, thereby assuring the heroes their victory. This is a case of conscience, turning both monster and shadow into a handful of sparkling diamonds and shadows, doubles of doubles, but at least the sentimental shadow's "soul was at rest" (p. 204). Brautigan's monster-shadow combination precisely conforms to the stereotypical narcissist-double pattern, as Otto Rank's formulation of the characteristics and devices of the double demonstrates: "We always find a likeness which resembles the main character down to the smallest particulars, such as name, voice, and clothing—a likeness which, as though 'stolen from the mirror' (Hoffmann), primarily appears to the main character as a reflection. Always, too, this double works at cross-purposes with its prototype; and, as a rule, the catastrophe occurs in the relationship with a woman, predominantly ending in suicide by way of the death intended for the irksome persecutor."[31]

In doggedly adhering to the formula, Brautigan mocks motifs grounded in the dualistic psychology of Freud and Jung. For both Freud and Jung the monster is the id, abandoning social or moral responsibility and acting irresponsibly, while the shadow is the superego, attempting to bring the host back into the proper sphere of social responsibility, trying to compensate for the monster's deficiencies. Insofar as the monster pursues its own vision at the expense of others, perpetuating this carnival nonsense, it represents negative narcissism in Freudian terms. But in Brautigan's use, this light-hearted, energetic narcissism is "good." Only when its potential for creative transformation is diminished by its desperate attempt to turn the heroines and heroes into "A Harem of Shadows" (p. 192) and control other forms of energy too closely does its own creative narcissism become crippling and stultifying. It is this kind of narcissistic solitude, "man's folding in on himself so much that he is unable to act decisively,"[32] that is criticized here.

The tendency to immobility and fixity may well have another

form. "Chemicals" almost certainly refers to the drug culture. Here the implications may be equally problematic. What may begin beautifully and innocently, inducing beatific feelings and assurances of utopian harmony, can become corrosive and self-destructive. Visions of imagination and fancy can become nightmarish, leading to serious disturbances (the mind bending of the Hawkline sisters), schizophrenia (the monster and his twin), catatonia (Professor Hawkline's becoming frozen as an elephant foot), and suicide (the shadow simultaneously killing the monster and himself). Using this means, Brautigan possibly hints that drugs lead to a solipsistic narcissism of a destructive sort, reducing rather than releasing creative energy.

The codified minimal use of twinship in the story follows a pattern similar to that of the chemicals and with similar emphasis on the twin aspects of narcissism—the negativeness of the static imagination and positiveness of boundless energy. The twins, perhaps the oldest form of double in folklore, are the Hawkline sisters and Cameron and Greer the main heroes of the tale. Brautigan treats these two sets of twins as minimalist stereotypical, one-dimensional figures, lacking psychological or sociological reality but fulfilling the criterion for the well-established tradition of mirror doubles. Traditional twins were said to have some spiritual affinity, and a "special genre of the manifest double is the mirror image, the projected self being not merely a similar self but an exact duplicate."[33] In fact, the words *umbra* and *imago*, used for shadow (or double) and reflection (or mirror image), were at one time interchangeable, suggesting the very old linkage between the shadow, the soul, and mirror images.[34]

The Hawkline sisters are exact mirror images, genuine look-alike and act-alike twins who move gracefully like "two birds gliding slowly on the wind" (p. 140). The rhetoric describing their reactions to events and circumstances indicates clearly that they shadow each other precisely, as do the monster and its double. In fact, playfully and self-reflexively, the rhetoric shadows itself, suggesting that the double is after all only a play of language. When the butler is suddenly struck down by the monster, their reactions are unquestionably shadowlike: "Miss Hawkline ran down the hall toward him. The other Miss Hawkline followed like a shadow in her footsteps. They crouched on their knees over the giant butler" (pp. 115–16). Both young and beautiful, they wear identical dresses and jewelry, even identical pearl necklaces in which the monster and shadow like to wander. And both show a "state of amused shock" when told by Cameron and Greer that the monster had been lighting on the necklaces. They share similar thoughts, voice similar concerns, smile in unison, and even seduce the heroes at precisely the same inappropriate moments. So completely and capriciously are they doubled by the monster that one is further transformed into Magic Child, the dusky shadow of the other Miss Hawkline, whose actions, even when journeying to Portland, many miles from Billy, Oregon, are still controlled by the monster. The citizens of Billy have taken this transformation in stride, though as with Cameron and Greer, they find Magic Child's and Miss Hawkline's identical looks a bit unnerving. Similarly, after the initial shock, Cameron and Greer accept as necessary the "death" of Magic Child and her reversion to the second Miss Hawkline.

Continuously identical, the two Miss Hawklines are only at the end of the book slightly individualized. When Cameron and Greer suggest that the Chemicals must be destroyed, the sisters have conflicting reactions. One agrees that they should be destroyed, but the other hesitates because she honors her father's memory and scientific enterprise. Once the Chemicals are destroyed and the monster's naming curse is removed, the sisters are individually identified as Jane and Susan, not really unique names and hardly indicative of strikingly separate personalities. Ultimately they choose different ways of life, though both are killed in similarly bizarre ways. The "real" world has its own way of doubling them in death. In depicting them, Brautigan seems to have something slightly different from the narcissism of the monster-shadow in mind, something integrally tied to the function of Cameron and Greer.

Cameron and Greer, the second set of mirror image twins, are depicted as nearly identical, though they are somewhat individualized by their dissimilar names. Both are sentimental and aggressive. Both go whoring in the same room in Portland. Both lament the passing of the Indian maiden, Magic Child, and both equally and quickly accept the existence of the new, emergent Miss Hawkline. Although of different height and stature, they are said to be indistinguishable. And finally both go in quest of the monster. Their situation is a parody of the view that "twins could only carry out their heroic deeds together, because it was precisely the magic significance of their twinship which assure[d] . . . them invincibility."[35]

The two are differentiated only enough to suggest that what one lacks the other has. In their close friendship, tantamount to twinship, they parody Jean Paul's "pairs of friends (in the original sense of 'fellows, two of a pair'), who together form a unit, but individually appear as a 'half', dependent on the *alter ego*."[36] For instance, although Greer often fails to notice recurrent patterns, Cameron does, counting everything at all times. The counting may suggest a higher intelligence and level of activity, for he notices the monster more quickly than does Greer and he pours the whiskey into the Chemicals to vanquish the monster and redeem the household. (Certainly he knows that whiskey and Chemicals [drugs] do not mix.) Then, too, after returning to the "real world," Cameron alone of the twins, male or female, survives and succeeds in producing movies. But more likely his counting means nothing, an empty signified for a neutral sign. In fact, his wife leaves her counting husband for a count when she divorces him and marries a Russian nobleman. This metonymous displacement reduces the signifiers of counting and count to absurdity.

Brautigan has still another way of doubling these heroes and heroines, for the four of them are in certain respects mirror reflections, the same image but reversed. While the two Miss Hawklines have no first names, Cameron and Greer have no last names. While the educated women come from the East, the uneducated men come from the West. Although they obviously differ in gender, their physical and verbal reactions to each other, to their sexuality, and the outside world are much alike, for the women are as sexually aggressive as the men and manage their four-letter vocabulary with the same panache. Their mirror likeness is even noted in the chapter "Mirror Conversations," in which in one bedroom one of the Misses Hawkline speaks to Greer exactly the same way that Cameron in the other bedroom speaks to the other Miss Hawkline. Female and male replicate each other, and language reproduces itself in apparently endless self-reflexive–reflective combinations. "In a world in which duplication, reflection, reproduction and resemblance are the generic norm," Chénetier argues, "the characters are stricken with closure through repetition, and they cannot avoid progressing in circles, misunderstanding everything or taking one word for another, repeating sentences already uttered."[37] Discourse reflects discourse, unsettling the doppelgänger tradition.

These doubles are a parody of twins such as Romulus and Remus, who were at one time "tabued and venerated, feared and worshipped"[38] as founders of civilizations and tamers of wild animals. Yet these twins are fictionally compelling, for as has been said of Jean Paul's fiction, they "add to the complications of the plot. But this heightens the unreality of his novels, and makes it seem as if his personages have been provided with duplicates, or 'spares' in case of accident."[39] This playfulness of Brautigan may be attributed to contemporary amorality: "The modern novelist, although conscious of using the Double motif technically, does not place a moral judgment upon the irrational; or, at least, he reveals a tension between his sympathy for amoral freedom and his judgment of the fictional creatures he has given life."[40] But it can just as easily be seen as the mark of minimalist postmodernism, a simple decoding of traditional signification and affirmation of narcissistic energy.

Yet the Hawkline twins and Cameron and Greer do exemplify a vision of traditional "projected wish-fulfillment" akin to "Dorian Gray's desire for permanent youth and beauty" and "Peter Schlemihl's yearning for riches and beautiful women."[41] In *The Hawkline Monster*, the wish fulfillment focuses on the twins' heroic quest to kill the monster. Such is the stuff of dreams. A primitive antinomianism is also involved. Moral scruples hardly matter more to Cameron and Greer than they do to the monster. Granted, Cameron and Greer have their moments of uplifting sentimentality, but most of the time the same routine prevails—killing men and visiting Portland whorehouses. Then too, the complete freedom of the libido is sheer self-reflexive wish fulfillment drawn directly from the sexual fantasies of *Penthouse*. In effect, the context of the book is one in which reason and social morality are severely battered and unfettered violence and sexuality, the traditional hallmarks of narcissism, are allowed full rein, at least until the monster and his conscience are finally "frozen" into a handful of diamonds. Then the romance world gives way first to surrealism (the destruction of the house and ice caves) and finally to "reality" itself (the death or imprisonment of most of the characters). Whether allowed freedom or not, the idlike monster will destroy the rational constructs of man.

It is precisely the freezing of the monster's creativity into a diamond hardness that is related to the most negative kind of narcissism—the human ironic striving for immortality by projecting an image onto creation. In "The Double as Immortal Self," Otto Rank asserts that fear of death and need for self-perpetuation lead to attempts to re-create oneself through offspring, to live eternally as an immortal soul (the double of the physical body), and to imprint one's image permanently on civilization ("an expression of the irrational self seeking material immortalization in lasting achievements").[42] The failure of such narcissistic attempts is clearly evident, as Rank has shown, in the world of art. Rank speaks of two sorts of people who would immortalize themselves: those he calls artists, talented individuals who are able to carry on the traditions of the hero and contribute significantly to the development of civilization, and those with little talent who simply want to project their image narcissistically onto culture, with little regard for what civilization really needs. According to Rank, the true artist is "the hero's spiritual double, who told in immortal works of art what the other had done and thus preserved the memory of it and himself for posterity."[43] "The real artist," says Rank, "finds his subject in the heroic life, whereas the artisan as a ready-made type finds his sole subject in himself."[44]

Minimalist postmodernism is extremely concerned with the problems of obsessive authority. Brautigan presents two examples of narcissistic attempts at self-perpetuation: those of Professor Hawkline, the sterotypical mad scientist, and the monster itself, the creative artisan. The professor's attempts to recreate his image through progeny is doomed to failure since as far as the reader knows, both of the daughters die childless and his attempt to create a fixed object in the future also goes awry.

Perhaps the most ingenious of the narcissistic artists is the monster, who creates fantasy for the entire Hawkline household. But when his artistic aims are narrowed and his wish to exert control over others becomes obsessive, he too fails. One genuine artist, however, manages to succeed, a true hero who saves the girls and a true artist who constructs reality through film. Cameron succeeds where the professor and other characters fail.

The Hawkline Monster: A Gothic Western is Brautigan's playful double as well. Like professor Hawkline, he creates his "Hawkline Monster"; but unlike the professor, Brautigan eschews the possibility of a utopia and regales the reader with the heroically anti-heroic life of several sets of doubles. In this respect, he resembles Cameron, counting the episodes of the doubles and creating clever illusions but making certain that the reader is aware of his constructions, his metadoubles. Self-parody enables Brautigan to keep his art from being elevated to the statically monumental.

Despite the negative values the reader may associate with narcissism, Brautigan does not altogether condemn it. He simply points out that narcissism is a characteristic part of the tissue of our culture. The narcissism of the monster is no greater than that of the western heroes, eastern heroines, the mad scientist, or Brautigan himself. These figures, so much a part of the American literary fabric, live within the confines, the rules, the prison bars, of their own and their culture's ideological frame of reference. No matter how much the individual attempts to escape, to create something of significance outside the cultural context, that very act of individualism, that attempt, is part of the characteristic narcissistic framework, even culturally determined ethos, of our Western tradition. In this respect Brautigan is self-parodic, his tongue-in-cheek manner directed at all artists and authors, including him. By parodying and exploiting the double, Brautigan explores much of the Western myth of individualism and puts it in its proper context of narcissism. He does not, however, suggest other, potentially more positive forms of behavior. He suggests that all forms of individual and social action are necessarily self-referential and narcissistic. In this way, Brautigan resembles Nabokov, Pynchon, Hawkes, and Barth, but he takes the issues further than they, undermining the double in both form and content. By proliferating doubles on every page and reducing them to certain figures, he parodies the traditional rhetoric and dualistic interpretations of the double. By drawing everything on a flat surface with no meaningful chiaroscuro, he works against the conventional opinion that all narcissism is "wrong." The minimalist metadouble exposes the reality of fiction and the fiction of reality in this postmodern work.

Ultimately, this book is about language itself, the endless circulation of signs. This process is perhaps the most narcissistic of all because language, as a self-referential system, points finally only to itself. Chock-full of literary stereotypes and parodies of literary langauge, *The Hawkline Monster* never allows the reader to forget that it is only a pastiche of forms that refer to nothing outside the closed circle of linguistic and literary expression. The question of narcissism is one of language, not sex or self-devotion. Brautigan's use of the double and his comments about narcissistic activities confirm that the speaker can never get outside language in understanding or assessing the world.

Surfictive Games of Discourse

7

Federman's Double or Nothing

BY HOLDING THE MIRROR SO CLOSE TO ITS ORIGINAL, RICHARD BRAUTI-gan's irrealistic parody of the double in *The Hawkline Monster* serves to short-circuit and mock both its own content and style and those of the original. As a result of this mockery, original and copy echo and reecho in a way that brings into question the validity of, and opposition between, the terms *original* and *copy*. Everything, being at once inter-textual and intratextual, interrogates the very status of texts and allu-sions. This self-conscious defamiliarization places Brautigan's work in the company of the postmodern works of Nabokov, Pynchon, Hawkes, and Barth, but Brautigan's novel surpasses them in the total freeplay of the signifier and the degree to which the book refuses to surrender traditional meaning or indeed any meaning at all.

Postmodernists have called into question many stable assump-tions more or less taken for granted by modernists and their precur-sors: for example, Oscar Wilde's, in *The Picture of Dorian Gray*, that the orders of art and life should not be confused. Although no postmod-ernist would deliberately confuse writing and life, neither would a postmodernist argue that art differs from life. The relevant question is not about similarity or difference but about the assumptions that underlie such truisms. While the margin between life and art may seem to have become more pronounced with modernism—the paint-ings of Picasso and the fiction of Joyce make it apparent that art is not life—postmodernists have chosen to ruminate upon the intellectual foundations that have created those centers and margins. It is true that some continue to use the abstractness and unreality of the mod-

167

erns, but they have done so for different purposes. Instead of agreeing that art depends upon verisimilitude or speculating that art differs wholly from life, the postmoderns either conclude with John Barth that life emulates art or with Richard Brautigan that both literature and life are less "real" and more fictive than traditionally perceived. Writing in a defamiliarizing, playful style and jumbling the orders of life and art, all of the authors considered in this study implicitly query ontological assumptions to highlight the process of constructing of knowledge and ways to put it under erasure. They wish to question arbitrary and binary distinctions to free up the play of fiction and life.

Arguing that the linkage between literature and reality or between new fiction and traditional realism has not been sufficiently uncoupled, Raymond Federman advocates fiction that explores fiction, challenges its traditions, queries its ontological status, emphasizes the role of imagination, and displaces rationality. This he calls *surfiction*—irreal postmodern literature that avoids mimesis and shows the fictionality of reality.[1] Texts that challenge realism and traditional conceptions of literary artifice and reality, now standard among postmoderns,[2] do so by self-consciously elevating their modes of representation and countering the romantic idea of selective genius, the principle of work, the belief in revision to perfection, a closed structure, and rational, significant meaning.[3] This fiction, consisting of textual ruptures, is emptied of former signification, given a metafictive purpose, and inscribed with what can be considered a new social and metaphysical referentiality: a demonstration of the distorting powers of reason and the basic irrationality of life. Unlike the fictions of Pynchon, Hawkes, Barth, and Brautigan, surfiction blurs the lines between the life of the author and narrators-protagonists not just to show the contamination of the real world by the literary one but also to show that everything is a fiction or construct of language. Specular images, traces, repetitions, and doubles of other writings call into question the original texts and reality to create new meanings. One of the most effective ways of accomplishing this task is through the presentation of an autotelic and demystified discourse of the double that is not only intrinsically playful but self-consciously ludic.

Conventional referential fiction for Federman is problematic because it often divides experience and interpretation into dualistic, or "duplicitous," categories. Surfiction (surrealistic-surface fiction) will not, he argues, fall into that trap because

all distinctions between the real and the imaginary, between the conscious and the subconscious, between the past and the present, between truth and untruth will be abolished. All forms of duplicity will
disappear. And above all, all forms of duality will be negated—especially duality: that double-headed monster which, for centuries now,
has subjected us to a system of values, an ethical and aesthetical system based on the principles of good and bad, true and false, beautiful
and ugly. Thus, the primary purpose of fiction will be to unmask its
own fictionality, to expose the metaphor of its own fraudulence, and
not pretend any longer to pass for reality, for truth, or for beauty.[4]

In making the case for a fiction that revels in its own fictionality and
avoids binary systematizing, Federman echoes other postmodernists,
but, if anything, he more explicitly insists that fiction no longer be "a
mirror taken out for a walk."[5] He advocates the elimination of coherent
sequentiality and verisimilitude and the disruption of causality
through a new arrangement of the various textual parts in fragmentary
and unshaped forms. By denaturalizing techniques, the author leaves
the fundamental role of establishing unity—ordering and interpreting—to the reader; the text no longer can determine its own reception.
These are techniques that Federman associates with an undermining
of explicitly dualistic, and implicitly realistic, premises.

While Federman is not likely to convince everyone that literature
will (or even should) abandon mimesis or suspend cultural and historical assumptions, his assertion has implications for the concept of the
double in literature. He takes such terms as *dual, double,* and *duplicity*
as evidence that society (and the realistic novel) operates in fixed
categories, especially opposing ones—good and evil, realistic and
unrealistic, true and false, light and dark. Federman hopes that fiction
can expose the weakness of these categorizations and embrace wider,
more comprehensive, pluralistic views. The simultaneous use and
parody of the double is one tool to accomplish a new orientation, to
unsettle the concept of dualism through the play of the double.[6]

Ill content with the general seriousness of the double, Raymond
Federman, in his *Double or Nothing: A Real Fictitious Discourse,* follows
closely in the footsteps of Richard Brautigan's *The Hawkline Monster,*
stripping the double of traditional associations by turning the device
into the elaborate play of discursive probing into the possibilities of
telling a fragmented, irrational, irrepressive, and autotelic story.[7] This
textual surface is a place where the author inaugurates a play of partial

meaning, where the traditional associations of the double are deferred, though the forms of doubling are recuperated.[8]

Arbitrary and elaborate rules of composition and genre—nonutilitarian in every respect and abundantly evident in many kinds of contemporary fiction, including science fiction, fantasy, detective fiction, and Harlequin romance—have often been deliberately obscured in the interest of assuring the illusion of completeness, enclosure, and significance.[9] The use of the first-person narrative point of view has provided the appearance of stability and singleness of purpose; the third-person narrative, historical accuracy and truth. One of a new breed of literary disrupters, Federman ignores traditional narrative discourses, reveals the "captivity of formulas," and exposes the process of fabrication. He writes metafiction, "fiction about fiction-making," which "proclaims and rejoices in its own fictiveness." By reveling in "the play of all communication,"[10] and reducing the doubles to nothing, Federman discloses the arbitrary, fragmentary, and nontelic rules of discourse, especially those that concern rules of composition, relationships between the text and its antecedents, and relationships among author, narrators, characters, and readers.

The subversion of the compactness, continuity, and coherence of fiction and emphasis on the "interplay" of the structure and meaning—the discourse—is apparent in *Double or Nothing*. Federman unsettles traditional views of narrators and narration by presenting several alternatives and then commenting upon them. Violating the narratorial basis upon which realistic and modernistic novels are built by separating recorder from narrator, the author has specifically called attention to narrative formulas. The proliferation of narrative voices has the effect of making the reader aware that all voices are contrived and ultimately projections of the author's imagination. He does not assume that the principal narrator is the author's second self but warns us, as Michel Foucault does in "What Is an Author?" about assuming any real or tangible connection between an author's "real" self and any fictional depictions. Each is the result of an author's imagination at play, no more and no less. The recorder comments on the narrator's telling of the tale, thereby making clear that fiction is play:

> THEREFORE the best thing for him to do was to start
> at the beginning wherever that might be allow nothi
> ng to interfere with his plans and keep going howev

er incoherent irrational all screwed up and so on w
hat he was doing became for indeed as an inveterate
gambler that he was why should he be ashamed when t
he dice or the cards fall in his favor and why shou
ld he ask himself AM I A DISHONEST PLAYER since fro
m the beginning he is willing to succumb if not imm
ediately at least eventually[11]

The narrator's tendency to gamble, to play a game with monetary stakes, is no different from the recorder's wish to alter textual discourse through the disruption of syllabic division and formatting, to play a game of fiction with its own emotional and intellectual gratification. So whether the issues are gambling or writing, winning or losing, playing or succumbing, the ontological questioning of *how* to play the game is paramount. The book attains its legitimacy through its self-proclaimed fictiveness and "its own becoming."[12]

The opening pages of the book establish implicit contradictions and discontinuities, and the double concerns the breaking down and metafictive reinscribing of dualistic patterns and closed structures associated with the realistic novel. The conventional opening of the text, "Once upon a time," followed by a parenthetical qualification, "(two or three weeks ago)," disrupt the patterning of conventionality, timelessness, and agelessness, and make the reader aware not only that fiction depends upon formulaic beginnings but that all writing is if not formulaic then certainly contrived. Fixed rules of characterization and plot are also exposed when the narrator cannot decide whether the protagonist should be named Jacques, Robert, Solomon, Boris, or Dominique; whether the heroine should be Mary, Marry, or Peggy; whether Uncle David or Arthur should be from Poland or elsewhere. He cannot decide whether the ending of the protagonist's story—and ultimately his own—should conclude with death or life, success or failure, hope or despair; he cannot even decide on the appropriate tense—past, present, conditional future, or a combination.

These myriad possibilities of voice, person, and tense help to position the grammatical structures of the text and satirize hierarchized possibilities and choices, and prevent the reader from discovering a center of consciousness or subject. The search for unity in narrative personae and the desire for linearity is disrupted through multiple narratorial subjectivity. Such examples indicate the possible moves in the game of fiction, which, when enunciated boldly for the readers, place the process of construction squarely before their eyes. Nothing in this fiction is permanently fixed but is open to review, revision, and demystification. The structure and grammar of the sentences and overall text is broken, and the rhetoric is anarchical and will not serve the traditional process of creating and sustaining a given textual illusion. Federman denies to his characterization, plot, and setting a singleness of identity by dissociating the fiction into "incompatible fragments" and distributing "the pieces according to completely new units."[13] He allows no stable element of fiction to go unchallenged, and nothing solid exists in sign and value.

This destabilizing and dislocating of traditional rules governing fiction denies poetic inspiration, rational discourse, or a perfectible text. Conversely, it affirms inspiration for everybody, the value of subconscious forces, the promotion of automatism, hypnotism, dream, and play in a literary text.[14] This mode tries to empty the game of discourse of seeming rationality, philosophy, and meaning, to create "a boundless, unruly discourse out of which proper meanings would be expelled by a proliferation of tropes, word-play, equivocation. Or collage, pure and simple, all attributions, any appropriation, gone. Theory could then claim the 'irresponsibility' of poetry and forsake the authority of philosophy."[15] This concept of discourse as meaningless, nonrational play differs radically from philosophical and linguistic discourse, which affirms the rational, rule-governed manner of linguistic utterance.

Despite this desire to overturn the stuffy, shopworn traditions of fiction and present a new "pluridimentionality," an unabashed pun on "mentioning" or "writing," by means of a playful sensibility, Federman is aware that novelistic impressions of life cannot be so easily abolished. They exist in uneasy tension with their formalistic doubles. Readers expect novelistic language to confirm their impressions of reality, but at the same time novels always "appresent" and distort the very reality they seek to affirm. The role of the novel is by these traits double, using forms of realism and social attitudes to criticize those very forms. Of course, in criticizing those forms while also using them, the author extends the novel's tradition. He is implicitly asking that it not be exterminated. What better mode to accomplish this task than fictional play that while alluding to life is at the same time one remove from, or a mirror of, life—or a mirror of itself.

The title itself continues the tradition while self-consciously remarking on the implicit game of artifice. An obvious allusion to gambling, it is chosen by the narrator, himself a gambler, who claims to have won $1,200 in a game of chance, perhaps blackjack in Los Angeles or craps in Las Vegas.[16] As a result of this phenomenal win, he has, he maintains, enough money for a full year, in which he writes this work of fiction. The project of writing this book and the title are supposedly a result of the narrator's decision to risk a $600 pot to go for the big one—or lose all in the attempt. So he will also write a book that is close to realism and undermine it or accomplish nothing. The title refers to the play of doubled intentions.

The main discourse conspicuously emphasizes the atmosphere of the game and deconstructs the conventional novel where problems of writing are separate from the story. Captured by the shrewd recorder, the book articulates the words and imaginings of the narrator, who stocks his apartment to provide for the days during which he will write his story. As he lists needs, multiplying weights by days, he mulls over what trade-offs he will have to make to afford them. The same decisions must be made about his fiction, about the sorts of themes, characters, and structures he can manage in a given time and space. In a sense, he lays odds on the best, most effective, and most economical combinations that will coalesce to form a workable fiction.

The structure and setting of the tale also relate to the plays of a game that cannot easily be broken down into such dualistic categories as text and nontext, serious and frivolous, original and parody, work and play. The events take place over a period of 365 days, during which the narrator isolates himself in his room to write his book. This period and the duration of the book are interludes, time and space taken out of his everyday working environment. At the end of his stint of writing, at the end of the book, life will resume where the narrator leaves off, but there will be leakage between them. Art takes from life, and life takes from art. The pattern is looping and circular, not linear or binary. When he writes of his protagonist, usually called Boris, the narrator includes details that will contribute to this cycle and rules out others that will "mess up the circular aspect of the trip" (p. 124). The room itself—a self-enclosed, self-contained space within which the narrator will work—cannot preclude other kinds of activities.

What transpires in the plot is also expressed in terms of doubled personal, social, and literary games. The narrator initially speaks of gambling, but this discussion concerns the purchase of a toothbrush and the composition of a work of fiction. This combination of topics illustrates his thesis that all areas of life, real and imagined, are interdependent and nonbinary. At their center are chance, improvisation, and indeterminacy, and victory requires more than skill. The narrator points out at least two kinds of social and personal games, both described as a hole. For Boris, recently arrived from France, America is a hole, a void, a completely alien, aporatic opponent that he must reckon with and if possible overcome. It is an absence that ought to have no significant bearing on his life, yet it asserts itself as a presence, as relevant if not transcendent. He dislikes America's materialism, its degrading commitment to work coupled with manufacturing, advertising, and consuming. For him, the New York subway with its teeming population is the "Belly of America," or the hole, representative of all that is both invigorating and undesirable about the culture. Sexuality too is identified as a part of the belly or hole of America, where the rules for Boris are uncertain and ambiguous, where he can be swallowed up and eliminated. As he contemplates the possibility of seduction, he realizes he does not know "if she really wants it. Or if she's simply playing a game" (p. 172). This element of ambiguity leads to traps in the game, and he is always skirting personal disaster. Boris views both the handsome black woman on the subway, whom he lusts after, and Ernest's mother, who initiates him into new sexual experiences, as honorable opponents in a game he must react to in a complicated fear-love relationship. The rules of these games, these holes, are no more clear-cut and absolute than those of novelistic writing. Each discourse has approximate doxas that can be used, abused, and violated. This arbitrariness of discourse is both exhilarating and threatening; it seems to allow endless possibilities, yet the violation of the rules of discourse can bring instant failure.

Ultimately the book is about succeeding in an arbitrary, risk-filled environment and staying alive—physically, mentally, and imaginatively. In this game of life, the question of risk is of paramount importance. The narrator often speaks of luck, though he realizes how capricious and unpredictable it is. Luck suggests that discourses are not driven by unbreakable and necessary laws and rational procedures. The narrator does not wish to restrict the role of radical contingency and uses chance to discover that "everything is at least double, split in two, plays a double and a triple game, is double-edged. In every unity and totality, there are inter-changeable, movable places and points which overlap and interlock."[17] This Wittgensteinian view of play disputes "the discrete, hermetic character of each game or 'language stratum' " in favor of the "blurred edges"[18] of indeterminacy and luck. Luck, like a game, exists by itself, unrelated to any external rationale in an existential void. Luck, combined with sure knowledge of the rules and a willingness to break or change them, is the essence of a game.

In *Double or Nothing*, this fictional discursive game is played primarily in terms of the double. This is evident in the ways the word itself is employed. It is used many times as "Double or Nothing" to suggest that the narrator views his problems as coming in sets of twos that if unresolved will reduce him to nothing. But *double* assumes pluralistic meanings. It refers to abstract concepts as well as mundane, even trivial things. "Double statement," "double problem," "double purpose," and "double time" indicate the complexity of an issue or a concept and the need to account for it in complex rather than simplistic ways. But more often the narrator uses the term as an indication of the triviality in American culture. He speaks of "double-ply" toilet paper, the "double-breasted suit," the "double bed," even a "doubled-up" portion. When used in conjunction with material objects, the term suggests ampleness, but often with negative connotations; for example, *double* is a term used in American advertising in touting a commodity as especially large or good. Sometimes words are doubled to suggest "chance luck the stars god heaven fate destiny or coincidence OR SIMPLY A JOKE" (p. 77). For example, ".04" is often doubled without explanation, almost as a magic number; "crap" frequently means excrement, a gambling game, or cultural sentimentality; "concentration" refers to a prison camp or mental alertness. These doublings suggest the displacement, dissemination, and deferral of meaning in our language and culture.

Federman's work is also the double of realistic fiction in a basically structural sense. The unbounded, ludic typescript and layout provide an alternative to or double of the traditional fictional framework, syntactical arrangement, compositional devices, and formal design, for, as the narrator insists,

  the
  whole

story
is
a
break
with the past.
(P. 48)

Most works of fiction use conventional print with a conventional typeface to guide the reader conventionally across the page from left to right, row after row, page after page, without any sort of interruption or disruption except for paragraph and chapter endings and beginnings. Federman's design and layout, however, are not so predictable because, first, the book lacks the appearance of having been typeset; rather, it resembles a typewritten notebook, with all the strikeouts, typos, and inserts of the amateur typist. Second, most of Federman's pages do not follow the left-to-right, line-by-line pattern. Some go from right to left, some from top to bottom, some around the sides. Some pages are jammed with words from corner to corner; others are entirely blank or present an admixture of filled and open spaces in random or pictorial patterns resembling free verse or concrete poetry. Some pages are filled with a single repeated word; some mix poetry and graphic design with prose, creating what Brian McHale calls concrete prose or concrete fictions;[19] others are crammed with English and French script. Most pages are white, with or without black print, but two are blue, one with print and one without. In short, while the pages themselves are uniform if somewhat oversized, what happens on the pages is rarely the same. Only blanks can claim to be identical (perhaps gaps, blank pages, and holes are ultimately the most important features for emphasizing irrelevancy and pure play). In this "concretism" graphics, visual display, and paginal space serve iconically to stand for the content.[20] Federman's "visual fictions"[21] create a discursive game between author and reader, and it is the reader who takes the most active role in construing pattern and meaning, which will vary from reader to reader and reading to reading.

Although the book consists of 202 numbered pages, there are an additional 33 eccentrically numbered, unnumbered, or blank pages of introduction, postscript, and text. Hence the book provides 235 opportunities for unique page formats, and the author capitalizes on nearly all of them. These pages present a collage or pastice rather than a neat, properly numbered, continuous narration. Early in the work, the author reflects on this alternative format by writing a "short (double) poetic statement" (p. 000000), in which the recorder intrudes into the narrator's discourse on masking reality by poetic illusion. Through this intrusion, the reader is explicitly warned that the book not only shatters conventional illusions but is *about* the shattering of illusions in fiction. The nature of fiction has been doubled so that the reader may perceive and feel the difference between fiction that hides its forms and fiction that overtly plays with them. Federman's piece may be the avenging double of customary prose, summoned to demonstrate fully the weaknesses of realistic fiction or the double as hero, come to rescue fiction from its sameness.

The apparently bipartite structure of the book carries the game of the double even further, for here the play is between the introduction and the text. Divided into this double structure, the book has two numbering systems: the introduction contains an 11-page preface numbered with an accumulating series of zeros, and the 202-page body is more conventionally paginated. This separate pagination suggests that these two sections flicker playfully between sameness and opposition in their range and use of numbers, though in continuing to use a numbering system at all the text proclaims itself partly conventional and comprehensible, within the framework of customary reader expectations.

The discursive freeplay of introduction and main text is confirmed in the first part, "THIS IS NOT THE BEGINNING," which seems to warn the reader that the essential story line will be deferred to the text, significantly labeled "BEGINNING." The appearance, however, belies the reality. "THIS IS NOT THE BEGINNING" in fact discloses the entire plot and cast of characters of the book, providing what in conventional fiction is reserved for the text. The text, on the other hand, is literally the introduction, for it indicates the circumstances under which the recorder and narrator undertake the telling of the story and the process by which it is told. Federman thus reverses the conventional order, as in the game Mad, in which the player wins with the greatest number of losses and the lowest score wins. Consequently, if readers are interested only in what John Hawkes calls the enemies of fiction, conventional plot and characterization, they can close the book after reading the introduction, for they will know about the "succession of exteriorities" that highlights the syntax of the book.[22] Should the reader, however, be interested in the ontology and play of fiction—that is, what its components are, how they operate, and what other alternatives exist, in addition to the author's spirit of play of vocabulary selection, sentence construction, and page layout—then the text will hold a special interest. The normal pattern of books is reversed, and this pattern virtually ignores any attempt to establish a well-plotted tale with interesting characters and a sense of enclosure, emphasizing instead the artist's struggles and defeats, triumphs and joys, in telling a story. Federman has disposed of the fiction, reserving the emphasis for the metafiction, the creative process by which a story comes to be told.

The cast of players is also ludically distorted and doubled to replace textual unity of the realistic novel with indeterminacy, incompleteness, and formlessness. Although fiction commonly depends upon the dualistic conflict of the antagonist and protagonist or the implied conflict between the narrator's and characters' observations and actions, Federman's strategy differs considerably because of the multiple narrative voices—what he calls the first-person recorder, second-person narrator, third-person protagonist, and fourth-person author. Rather than realistic, believable characters in conflict, these players or actants are defined by their structural roles and call into question the interpretive and stabilizing function of conventional narrators. The player "is at once the subject and the object of the play. The pronouns I, you, he are the different modes of the play structure. The subjectivity-objectivity dualism is abolished because it is inoperative."[23]

The protagonist has the narrowest role, for he must patiently and passively wait to be drawn by the narrator, submitting to his fictional fate, although he might like a "life" of his own in order to "come alive" to other narrative possibilities. The narrator enfolds the protagonist and has the responsibility of creating, inventing, and sustaining the fictional life of the narrator at the same time that he must furnish his room and buy his supply of noodles so that he can totally isolate himself long enough to create and sustain his fiction. The recorder attempts to be as faithful as he can in replicating the thoughts and actions of the narrator and his account of the protagonist, but he cannot help making interpretive comments about this activity and on occasion finds that he must subjectively intrude into the narrator's world. The assumed author is the most comprehensive figure, containing all the characters and narrative possibilities, which at times become confused with his life in the real world. He stands back, slightly bemused, trying to maintain the stance of a detached observer of all the activity happening under his nose and beyond his control, but ultimately he knows that he is the fiction master and that his life and his art cannot be neatly separated. Quite clearly, this "intramural set up," as Federman calls it, is a game in which each of the players has an assigned role circumscribed by the roles of the other players. And in these roles the protagonist is doubled by the narrator, who is doubled by the recorder, who is doubled by the assumed author, who is doubled by all of the narrative agents and roles. Outside the text is the real author whose imagination generates the construct but whose imagination is in turn generated by his culture.

The roles of the personae may be fixed, but as players in the game, they are still maneuverable within the overall framework, and the possibility always exists that one or more of them will be allowed to cheat and so alter the response of another, thus reminding the readers that fiction is a game spun out of the real author's mind. That game is essentially a narcissistic one in which the personae are fabricated extensions of the author's conscious ideas and unconscious needs and desires. The author-persona seems to suggest this possibility, though without any Freudian implications about the paranoia of artists. This narcissistic urge is symbolized by the protagonist's masturbating in the bathroom while "he waited to see how he and his story were going to develop be handled by the SECOND PERSON his creator his maker" (p. 000000000), who is similarly locked up in his sparsely furnished room beginning a year's labor of writing. These personae may be extensions of the author and are designed to help him gain more objectivity about himself, just as Boris, standing before the mirror after escaping from the prison train, is shocked by, and therefore detached from, his ugly, unkempt image in the mirror. The characters are, however, just as likely to have a life of their own, for the author cannot control them as he wills. All four of these personae are "anxious to be to go to exist to invent to write to record to survive to become" (p. 000000000). The fear of death and extinction and the love of imagination underlie their will to exist in this game of art.

The role of the first person, the middle-aged recorder, is to exercise judgment in selecting and editing the thoughts and jottings of the narrator. His is a specifically literary role as he tries to stand outside the fiction striving for objectivity, detachment, and literacy, though the intrusive author accuses him of being "a poor recorder, a lousy designer, a weak scribbler, and . . . on top of that . . . a very bad typist" (p. 00). The recorder's interest in fiction is, however, catholic (or indiscriminate) enough to cause him to acknowledge and record the imperfect and unsound ideas and procedures of the narrator. He includes the narrator's alternative suggestions for plot sequence, character descriptions, and word choices, as well as his characteristic personal activities, even the narrator's mind-boggling decision to live on spaghetti every day for one entire year—all the factors that an aspiring writer must take into consideration to free up his time and prime his imagination.

Still, the recorder has a decided problem in remaining objective, detached, and scrupulously honest in his judgment. When on one occasion the narrator reveals that his jottings are autobiographical and self-referential, the recorder intrudes, claiming that same self-referentiality. As a result, the narrator's personal poem, "Reflection," becomes a short double statement in which the recorder intrudes, parenthetically altering the personal pronoun and consequently distancing the entire piece:

> Forging
> with my (his) hands
> from the experiences
> of my (his) skin
> a mask for reality
> Carving
> in my (his) bones
> a meaning for life
> I (he) heard something whispered
> and my (his) fingers burned
> at the touch of flesh
>
> (P. 000000)

Similarly, when the narrator tells of the protagonist's escape from a train bound for a concentration camp, he (or the recorder) interjects, "AND I FOLLOWED MY SHADOW" (p. 7.1). This mystifying interjection, used later in reference to Boris's first sight of himself in the mirror after jumping from the prison train, removes the readers from a growing attachment to the protagonist and sentimental feelings over this dramatic escape even as it also suggests that the protagonist is the projection or shadow of the narrator. This distancing reminds the reader that the protagonist's and narrator's characters, emotions, and styles are inventions and mere illusions created from words, and it raises the possibility that the assumptions made about one character can just as easily be made about another, for they are all finally the author's projections.

Within this ludic discourse, the role of the second-person narrator is to create the appearance of an inner psychological discourse.[24] But the narrator is not the source of the text; he is an assemblage, a trace of the author's own consciousness, and needs finally to be linked to that absence. Here the narrator's consciousness and his subconscious are available to the reader, captured in their pristine purity by the recorder. An odd and eccentric gambler, the narrator emphasizes the role of chance and luck in life. He ruminates on various alternatives to his decisions regarding gambling, life, and fiction before taking a leap in any one direction. His view of the various alternatives is captured in his term "Double or Nothing," which reflects his "either-or" mentality. But the narrator attempts to go beyond these limited alternatives by overcoming the implied opposition between "nothing" and "everything." One of the narrator's favorite uses of the term is his "noodling around," which suggests the noodles the narrator must feed himself while he attempts to free his head (his noodle). He will not be able to keep track of time unless, like Robinson Crusoe, he notches a stick for each passing day. In so doing, he argues, he fulfills "a double purpose on the one hand to save his life, on the other to escape alive It may be double work but eventually it pays IT'S DOUBLE OR NOTHING" (p. 10).

By postulating these "double" problems, the narrator indicates that if he cannot resolve the split between physical well-being and imaginative creativity, he will die. If he solves the problem, he will live. If he can set aside enough money for one year and stock his room with the required articles, he will have enough time to write his fiction. He also needs to devise the rules of fiction as he goes along, thinking out alternative plot ideas, characterizations, and details to continue his daily writing. These are his conscious aims, but his subconscious desires serve to disrupt the process of writing. His yearning for sex and companionship; his obsession with the bathroom, toilet paper, and excrement; and his deeply felt attitudes about the spiritual void in America disturb his imagination. But these details, while intensifying his dilemma, make it fruitful and creative. The subject of the book, the labor of writing, makes for apt and interesting, if disruptive and collagelike, fiction. If the narrator can turn dilemma, disruptiveness, and distortion against themselves, he can go on writing and living. The process is not one of "either-or" but rather, as one of Federman's main metaphors has it, "up and down," a matter of getting out of the hole (in gambling and writing) to win the big one but, repetitiously, sliding back. This too is a double procedure, doubling and redoubling continually (p. 57).

Of the three speakers, the youthful protagonist has the most inherently limited role. All decisions have been made by the narrator and the recorder, who have constituted themselves as subjects. He is merely an object to be "invented, told, composed, and eventually written" by the second person. Physically, he is "shy not bad looking dark hair strong nose bright dark eyes straight white teeth height: 5' 10" weight: 156 lbs. strong nails long fingers size 40, shoe 10½ socks 9½ arms 33" neck 15¼ a little scar on left knee heavy beard waist 32 20/20 vision" (p. 72). Psychologically, he is said to have a castration complex, a mother complex, and a father complex, but these are merely words that do nothing to fill out his character or establish a meaningful psychological profile. A Jew born and bred in France, he escaped concentration camps by jumping from a train; he was harbored for years by a French farmer; and at nineteen he came to New York where he met his uncle, afterward settling in Detroit and attending Northern High School. The narrator develops none of his emotions but mentions that he felt "Anguish Fear Hesitation Loneliness Anxiety Homesickness Alienation" (p. 142).

This thumbnail sketch gives him a certain "dimentionality," but still, "All he has *to do*, in fact, is submit to the second person's imagination and sense of organization as he (the inventor) invents, projects, organizes, composes, and (eventually) writes everything that will happen to him" (p. 00000). He is merely the doubled projection of others. He may yearn for a meaningful role and an artistic narrative, but since he has historically no voice of his own, he cannot directly influence his fate; he is only a moveable pawn: "In other words, he is NOTHING in the double setup, the interplay between the first and second person" (p. 00000). The narrator notes that while the protagonist would like to have a hand in the writing of the story and the formation of his own character, he can just as easily be eradicated: "But since I have a great advantage over BORIS as his progenitor. Since I literally control his existence. If for some reason he argues with me and I find I do not like what he says to me I destroy him. One Two Three. I tear him up and throw him away. I wipe him out" (p. 112).

In mainline realistic fiction, the protagonist is usually the primary person, behind whom the narrator and recorder hide; his are the fears and aspirations with which the readers identify. But here his character and life are too obviously contrived and circumscribed by the recorder and narrator to warrant complete identification. In fact, the details of his life are for the most part described offhandedly as if ordinary and commonplace. True, his escape from the prison train bound for the concentration camp carries genuine interest, but his characterization depends less upon the pathos of that incident than the portrayal of his libido (the narrator worries about sustaining his fiction, the protagonist about maintaining his sexual vigor).[25] The narrator treats the sexual drive of the protagonist with some intensity: his adolescent fondness for the young blonde from Wisconsin, his lust after the black girl on the subway, his occasional masturbation, and finally his seduction of a black friend's mother. But while these fantasies and activities are realistically described, the irrealistic format of the book reminds readers that they are literary clichés. The protagonist is like most adolescent protagonists in American fiction—fleeing from his historical and geographical base, striving to create a new identity although caught up in his own adolescent inexperience and sexualilty, wishing for an *affaire de coeur*, and only slowly coming to self-knowledge and awareness of cultural conventions. Such a pattern exemplifies an impulsive, anarchic, and troubled vision of the hero, but it is also a variation on the old-fashioned heroic quest motif of traditional fiction. However much the protagonist might like to be an individual, to escape from this pattern of fiction as he escaped from a concentration camp, he has severely limited options. More than willing to take a chance, at times he is utterly subject to the limitations of the game, especially the rules of characterization.

The function of the protagonist is not, however, as limited as he (or the narrator and recorder) thinks, for standing on the edges of the fiction is the primary puppeteer, a fourth person, the assumed author. It is only by the author's permission that the recorder and narrator manipulate and control the protagonist, a permission revocable at any moment. The protagonist can, according to the intrusive author, be more than NOTHING in the double setup:

> However, if eventually, for personal reasons (man is indeed free to choose his own destiny, free to propose and dispose), the third person (the shy young man) is not satisfied with the way the second person is writing him, or what he is saying about him (and by simple extension how the first person is recording him), then he might (quite possibly) disagree with him, argue with him, and even try to convince him to change the way *his* story is being told, shaped, written (and beyond that scribbled, designed, and recorded). (P. 00000)

At two points in the text the author does permit the protagonist to break the rules imposed by the narrator. In the first of these instances, Boris, speaking in demotic French, describes his terrible angst, his hatred of this new America to which he has come, and the phony platitudes mouthed by Peggy. He also indirectly attacks the narrator, saying, "*Les nouilles pour les cons-tipés*" (p. 123) (noodles are for the constipated). Later, he uses more dense, poetic French and reveals the full extent of his misery. Presented in strongly negative images, the game of life he sees is ultimately controlled by an Eater of Children, a god who lurks behind the stage scenery. Life for the protagonist has consequently lost any meaning. Although he longs for innocent youth, for pastoral nature, he can see life through his ennui only as a *cul de sac* and himself only as a failure (p. 180).

The author, however, limits such disruptions of the game, seemingly granting the characters consistent roles and hiding his own. He claims that he has no creative power of his own, an attitude that speaks to the issue that once a character has been invented, given a location, language, and personality, that essential being develops in accordance with those rules that may seem beyond the author's control. More than that, the fiction continually affirms the principle of indeterminacy, a celebration of the randomness involved in composition and the way characters often evade the best-laid rational plans of composition.

At several points, the illusion of separate people fades, revealing an essential sameness to the characters, so that the reader always bears in mind that the author and characters are more or less one. (Certainly the narrator and recorder are one; only their narrative functions differ.) The rough outline of the protagonist's experiences follows that of the author. Both main character and author apparently escaped from the Nazi oppression in France and came to North America to begin a new and difficult life. In one instance the narrator reveals that "Boris will do the same eventually since he and I will coincide It's inevitable with us" (p. 189). In another, the narrator reveals that Boris's coming to America resembled his own: "Like that suit I bought at Klein's. His first American suit. $48.98. With the 50 bucks I had he didn't even have enough for a tie" (p. 18). Moreover, that suit of the protagonist-narrator's is probably the author's. Such metafictive remarking on narrative roles implicitly provides a critique, and a doubling, of fiction.[26] It does not allow for distinctions between author and character or subject and object, for according to McHale, "Authority and subjectivity are dispersed among a plurality of selves, in a way apparently quite compatible with the contemporary awareness of authorial eclipse and displacement."[27]

The unseen players in this text—the fifth person, who is the real author, and the sixth person, who is the reader—double all the others. The real subject of any game is the player, and in any published piece of fiction that is the reader and the author combined.[28] The real author is unknown and therefore indeterminate, just as the "user" of the text is indeterminate, diachronically varying, so that the text itself is never fixed but always dependent upon the play according to the user's own "system of resonance."[29] The author creates the various roles or possible moves in the game, and the reader has to sort them out, determine if the narrator is cheating the protagonist, and recognize how the protagonist evens the odds. The narrator no longer appears to control the fiction; rather, the medium itself controls the narrator, author, subject, and reader in the field of interaction.[30] This collapsing of the traditional functions and persona is typical of surfiction. Author, text, and reader are infinitely dispersed, disseminated, and displaced, and the doubling of signs leads simultaneously to nonmeaning and meaning. Both author and reader must recognize the truly ludic scope of life and fiction in which we participate.

What Federman has neatly accomplished in *Double or Nothing* is to push the double and the play of literary signification beyond what we have seen in the other works. The author has created a space the reader enters at will, becoming a player in a textual game that also involves every aspect of the fiction, including structure, plot, and format. While this game is important in itself, it also relates to the larger question of perception, artistic endeavor, and survival in life. In playing the game of life, each person naturally wishes to win, but to win, to survive, depends upon a proper perception of the limits, the rules, and the risks. At least since Plato and Aristotle, the tendency has been to view life through the lens of dualism, with reality constituted on a grid of opposites or contraries. This double perspective, Federman implies, no longer suffices. A new pluridimensionality is required if we begin to question the basis of perception and action.

The upshot is that Federman simultaneously strips the double of meaning and paradoxically reinvests it with his antimetaphysical metaphysic. He insists that literature and life are games, that the play of the double should push readers beyond all laws of contraries so that they can embrace a host of possibilities, for Federman advocates the policy of double or nothing. People must double, and redouble, their perspectives and hence risk the possibility of the big loss—or the big win. As a result, the double in its metafictive form is a device that works against and parodies itself and ultimately erases the notion that phenomena can be seen as double. Everything is in fact simultaneously nothing and pluridimensional. By undermining the traditional concept of the double, this metafictive doubler has emptied the device of meaning, exhausting it, but he has also reconstituted it. He has cleared the way for fiction to use the device not simply to explore dualistic beliefs but to enunciate multiple perspectives for re-viewing life and literature. Ultimately, in emphasizing the process of doubling rather than the double itself—becoming rather than being—he has changed the form of the word from a noun to a verb and has altered its definition and hence its function as a fictional device. Federman would argue that only by breaking free of the inherent limitations of a theory of opposites or contraries can fiction renew itself or can one hope to survive in this world of pluralistic possibilities.

Postscript
Re-viewing the Double

IN ASSESSING THE AUTOTELIC, NONREFERENTIAL CHARACTER OF POST-modern fiction, Philip Stevick centers on the game as the most important element: "Saying that the novel is a game means that the composition is a playful activity circumscribed by certain arbitrary rules, that the novel itself is in certain ways autotelic, the source of its own laws, a repository of 'fun,' and that the reading of the novel is like learning the rules of, then playing, a game."[1] This game, however, is not as stable as Stevick suggests and can always be opened to new play.

The basis for the play of fiction is language itself (*langue*), which Richard Macksey describes as a playing field or board with "local rules of association, articulations of similar and dissimilar moves, paradigmatic alternatives, and so on."[2] Different discourses within this total field produce different rules and kinds of signification. The specific "environment," "region," and "linguistic topography" matter appreciably in this game, as does the individual speech act (*parole*) that uses some of the basic rules while distorting and omitting others—those that "bend in play, which are sometimes improvised or even forgotten."[3]

Within this context the rhetorical figure of the double is not only a specific signifier but also a field of discourse. Its status as signifier may appear not to have changed diachronically, but its signifying values and rules of discourse certainly have. The epistemology that characterized the premodern and modern double depended upon a discourse of unity, whether based on Platonistic or Freudian-Jungian dualism. Dealing with man's external world and internal psyche, these discourses of unity sought completeness and wholeness. But postmodernism has demolished this previous epistemology and built anew on what the authors believe to be the chaos and rubble of exhausted, shattered novelistic forms. The postrealist writers mine the very foundations of these previous discourses in order to assert the validity and the vitality of other literary constructs. They declare that the device of the double is alive and well; it has, they say, broken through the cocoon of allegory and realism, emerging as a new and beautiful form, although obviously still bearing its old genetic traits.

This new antimimetic double is opposed to the idea of a knowable, integrated self within a comprehensible self-contained frame of historical reality and metaphysics. Such fiction is, as Stevick argues,

> against realism and the visible world and against a verisimilar, or credible, rendering of the inner world; an autotelic, nonpragmatic aesthetic motive, in which fiction aspires to the condition of abstract painting or music, answerable only to itself; the cultivation of a range of verbal activities that place a high premium on nonpurposive ingenuity, activities that another period would have called cuteness, cleverness, mere facility, and worse; and the cultivation of a tacit pact in which reader and writer agree to suspend certain expectations about each other, out of a shared mistrust of old modes of literary high seriousness.[4]

Although there is in the United States a long-standing tradition of authors who write against the grain of realistic and moralistic fiction, it was not until the arrival of Vladimir Nabokov that the novel became self-consciously and ludically postmodern. For Nabokov, the novel is the signifying domain of one shaper, one author, whose vision deliberately defamiliarizes, decodes, and demystifies those of others. As citizen and sojourner of many countries—Russia, England, Germany, the United States, and Switzerland—he came to know unusually well the strengths and weaknesses of the dominant language systems in those countries, and he experienced the benefits and disadvantages of a full range of political and economic ideologies, from totalitarianism to anarchy, monarchy to representational democracy, communism to capitalism. Having experienced pluralistic cultural structures, lived through the most traumatic political upheavals of twentieth-century Europe, and nurtured a natively skeptical temperament, he could not attribute *sens* to any collective form of behavior or ideology. What he could affirm was his existence, imagination, and literary constructs, and even those he occasionally questioned.

Given this existential ground of being and beyond it a qualified solipsistic frame of parody and self-referentiality, Nabokov's works involving the double reject the traditional implications of the device. They implicitly dispute the symbolists' adherence to a mystical logos and higher range of significance, and finally do not even accept the view that two people can perceive anything in fundamentally cognate terms. For Nabokov, therefore, the very idea that two people can be double in any meaningful physical, moral, psychological, or metaphysical sense is patently absurd; all doubles are false. Given these working premises, his task in *Despair* is to strip and reduce to zero the significations, the constructs of meaning, governing the double and to suggest that all such attributions are untenable. He leads his readers to understand that resemblances and signifying associations are not inherent in the objects themselves but lie in the perceptions, deliberate and intentional misconceptions, metaphorical linkings, and acts of the viewer. In this case, the creation of any sort of idealist system resulting from a theory of resemblances is baseless fancy. Asserting that man's vision is always subjective, Nabokov nevertheless concurs with Sartre's view in *Being and Nothingness* that it is necessary to validate one's perceptions against others' to prevent the rampant growth of a system of idealism stemming from solipsism. In *Despair*, Hermann's enthusiasm for finding and killing his double is the result of perceiving false resemblances, failing to check his own view of his double against others', and then generating an idealist philosophical system from those faulty resemblances. Hermann's is a corrupted mode of thinking and a dishonest use of his subjectivism, resulting in questionable analogues and false attributions. The double defamiliarizes and designifies traditional literary, psychological, and mystical uses, warning readers against restricting meaning to a single signified. By designifying idealistically perceived resemblances, Nabokov has essentially removed meaningful, consistent signification from the metaphor of the double.

Some authors may deplore this reduction and continue to view the double along traditional lines with conventional values of signification and goals of explaining immediate or ultimate reality. Others, like Thomas Pynchon, further demystify the linking of literary, psychological, social, and political significances, and involve questions of aesthetics to pursue the most radical problem of all, the overall shaping of our minds through cultural beliefs and attitudes, the problem of one's mind as the double of culture. The root problem in Pynchon is our tendency to place experience into any *form* at all. At the heart of his fiction is the revolutionary impulse to unmake readers' concepts of reality through exposing fundamental bipolar structures as well as contradictions and lacunae within the structures in our culture. Through this awareness of culture and its semiotic values, Pynchon and the reader can begin to break down the structure of duality and move beyond it.

The key to understanding and partially overcoming this structure is not only the demystification of dualism but the principle of indeterminacy itself, the feature that, according to Ihab Hassan, especially characterizes postmodernism.[5] Indeterminacy—the principle of chance, accident, disorganization, and randomness—operates in any situation, in science, the creation of works of art, or the regulation of mental and social structures.[6] For every law, there is finally the counterpresence of indeterminacy. The fault at the heart of Western civilization that Pynchon's work explores is that the *cogito*, rationalism, or what D. H. Lawrence calls "white-consciousness," has created an inherently dualistic and limited way of perceiving and defining reality, one that has not allowed for aleatoric principles. This self-enclosed frame of reference cherishes all the philosophical and idealistic concepts of rationalism—cause and effect, coherence, order, and balance—and specifically denigrates or excludes those aspects that are irrational, animallike, incoherent, orderless, and chaotic. In going beyond duality itself, Pynchon affirms the paradox of antitelic indeterminacy articulated by Leonard B. Meyer: "Here another difference between the anti-teleological position and that of existentialism becomes apparent. In the anti-telelogical [*sic*] view, existence is *one*. Being and non-being are not opposites, but merely different states which may happen to something. Death is a change in existence, not the negation of it."[7]

The paranoiac terror at the heart of Thomas Pynchon's fiction springs from the realization that although existence is probably not a unity, people perversely try to make it so, developing links between various social structures that are deeper, more pervasive, and more sinister than anyone suspects. Pynchon is of the opinion that serious, teleological, referential fiction has been used too often in support of what we might call cultural hegemony and structural oppression, the combination and collusion of structures. Like the statue of the angel in Lübeck that oversees the daily activity of the people and the carnage of the war, the conventional novel cannot be considered as existing apart from, or innocent of, its culture. Fiction is a created part of the Western cultural consciousness and shares society's commitments and its failures. Assumptions about fiction, like those of life (and even the teleological link presumed to exist between the novel and social views), need to be disrupted and demythologized. Pynchon has demonstrated that the patterns of Western thought taken the most seriously are the most ludicrous. A comic undercutting of binarity is necessary for an adequate understanding of the human condition. He accomplishes this task in *Gravity's Rainbow* through various devices involving excess: length, fragmentation of plot lines, multiple characters, and bizarre elements (such as the huge behavioristically trained octopus). He challenges systems, institutions, and establishments— the military-industrial complex, scientific methodologies, Christianity, and language usage itself.

One specific way Pynchon disrupts conventionally held beliefs is through doubles and doubling. By employing a device that has conventionally been used to confirm socially conservative views of spirituality, morality, and identity (usually Platonic and Cartesian), Pynchon questions the governing rules of Western binary thought. His use of the double itself redoubles in a way that mocks coherence, order, and balance based upon dualism and highlights the presence of chance and randomness. This pervasive use is simultaneously playful and serious, for the perspective, goals, and signifying patterns of a literary device are often similar to if not identical with those of the culture itself. To free fiction from its conventional associations involving the double is in some small way to free culture from its dependency on the binary perspective.

John Hawkes's works provide a similar perspective for the reader. By using the double in so many ways, they indicate the full range of pluralistic signification rather than the limited range of bipolar opposition. This demystification of dualism is not accomplished through an anlysis of patterns of writing or the interchangeable personal, corporate, and business "systems" of Western culture such as Pynchon portrays but through a consideration of the complex interrelationship of the id and ego, life and death instincts, imaginary and symbolic stages of development. In exploring these parts and developmental stages of the human personality, Hawkes implicitly assumes the fragmentary and provisional rather than wholeness and completeness. The self is not knowable and integrated but so deeply divided and fractured that the id and ego remain embattled. Hawkes does not, however, leave the self-divided personality in a traditionally Freudian and dualistic framework. Using principles that reflect a contemporary, neo-Freudian understanding of the self, Hawkes suggests the presence of intersubjective transference among the parts of the personality. Not only is the unconscious structured like a language, as Lacan would say, but several different discourses constitute the human personality. Cyril, of *The Blood Oranges*, is not simply opposed to and the double of Hugh; he is complemented and doubled by Fiona and Catherine. And Cyril and Fiona are, as a pair, doubled by Hugh and Catherine. In this psychodrama, the personality is divided not binarily but multiply.

The tapestry of self is always fragmentary and indeterminate. One is multiply self-divided, and only in one's imagination (the imaginary stage) can the self be considered whole. It would be wrong to view these personality divisions as totally irreparable or to see them as totally reparable, for to believe that the personality can be completely separated is to believe in an impossible absolute, just as to believe in a whole personality or identity is to accept an equally impossible absolute. Hawkes's vision is of a personality where the component parts interract with each other, where the id and ego, self and other, engage in intersubjective transference. The language of one never completely becomes the language of the other, and there is always a separation, always an abyss, always a lack—but there always remain links. The pluralistic double for Hawkes is psychological, but it is no more binary than are social systems for Pynchon.

Similarly, John Barth uses ground-point-zero as the foundation on which to build a new strategy of the double, one inherently formalistic, self-referential, and intertextual. Although many of his early texts are tributes to, and stylizations of, early treatments of the double, his later ones parody that earlier tradition and suggest various new significations. This double postulation—simultaneous use and displacement of signs—is especially crucial, for in *Lost in the Funhouse* Barth deploys exhaustion against itself, presenting not one but a series of doubles illustrating the ways literature ultimately depends upon form and pattern, regardless of what content the author or society finally attributes to them. By grounding *Lost in the Funhouse* in classical myth and extending it to embrace the initiation of young Ambrose, who lives in modern Maryland (or is it Merry-land?), Barth declares that the structure of myth partially accounts for the structure of modern literary conventions and social attitudes. This ahistoricity decenters meaning, replacing it with aesthetic devices and literary techniques and confirming the gaps between signifying systems as well as between signifiers and signifieds. In capitalizing upon the tale of Echo and Narcissus and using the story line of the *Odyssey*, for instance, Barth demythologizes myth, implying that its structure, characters, and literary devices have been used over and over and will be used again and again, each author or period attributing to them differing significations. As signifiers, myths are essentially protean and may be adapted to any context, taking on any number of significations. The nature and function of Barth's art is to take both signifier and signified, playing them as many times as possible, incorporating subtle distortions, in order to provide the reader with an endless source of entertainment and enjoyment, but not stable meaning. Dismantling the bourgeois myth to which Barth and his readers are bound, Barth refuses to invest literature with another myth or presence, preferring signifier to signified, form to substance, game to meaning. Barth's technique, for example, is to take one story and double it in others, thereby emphasizing the act of doubling itself.

Clearly enjoying wit and verbal pyrotechnics, Barth is for the most part an author of "silence," evading the social and historical criteria that have characterized the avant-garde in the past two centuries. He does so because he so patently distrusts the bourgeois myth and its generating of cohesive cultural expectations and because he perceives the narcissistic self-reflexiveness of culture and literature. As Ihab Hassan remarks in *The Literature of Silence*, this "force of evasion, or absence, in the new literature is radical indeed; it strikes at the roots and induces, metaphorically, a great silence."[8] Although Barth strives in his early fiction to be apolitical, asocial, and ahistorical, he does tackle the basis of perception and the aesthetic problems of fiction, the foundations upon which society and literature are constructed. In Barth's later fiction, less noticeably realistic and more self-consciously postmodern in political, social, and historical reassessments, he continues to address issues of aesthetics. He sees these issues as *the* most pressing for author and reader. He is especially concerned with aesthetics, for aesthetics can claim some universality and timelessness, bridging space and historical periods. The literary double is inexhaustible, capable of being renewed an infinite number of times. It may be mirrorlike, reflecting itself through countless stages; circular, forever employed along the same repetitious lines; and labyrinthine, using innumerable related paths, some dead-ended, some leading to exhaustion and death, others to reinvigoration. For like the egg waiting patiently for the sperm at the end of the fallopian tube in "Night-Sea Journey," the source of exhaustion and death, the minotaur of the modern novel, is simultaneously its apotheosis.

The parodies that distinguish Barth's fiction are not silly and self-defeating. He does not mock the double device to abandon it; he mocks the traditional signification of the double to use this device again for other purposes. The recognition of indeterminacy in the signifying process, reduction of content to form, does not leave zero value but allows for a reconstitution of meaning in other ways. To suggest that one's experiences create an intertextual system based on a literary one is finally to enunciate the process of repetition and doubling itself. Being aware of this tendency to pattern allows the writer the freedom to use and subvert pattern at will. Knowledge may lift him above necessity and allow him the full play of supplementation.

The fiction of Richard Brautigan is similarly self-consciously and deconstructively playful in its use of culture and literary signs but goes even further in emphasizing a reductiveness of signifier and signified, giving readers no hint of a vision exceeding the boundaries of the fiction that might inform a perception of life or help formulate appropriate kinds of action. Brautigan's mode is ultimately autotelic, intertextual, and metafictive, presenting characters and situations widely separated from the daily affairs and understandings of readers. As metafiction, *The Hawkline Monster* does not pretend to imitate the lives of those in the real world. The only operative principle of imitation is the self-conscious imitation of other fiction and displacement of signification. With its superabundance of mirror doubles—the Hawkline sisters, Cameron and Greer, the sheepmen and the cattlemen, the monster and his shadow, the towns of Billy and Brooks—this fiction is a mirror reflection of other fictional versions of the double. *The Hawkline Monster* is in itself an imitation of other imitations, a parodic, self-referential, metafictive book of metadoubles, that celebrates the very existence of literary imagination and imitation.

Because this text is comically minimalistic, it too can repudiate the implications of the traditional significations of the double. The issues of dualism and psychological narcissism and narcissistic wish fulfillment are posed as false issues. Whereas Freud in interpreting the significance of the mirror image and the double postulates that the adult manifesting narcissistic behavior needs to undergo psychiatric treatment to become normalized, Brautigan asserts that narcissism is the norm. In the fiction many of the characters are narcissistic, especially the playful monster. Creating dramatic roles for those whose lives he touches, manipulating their codes of conduct and actions, this monster is a thinly disguised writer of fiction who creates characters and manipulates them in accordance with the laws of his own self-contained fictional game. But even this creature of "dark invention" cannot control the situation all of the time. The alter ego, the shadow of darkness, takes over as his opposing double and helps Cameron sabotage the worst intentions of the manipulative inventor and controlling author. Even within this game, the principle of indeterminacy subverts carefully planned rules.

But the end of one fiction is always the beginning of another. It is Cameron who lays to rest the monster's designs, and it is Cameron who becomes a producer of films, quite literally projecting the fantasies of his imagination into the lives of millions. The pleasure of this text is the way Brautigan lays bare the double device, exposing the error of the Freudian view of narcissism and spinning an interesting, readable, self-referential fantasy. For Brautigan, as for Barth, literature can only reflect and be about the role of the creative imagination.

Raymond Federman's contribution to the double is also mirror-like, antitelic, and self-reflexive, but it is a further step from realism, philosophy, or rationality, from predictable, significant, and telic meaning. The central metaphor of gambling-doubling boldly enunciates the book's game and underlines Federman's emphasis on the *form* of doubling and his lack of concern about an issue like narcissism. This is a discourse, a dialogue, a multiple conversation between elements of the text and between the text and readers.

The narrative personae provide a major focal point of the doubling in this textual discourse. The recorder, the narrator, the protagonist, the assumed author, and the real author are doubles of one another. Although Federman assigns specific character parts to the personae, he makes it clear that their personalities and functions blur, thereby signaling to readers that they are in fact projections of the author's single and singular imagination. These doubles go beyond the mere fact of doubling to erode categorical distinctions and to indicate that although not much of the author's life is specifically identifiable, the speakers stem from his own real or imagined life. In a word, each person is only a projection or double of a single consciousness.

Even here, however, the principle of indeterminacy functions. Each person has a given function in this game of discourse, but the author cannot contain or rationalize them all, cannot hold them hostage to a governing principle. The personae will every now and again escape their typecast roles, just as the fiction escapes the planning of the author. Despite the rationale for the book, the elaborate plans for composition—the character portraits, plot, and arrangement of words on the page—the discourse will not conform. No matter how perfectly executed, no system can escape the fact of chance, accident, or irregularity. So Federman does not attempt to contain the narrative discourse within a conventional format and typescript. He allows it to disrupt traditional plotting and formatting, to create a fictional collage that lacks overall rational coherence.

By this posture of the narrative, the author can demonstrate his interest in narration, in the play of literary and compositional rules and techniques, in creating an environment that will foster an interaction between text and reader, the sixth projected persona of the book. Here is another kind of doubling in which the reader becomes a projection of the text or, conversely, the text becomes a projection of the reader. Without the reader's reading of the text, it dies, and unless the reader perceives the play and attributes order and coherence to it, it quite literally has none. Seen from this perspective, the interaction between author and reader, between text and interpretation, is in fact double. The various structural doubles within the text—for example, the relationship of "THIS IS NOT THE BEGINNING" and the "BEGINNING"—simply attest to and celebrate this kind of double interaction. This double, an obvious metadouble, emphasizes the many double encounters, the double discourses, of literary texts.

The conclusion to be drawn from this extraordinary double discourse is something more than that to be derived from the customary double. Federman actively courts pluralistic interpretations even as he allows for the blurring and breaking down of assigned narrative roles. This text is, after all, double or nothing. The readings of its discourse must go beyond doubling. Paradoxically, its twin strains must nullify each other to open the way for a new principle of discourse.

The literature of the double, then, has moved well beyond its traditional dualistic moorings. Carnivalized parody has functioned to undermine those traditional categories of meaning and has paved the way for new possibilities. Some authors have used the device of the double to comment on the way we construct systems of selfhood, language, and culture. For others, the techniques of parody are pleasure enough. Deconstruction is a game with inherent principles of pleasure.

But that deconstruction can also implicitly lead to recuperation, for none of the authors utilizing the double ever deconstruct it so that it is incapable of further use. Those who have abandoned some of the seriousness cloaking the device of the double have substituted humor. In so doing they have commented on the structure and forms of our lives and literature, but they have not rendered it obsolete. They have used the device to question humanist certainties and to speak of the radical crisis in our culture and our literature.

But even Federman paradoxically suggests a new interpretation of the double. When he uses the device as a game to end its implications of dualism, he either stops short of, or goes beyond, dualism to recognize pluridimensional possibilities and meanings. In fact, he introduces a new sort of metaphysic through the ludic. It is this new metaphysic that intrigues Wayne Booth, who discovers in the "cosmic irony" of the postmodern era the deflating of the centrality of man in rhetoric reminiscent of traditional religions.[9] All signification is provisional, so it will be most interesting to observe new variations of the double as in its literary manifestations it continues to follow the pattern of the Möbius strip.

Notes

Bibliography

Index

Notes

Prescript: Rewriting the Double

1. Guerard, p. 1.
2. Hallam, p. 11.
3. Hallam, p. 17.
4. Todorov, *The Fantastic*, pp. 143–44.
5. Rogers, pp. 161–74.
6. de Man, p. 191.
7. Malmgren, p. 13.
8. Hutcheon, *Canadian Postmodern*, p. 2.
9. Lyotard.
10. Jameson, "Postmodernism," pp. 53–92; Eagleton, *Against the Grain*.
11. Jameson, "Postmodernism," p. 58.
12. Tiffin, p. viii.
13. Jencks.
14. Klinkowitz, *Literary Subversions*, p. xix.
15. Gitlin.
16. Hassan, "Pluralism in Postmodern Perspective," pp. 504–8.
17. Stark, *Literature of Exhaustion*, p. 160.
18. Coates, pp. 1–31.
19. Higgins, p. 5.
20. Hutcheon, *Poetics of Postmodernism*, pp. 163, 167.

1. The History of the Double: Traditional and Postmodern Versions

1. Foucault, *Archaeology of Knowledge*, p. 7.
2. Barth, "Some Reasons Why I Tell the Stories I Tell the Way I Tell

Them Rather Than Some Other Sort of Stories Some Other Way," in *Friday Book*, p. 3. See also, for example, Rank, "Double as Immortal Self," p. 84, as well as the whole of his *Myth of the Birth of the Hero*; Tymms pp. 24–26; Keppler, pp. 14–26; and Hallam, p. 6.

3. See Frazer, pp. 76–77.

4. Plato, *Symposium*, pp. 59–65.

5. This idea is echoed by Rank in "Double as Immortal Self."

6. See Vinge.

7. Frazer, p. 207.

8. See Borges's comment on the fetch and wraith, p. 80.

9. Miyoshi, p. ix.

10. Karl Miller, p. 21.

11. Keppler, p. 161.

12. This is something like the position of William Blake, who asserted in "The Marriage of Heaven and Hell" that "without Contraries is no progression. Attraction and Repulsion, Reason and Energy, Love and Hate, are necessary to Human existence."

13. Eichner, p. 70.

14. Wain.

15. Nietzsche, p. 225.

16. Marcus.

17. Rogers, pp. 68–69.

18. See Rogers, esp. "The Mirror Self"; also see Tymms, pp. 40–41.

19. Wilson, p. 10.

20. Rogers, pp. 20–23, 99.

21. Freud, " 'Uncanny,' " p. 238, and "Beyond the Pleasure Principle," p. 36.

22. Freud, "Beyond Pleasure Principle," p. 36.

23. Freud, " 'Uncanny,' " p. 235.

24. Freud, "Beyond Pleasure Principle," pp. 49, 50. Such images and understandings of the personality are presented by Rank, Rogers, Rosenfield, and Keppler in their interpretations of the id, superego, and ego.

25. Rank, "Double as Immortal Self," pp. 62–101; Rosenfield, "Shadow Within, pp. 311–31; and Keppler.

26. Rogers, p. 29.

27. Ibid., pp. 31, 161–74.

28. Jung, "Shadow," p. 8.

29. Ibid., p. 9.

30. Jung, " Syzygy," pp. 20–21.

31. Jung, *Dreams*, p. 52.

32. LeGuin, p. 63.

33. Ibid., p. 64.
34. Keppler, p. 106.
35. Scholes, p. 52.
36. Keppler, p. 56; Rogers, p. 138.
37. Marcuse, pp. 35–36.
38. Irwin, pp. 4, 15.
39. Jackson, p. 4.
40. Bowie, p. 127.
41. Coates, p. 4.
42. Blum, p. 1.
43. Durham, p. 38.
44. Barthes, *Mythologies*, p. 45.
45. Barthes, *Elements of Semiology*, p. 12.
46. Johnson, p. viii.
47. Derrida, *Dissemination*, p. 221.
48. Ibid., pp. 186, 188; Derrida, "Living On," p. 164.
49. See Foucault, *Care of the Self*, p. 198.
50. Foucault, "Subject and Power," p. 208.
51. Foucault, *Language, Counter-Memory*, p. 56.
52. Foucault, *Order of Things*, p. 340ff.
53. Foucault, *Language, Counter-Memory*, pp. 182–83.
54. Ibid., p. 117.
55. Rosolato, p. 202.
56. Foucault, *Order of Things*, p. 325.
57. Ibid., p. 326.
58. Ibid., p. 318.
59. Ehrmann, "Tragic/Utopian Meaning," pp. 17, 30.
60. Derrida, *Writing and Difference*, p. 280.
61. Coates, p. xi.
62. Tiffin, p. viii; Eagleton, "Capitalism, Modernism," pp. 60–73; Jameson, "Postmodernism and Consumer Society."
63. Hutcheon, *Poetics of Postmodernism*, p. 35.
64. While the nineteenth-century use of the double is dualistically oriented, a few works are noticeably parodistic. For instance, the parody of the double at the heart of Brentano and Jean-Paul Richter. To Brentano's *Die Mehreren Wehmüller*, Tymms (p. 70) attributes mockery of "the whole stock-in-trade of romantic coincidences and mystifications, including (with a comic abuse of the modish technique of the tale-within-a-tale) a tilt at the supernaturalism with which Hoffmann invests the *Doppelgänger*." The consequence of the doubling in Brentano's tale is not only a parody of the typical romantic treatment of the double but finally a self-reflexive parody, mocking the very devices

it uses. Even the doubles of Edgar Allan Poe are playful and antidualistic. In "William Wilson" and "Ligeia," Poe wraps the apparent contraries of human nature in a tissue of indeterminacy and subterfuge.

65. Lacan, "Of Structure," p. 194.
66. Derrida, *Dissemination*, pp. 243, 268.
67. McHale, p. 134.
68. Ibid., pp. 10, 73.
69. Lodge, pp. 220–45.
70. Fokkema, *Literary History*.
71. Rosolato, p. 217.
72. Barth, "Literature of Exhaustion," in *Friday Book*, p. 74.
73. Klinkowitz, *Literary Disruptions*.
74. Said; Rorty.
75. McHale, p. 190.
76. Kline, pp. 72–73.
77. Derrida, "Living On," p. 78.

2. Analogy and the False Double: Nabokov's *Despair*

1. Eagleton, *Literary Theory*, p. vii.
2. McHale, p. 18.
3. Erlich, p. 18.
4. Shklovsky, p. 11.
5. Appel, "Interview with Vladimir Nabokov," pp. 22–23.
6. Nabokov, *Strong Opinions*, pp. 160–61.
7. Appel, "Interview with Vladimir Nabokov," p. 30.
8. Hutcheon, *Theory of Parody*, pp. 72–83.
9. Rosenfield, "*Despair* and Lust," pp. 66–84; Rogers, pp. 164–66; Williams, pp. 165–82; Field, pp. 219–36; Nicol; Gordon; Appel, "Interview with Vladimir Nabokov"; and Roth, pp. 204–28; Appel ("Lolita," p. 131) makes it clear that he does not accept the psychological interpretation of Nabokov's doubles. He finds them all parodies and self-parodies of that angle.
10. Appel, "Lolita," pp. 127, 131.
11. Ibid., pp. 131, 133.
12. Gordon, pp. 155–56.
13. Appel, "Interview with Vladimir Nabokov," p. 37.
14. Ibid., p. 37.
15. Ibid., pp. 41–42.
16. Rogers, p. 165.
17. Smock, *Double Dealing*, pp. 47–69.
18. Arana, p. 127.

19. Stuart.

20. Derrida, *Margins of Philosophy*, p. 242, and *Archaeology of the Frivolous*, pp. 73–74.

21. Derrida, *Archaeology of the Frivolous*, pp. 76, 83.

22. Wittgenstein, p. 17.

23. Nabokov, *Despair*. Hereafter, references to this book will be cited in the text.

24. Other examples of the way Hermann seeks resemblances include the nonsensical equation of the formula "minus X minus = plus" and mirrors; his inability to separate current experiences in Tarnitz with those of his childhood in St. Petersburg; and his confusion of Ardalion's picture of peaches and an ashtray with another of two roses and a briar pipe.

25. Compare, for example, Plato's analysis of the poet and the mirror metaphor in *The Republic* X, *Ion* 535–6, and *Apology* 22 with Abrams's discussion of Neoplatonism, pp. 42–46.

26. Todorov, *Fantastic*, p. 113.

27. Ibid., p. 115.

28. McHale, p. 231.

29. Alter, p. 198.

30. Appel, "Interview with Vladimir Nabokov," p. 25. Popper, *Open Society*, vol. 1, discusses Platonic thought as it can contribute to a totalitarian state.

31. Dolores M. Burdick, "'The Line Down the Middle': Politics and Sexuality in Fassbinder's *Despair*," *Fearful Symmetry*, p. 138.

32. Ibid.,p. 139.

3. Binary Intersubjectivity: Pynchon's *Gravity's Rainbow*

1. Hutcheon, *Poetics of Postmodernism*, p. 4.

2. Redfield, p. 159.

3. Hite, p. 10.

4. Davis, p. 410.

5. Derrida, *Dissemination*, p. xxvii.

6. Foucault, "Discourse on Language," p. 229.

7. Culler, *On Deconstruction*, p. 140.

8. Cooper, p. 3.

9. Tanner, p. 54.

10. Slade, *Thomas Pynchon*, p. 69.

11. Pynchon, *Crying of Lot 49*, p. 136.

12. Stark, *Pynchon's Fictions*, p. 17.

13. McHale, p. 25.

14. Fowler, p. 112.

15. Slade, *Thomas Pynchon*, pp. 185–86.

16. Clerc, p. 24.

17. Hite, p. 128.

18. Pynchon, *Gravity's Rainbow*, p. 555. All references to *Gravity's Rainbow* in the text refer to this edition.

19. Slade, "Religion, Psychology," p. 167.

20. Wilde, p. 82.

21. McHoul and Wills, p. 57.

22. Tanner, p. 82.

23. Cooper, p. 188.

24. Stark, *Pynchon's Fictions*, p. 48.

25. Bersani, p. 108.

26. Cooper, p. 166.

27. Horkheimer, p. 176.

28. Bersani, pp. 101–2.

29. Lyotard, p. 12.

30. Siegel, p. 19.

31. Bersani, p. 112.

32. Derrida, "Structure, Sign, and Play," p. 289.

33. Fowler, p. 19.

34. One of the recurrent terms in the book is "mystery." It is used in the conventional Christian sense of sacrament but also in the sense of "hidden"—an idea whose origin is not revealed and is consequently elusive and difficult to contest or combat. In this sense, it is what Barthes calls culture trying to pass itself off as nature. It is also used in a parodic way when the members of the group working on the rocket are described as initiates of religious mysteries. It might be fair to say that Pynchon uses the term in much the same way as Blake in his poem "The Human Abstract," where the Tree of Mystery represents an abstract and inhuman view of religion that has its roots only in the human brain.

35. Cooper, p. 53.

36. Eagleton, *Literary Theory*, p. 131.

37. Tanner, p. 25.

38. Russell, p. 268.

39. Tanner, p. 76.

40. Foucault, "What Is an Author," in *Language, Counter-Memory*, p. 130.

41. Dugdale, p. 189.

42. Foucault, "What Is an Author," in *Language, Counter-Memory*, p. 138.

43. Schaub, p. 116.

4. Eros and Thanatos: Hawkes's *Blood Oranges*

1. Barthelme.
2. McGuane, p. 1.
3. Greiner, *Understanding Hawkes*, p. 1.
4. Fielding.
5. Fiedler, p. xi.
6. O'Donnell, p. 19.
7. Graham.
8. Hawkes, "Conversation, *Blood Oranges*," p. 200.
9. Greiner, *Understanding Hawkes*, p. 125.
10. O'Donnell, p. 122; Kuehl, pp. 158–59.
11. Kuehl, p. 171.
12. Hawkes, *Blood Oranges*, p. 203.
13. O'Donnell, p. 2.
14. Kuehl, pp. 164–65.
15. Freud, "Ego and Id," p. 373.
16. Lacan, "Mirror Stage," p. 3.
17. According to Freud, each human being consists of two basic instincts that are linked to the primal origins of the inorganic state and organic development. He defines *instinct* as "an urge inherent in organic life to restore an earlier state of things," and there is no instinct whatsoever that moves mankind to the higher level of superman (Freud, "Beyond the Pleasure Principle," p. 308). The sexual instinct has as its goal—this anthropomorphization is Freud's—the genetic continuation of each creature. Working for the limited immortality offered by reproduction, the sexual instinct seeks the originary pattern of organic growth. Because immortality is possible only through combination of two germ cells, the sexual instinct is also responsible for "death" or termination of individual development and for the continuation of the species. The death instinct seeks something still more primal, for "inanimate things existed before living ones," a fact that suggests to Freud that "the aim of all life is death" ("Pleasure Principle," p. 311). Death is ultimately stronger than sex, in Freud's view, and instinctual life serves to bring about death. Indeed, the potential immortality offered by the sexual instinct may be "no more than a lengthening of the road to death" ("Pleasure Principle," p. 313), a way of allowing each creature to pursue its own way to death.

18. Emmett and Vine, p. 168.

19. Lacan, "Function and Field of Speech," in *Écrits*, p. 67.

20. Hawkes's choice of the word *faun*, instead of *fawn*, is interesting. Technically, the faun of mythology is male, although there is a goddess named Fauna (Bona Dea), patroness of chastity and fruitfulness. It is difficult to tell whether Hawkes has made a spelling error or is conscious of the irony.

21. Barthes, *Mythologies*.

22. Lacan, "Function and Field of Speech," p. 66.

23. Lacan, "The Subversion of the Subject and the Dialectic of Desire in the Freudian Unconscious," in *Écrits*, p. 321.

24. Lacan, "Aggressivity in Psychoanalysis," in *Écrits*, p. 28.

25. Greiner, *Comic Terror*, p. 221.

26. Lacan, "Aggressivity in Psychoanalysis," p. 16.

5. "Neither one nor quite two": Barth's *Lost in the Funhouse*

1. Barthes, *Writing Degree Zero*, p. 93.

2. Barth, "Some Reasons Why I Tell the Stories," in *Friday Book*, pp. 7, 159.

3. Le Clair and McCaffery, pp. 9–19. See also Barth's discussion of the similar structures of regression and return, theme and variation, that he perceives in most phenomena; "Tales Within Tales Within Tales," in *Friday Book*, p. 237.

4. Comments by Johan Huizinga tend to support Barth's view of music as play. In *Homo Ludens* (p. 62), he persuasively argues that "music bears at the outset all the formal characteristics of play proper: the activity begins and ends within strict limits of time and place, is repeatable, consists essentially in order, rhythm, alternation, transports audience and performers alike out of 'ordinary' life into a sphere of gladness and serenity, which makes even sad music a lofty pleasure. In other words, it 'enchants' and 'enraptures' them."

5. Barth, "More Troll Than Cabbage" and "Algebra and Fire," in *Friday Book*, pp. 79, 167.

6. Barth, "Historical Fiction, Fictitious History," in *The Friday Book*, p. 191.

7. Cf. Lewis, p. 134.

8. Fink, pp. 20–21.

9. Barth, "More on the Same Subject," in *Friday Book*, p. 29.

10. Ziegler, p. 19.

11. Terrence Hawkes, p. 71; Todorov, *Littérature et Signification*, p. 49.

12. Cf. Enck, p. 6; Barth, "The Literature of Exhaustion" and "The Spirit of Place," in *Friday Book*, pp. 68, 127–29; Bellamy, pp. 3, 7; and Barth, "Literature of Replenishment," in *Friday Book*, p. 203.

13. Barth, "Literature of Replenishment," in *Friday Book*, p. 205.

14. Ibid., p. 203.

15. Derrida, *Margins of Philosophy*, p. 329.

16. Baxtin, pp. 184, 185.

17. Harris, p. 26.

18. Ibid., p. 32.

19. Prince, pp. 56–57; Barth, "The Self in Fiction," in *Friday Book*, pp. 207–14.

20. Barth, *Giles Goat-Boy*, p. xx.

21. Barth, "Literature of Exhaustion," in *Friday Book*, p. 74.

22. Joseph, pp. 7, 29. See also Scholes, pp. 75–102, and Stark, *Literature of Exhaustion*, p. 160.

23. *New Yorker* 48 (September 30, 1972): 125.

24. Rovit; Joseph, pp. 7–9; Russell Miller; and Stark, *Literature of Exhaustion*, pp. 118–75, esp. 142.

25. Alter, p. 159; Rogers, p. 130.

26. Other such opposing doubles in the book include Charley Mattassin and Cohunkaprets, Lord Baltimore and John Coode.

27. Spivak, p. xix; Ricardou, p. 119.

28. Barth, *Sot-Weed Factor*, p. 556.

29. Barth, "Tales Within Tales," in *Friday Book*, p. 220.

30. Barth, "Literature of Replenishment," in *Friday Book*, pp. 200, 203.

31. Terence Hawkes, p. 144.

32. Barth, "Literature of Exhaustion," in *Friday Book*, p. 63.

33. Barth, *Lost in the Funhouse*, pp. 32–34. Hereafter, all references to *Lost in the Funhouse* in the text refer to this edition.

34. Barth, *Chimera*, p. 138.

35. Barth, "Tales Within Tales," in *Friday Book*, pp. 222–23.

36. Harris, p. 165.

37. Ibid., p. 165.

38. Barth, "My Two Problems: 2," in *Friday Book*, p. 147.

39. Barth, "Literature of Replenishment," in *Friday Book*, p. 204.

40. Slethaug, "Floating Signifiers."

41. Barth, *Sabbatical*, p. 199.

42. Slethaug and Fogel, pp. 190–212.

43. Malmgren, pp. 176–77.

44. Stevick, p. 18.

45. Cf. Lacan, "Of Structure as an Inmixing," p. 192, and Derrida, "Ellipsis," in *Writing and Difference*, p. 296.

46. Barth, "Getting Oriented" and "Algebra and Fire," in *Friday Book*, pp. 134, 139, 170.

47. Derrida, "Ellipsis," p. 280.

48. Ibid., pp. 297, 299.

49. Caramello, p. 118.

50. Morrissette, pp. 159–60.

51. McConnell, p. 111; Lewis, p. 137; Barth, "Tales Within Tales," p. 224.

52. Rosolato, p. 203.

53. In the discussion of Rosolato's "Voice and the Literary Myth," p. 216, Jean Hippolyte asks whether the double within a literary work does not demonstrate the problematic of literature as the double of society.

54. Bienstock.

55. Derrida, *Writing and Difference*, pp. 289, 291.

56. For the critique of *Lost in the Funhouse* as a *Künstlerroman*, see Kiernan; Barth, "Self in Fiction," in *Friday Book*, pp. 208–9.

57. Foucault, "Man and His Doubles," in *Order of Things*; p. 308; Rosolato, p. 204.

58. Rosolato, p. 202.

59. Barth, "Self in Fiction," in *Friday Book*, p. 210; Derrida, *Margins of Philosophy*, p. 248.

60. Hansen, esp. pp. 9–10; Hauck, pp. 201–10.

61. Rosolato, p. 207.

62. Barthes, *Pleasure of the Text*, p. 32.

63. Ehrmann, "Death of Literature," pp. 245, 247; Rosolato, p. 208.

64. Derrida, *Positions*, p. 12; Derrida, *Grammatology*, p. 55; Terence Hawkes (p. 148) remarks of Derrida's *différence/différance* that "speech cannot stand as the reality to writing's shadow, for speech already *itself* appears to be a shadow of some *prior* act of signification, of which it manifests the 'trace,' in an infinite regression."

65. Barth, *End of the Road*, p. 110.

66. Jameson, *Prison-House of Language*, p. 105.

6. Minimalism, Metadoubles, and Narcissism: Brautigan's *Hawkline Monster*

1. Chénetier, p. 19.

2. Barth, "Role of the Prosaic in Fiction," in *Friday Book*, p. 83.

3. McHale, p. 190.

4. Derrida, *Grammatology*, p. 7.

5. Chénetier, pp. 30, 32.

6. Hutcheon, *Poetics of Postmodernism*, p. 26.

7. Baxtin, p. 176.

8. Barthes, *Pleasure of the Text*, p. 6.

9. Chénetier, p. 21.

10. Foster, p. 91. The reviewers tend to view *The Hawkline Monster* as altogether playful and unsubstantial. See Adams, Nordell, and Yohalem. Willis thinks the story is Brautigan's pronouncement on America's failed dream.

11. Malley, p. 35.

12. Bruce Cook, p. 208.

13. Rockwell, p. 115. See also Perreault, p. 260, and Eagleton, "Capitalism, Modernism and Postmodernism."

14. Goossen, p. 169.

15. Chénetier, p. 21.

16. Malley, p. 128.

17. Fried, p. 145.

18. Sharp, pp. 344–45.

19. Chénetier, p. 31.

20. David Cook, p. 620; Bochner, p. 101.

21. O'Doherty, p. 253.

22. Nyman, p. 24; Cage, p. 345.

23. Clayton, p. 59.

24. Klinkowitz, *Literary Subversions*, p. xxix.

25. Rose, p. 293.

26. Bochner, p. 100.

27. See my "*Hawkline Monster*."

28. Stevick, p. 120.

29. Chénetier, p. 31.

30. Brautigan, *Hawkline Monster*, p. 173. Hereafter, all references to this book are cited in the text.

31. Rank, *Double: Psychoanalytic Study*, p. 33.

32. Foster, p. 102.

33. Rogers, p. 19.

34. Vinge, p. 12.

35. Rank, "Double as Immortal Self," p. 91.

36. Tymms, p. 29.

37. Chénetier, p. 60.

38. Rank, "Double as Immortal Self," p. 84.

39. Tymms, p. 33.

40. Rosenfield, "Shadow Within," p. 325.

41. Rogers, p. 30.
42. Rank, "Double as Immortal Self," p. 84.
43. Ibid., p. 97.
44. Ibid., p. 101.

7. Surfictive Games of Discourse: Federman's *Double or Nothing*

1. Federman, "Surfiction," p. 7.
2. Hassan, "Pluralism," p. 506.
3. Beaujour, "Game of Poetics," p. 63.
4. Federman, "Surfiction," p. 8.
5. Ricardou, p. 130.
6. Ehrmann, "Death of Literature," p. 239.
7. Federman, "Surfiction," p. 13.
8. Culler, "Towards a Theory," p. 258.
9. Huizinga, *Homo Ludens*, p. 12; Derrida, *Dissemination*, p. 63. Although the indebtedness of *Double or Nothing* to Laurence Sterne's *Tristram Shandy* deserves a treatment I cannot give it here, there are certain major features of resemblance that may be touched on. The coupling of rhetoric and game is one such aspect. As Richard A. Lanham (*Tristram Shandy: The Games of Pleasure* [Berkeley: University of California Press, 1973], p. 43) notes of *Tristram Shandy*: "It is interesting to pair rhetorical theory for a moment with game theory. . . . Both are theories of conflict-analysis and conflict-resolution. Both try to reduce conflict to pattern, defuse it by stylizing it." Federman follows this tradition by pairing discourse and game, though he is not especially concerned with the central proposition of conflict analysis. Another point of similarity is an emphasis on a 365-day pattern, which in certain respects governs each of the two books. About midway in his narrative, Tristram complains that in his writing he has been able to cover only the first day of his life. The narrator of *Double or Nothing* seems to get nothing on paper. It is only the recorder who is able to capture the narrator's hopes and plans for the book, and behind that, only the author who has really written anything. The game of empty pages, doodles, and scribbles also may be traced to Sterne, who may rightfully be called the father of the novelistic game in English literature.
10. Klinkowitz, *Literary Disruptions*, pp.129–53; Eder, p. 153; Ehrmann, "Death of Literature," p. 239.
11. Federman, *Double or Nothing*, p. 00000000. Hereafter, this book will be cited in the text.

12. Klinkowitz, *Literary Disruptions*, p. 132.

13. Ricardou, p. 103.

14. Beaujour, "Game of Poetics," pp. 62–63. That Federman adheres to such a premise is apparent from the format of *Double or Nothing*. But his use of such a procedure is also overtly supported by a hidden "game" reference to Jacques Ehrmann. When the narrator goes through the motions of choosing a name for his protagonist, he centers on Jack or Jacques, a name he loves. The significance of that name is not made altogether clear, however, until *The Twofold Vibration*, where it again emerges. In this futuristic novel, the protagonist, the same character as the narrator of *Double or Nothing*, is, everyone supposes, about to be removed to the developing space colonies as a form of social control or punishment for some unknown infraction he has committed. While he waits his turn at the launching center, other less lucky ones are taken away. These include Jacques Ehrmann, Larry McCaffery, and Ihab Hassan, literary dissidents who, we must suppose, are dangerous to the state of art because they deconstruct the game and expose the arbitrariness of the rules.

15. Beaujour, "Introduction," pp. 6–7.

16. There are many lesser games referred to or played in this fiction. For example, the narrator plays a picture game with the typescript when he notes that in Detroit Boris walks into a school filled with fifteen blacks and when he mentions that the wallpaper of the room is covered with horses and gives them numbers, suggesting a horse race.

17. Axelos, p. 14.

18. Macksey, "Lions and Squares," p. 12.

19. McHale, p. 184.

20. Malmgren, p. 180.

21. Kostelanetz, p. 96.

22. Derrida, *Dissemination*, p. 180.

23. Ehrmann, "Homo Ludens Revisited," p. 56.

24. Beaujour, "Game of Poetics," p. 64.

25. On p. 14 of the text, it is unclear whether the difficulty described pertains to the narrator's problem in getting on with the fiction or the protagonist's getting on with his sex life. The two are strangely combined.

26. Werner, p. 107.

27. McHale, p. 201.

28. Ehrmann, "Homo Ludens Revisited," p. 55.

29. Ehrmann, "Death of Literature," p. 241.

30. Pearce, "Enter the Frame," p. 48.

Postscript: Re-viewing the Double

1. Stevick, pp. 8, 12.
2. Macksey, "Lions and Squares," p. 11.
3. Macksey, "Lions and Squares," pp. 11–12.
4. Stevick, p. 45.
5. Hassan, "Pluralism," pp. 504–5.
6. See, for instance, Meyer, whose comments on indeterminacy in painting and music as well as literature are directly applicable.
7. Meyer, p. 178.
8. Hassan, *Literature of Silence*," p. 4.
9. Booth, pp. 719–37.

Bibliography

Abrams, M. H. *The Mirror and the Lamp: Romantic Theory and the Critical Tradition*. New York: Oxford University Press, 1953.

Adams, Phoebe. Review of *The Hawkline Monster: A Gothic Western*, by Richard Brautigan. *Atlantic Monthly* 234, no. 4 (October 1974): 119–20.

Alter, Robert. *Partial Magic: The Novel as a Self-Conscious Genre*. Berkeley: University of California Press, 1975.

Appel, Alfred, Jr. "An Interview with Vladimir Nabokov." In *Nabokov: The Man and His Work*, edited by L. S. Dembo, 19–44. Madison: University of Wisconsin Press, 1967.

———. "Lolita: The Springboard of Parody." In *Nabokov: The Man and His Work*, edited by L. S. Dembo, 106–43. Madison: University of Wisconsin Press, 1967.

Arana, R. Victoria. " 'The Line Down the Middle' in Autobiography: Critical Implications of the Quest for the Self." In *Fearful Symmetry: Doubles and Doubling in Literature and Film*, edited by Eugene J. Crook, 125–37. Tallahassee: University Presses of Florida, 1981.

Axelos, Kostas. "Planetary Interlude." *Yale French Studies* 41 (1968): 6–18.

Barth, John. *Chimera*. New York: Random House, 1972.

———. *The End of the Road*. Garden City, N.Y.: Doubleday, 1967.

———. *The Friday Book: Essays and Other Nonfiction*. New York: G. P. Putnam's Sons, 1984.

———. *Giles Goat-Boy*. Garden City, N.Y.: Doubleday, 1966.

———. *Lost in the Funhouse: Fiction for Print, Tape, Live Voice*. Garden City, N. Y.: Doubleday & Co., Inc., 1968.

———. *The Last Voyage of Somebody the Sailor*. Boston: Little, Brown, 1991.

———. *Sabbatical: A Romance*. New York: G. P. Putnam's Sons, 1982.

———. *The Sot-Weed Factor*. Garden City, N.Y.: Doubleday, 1967.

Barthelme, Donald. "The Most Wonderful Trick." *The New York Times Book Review*, November 25, 1984, p. 3.

Barthes, Roland. *Elements of Semiology*. Translated by Annette Lavers and Colin Smith. London: Jonathan Cape, 1967.

———. *Mythologies*. Translated by Annette Lavers. London: Jonathan Cape, 1972.

———. *The Pleasure of the Text*. Translated by Richard Miller. New York: Hill and Wang, Farrar, Straus, and Giroux, 1975.

———. *Writing Degree Zero*. Translated by Annette Lavers and Colin Smith. London: Jonathan Cape, 1967.

Battcock, Gregory, ed. *Minimal Art: A Critical Anthology*. New York: E. P. Dutton, 1968.

Baxtin, Mixail. "Discourse Typology in Prose." In *Readings in Russian Poetics: Formalist and Structuralist Views*, edited by Ladislav Matejka and Krystyna Pomorska, 176–96. Cambridge, Mass.: MIT Press, 1971.

Beaujour, Michel. "The Game of Poetics." *Yale French Studies* 41 (1968): 58–67.

———. "Introduction." *Yale French Studies*, 58 (1979): 6–14.

Bellamy, Joe David, ed. "John Barth." In *The New Fiction: Interviews with Innovative American Writers*, 1–18. Urbana: University of Illinois Press, 1974.

Bersani, Leo. "Pynchon, Paranoia, and Literature." *Representations* 25 (Winter 1989): 108.

Bienstock, Beverly Gray. "Lingering on the Autognostic Verge: John Barth's *Lost in the Funhouse*." *Modern Fiction Studies* 19, no. 1 (Spring 1973): 69–78.

Blum, Joanne. *Transcending Gender: The Male/Female Double in Women's Fiction*. Ann Arbor, Mich.: UMI Research Press, 1988.

Bochner, Mel. "Serial Art, Systems, Solipsism." In *Minimal Art*, edited by Gregory Battcock, 92–102. New York: E. P. Dutton, 1968.

Booth, Wayne. "The Empire of Irony." *Georgia Review* 37 (Winter 1983): 719–37.

Borges, Jorge Luis. *The Book of Imaginary Beings*. Translated by Norman Thomas di Giovanni. New York: E. P. Dutton, 1969.

Bowie, Malcolm. "Jacques Lacan." In *Structuralism and Since: From Lévi-Strauss to Derrida*, edited by John Sturrock, 116–53. Oxford: Oxford University Press, 1979.

Brautigan, Richard. *The Hawkline Monster: A Gothic Western*. New York: Simon and Schuster, 1974.

Burdick, Dolores M. " 'The Line Down the Middle': Politics and Sexuality in Fassbinder's *Despair*." In *Fearful Symmetry: Doubles and Doubling in Literature and Film*, edited by Eugene J. Crook, 138–48. Tallahassee: University Presses of Florida, 1981.

Cage, John. "Interview with Roger Reynolds, 1962." In *Contemporary Composers on Contemporary Music*, edited by Elliott Schwartz and Barney Childs, 336–48. New York: Holt, Rinehart and Winston, 1967.

Caramello, Charles. *Silverless Mirrors: Book, Self and Postmodern American Fiction*. Tallahassee: University Presses of Florida, 1983.

Chénetier, Marc. *Richard Brautigan*. London: Methuen, 1983.

Clayton, John. "Richard Brautigan: The Politics of Woodstock." In *New American Review*, edited by Ted Salotaroff, 56–68. New York: Simon and Schuster, 1971.

Clerc, Charles. Introduction to *Approaches to Gravity's Rainbow*, edited by Charles Clerc. Columbus: Ohio State University Press, 1983.

Coates, Paul. *The Double and the Other: Identity as Ideology in Post-Romantic Fiction*. London: Macmillan, 1988.

Cook, Bruce. *The Beat Generation*. New York: Charles Scribner's Sons, 1971.

Cook, David A. *A History of Narrative Film*. New York: W. W. Norton, 1981.

Cooper, Peter L. *Signs and Symptoms: Thomas Pynchon and the Contemporary World*. Berkeley: University of California Press, 1983.

Crook, Eugene, ed. *Fearful Symmetry: Doubles and Doubling in Literature and Film*. Tallahassee: University Presses of Florida, 1981.

Culler, Jonathan. *On Deconstruction: Theory and Criticism after Structuralism*. Ithaca, N.Y.: Cornell University Press, 1982.

———. "Towards a Theory of Non-Genre Literature." In *Surfiction: Fiction Now . . . and Tomorrow*, edited by Raymond Federman, 255–62. Chicago: Swallow Press, 1981.

Davis, Robert Con. "The Poststructuralist 'Texte.' " In *Contemporary Literary Criticism*, edited by Robert Con Davis. New York: Longman, 1986.

de Man, Paul. "The Rhetoric of Temporality." In *Interpretation: Theory and Practice*, edited by C. S. Singleton. Baltimore: Johns Hopkins University Press, 1969.

Derrida, Jacques. *The Archaeology of the Frivolous: Reading Condillac*. Translated by John P. Leavey, Jr. Pittsburgh: Duquesne University Press, 1980.

———. *Dissemination*. Translated by Barbara Johnson. Chicago: University of Chicago Press, 1981.

———. *Of Grammatology*. Translated by Gayatori Chakravorty Spivak. Baltimore: Johns Hopkins University Press, 1976.

———. "Living On: *Border Lines*." In *Deconstruction and Criticism*, edited by Harold Bloom et al., 75–176. New York: Continuum, 1979.

———. *Margins of Philosophy*. Translated by Alan Bass. Chicago: University of Chicago Press, 1982.

———. *Positions*. Translated by Alan Bass. Chicago: University of Chicago Press, 1972.

———. *Writing and Difference*. Translated by Alan Bass. Chicago: University of Chicago Press, 1978.

Dugdale, John. *Thomas Pynchon: Allusive Parables of Power*. Houndsmills, England: Macmillan, 1990.

Durham, Carolyn A. "Fearful Symmetry: The Mother-Daughter Theme in *La Religieuse* and *Paul et Virginie*." In *Fearful Symmetry: Doubles and Doubling in Literature and Film*, edited by Eugene J. Crook, 32–40. Tallahassee: University Presses of Florida, 1981.

Eagleton, Terry. *Against the Grain: Essays 1975–1985*. London: Verso, 1986.

———. "Capitalism, Modernism, and Postmodernism. " *New Left Review* 152: 60–73.

———. *Literary Theory: An Introduction*. Oxford: Basil Blackwell, 1983.

Eder, Doris L. "*Surfiction*: Plunging into the Surface." *Boundary 2*, 5, No. 1 (Fall 1976): 153–64.

Ehrmann, Jacques. "The Death of Literature." In *Surfiction: Fiction Now . . . and Tomorrow*, edited by Raymond Federman, 229–53. Chicago: Swallow Press, 1981.

———. "Homo Ludens revisited." *Yale French Studies* 41 (1968): 31–57.

———. "The Tragic/Utopian Meaning of History." *Yale French Studies* 58 (1979): 15–30.

Eichner, Hans. *Friedrich Schlegel*. New York: Twayne, 1970.

Emmett, Paul, and Richard Vine. "A Conversation with John Hawkes." *Chicago Review* 28 (1976): 163–71.

Enck, John. "John Barth: An Interview." *Wisconsin Studies in Contemporary Literature* 6, no. 1 (Winter-Spring 1965): 3–14.

Erlich, Victor. *Russian Formalism: History-Doctrine*. 'S-Gravenhage, Netherlands: Mouton, 1955.

Federman, Raymond. *Double or Nothing: A Real Fictitious Discourse*. Chicago: Swallow Press, 1971.

———. "Surfiction—Four Propositions in Form of an Introduction." In *Surfiction: Fiction Now . . . and Tomorrow*, edited by Federman, 5–15. Chicago: Swallow Press, 1981.

Fiedler, Leslie A. "The Pleasures of John Hawkes." Introduction to *The Lime Twig*, vii–xiv. New York: New Directions, 1961.

Field, Andrew. *Nabokov: His Life in Art*. Boston: Little, Brown, 1967.

Fielding, Andrew. "John Hawkes Is a Very Nice Guy, and a Novelist of Sex and Death." *Village Voice*, May, 24, 1976, p. 47.

Fink, Eugen. "The Oasis of Happiness: Toward an Ontology of Play." *Yale French Studies* 41 (1968): 19–30.

Fokkema, Douwe. *Literary History, Modernism, and Postmodernism*. Amsterdam: John Benjamins, 1984.

Fokkema, Douwe, and Hans Bertens, eds. *Approaching Postmodernism*. Amsterdam: John Benjamins, 1986.

Foster, Edward Halsey. *Richard Brautigan*. Boston: Twayne, 1983.

Foucault, Michel. *The Archaeology of Knowledge*. Translated by A. M. Sheridan Smith. London: Routledge, 1972.

———. *The Care of the Self*. New York: Vintage, Random House, 1988.

———. *Language, Counter-Memory, Practice: Selected Essays and Interviews*. Edited by Donald F. Bouchard. Ithaca, N.Y.: Cornell University Press, 1977.

———. *The Order of Things: An Archaeology of the Human Sciences*. New York: Pantheon, 1970.

———. "The Subject and Power." In *Michel Foucault: Beyond Structuralism and Hermeneutics*, edited by Herbert L. Dreyfus and Paul Rabinow, 208–26. Chicago: University of Chicago Press, 1982.

Fowler, Douglas. *A Reader's Guide to "Gravity's Rainbow."* Ann Arbor, Mich.: Ardis, 1980.

Frazer, Sir James. *The Golden Bough*. Abridged ed. New York: Macmillan, 1960.

Freud, Sigmund. "Beyond the Pleasure Principle.," In *Complete Psychological Works*, edited by James Strachey et al., vol. 18. London: Hogarth Press, 1962.

———. "The Ego and the Id." In *On Metapsychology: The Theory of Psychoanalysis*. Middlesex, England: Penguin, 1984.

———. "The 'Uncanny.' " In *Complete Psychological Works*, edited by James Strachey et al., vol. 17. London: Hogarth Press, 1962.

Fried, Michael. "Art and Objecthood." In *Minimal Art: A Critical Anthology*, edited by Gregory Battcock, 116–47. New York: E. P. Dutton, 1968.

Gitlin, Todd. "Hip Deep in Post-modernism," *The New York Times Book Review*, November 6, 1988, p. 35.

Goossen, E. C. "Two Exhibitions." In *Minimal Art: A Critical Anthology*, edited by Gregory Battcock, 165–79. New York: E. P. Dutton, 1968.

Gordon, Ambrose, Jr. "The Double Pnin." In *Nabokov: The Man and His Work*, edited by L. S. Dembo, 144–56. Madison: University of Wisconsin Press, 167.

Graham, John. "John Hawkes on His Novels." *Massachusetts Review* 7 (1966): 459–60.

Greiner, Donald J. *Comic Terror: The Novels of John Hawkes*. Memphis: Memphis State University Press, 1973.

———. *Understanding John Hawkes*. Columbia: University of South Carolina Press, 1985.

Guerard, Albert J. "Concepts of the Double." In *Stories of the Double*, edited by Albert J. Gerard, 1–14. Philadelphia: J. B. Lippincott, 1967.

Hallam, Clifford. "The Double As Incomplete Self: Toward a Definition of Doppelgänger." In *Fearful Symmetry: Doubles and Doubling in Literature and Film*, edited by Eugene J. Crook, 1–31. Tallahassee: University Presses of Florida, 1981.

Hansen, Arlen. "The Celebration of Solipsism: A New Trend in American Fiction." *Modern Fiction Studies* 19, no. 1 (Spring 1973): 5–15.

Harris, Charles B. *Passionate Virtuosity: The Fiction of John Barth*. Urbana: The University of Illinois Press, 1983.

Hassan, Ihab. *The Literature of Silence: Henry Miller and Samuel Beckett*. New York: Alfred A. Knopf, 1967.

———. "Pluralism in Postmodern Perspective." *Critical Inquiry* 12 (Spring 1986): 503–20.

Hauck, Richard Boyd. *A Cheerful Nihilism*. Bloomington: Indiana University Press, 1971.

Hawkes, John. *The Blood Oranges*. New York: New Directions, 1971.

———. "A Conversation on *The Blood Oranges* between John Hawkes and Robert Scholes." *Novel* 5 (1972): 197–207.

Hawkes, Terence. *Structuralism and Semiotics*. Berkeley: University of California Press, 1977.

Higgins, Dick. *Horizons: The Poetics and Theory of the Intermedia*. Carbondale: Southern Illinois University Press, 1984.

Hite, Molly. *Ideas of Order in the Novels of Thomas Pynchon*. Columbus: Ohio State University Press, 1983.

Horkheimer, Max. *Eclipse of Reason*. New York: Oxford University Press, 1947.

Huizinga, Johan. *Homo Ludens: A Study of the Play Element in Culture*. London: Maurice Temple Smith, 1970.

Hutcheon, Linda. *The Canadian Postmodern: A Study of Contemporary English-Canadian Fiction*. Toronto: Oxford University Press, 1988.

————. *A Poetics of Postmodernism: History, Theory, Fiction*. New York: Routledge, 1988.

————. *A Theory of Parody: The Teachings of Twentieth-Century Art Forms*. New York: Methuen, 1985.

Irwin, W. R. *The Game of the Impossible: A Rhetoric of Fantasy*. Urbana: University of Illinois Press, 1976.

Jackson, Rosemary. *Fantasy: The Literature of Subversion*. London: Methuen, 1981.

Jameson, Frederic. "Postmodernism and Consumer Society." In *The Anti-Aesthetic: Essays on Postmodern Culture*, edited by Hal Foster, 111–25. Port Townsend, Wash., 1983.

————. "Postmodernism, or the Cultural Logic of Late Capitalism." *New Left Review* 146 (July–August 1984): 53–92.

————. *The Prison-House of Language: A Critical Account of Structuralism and Russian Formalism*. Princeton, N.J.: Princeton University Press, 1972.

Jencks, Charles. *Post-Modernism: The New Classicism in Art and Architecture*. New York: Rizzoli, 1987.

Johnson, Barbara. Translator's introduction to Jacques Derrida, *Dissemination*, vii–xxxiii. Chicago: University of Chicago Press, 1981.

Joseph, Gerhard. *John Barth*. Minneapolis: University of Minnesota Press, 1970.

Jung, C. G. *Dreams*. Princeton, N.J.: Princeton University Press, 1974.

————. "The Shadow." In *Aion: Researches into the Phenomenology of the Self, Collected Works*, translated by R. F. C. Hull, vol. 9. New York: Pantheon, 1959.

————. "The Syzygy: Anima and Animus." In *Aion: Researches into the Phenomenology of the Self, Collected Works*, translated by R. F. C. Hull, vol. 9. New York: Pantheon, 1959.

Keppler, Carl F. *The Literature of the Second Self*. Tucson: University of Arizona Press, 1972.

Kiernan, Robert F. "John Barth's Artist in the Fun House." *Studies in Short Fiction* 10, no. 4 (Fall 1973): 373–80.

Kline, T. Jefferson. "Doubling *The Double*." In *Fearful Symmetry: Doubles and Doubling in Literature and Film*, edited by Eugene J. Crook, 65–83. Tallahassee: University Presses of Florida, 1981.

Klinkowitz, Jerome. *Literary Disruptions: The Making of a Post-Contemporary American Fiction*. Urbana: University of Illinois Press, 1975.

————. *Literary Subversions: New American Fiction and the Practice of Criticism*. Carbondale: Southern Illinois University Press, 1985.

Kostelanetz, Richard. "New Fiction in America." In *Surfiction: Fiction*

Now . . . and Tomorrow, edited by Raymond Federman, 85–100. Chicago: Swallow Press, 1981.

Kuehl, John. "Interview." In *John Hawkes and the Craft of Conflict*, 155–83. New Brunswick, N.J.: Rutgers University Press, 1975.

Lacan, Jacques. "The Mirror Stage as Formative of the Function of the I as Revealed in Psychoanalytic Experience." In *Écrits: A Selection*, translated by Alan Sheridan. New York: W. W. Norton, 1977.

———. "Of Structure as an Inmixing of an Otherness Prerequisite to Any Subject Whatsoever." In *The Structuralist Controversy: The Languages of Criticism and the Sciences of Man*, edited by Richard Macksey and Eugenio Donato, 186–200. Baltimore: Johns Hopkins University Press, 1972.

Lanham, Richard A. *Tristram Shandy: The Games of Pleasure*. Berkeley: University of California Press, 1973.

Le Clair, Thomas, and Larry McCaffery eds. "A Dialogue: Hawkes and Barth Talk About Fiction." In *Anything Can Happen: Interviews with Contemporary American Novelists*, 9–19. Urbana: University of Illinois Press, 1983.

LeGuin, Ursula. "The Child and the Shadow." In *The Language of the Night*, edited by Susan Wood. New York: G. P. Putnam's Sons, 1979.

Lewis, Philip E. "La Rochefoucauld: The Rationality of Play." *Yale French Studies* 41 (1968): 133–47.

Lodge, David. *The Modes of Modern Writing: Metaphor, Metonymy, and the Typology of Modern Literature*. Ithaca, N.Y.: Cornell University Press, 1977.

Lyotard, Jean-François. *The Post-Modern Condition: A Report on Knowledge*. Translated by Geoff Bennington and Brian Masscami. Minneapolis: University of Minnesota Press, 1984.

MacCannell, Juliet. *Figuring Lacan: Criticism and the Cultural Unconscious*. London: Croom Helm, 1986.

McConnell, Frank D. *Four Postwar American Novelists: Bellow, Mailer, Barth, and Pynchon*. Chicago: University of Chicago Press, 1977.

McGuane, Thomas. "The Blood Oranges," *The New York Times Book Review*, September 19, 1971, p. 1.

McHale, Brian. *Postmodernist Fiction*. New York: Methuen, 1987.

McHoul, Alec, and David Wills. *Writing Pynchon: Strategies in Fictional Analysis*. Urbana: University of Illinois Press, 1990.

Macksey, Richard. "Lions and Squares: Opening Remarks." In *The Structuralist Controversy: The Languages of Criticism and the Sciences of Man*, edited by Richard Macksey and Eugenio Donato, 1–14. Baltimore: Johns Hopkins University Press, 1972.

Macksey, Richard, and Eugenio Donato, eds. *The Structuralist Controversy: The Languages of Criticism and the Sciences of Man*. Baltimore: Johns Hopkins University Press, 1972.

Malley, Terence. *Richard Brautigan*. New York: Warner, 1972.

Malmgren, Carl Darryl. *Fictional Space in the Modernist and Postmodernist American Novel*. Lewisburg, Pa.: Bucknell University Press, 1985.

Marcus, Mordecai. "Melville's Bartleby as a Psychological Double." In *Bartleby The Inscrutable: A Collection of Commentary on Herman Melville's Tale "Bartleby the Scrivener,"* edited by M. Thomas Inge, 107–13. Hamden, Conn.: Archon Books, 1979.

Marcuse, Herbert. *An Essay on Liberation*. Boston: Beacon Press, 1969.

Meyer, Leonard B. "The End of the Renaissance?" *The Hudson Review* 16, no. 2 (Summer 1963): 169–86.

Miller, Karl. *Doubles: Studies in Literary History*. Oxford: Oxford University Press, 1985.

Miller, Russell. "*The Sot-Weed Factor*: A Contemporary Mock-Epic." *Critique* 8, no. 2 (Winter 1965–1966): 88–100.

Miyoshi, Masao. *The Divided Self: Perspective on the Literature of The Victorians*. New York: New York University Press, 1969.

Morrissette, Bruce. "Games and Game Structures in Robbe-Grillet." *Yale French Studies* 41 (1968): 159–67.

Nabokov, Vladimir. *Despair*. New York: G. P. Putnam's Sons, Capricorn, 1970.

———. *Strong Opinions*. New York: McGraw-Hill, 1973.

Nicol, Charles. "The Mirrors of Sebastian Knight." In *Nabokov: The Man and His Work*, edited by L. S. Dembo, 85–94. Madison: University of Wisconsin Press, 1967.

Nietzsche, Friedrich. *On the Genealogy of Morals and Ecce Homo*. Translated by Walter Kaufmann and R. J. Hollingdale. New York: Vintage, 1989.

Nordell, Roderick. "American Gothic Comes of Age." Review of *The Hawkline Monster: A Gothic Western*, by Richard Brautigan. *Christian Science Monitor*, November 8, 1974, p. 10.

Nyman, Michael. *Experimental Music: Cage and Beyond*. London: Studio Vista, 1974.

O'Doherty, Brian. "Minus Plato." In *Minimal Art: A Critical Anthology*, edited by Gregory Battcock, 251–55. New York: E. P. Dutton, 1968.

O'Donnell, Patrick. *John Hawkes*. Boston: Twayne, 1982.

Pearce, Richard. "Enter the Frame." In *Surfiction: Fiction Now . . . and Tomorrow*, edited by Raymond Federman, 47–57. Chicago: Swallow Press, 1981.

Perreault, Jean. "Minimal Abstracts." In *Minimal Art: A Critical Anthology*, edited by Gregory Battcock, 256–62. New York: E. P. Dutton, 1968.

Plato. *The Symposium*. Translated by Walter Hamilton. Harmondsworth, England: Penguin, 1979.

Popper, K. R. *The Open Society and Its Enemies*. Vol. 1. London: Routledge and Kegan Paul, 1957.

Prince, Alan. "An Interview with John Barth." *Prism* (Spring 1968): 42–62.

Pynchon, Thomas. *The Crying of Lot 49*. New York: Bantam, 1972.

———. *Gravity's Rainbow*. New York: Viking, 1973.

Rank, Otto. "The Double as Immortal Self." In *Beyond Psychology*. New York: Dover, 1958.

———. *The Double: A Psychoanalytic Study*. Translated by Harry Tucker, Jr. New York: New American Library, 1971.

———. *The Myth of the Birth of the Hero and Other Writings*. New York: Random House, 1964.

Redfield, Marc W. "Pynchon's Postmodern Sublime," *PMLA* 104, no. 2 (March 1989): 152–62.

Ricardou, Jean. "Nouveau Roman, Tel Quel." In *Surfiction: Fiction Now . . . and Tomorrow*, edited by Raymond Federman, 101–33. Chicago: Swallow Press, 1981.

Rockwell, John. *All American Music: Composition in the Late Twentieth Century*. New York: Alfred A. Knopf, 1983.

Rogers, Robert. *A Psychoanalytic Study of the Double in Literature*. Detroit: Wayne State University Press, 1970.

Rorty, Richard. "Texts and Lumps," *New Literary History* 17, no. 1 (1985): 1–16.

Rose, Barbara. "ABC Art." In *Minimal Art: A Critical Anthology*, edited by Gregory Battcock, 274–97. New York: E. P. Dutton, 1968.

Rosenfield, Claire. "*Despair* and the Lust for Immortality." In *Nabokov: The Man and His Work*, edited by L. S. Dembo, 66–84. Madison: University of Wisconsin Press, 1967.

———. "The Shadow Within: The Conscious and Unconscious Use of the Double." In *Stories of the Double*, edited by Albert J. Guerard, 311–31. Philadelphia: J. B. Lippincott, 1967.

Rosolato, Guy. "The Voice and the Literary Myth." In *The Structuralist Controversy: The Languages of Criticism and the Sciences of Man*, edited by Richard Macksey and Eugenio Donato, 201–17. Baltimore: Johns Hopkins University Press, 1972.

Roth, Phyllis Ann. "Lunatics, Lovers, and a Poet: A Study of Doubling and the Doppelganger in the Novels of Nabokov." Dissertation, University of Connecticut, 1972.

Rovit, Earl. "The Novel as Parody: John Barth." *Critique* 6, no. 2 (Fall 1963): 77–85.

Russell, Charles. "Pynchon's Language: Signs, Systems, and Subversion." In *Approaches to Gravity's Rainbow*, edited by Charles Clerc, 251–72. Columbus: Ohio State University Press, 1983.

Said, Edward. "An Ideology of Difference." *Critical Inquiry* 12, no. 1 (1985): 38–58.

Schaub, Thomas H. *Pynchon: The Voice of Ambiguity*. Urbana: University of Illinois Press, 1981.

Scholes, Robert. *Fabulation and Metafiction*. Urbana: University of Illinois Press, 1979.

Sharp, Willoughby. "Luminism and Kineticism." In *Minimal Art: A Critical Anthology*, edited by Gregory Battcock, 317–58. New York: E. P. Dutton, 1968.

Shklovsky, Viktor. "Art as Technique." In *Russian Formalist Criticism: Four Essays*, edited by Lee T. Lemon and Marion J. Reis, 3–57. Lincoln: University of Nebraska Press, 1965.

Siegel, Mark Richard. *Creative Paranoia in Gravity's Rainbow*. Port Washington, N. Y.: Kennikat Press, 1978.

Slade, Joseph W. "Religion, Psychology, Sex, and Love in *Gravity's Rainbow*." In *Approaches to Gravity's Rainbow*, edited by Charles Clerc, 153–98. Columbus: Ohio State University Press, 1983. 153–198.

———. *Thomas Pynchon*. New York: Warner, 1974.

Slethaug, Gordon E. "Floating Signifiers in John Barth's *Sabbatical*." *Modern Fiction Studies* 33 (Winter 1987): 647–55.

———. "*The Hawkline Monster*: Brautigan's 'Buffoon Mutation.' " In *The Scope of the Fantastic—Culture, Biography, Themes, Children's Literature*, edited by Robert A. Collins and Howard D. Pearce, 137–45. Westport, Conn.: Greenwood Press, 1985.

Slethaug, Gordon E., and Stan Fogel. *Understanding John Barth*. Columbia: University of South Carolina Press, 1990.

Smock, Ann. *Double Dealing*. Lincoln: University of Nebraska Press, 1985.

Spivak, Gayatri Chakravorty. Translator's preface to Jacques Derrida, *Of Grammatology*, ix–lxxxvii. Baltimore: Johns Hopkins University Press, 1976.

Stark, John O. *The Literature of Exhaustion: Borges, Nabokov, and Barth*. Durham, N.C.: Duke University Press, 1974.

————. *Pynchon's Fictions: Thomas Pynchon and the Literature of Informa-tion*. Athens: Ohio University Press 1980.

Stevick, Philip. *Alternative Pleasures: Postrealist Fiction and the Tradition*. Urbana: University of Illinois Press, 1981.

Stuart, Dabney. "Nabokov's *Despair*: Tinker to Evers to Chance." *The Georgia Review* 30, no. 2 (Summer 1976): 432–46.

Tanner, Tony. *Thomas Pynchon*. London: Methuen, 1982.

Tiffin, Helen. Introduction to *Past the Last Post: Theorizing Post-Colonial-ism and Post-Modernism*, edited by Ian Adam and Helen Tiffin, vii–xx. Calgary, Alberta: University of Calgary Press, 1990.

Todorov, Tzvetan. *The Fantastic: A Structural Approach to a Literary Genre*. Translated by Richard Howard. Cleveland: Press of Case Western University, 1973.

————. *Littérature et signification*. Paris: Larousse, 1967.

Tymms, Ralph. *Doubles in Literary Psychology*. Cambridge, England: Bowes and Bowes, 1949.

Vinge, Louise. *The Narcissus Theme in Western Literature up to the Early Nineteenth Century*. Lund, Sweden: Gleerups, 1967.

Wain, Marianne. "The Double in Romantic Narrative: A Preliminary Study." *The Germanic Review* 36, no. 4 (December 1961): 257–68.

Werner, Craig Hansen. *Paradoxical Resolutions: American Fiction since James Joyce*. Urbana: University of Illinois Press, 1982.

Wilde, Alan. *Middle Grounds: Studies in Contemporary American Fiction*. Philadelphia: University of Pennsylvania Press, 1987.

Williams, Carol T. "Nabokov's Dialectical Structure." In *Nabokov: The Man and His Work*, edited by L. S. Dembo, 165–82. Madison: University of Wisonsin Press, 1967.

Willis, Lonnie L. "Brautigan's *The Hawkline Monster*: As Big as the Ritz." *Critique* 23, no. 2 (Winter 1981–1982): 37–47.

Wilson, R. Rawdon. *In Palamedes' Shadow: Explorations in Play, Game, and Narrative Theory*. Boston: Northeastern University Press, 1990.

Wittgenstein, Ludwig. *The Blue and Brown Books*. Oxford: Basil Black-well, 1960.

Yohalem, John. "Cute Brautigan." Review of *The Hawkline Monster: A Gothic Western*, by Richard Brautigan. *The New York Times Book Review* 8 (September 1974): 6.

Ziegler, Heide. *John Barth*. London: Methuen, 1987.

Index

GORDON E. SLETHAUG teaches in and chairs
the Department of English at the University of
Waterloo, Ontario, where he is engaged in the
study of contemporary American fiction, the
American Renaissance, and literary theory.
His previous publications include works on
Barth and Brautigan as well as other American
authors, modernist and postmodernist, including Knowles, Salinger, and Updike.